The Complete Tales of Dulditch

by Mary E. Mann

Other books by Mary E. Mann available from the Larks Press

The Parish of Hilby

The Patten Experiment

Rose at Honeypot

The Complete
Tales of Dulditch

by Mary E. Mann

Foreword by D.J.Taylor

Introduction by Patience Tomlinson

Larks Press

Published by the Larks Press
Ordnance Farmhouse
Guist Bottom, Dereham

Printed by the Lanceni Press, Garrood Drive,
Fakenham,
Norfolk. 01328 851578

British Library Cataloguing-in-Publication-Data
A catalogue record for this book is available from the British Library

A full catalogue of Larks Press books is available at
www.booksatlarkspress.co.uk

Front cover photograph, 'A Stiff Pull' by P. H. Emerson, kindly supplied by
Norfolk County Council Library and Information Service
from the Picture Norfolk Archive

Acknowledgements

Grateful thanks to D.J. Taylor for providing the Foreword to this volume; to
Patience Tomlinson for encouragement, for help in finding the stories, and
for her Introduction; to Mary Fortune for directing me to some of the less
well-known tales; and to Diana Hyde for sharing her memories of her
grandmother and for giving Patience Tomlinson permission to quote from
letters diaries and other unpublished material. Susan Yaxley

ISBN 978 1 904006 43 5

Foreword by D.J.Taylor

As a writer Mary Mann (1848-1929) made the fatal mistake of excelling in the wrong genre. For some reason literary reputations are nearly always made on the strength of full-length novels, and while Mann's fiction is always interesting – see in particular *The Patten Experiment* (1899) – her real genius lies in the short story. At their best, the pieces collected here are as good as anything by Thomas Hardy, George Gissing, George Moore or any other English writer at work in the last decade of the nineteenth century. But if one or two of Mann's heroines can be marked down as the south-west Norfolk equivalent of Tess of the d'Urbervilles, her approach to the human condition, as displayed in these accounts of late-Victorian rural life, is very different. Hardy's characters – to make the obvious comparison - are at the mercy of vast, unappeasable natural forces – that 'president of the immortals' who had 'finished his sport' with Tess. Mann's sense of determinism is much less obtrusive. What distinguishes the final paragraphs of *'Little Brother'*, a brief, five-page sketch that even now sends shivers down your spine, is not its tragic glamour, but its matter-of-factness. Mrs Hodd, reproached for allowing her children to commit what most 'civilised' people would regard as an act of desecration, simply cannot see what the fuss is about. The Dulditch tales are full of these moments - paralysing glimpses of human elementals that are sometimes terrifying in their refusal to respect the moral conventions of Victorian story-telling. Over the past thirty years several attempts have been made to push Mary Mann into the late-Victorian literary pantheon. A.S. Byatt included *'Little Brother'* in *The Oxford Book of the English Story,* one or two of her stories have been anthologised, the actress Patience Tomlinson, who contributes an introduction to this collection, has devised a fascinating one-woman show about her life and she rates a modest entry in the *New Oxford Dictionary of National Biography.* This is a start, but it is nowhere near the recognition she deserves. We should read her work not because she is one of those 'interesting' but neglected local writers whom practically every county in the British Isles periodically throws up, but because, in her chosen form, she is one of the greatest talents of the late-Victorian age. This is a substantial claim, but I have never met anybody compelled to read *'Little Brother'*, *'Wolf Charlie'* or *'Dora o' the Ringolets'* who didn't share it.

Foreword to the first edition of
The Fields of Dulditch by Mary E. Mann

We, whom the hand of the great Disposer has tossed among the fields of Dulditch, who pass our lives in a silence and solitude so remote from the living world, bear with us through the peace of nature hearts not always peaceful. It is not a matter of indifference that for us the Book of Life is practically closed, that only tantalisingly and at moments have we been permitted to peep within its pages; that only an echo of the distant hum of the toiling, marching multitude reaches our ears. The consciousness of that stirring sound, made up of laughter and weeping, of the clash of arms and of tools, of the pantings of struggling, heaving existence, of choruses of triumph, of suffering, of despair, does but chafe our spirits into restlessness, fills us with a graceless discontent.

In accordance with that pleasant superstition which allots impartially to each unit its regulation stock of happiness, we are inclined to look around us for the compensation which should adjust the balance of our impoverished lives. Does it lie in the fact that in slow process of time and without intellectual effort we become apathetically resigned, that we cease to look out wistfully at a larger existence, but hug ourselves sullenly in silence and shrink from the noises of the world? Is it in the certainty that the poor scenes always before our eyes become dear to us at last as the most glorious prospects in the world never could have become dear? That the insignificant landscape, bleak fen-land, gorse-choked heath, familiar ponds and "pits" and puddles, rank turnip-fields, flat distances, lamb-dotted meadows shall be imprinted on our very hearts – shall be, indeed, part of our vital selves so that severance might be fatal?

Is this to be our recompense for the joy of the struggle, the intoxication of the fight, the fierce excitement of life? This, and the sound of the rain upon the roof, the rustle of falling leaves, the chirp of the swallow darting to and fro beneath our eaves, the caw of the rooks in the elms by our gate, the bleat of the lamb in the meadow, the soft stir of scented summer breeze, the rush of the winter storm? These, and a repetition of the peasant's gossip over the ale-house fire, his wife's tittle-tattle at the village shop, the sight of girl and boy keeping company in the lanes, the sound of the tolling bell?

This to be all? For this and this only are we condemned to lose the race we have not run?

Yet do such trivialities move us strangely. Our emotions are stirred by the joys and sorrows of the toilers by field and hedgerow as they might never be stirred by the tragedies of the streets. We may not see and hear and pass on. We are compelled to live side by side with the suffering we see, to take the joy into our own bosoms, to feel the oppression in our hearts.

Then is this our requital perhaps?

In that sympathy which the fullest knowledge gives, does our consolation lie?

To understand is to forgive, and it is also to love.

Of the lives of the simple folk who are born, grow up, grow old around us, every incident is known. The slow working of their untilled minds, the joy, the sorrow, the sin, the foolishness – above all, the patience and the goodness of their lives.

So may we not humbly hope that, having missed the greater knowledge to be gained only from contact with the world, we yet may have acquired some letter of that large wisdom of Nature who counts nothing that she meets with base?

CONTENTS

Introduction

'And He that tossed thee down into the field,
He knows about it all - He knows – He knows.'

The above inscription was chosen by Mary Mann to go on the title page of the first edition of *The Fields of Dulditch*, a collection of some of her best short stories, which was published in 1902. In her Afterword to the edition Mann writes, 'In chronicling such trifles as these from the simple annals of the poor, there is danger of much monotony of shade.'

Fortunately for us she avoids that danger. There is no monotony of shade here. This chronicler has a sense of humour, a sharp ear for dialogue and the Norfolk dialect, and a dry economical style. These stories are often extremely funny. A lesser writer would have taken a moral or perhaps political tone. How tedious and indeed monotonous that might be. Mann straightforwardly offers often shocking facts of poverty and deprivation without judgement or comment, but threaded throughout these pages is wry irony and amusingly detailed characterization, revealing her personal involvement with the people she knew so well. These stories may be found in the library catalogued under fiction, but like most of the best fiction, they are telling us the truth. When I recorded some of the stories, which were broadcast on BBC Radio 4, I was impressed that each one of them was like a perfect one-act play, a small masterpiece of both tragedy and comedy. Thomas Hardy with laughs. Mann has been compared favourably to Hardy – here I think she exceeds him.

This new complete collection of all the Dulditch stories makes a fascinating and very entertaining account of rural Norfolk life in the late 19th century. The characters and events of a whole village are brought into focus as if Mann were presenting it to us under a Victorian glass dome. She wrote, 'the history of individuals stirs me more than the history of the masses.' Here is the Rector, and his spinster sister, bent on doing good; here are their maids; the schoolmistress and her charges; the tenant farmer and his men, particularly his men, and their struggling wives and families, the old and the very young. The Squire however is notable mostly for his absence. He can no longer afford to live in the Hall, like so many of his class at the time, and rents out the family seat to raise funds.

Mary Elizabeth Rackham was born in Norwich in 1848 into a wealthy middle class family. Her father William Rackham was a wholesale tradesman in the textile business. She was brought up surrounded by six brothers and she had an unusually good education for a girl of that period. The family went to the theatre and concerts and the house was full of books. She was confident, articulate and very well read.

When, at the age of 23, she married Fairman Mann, she moved with him to Shropham, a small village near Attleborough in Norfolk. Fairman was 10 years older than her but there was something about this more mature gentleman farmer that attracted her. He came from a big yeoman farming family and they set up home together first at Church Farm and then later moved to the larger and grander Manor Farm. At first the prospects seemed good: 'when we first came here everything looked so promising.' However, by the 1880s the agricultural depression began to take hold, deeply affecting the Manns and the lives of everyone around them from labourer to tenant farmer to landowner. Mary Mann wrote, 'A farmer in the adjoining parish who had looked ruin in the face through weary days and wakeful nights, till he could endure the hideous prospect no longer, got up with the dawn one morning, and, while the lark sprang up with its joyful cry to the blue above him, and the sparrows twittered familiarly about the eaves of the old house where he had heard them as a boy, blew out his brains in the pretty summer-house upon his lawn.' Bad harvests, land taxes, high rates and free trade had all contributed to this. The youngest and strongest of the men deserted their villages to seek work in towns.

Henry Rider Haggard farmed nearby and in his book *A Farmer's Year of 1898* he writes of the devastating effects of this rural decline. He outlines the life of an average labourer who, having received little education, starts work on a local farm when he's not much more than a child. By the time he is married at the age of 19 or so he would earn 13 shillings a week and within 12 years he'd be supporting seven or eight children. 'It is during these first 17 or 18 years of his married life that the burden of existence falls so heavily upon him, since there are many mouths to feed and only one pair of hands to provide the food.' Life becomes a little easier when his children start earning but he still needs to carry on working. By the age of seventy 'too frequently the real tragedy of life strikes him. He is no longer able to do a full day's work, and in these times, when the best of farmers can scarcely make ends meet and earn a living, it is not to be expected, indeed it is not possible, that they should continue to pay him for that he cannot perform. Therefore if help is not forthcoming from his children or other sources, he must sink to the workhouse.'

Mann describes her husband Fairman as 'a man well-to-do, kind and generous once, an excellent husband, master, farmer, getting now poorer in pocket, shorter in temper, year by year, a man who has struggled in a quiet, dogged fashion but who is beaten and knows it, finding the knowledge bitter and self deteriorative to a degree.' And, despite being very busy with four children she took up her quill pen, which she always used, and started writing in order to supplement the family income. 'We perish of dullness here,' Mann wrote, so 'Dulditch' became her name for Shropham and its inhabitants were her inspiration. She certainly needed the money but she also needed the intellectual stimulation, which she missed so much on moving away from the city.

Her first novel, *The Parish of Hilby* was published in 1883 and she went on to write another 38 novels for which she became very well known by the beginning of the new century. The constraints of agent and publisher, however, sometimes forced her to write to a more romantic and sentimental formula than she wished. In 1899 she was very taken up with the events of the Boer War. 'The poor, pious, mistaken Boers, they are brave men too and the spectacle is altogether horrid. These are the sorts of things I would like to write about but my agent constantly demands cheerful stories.' She wrote a large number of short stories published in many different magazines and periodicals including *The Ladies Field, The Athenaeum, The World, The Daily Mail, Cornhill, Temple Bar* etc. The Dulditch stories seem to have escaped censure however and form the strong core of her writing for which she so deserves to be remembered.

In her unpublished foreword to *The Fields of Dulditch* Mann wrote, 'The little Norfolk village about some of whose inhabitants I propose to write is to be warrantable only in its lack of interest. As I detail its several features I am appalled at the bleakness, the dreariness of the prospect. And it is certain that we who pass our lives here in the silence and the solitude are not always content. These simple folks that are born, grow up, grow old around us - every incident of their history is known to us: the slow working of their untilled minds, the toils and sorrows, the sins and foolishness and goodness of their lives.'

In April 1902 Mary Mann wrote to her husband's nephew Thomas Ordish, 'You will, I am sure, be pleased to hear that Mr Edward Garnett thinks very highly of the Dulditch sketches. He writes me a

13

long letter so full of nice things that I cannot pick and choose among them. He asks for some more of my writings and speaks of writing a paper on them which will be fine if only he keeps it in mind.'

Ordish was the son of her husband's sister and a great admirer of her writing. He was only six years younger than Mann and was her lifeline and inspiration in her literary work. He was in London, a journalist and writer himself, and a well respected Shakespearian scholar. They corresponded regularly and he acted as a go-between for her with London publishers. She wrote to him, 'It is as certain as anything that I should never have attempted to write or do more than pester my friends with long letters if it had not been for you, my old friend and sympathiser, the champion of my poor powers and defender of all my scribblings. It is very flattering of you to imagine anyone will want to hear anything of me when I am dead. I'm quite sure they won't – except perhaps in the Norfolk papers, a small paragraph.'

In the *Eastern Daily Press* the Suffolk novelist Adrian Bell wrote, 'whatever the weather and the season, the blizzard of necessity never ceases to blow on the inhabitants of Dulditch. It would be truer to say that I lived this book rather than read it. The people are more real to me than Hardy's. Although the record of rural penury is so shocking that it awes the writing to simplicity, it leaves an epic quality in the mind, a sort of noble rage which makes for life.' In 2004, also in the *EDP*, Ian Collins refers to Mann's 'superbly crafted stories with their acute feeling for rich dialect and ruined lives, that are as haunting as the East Anglian ghost stories of MR James.'

But Mann not only wrote about the shockingly impoverished conditions so many of the farm labourers and their families lived in, she and her husband Fairman did their best to do something about them. Fairman was a workhouse Guardian and overseer of the poor and founded the village school. For the 42 years they lived there Mann constantly visited and helped in the village and further afield. She must have been a welcome visitor. People talked to her and she listened. Her stories, full of such real people and their conversations are evidence of that. She uses the Rector's spinster sister as her narrator, but it is undoubtedly her own voice.

She describes with affection Old Angel in *A Dulditch Angel*: 'he was a little old man, blue eyed, white haired, apple-cheeked. As gently and as wisely as a good mother waits on her stricken child did the old husband wait upon his ailing wife. He made no protest or complaint, cheerfully and alone he laboured on. "I'll tell you how it be," he said one day when I had been moved to express to him my appreciation of his untiring care; "I'll tell ye th' wuds I used to say ter my old wumman in our young time, when her and me, happen, di'nt allust think alike, Meery' I'd say, Meery, (these hare be th' wuds), theer's on'y one thing to be put down to yar favour, Meery, bor, I'd say, and that be – I love yer.'"

Wolf-Charlie is a less appealing looking character, 'by reason of the famished look in his melancholy eyes, of the way in which the skin of his lips, drawn tightly over his gums, exposes his great yellow teeth. He is in a word, the poorest of the poor – a most wretched and pitiable object.' Despite his poverty, after being forced to spend the winter in the workhouse he leaves there with a new responsibility. 'She was a middle-aged woman, with a red and foolish face. She had a wooden leg and six children.' And the Wolf somehow provides for them all. 'There is something too melancholy in the history of such sordid lives,' says Mann. 'One stands aghast for the moment, frightened at the privation which those fashioned like ourselves in outward seeming, can bear and live. Perhaps never having had enough to eat, Wolf-Charlie does not understand how bad it is to be hungry. It is comforting to reflect that if Wolf-Charlie is not thoroughly contented, he at any rate does not complain.' So it is with most of the people in these stories – struggling to make a life against almost impossible odds, finding ways of coping, being stoical and accepting and yet never complaining.

In *Ben Pitcher's Elly* we see the gradual transformation of young Elly. She was a fair and 'winning' child who showed such promise at school she might have been kept on to train as a pupil teacher, had her mother not needed her help with a new baby at home. By the end of this tragic tale Elly, the victim of a brutal father, is an exhausted, half-starved, beaten and misunderstood 17-year-old, responsible, really through no fault of her own, for the death of her baby.

'*Women O'Dulditch* is absolutely true in its essentials,' said Mann, '*Dora O' the Ringolets* true with the exception of the denouement, which is a concession to popular taste.' Her comic characters are a delight and the Norfolk dialect is used to great effect to achieve this. Gentleman George in *The Witch of Dulditch* describes an old print on his wall, which he calls 'the Cleopatrick': ''Tis an antikity. Tain't on'y th' gentry that keer for such. This here is a French party,' he explains, his broad fingertip on the principal figure. 'That theer little sarpent she've ketched hold on, she's about to swallow it fer a merracle. This here young person aside on her she be a-washhuppin o' Cleopatrick. 'Tis a Scripter subject, and bein' antikity is wallable. 'Twas th' postman, a-callin to ax me for the faviour of an apple, come ten year last Janiwary, as giv' me th' hist'ry.' In *Our Mary*, the maid at the rectory 'has a curious terror of music'. When the piano is opened Mary takes refuge in the cellar and muffles her head in a shawl. She calls music a 'terrufic n'ise' and says it gives her 'a sinkin in 'er in'ards.'

These, and many other characters and their friends, relatives and descendants all filled the church at Shropham when Mann was taken back to be buried there beside her husband in 1929. Her gravestone, in the form of an open book, was cleaned and made legible again in 2005 after many years of neglect. On it a quotation from Psalm 90 reads 'We bring our years to an end as it were a tale that is told.' A fitting memorial for this unique teller of tales.

Mary Mann's son Rackham had one child, Diana Hyde. I visited her recently. Although she was only three when Mann died she vividly remembers being taken to see her grandmother in Sheringham. (Mary Mann had moved there in 1915.) At first she was frightened of the dog barking and the keys rattling behind the front door, but when her grandmother opened it and looked at Diana she felt an immediate rapport with her. Diana told me that when Rackham was a baby his mother had hired a girl from the village to look after him. The girl was found fast asleep by the fire with Rackham, far too close to the flames, safety-pinned not very securely to her apron. Mary Mann uses this incident in *The Gal La'rences*, a story that, along with *A Dulditch Rose*, shows her admiration for the women who 'not realising how hard the struggle was, fought a brave fight.' They did everything they could to avoid the workhouse or the 'disgrace of asking for alms.'

Mary Mann had three daughters. One of them, Berthalina, was an artist and through her writing Mann was able to finance her training at the Slade. Diana remembers her Aunt Bertie standing beside a chest of drawers full of manuscripts and telling her how precious they were and that her grandmother had left strict instructions that they be preserved after her death because she knew that her writing was important. Mann said: 'I am glad to have aspired to something that mattered even if I don't attain it.'

Despite complaining of its dullness she writes about the Norfolk countryside with obvious appreciation. In the opening paragraphs of *The Country Doctor* she describes a ride in a gig through a perfect early spring morning. 'We see the woods and copses this morning, the village on the low crest of the gently rising ground, the grey church tower, the far-off mill with its white sails, through the purple haze which painters love to imitate. Upon the tree-tops in the plantation there is a tender shimmer of greenness. There is a blessing in the air.

We feel the south wind, soft and fragrant on our faces. The gorse bordering each side of the road is alive with linnets.'

'I have two short stories to write this week and one, which ought to be written next week,' Mann writes to Ordish in 1907. 'But my powers of invention are exhausted. If an incident strikes you please put it on a postcard and send on. I like to keep my short stories to an incident not to make of them a history.' Certainly the shorter of the stories, featuring one incident, make a strong impact. In *Rats!* Alick, the odd-job boy, 'tall with hard-shining expressionless eyes and an ever-open mouth' very satisfyingly outwits a party of upper class 'young men and maidens' who barely speak the same language as him; in *A Gentleman at Large,* old Bob, retired, sees the new man who has taken on his job, sitting 'atop the hay cutter.' Grieving for the horses who had been his life's work, 'he looked wistfully at Joe on his coveted perch. He would rather have sat there than on the throne of kings.' And in *Levenses* the understated reunion between an estranged couple is very moving, as indeed is that between the couple in the much longer *David Peck's Love Affair.*

'The reviews are saying kind things about my short stories. I am glad critics at last discover I can write the short story because I have made a study of what it should be and always felt that I was more successful in my efforts than most.' That was written to Ordish in 1910, and still writing to him when she was in her late seventies, Mann says, 'I figure in a book called *31 Stories by Thirty and One Authors.* (Appleton & Co 1923) Have you seen it? It is supposed to contain the best short story of the best short story writers, some of them very good.' She is right, they include H.G. Wells, G.K. Chesterton and A.E. Coppard. The story of Mann's selected for this American publication is *The Blue Beads,* a good one certainly, but arguably not her best. That accolade must surely go to *Little Brother* chosen by A.S. Byatt for her *Oxford Book of English Short Stories* in 1998. Byatt describes the story as, 'plain, and brief, and clear and terrible, though the narrator's tone is not simple. She is recording, not judging, but her telling is spiky with morals and the inadequacy of morals.' In a dazzling economy of a mere 1,426 words *Little Brother* is very powerful and unforgettable. This story alone would be enough to secure her reputation.

In January 1923 at the age of seventy-five, Mann wrote to Ordish, 'we drove to dear Shropham in the summer, had lunch at the Vicarage and looked at all the familiar places. What a safe and comfortable and generally happy time I had there! Such things are never valued until they are past. I love every stick and stone of the place now, and all the dear people who were so kind to me there.' And later that year, 'I have tried once or twice to get *The Fields of Dulditch* republished – but without success. They tell, faithfully of a countryside absolutely altered now and I have thought, therefore, these tales should have a sort of value. But it appears not.'

In 1976, fifty-three years after that letter was written, her wish came true, the Boydell Press in Ipswich republished *The Fields of Dulditch*, with an introduction by Ronald Blythe, who describes the stories as 'bitter and remarkable, the writing very accomplished and vivid.' Fifteen years later Morrow and Co. of Bungay published *Tales of Victorian Norfolk,* which included some stories that did not appear in the 1902 edition. Both these publications owed a lot to the enthusiasm and tenacity of a small group of people, chiefly E.A. Goodwyn, John Baxter and Diana Hyde. Mary Mann would no doubt have been delighted that at last, in 2008, a Norfolk publishing house is producing a complete collection of all her Dulditch stories, in one volume. Now, surely, her talents will be more widely recognised and she can take her proper place in the canon of English Literature.

Patience Tomlinson
Stanhoe, Norfolk 2008

Patience Tomlinson has created a one-woman show about the life and work of Mary E. Mann entitled *A Tale That Is Told,* which she has performed in many venues in and out of Norfolk. A frequent performer on BBC Radio 3 and 4, she has broadcast several of Mary Mann's short stories and four of these are available on CD under the title *The Fields of Dulditch.* Further recordings will include more Dulditch stories and audio books of *Rose at Honeypot* and *Astray in Arcady.*

OUR MARY

SHE is not indigenous to the soil of Dulditch, our Mary having been sent to us from a distant part of the country, a Heaven-given reply to our urgent need of someone to come and help us out of our muddle and take care of us.

It was the winter of our direst necessity. The rector's wife newly dead; her baby left to me, the rector's sister, a maiden lady with no knowledge of babyhood, to bring up as best I could. Guy, the other child, ill with whooping-cough; the rector himself – always an unpractical, dreary-natured man, almost paralysed by the trouble which had befallen him – nearly useless as a guide or support of his disorganised household. The servants, as is the nature of their class, deserting us in our sorest need.

She was not a person of a promising appearance – the new 'general'. We groaned in spirit when she first made her appearance among us – an overgrown, freckle-faced, sandy-haired girl of sixteen, wearing her best frock, a garment of green merino trimmed with black braid, far above the tops of her heavy boots; her short white apron – there were no bibs to aprons in those days and no embroidery to adorn them – standing out stiffly from a huge waist; a lace tucker in the neck of her dress and round her beef-red wrists. I look back with a smile still to Mary's advent upon the scene.

I was sitting, the baby in her wicker cradle by my side, over the dining-room fire, the nursery having been made over to Guy and his whooping-cough, when a startling knock at the door announced the new servant's arrival. To the present day our Mary insists on hammering at doors with a knuckle as hard as a poker and with a vigour that is like to splinter the panels. A rush of cold air always enters with her.

'Ef ye plase, miss, I'm come,' she announced.

With a sinking of the heart I murmured that I was pleased to see her, and was going on faintly to speak to her about her future duties in the house – an oration upon which she intruded without any ceremony.

'Ye look rare and comf'table – don't ye?' she inquired.

Her pale blue eyes, with the glitter in them, roved about the room. They fell at last upon the brown wicker cradle, and with a whoop and a swoop Mary had hurled herself into the room and fallen, so to say, upon the baby.

'Well, ain't she a rare po'r little thing!' she remarked, with no consideration whatsoever for the feelings of the relatives of the infant under discussion. 'Ain't she got big eyes, nayther! My mother's little Uthel, she ha' got eyes almost as blue, but they ain't so trumenjuous large!'

Upon these signs of friendly interest I asked her if she was specially fond of babies, and Mary, on her knees by the cot, looked up at me with her sidelong glance, which, darting forth from between her white lashes, has something sly and yet deprecating in it.

'I'm fond of 'em – bain't yew?' she inquired.

She had and has an incurably familiar manner; it is difficult to keep at a dignified distance from Mary.

'She be a chokin'!' she cried, looking back at the child. Her words filled me with terror. In my inexperience each fresh development of infantile ways was a cause of new alarm. 'Tha's 'cos she's a laying on her back. Yew shouldn't put little uns like her on their backses.'

Paying no heed to my feeble protests, she pulled the baby from the cradle. Her arms, awkward as they look, appear to have been made for the holding of children. The child, rocked in them, its little face pressed against the green frock, tight to bursting across Mary's bosom, was soon asleep, and lay peacefully on Mary's knees. She had seated herself upon the hearthrug at my feet, her own tucked under her, and she now looked critically down upon the infant, whose tiny hands she held locked in her own red fists.

'My mother's little Uthel, she 'ud make tew on her,' she soliloquised. 'Well, she du fare a po'r little thing! I 'spec' she bain't long for this warld,' she continued; 'and 'ont that be a mussy, neither, when th' Lord'll take 'er?'

I thought it less painful to decline the discussion of the baby's future, and talked to Mary instead upon what would be her duties in the house. They were duties, I took occasion to remark, with which the nursery and the children had nothing to do.

Mary gave me that sidelong glance which would so prejudice a physiognomist against her.

'When I ha' done my work I shall hold 'er though,' she said, indicating the baby on her knees. 'I shall ha' ter hold her, tu, I shall miss my mother's little Uthel so trumenjuous!'

We thought from former experience that the work which fell to her share would probably exhaust the 'general's' energies, but we did not know our Mary. No amount of dishes to wash, of bread to bake, of floors to scrub, would keep her out of the nursery if Margaret cried, no remonstrance or entreaty or command. Nurse after nurse left on account of the 'general's' unwarrantable interference. Roused to indignation at last by the resignation of a really efficient nurse, by whose experience we particularly desired the baby to profit, I gave Mary notice to quit.

Her sense of injury was great. She argued the point with me with much spirit.

'Ain't I kep' you straight and looked arter things?' she demanded. 'Don't your tea and sugar last twice as long since I'm here? Yew said it yerself. Bain't there as much again bread ate in the house since I ha' baked it? An' if so be as yew ate bread ye can't ate mate, and so your butcher's bill is seft.'

I acknowledged our indebtedness to her in various ways, and commended her honesty and fidelity, but pointed out that the baby's nurse would not brook her interference.

'Yew and her want me niver so much as to touch th' baby, then?' she inquired slowly; and I confessed that that was the plain state of the case.

Mary said no more, but for a couple of days went about her work in a very half-hearted and indifferent fashion – pale of face, pink of eye and nose. At length, seeing her tears fall like rain into her wash-tub one morning, I weakly inquired into the cause of her grief.

'I miss my mother's little Uthel trumenjuous!' she said.

It has been told of me that I am always to be conquered by the sound of a snuffle – by the sight of a falling tear. I certainly succumbed on this occasion, leaving the girl triumphant, with permission to sit with the baby when her work was done, so long as she did not infringe nurse's rules.

When Guy came down from nursery regions that afternoon we learnt of fearful things there. Over the unconscious body of the infant it seemed that the nurse and the 'general' had actually fought. Nurse had thrown the baby's bottle at Mary; Mary had slapped nurse's face. Nurse had thereupon left the 'general' master of the field and had gone to pack up her boxes; and almost immediately here she was at the door, very injured and angry, and insisting on leaving the Rectory at that very instant.

After that no reproaches had the effect of damping Mary's ardour. In the flush of victory she did the work of two people, and did it in such a thorough fashion as no two people at the Rectory had ever done it before. She arose before daybreak, that, her own legitimate labours being over, the coveted privilege of washing, dressing, and nursing the

21

infant till it slept again might be hers. Hour after hour of nights when the weakly child was fretful she, untired, carried it about in her arms. In such fashion her 'month's notice' crept away, and the day came on which she must go. We talked among ourselves of how she would bring herself to part from her precious charge.

'Let her stay,' pleaded the rector, always tempted to do the easy thing, always yielding to pressure. I had to remind him that Mary in many things had behaved badly; that while she remained I could not uphold authority; that in the end it would be bad for Margaret. Upon which representations he turned his back, as his habit is in all controversy, and went out of the room. I had once or twice attempted a word with Mary herself on the subject of her approaching departure. She heard me in stolid silence as far as her tongue was concerned, but it must be confessed she made the plates and dishes, the kitchen doors, and the tinware to speak.

Margaret, grown a year old now, was unusually fretful on the eventful day which was to see the last of the 'general'. It is a humiliating fact that in spite of all my love and devoted care, my anxious desire to please, the child would always turn from my blandishments to the rough arms, the hard bosom of Mary – a curious freak of preference a little difficult to bear.

She was sitting on my lap, resisting all my efforts to amuse her, when Mary, announced by her habitual attack on the door, appeared. The 'general' was attired in the green merino, grown shorter now, the black hat and white feather which on Sunday afternoons in the Rectory servants' pew were such an offence in my eyes, but which Mary had stoutly refused to relinquish. She was equipped for her journey, down to her white cotton gloves and her horn-handled umbrella.

So she stood for a minute silent in the doorway, and in her eyes was a great scorn of my ineffectual efforts to comfort the fractious child – a great longing was in them too.

In my own eyes, somewhat to my astonishment, the tears rose. The girl had been a comfort in many ways, although so impossible in others. To be going away from Dulditch, to be leaving for ever little Margaret, was not that a fate to awake compassion in the hardest heart?

'You have been a good girl, Mary,' I said. 'We shall be glad to hear that you are doing well. We shall not forget you.'

On Mary's part ungracious silence; on that of little Margaret loud cries and a passionate struggle to get out of my arms and to escape to Mary.

'Put 'er down and let 'er crape,' Mary cried with a kind of contemptuous authority. 'Yew be a hurtin' on 'er like that.'

'You'll have your mother's little Ethel, you know,' I reminded her, determined not to show offence, while Margaret, being put upon the floor, had hushed her crying and was putting much energy and enthusiasm into the exercise of 'craping'. I had hold of her dress, but she had bolted under the table, and, finding it inconvenient to follow, I perforce let her go. Running round to catch the child as she emerged, I found myself too late. With a crow of delight the little thing had made for Mary and clutched the green merino dress.

Triumphantly Mary flung down her umbrella and clawed the baby to her heart.

'I ha' got 'er,' she cried with a defiant look at me. She held the child tightly with one arm and pulled off her hat and feather. 'I bain't a goin' to lave her, nayther,' she declared, glaring at me. 'Nothin' 'ont make me lave her, and so I tell yer.'

And, although this was by no means the only effort made to get rid of our Mary, she never did leave us.

'Time little Margaret live I'm agoin' to stop along of her,' she always said. 'When she be gone I'll go if yer like.'

But although Margaret has been gone this many a year, Mary is with us still.

She is a hard-featured, middle-aged woman now, speaking always of herself as a 'gal' still. She has contrived to save money in our service, the green merino having had few successors, and Mary being always 'wunnerful keerful' over her things. When savings are spoken of suitors will appear, and more than once the household has been disturbed to its foundation by the announcement that its prop and mainstay was about to be wrenched from it – that our Mary was going to be married.

Experience of the worth of such intimations enables us now to treat the news with outward respect, but without any undue disturbance of equanimity.

'I ha' got another young man. I be goin' to git married, come Michaelmas,' is a sentence with which we are pretty familiar.

Mary's courting exercises run about the same course, and we can watch the proceedings without any too lively an interest, knowing well what will be the end. They generally begin, as in the case of Teddy Pyman, a young man of blameless character, but of rather weak intellect, over the chickens in the spring. Mary is clever in the rearing of fowls, and in the spring of the year a good deal of her time is spent on the 'drying-ground' where the hencoops are. Teddy, who makes a short cut through the small enclosed meadow on his way home from work, sits on the gate beneath the April sky and, with an abstracted air, pulls off a twig from the thorn-hedge beside him, or a gummy chestnut bud from the great tree above his head, and flings it at Mary's dress as she busies herself about the chickens. Mary, muttering to herself, with her eyes dropped to the little yellow chicks she has gathered in her apron, is as unresponsive as a stone wall. Having presently finished with the chickens, and without so much as a glance in Teddy's direction, Mary twitches some clothes off the linen line, stoops to pick up a large turnip which has fallen from a passing tumbril, and walks towards the house. The young man has slipped from the gate now, and, slouching behind her, still endeavours to attract her attention by missiles – pebbles now, or dry lumps of earth – despatched in her direction, and which hit her now and again on cheek or shoulder or in the small of her back.

Having reached the safe shelter of the kitchen door, Mary turns, and without the slightest warning responds to the above delicate attentions by flinging the turnip she carries straight in his face. The turnip is so large and she despatches it with so hearty a force that it looks like taking Teddy's head off. He is not a quick lad, but he manages to duck the ugly head in time to save it, and he greets the loud slamming of the door as Mary retreats with a yell of laughter.

When the next evening comes he is on the gate again: and the next, and the next.

Presently Mary goes out to shut up her chickens for the night without her cap. The cap is an immense improvement to Mary's appearance, but she does not recognise the fact, and always doffs it when admirers are about. Soon there comes an evening when, the grass in the drying-ground being slippery from the late rain, Mary tumbles over a refractory chicken which refuses to be tucked under its mother's wing, and measures her length upon the ground. Whereat the gallant gentleman upon the gate roars with an uncouth laughter.

'Don't set a goldering theer,' Mary says, with a stiff smile upon her own long lip and a sidelong glance from beneath her white lashes. 'Come and ketch it yerself, yer chump-hid!'

So encouraged, Teddy slides slowly from the gate, secures the refractory chicken, while Mary wipes the effects of her fall from her afternoon frock; and a recognised stage in the courtship has been reached.

After this, although he makes no more effort to assist her than lies in the sticking out of a heavy foot to prevent the escape of one of the brood, or the lazy kicking towards her of the sacks with which she secures the coops from the night air, the young man always slouches at Mary's back instead of lounging on the gate, and he is reported to be 'helping Mary with the chickens'.

'Tha's a rare bad job he ha' got that theer cross in's eye, ain't it?' Mary inquires of me soon, by way of introducing the important subject. 'That young chap – *yew* know – Tedder, then, Tedder Pyment,' she explains with the sidelong glance and the wriggle which portend the discussion of the tender passion; 'I'm a kapin' comp'ny 'long o' him – him and me's goin' to git married come Michaelmas.'

In Mary's preparations for marriage there is a peculiarity which I mention with diffidence, because of the censoriousness of the world. I must only entreat the charitable reader at this point not to give way to doubts which wrong her, but to hold our Mary to be, like the wife of Cæsar, above suspicion. Instead, then, of getting her *trousseau* ready, turning her thoughts to the making and laying-by of body-linen and dresses, as is the world-wide, time-honoured custom of intending brides, Mary devotes all her thought and ingenuity to the formation of the *layette*. In her bedroom she has a box devoted to her stock of baby-linen. In all her spare moments after the appearance of a lover she is to be seen busily cutting out and sewing little garments which her clumsy fingers most cleverly fashion and adorn. She mutters to herself over her needle with a very happy look.

'Ef so be as 'tis a gal – and I want it to be a gal – 'tis to be called Marg'ret,' she says, displaying some of the handiwork. 'Marg'ret and me used ter talk over how I were to have a little gal o' my own that were to be called arter her.'

It is useless to remonstrate with her on the premature nature of her work.

'Oh, ah! Some people is allust a puttin' orf,' she says with contempt.

The chance that her union might not be blessed with children has been pointed out to her.

'There bain't no sense i' getting married onless ye're to have child'en. I don't hold wi' no such a foolishness as that come tu, nayther,' she says.

So for a little she stitches busily away, and then, as in the case of Teddy, the chickens being reared and Michaelmas near, a change comes over the young dream of love which periodically visits our

Mary. The baby-linen is locked away in the box. Teddy may wait in vain, slouching about the kitchen door, lounging against the drying-ground gate. She takes the precaution to hang out her linen and to gather it in at an hour when the young man's occupation detains him at a safe distance. She has no quarrel with him, enters into no argument on the subject, listens to no lover's appeal. He may linger in the autumn air amid the flapping, wet sheets, may even, urged by the desperation of his case to show the reality of his love, re-erect her linen props for her, blown down in last night's gale; or, way-laying her in an unwary moment, attempt to carry her basket of linen.

Without any compunction for the false hopes she has raised and the havoc she has wrought in his affections, she elbows him out of her way, tells him she has no longer time to play the fool, and gives him various salutary but blunt pieces of advice as to his future conduct.

Teddy is convinced at last that his luck is to be no better than that of his predecessors; that his chances, for that year at any rate, are over. If he stay in the same mind till the chickens come again – no newer admirer being beforehand with him on the drying-ground – he can resume his *rôle* for the season. At the end of it he will meet with the same fate.

Poor Mary! That visionary baby of hers, which was to bear the beloved name, short-coated long ago, should be old enough by now to wear the green merino in which her mother came to Dulditch. Each time that the swain is sent about his business and Mary turns to the sober duties of her life again, she presents the greater part of those shirts and gowns and flannel head-pieces to some expectant mother in the village, whose hopes are more certainly fulfilled than Mary's. But in the spring-time, when the world that was dead, with all its hopes and promises, lives again, she is bound to set to work to fill her box once more.

While she lives, I suppose, the maternal instinct will cry out in Mary. She is so constructed that the blandishments of the rustic lover beguile her only partially and for a little while; she wearies of the 'fuleries' of the mate apportioned her; but the attractiveness of that baby head which should lie against her breast, of the helpless feet that should dance in her lap, of the clinging hands in her own, will fascinate her imagination till her death-bed.

It is said in the village that Mary rules the Rectory. At the Rectory it is known that she does not rule with a gentle hand. There is an air of contemptuousness in her management of us which is a little hard to bear. We cannot always do what we will with our own: there are certain days on which we dare not invite visitors to our house; there are one or two parishioners to whom we have to show attention *sub rosa*, Mary not approving of their persons or characters or ways of 'goin' on'; there are others who are pushed forward for soup and brandy and 'pieces' on all occasions. There was one summer-time, she being for some reason unusually crusty ('short-waisted' she calls this state of mind herself), when she would not sanction our giving the annual school treat. We dared not undertake it without her approval.

She is always specially 'difficult' when the church bells ring; can barely tolerate their tolling for church, and is rendered furious by the practice for Christmas, the New Year, and other festivals. She has, indeed, a curious terror of music. It is not often now that there are any to make music at the Rectory, but on those occasions when Guy runs down, and old friends of his look in upon us; when the piano is opened again, and again the

> 'Plaintive numbers flow
> For old unhappy, far-off things,
> And battles long ago,'

then Mary takes refuge in the underground cellar and muffles her head in a shawl.

It may be that the 'melancholy madness' is trying to Mary's nerve; it may be that she is unusually susceptible of the charm of music; she is, perhaps, dimly conscious that, if she ceased to withstand its sway, its power over her might become irresistible; perhaps the 'measured malice' awakes within her longings which tear her breast with unspeakable pain. Mary does not plead any of these excuses. She calls music a 'terrufic n'ise,' and says it gives her a 'sinkin' in 'er in'ards.'

She might be induced to go to the church oftener but for the music, she thinks, but she speaks with no certainty on the point. Familiarity, I fear, has accomplished its usual office, and bred contempt in the Rectory servant of the forms of that religion which is the Rectory 'consarn,' as she puts it. She is unable to separate the master in the pulpit, with his learning, his ascendancy, his voice of authority, from the master of the home, who has to be scolded for forgetting to put a comforter round his neck; whose study fire has to be lit six times a day because he is not to be trusted to put on the coals; who is so wickedly unpunctual about meals.

'I don't want him a-setting up ter tache me,' Mary says with frank disdain; 'ef so be as ivver I want ter pray, I take it I kin pray without such as him.'

So, instead of going to church, Mary sits over the kitchen fire on the Sabbath with her Bible in her lap. It is, in fact, a monster Bible, being one which she bought at the door of a travelling agent, expending all her earnings upon it – long ago, when Margaret was a baby.

There never was a Sunday afternoon after the acquisition of this treasure which Mary and Margaret did not spend over its vilely illuminated sheets. The tiny fingers could point out Noah on his knees before his fire of sticks, the rainbow over his head, Abraham with the abnormal muscular developments, the sacrificial knife raised above his son, long before her baby tongue could speak their names. On the very last Sunday afternoon of the child's life she and Mary went through the pages with as much interest as if they had never seen them before.

On that day, coming home from church, I entered the Rectory by the kitchen door. The kitchen had that inexplicable, indescribably Sabbath air which places have on the hallowed day, which Nature herself always wears. On the much-scrubbed deal table was a great brown gotch full of lilac, and the Bible, with Margaret, her head propped on her hand, leaning over it; one of Mary's hard red hands rested on the book waiting to turn the leaves. (She always honours the Sabbath day by wearing in the afternoons a brass watch-chain which one of her lovers gave her.) I remember that Margaret's brown hair, turned to bronze and gold in places by the kiss of the afternoon sun, fell upon the picture of the Flood.

It is partly the possession of that enormous Bible which gives Mary such a feeling of superiority to the rector. Once, in a moment of expansion, anxious to share the blessings that were hers, she carried the book, wrapped in the cloth which always enveloped it, into the dining-room and laid it proudly down before her master's chair.

'The gays are wonnerful instructin',' she said, her eyes on her treasure, her person modestly withdrawn from its neighbourhood. 'There's in ut Angels, and Balum's dicky a crunching of his master's fut.'

The rector, who does not care to tackle Mary herself, was very severe when her back was turned on the sin of vulgarising Holy Writ by such abominable caricatures. As he turned from one illustration to another he grew reproachful as well as severe. Surely, he said, we who for so many years had enjoyed the inestimable privilege of sheltering this good and faithful servant beneath our roof should have done something to correct her taste, to elevate her understanding. She had given us her best, and we – what had we done in return? The duties we felt called upon to perform towards our inferiors were only gross, material ones. If we had fed sumptuously, knowing that one among us was perishing for want of food, we should be called culpable, and the world would cry out on us. But here was one, starved of all culture, associating with us who boasted of our refinement, yet a savage in matters of taste. 'Shame! Shame!' said the rector, having turned his back on the book, and mildly lecturing his son and me as he paced the room.

And then Guy, who happened to be at home on that occasion, and who had lounged up to inspect the cause of so much eloquence, gave a shout of laughter and called on his father to admire with him the representation of Lot's wife.

And while the Rector, his homily forgotten, an unwilling smile on his lips, stood there with a hand upon Guy's shoulder, I took heart to tell him how, for all her little life, Margaret had loved the blue and red and yellow daubs; and I told him too of that picture, always present to my mind, of the child on that last Sunday afternoon with her rippled hair falling upon the picture of the Flood.

After that the rector sat down by Guy's side, and silently and in reverence looked at the dreadful plates, and said no other word of condemnation. And presently, when the end was reached, he arose and himself carried back the book into the kitchen. Then, in that polite and deferential manner he always exhibits to Mary, he thanked her for her kindness in lending the book and for all her kindness.

'I don't want ter fluster myself to go to church now I ha' got that, do I now?' Mary calls after him, gratified and triumphant, as he departs. The rector hastens his steps a little; he always shirks an argument with Mary.

'So long as I ha' got 'em all theer, and kin see th' devil a temptin' o' Ave, and th' 'arth a-opinin' ter swaller Abiram, I bain't a-goin' ter trouble no fudder about 'em,' Mary mutters to herself, turning back to her book.

WOMEN O' DULDITCH

DINAH BROME stood in the village shop, watching, with eyes keen to detect the slightest discrepancy in the operation, the weighing of her weekly parcels of grocery.

She was a strong, wholesome-looking woman of three- or four-and-forty, with a clean, red skin, clear eyes, dark hair, crinkling crisply beneath her sober, respectable hat. All her clothes were sober and respectable, and her whole mien. No one would have guessed from it that she had not a shred of character to her back.

The knowledge of this incontrovertible fact did not influence the demeanour of the shop-woman towards her. There was no better payer in the village, nor a more constant customer than Dinah Brome. In such circumstances, Mrs Littleproud was not the woman to throw stones.

'They tell me as how Depper's wife ain't a-goin' to get over this here sickness she've got,' she said, tucking in the edges of the whitey-brown paper upon the half-pound of moist sugar taken from the scales. 'The doctor, he ha'n't put a name to her illness, but 'tis one as'll carry her off, he say.'

'A quarter pound o' butter,' Dinah unmovedly said, 'The best, please. I don't fancy none o' that that ha' got the taste o' the shop in it.'

'Doctor, he put his hid in at the door this afternoon,' Mrs Littleproud went on; 'he'd got his monkey up, the old doctor had! "'Tis a rank shame," he say, "there ain't none o' these here lazy women o' Dulditch with heart enough to go to help that poor critter in her necessity," he say.'

'Ler'm help her hisself,' said Mrs Brome, strong in her indifference. 'A couple o' boxes o' matches, Mrs Littleproud; and you can gi' me the odd ha'penny in clo' balls for the digestion.'

'You should ha' heered 'm run on! "Where be that Dinah Brome?" he say, "that ha' showed herself helpful in other folks' houses. Wha's she a-doin' of, that she can't do a neighbour's part here?"'

'And you telled 'm she was a-mindin' of 'er own business, I hope?' Mrs Brome suggested, in calmest unconcern.

'I'll tell you what I did say, Dinah, bor,' the shopwoman said, transferring the sticky clove-balls from their bottle to her own greasy palm. 'Dinah Brome, sir,' I say, 'is the most industrousest woman in Dulditch; arly and late,' I say, 'she's at wark; and as for her floors –

you might eat off of 'em.' She screwed the half-dozen hard red balls in their bit of paper, and stowed them lightly in the customer's basket. 'That the lot this week, Dinah?'

Dinah removed her basket from counter to arm. 'What'd he got to say for hisself, then?' she asked.

' "A woman like that can allust make time," the old doctor he say. "Tell her to make time to help this here pore sufferin' woman." I'm a-sayin' it as he said it, Dinah. I ain't a-hintin' of it myself, bor.'

'Ler'm tell me, hisself, an old interfarin' old fule, and he'll ha' the rough side o' my tongue,' the customer said; and nodded an unsmiling good-afternoon, and went on her way.

Her way led her past the cottage of the woman of whom they had spoken. Depper's cottage, indeed, was the first in the row of which Dinah's was the last – a half-dozen two-roomed tenements, living-room below, bedroom above, standing with their backs to the road, from which they were divided by no garden nor even so much as a narrow path. The lower window of the two allotted to each house was about four or five feet from the ground, and was of course the window of the living-room. Mrs Brome, as she passed that of the first house in the row, suddenly yielded to the impulse to stop and look within.

A small interior, with furniture much too big for it; a huge chest of drawers, of oak with brass fittings; a broken-down couch as big as a bed, covered with a dingy shawl, a man's greatcoat, a red flannel petticoat; a table cumbered with the remains of wretched meals never cleared away, and the poor cooking utensils of impoverished, shifty housekeeping.

The woman of whom they had been speaking stood with her back to the window. A stooping, drooping skeleton of a woman, who, with weak, shaking hands, kneaded some dough in which a few currants were stuck, before laying it on a black-looking baking tin.

'A fine time o' day to bake his fourses cake!' the woman outside commented, reaching on tiptoe, the better to look in at the window.

The tin, having its complement of cakes, the sick woman essayed to carry it to the oven. But its weight was too much for her; it hung limply in her weak grasp; before the oven was reached the cakes were on the ragged carpet of the hearth.

'God in heaven!' ejaculated the woman looking in.

She watched while the poor woman within dropped on all-fours, feebly trying to gather up the cakes spreading themselves slowly over the dirty floor.

31

'If that don't make me sick!' said Dinah Brome to herself as she turned and went on her way.

The cottage of Dinah Brome, distant from that of Depper's wife by a score or so of yards, was, in its domestic economy, as removed from it as the North Pole from the South. Small wonder that Depper – his name was William Kittle, a fact of which the neighbourhood made no practical use, which he himself only recalled with an effort – preferred to the dirt, untidiness and squalor of his own abode the spick-and-span cleanliness of Dinah Brome's. Small wonder that in this atmosphere of wholesomeness and comfort, he chose to spend the hours of the Sabbath during which the public-house was closed; and other hours. Small wonder, looking at the fine, capable figure of the woman, now bustling about with teapot and cups, he should esteem Mrs Brome personally above the slatternly skeleton at his own hearth.

Having made a cup of tea and cut a couple of slices of bread-and-butter, the owner of the fresh-scrubbed bricks, the fresh polished furniture, the dazzlingly white hearth, turned her back on her household gods, and, plate and cup in hands, betook herself, by way of the uneven bricked passage separating the row of houses from their rows of gardens at the back, to the house of the wife of Depper.

'I swore I wouldn't,' she said to herself as she went along; 'but I'm dinged if the sight o' Depper's old woman a-crawlin' arter them mamucked up bits o' dough ha'n't tarned my stomach!'

She knocked at the door with the toe of her boot, her hands being full, and receiving no answer, opened it and went in.

Depper's old woman had fallen, a miserable heap of bones and dingy clothing, upon the broken-down couch, and had fainted there.

'I'd suner 'twas anyone in the warld than you a-waitin' on me like this,' she said, when, consciousness having returned during the ministrations of the other woman, her weary eyes opened upon the healthy face above her.

'And the las' time you told me to walk out o' your house, I swore I'd never set fut in it again,' Mrs Brome made answer. 'But I ha' swallowed worse things in my time than my own wards, I make no doubt; and you ha' come to a pass, Car'line Kittle, when you ha' got to take what you can git and be thankful.'

'Pass? I ha' come to a pass, indeed!' the sick woman moaned. 'You're wholly right there, bor; wholly right.'

'So now you ha' got to drink this here cup o' hot tea I ha' brought ye; and let me help ye upstairs to yer bed as quick as may be.'

'When I ha' baked Depper's fourses cake, and sent it off by 'Meelyer's little gal – she ha' lent her to me to go back and forth to the harvest-field, Meelyer have – I kin go,' the wife said; 'not afore,' hiccoughing loudly over the tea she tried to drink; 'not afore – not afore! Oh, how I wish I could bor; how I wish I could!'

'You're a-goin', this instant minute,' the masterful Dinah declared.

The other had not the strength to resist. 'I'm wholly done,' she murmured, helplessly, 'wholly done at last.'

'My! How ha' you got up these here stairs alone?' Dinah, having half-dragged, half-carried the feeble creature to the top, demanded of her, wiping her own brow.

'Crawled, all-fours.' Depper's wife panted out the explanation. 'And to git down 'em i' the mornin's – oh, the Lord alone knows how I ha' got down 'em i' th' mornin's. Thankful I'd be to know I'd never ha' to come down 'em agin.'

'You never will,' said Mrs Brome.

'I don't want to trouble you, no fudder. I can fend for myself now,' the poor woman said, when at length she lay at peace between the sheets; her face bathed, and the limp grimy fingers; the scant dry hair smoothed decently down the fallen temples. 'I'd rather it'd ha' been another woman that had done me the sarvice, but I ain't above bein' thankful to you, for all that. All I'll ask of ye now, Dinah Brome, is that ye'll have an eye to Depper's fourses cake in th' oven, and see that 'Meelyer's gal take it and his home-brew, comf'table, to the field for 'm.'

Dinah, having folded the woman's clothes, spread them for additional warmth upon the poor bedcovering. 'Don't you worrit no more about Depper,' she said. 'Strike me, you're the one that wants seein' to now, Car'line.'

The slow tears oozed beneath Car'line's closed lids. 'I kin fend for myself if Depper ain't put about,' she said.

When Depper returned, with the shades of night, from the harvest-field, he might hardly have known his own living-room. The dirty rags of carpet had disappeared, the bricks were scrubbed, the dangerous-looking heap of clothing had been removed from the sofa, and a support added to its broken leg; the fireside chairs, the big chest of drawers, redolent of the turpentine with which they had been rubbed, shone in the candlelight; the kettle sang on the bars by the side of a saucepan of potatoes boiling for the meal. It was the sight of Dinah Brome at the head of affairs, however, which drew his attention from these details.

'Well, I'm jiggered!' Depper said, and paused, door in hand, on his own freshly-washed step.

'You wipe your feet, afore you come in,' said Mrs Brome, masterful as ever. 'Here's yer supper ready. I ain't a-goin' to ate it along of you, Depper; but I ha' got a ward or two to say to you afore I go.'

Depper entered, closed the door behind him, sat down, hat on head, in the freshly-polished chair by the hearth; he fixed his eyes, his mouth fallen open, on the fine form of Dinah standing before him, with hands on hips, arms akimbo, and the masterful gleam in her eyes.

'Depper, yer old woman's a-dyin',' Dinah said.

'Marcy on us! Ye don't tell me that! Kind o' piney, like, fer the las' six months, my missus ha' bin', but –'

'Now she's a-dyin'. D'ye think I ha'n't got the right use o' my senses, arter all these years? Wheer ha' yer own eyes been? Look at 'er! No better'n a skeercrow of a woman, under yer very nose! She's a-dyin', I tell ye. And, Depper, what du I come here to find? I find a bare cupboard and a bare board. Not a mite o' nouragement i' th' house, sech as a pore suff'rin' woman like Car'line's in need of.'

'Car'line's a pore manager, as right well you know, Dinah. Ha'n't I telled ye –?'

'You ha' telled me – yes. But have you played th' husban's part? You ha' telled me – and I ha' put the fault o' yer poverty home on ter yer pore missus' shoulders. But since I been here, I ha' seen 'er crawlin' on 'er han's and knees to wait on you, wi' yer fourses i' th' harvest-field. I ha' heered her manderin' on, "let things be comf'table for Depper," and let her fend for herself. And I can see with half an eye the bute is on t'other fut, Depper. And this here is what I'm a-goin' to say to you, and don't you make no mistake about it: I'm yer wife's woman while she wants me, and none o' yours.'

Depper was a small, well-made man, with a curling, grizzled head, and a well-featured face. It is possible that in his youth the word 'dapper' may have applied to him; a forgotten fact which perhaps accounted for his nickname. He gazed with an open mouth and puzzled, blear eyes at the woman before him.

'You and me,' he said slowly, with an utterance suspiciously slow and thick – 'you and me ha' kep' comp'ny, so to speak, for a sight o' years, Dinah. We never had no fallin's out, this mander, afore, as I can call ter mind. I don't rightly onderstan' what you ha' got agin me – come ter put it into wards.'

'I ha' got this agin ye,' the valiant Dinah said: 'that you ha' nouraged yer own inside and let your missus's go empty. You ha' got too much drink aboard ye, now, an' her fit ter die for the want of a drop o' sperrits. And I ha' got this ter say: that we ha' come to a pass when I ha' got to make ch'ice twixt you and yer old woman. Arter wha's come and gone, we t'ree can't hob an' nob, as ye may say, together. My ch'ice is made, then, and this is how I ha' fixed it up. When yer day's wark is done, and you come home, I go out o' your house. Sune as ye up an' away i' th' mornin', I come in and ridd up yer missus and wait on 'er, while the woman's in need of me.'

Whether this plan met with Depper's approval or not, Dinah Brome did not wait to see. 'For Car'line's peace o' mind, arter what's come and gone, 'tis th' only way,' she said to herself and to him; and by it he had to abide.

It was not for many weeks. The poor unlovely wife, lying in the dismantled four-poster in the only bedroom, was too far gone to benefit by the 'nouragement' Mrs Brome contrived to administer. The sixpenn'orths of brandy Depper, too late relenting, spared from the sum he had hitherto expended on his own beer – public-house brandy, poisonous stuff, but accredited by the labouring population of Dulditch with all but magical restorative powers – for once failed in its effect. Daily more of a skeleton, hourly feebler and feebler, grew Depper's old woman; clinging, for all that, desperately to life and the hope of recovery for the sake of Depper himself.

'Let go the things of this life, lay hold on those of Eternity,' the clergyman said, solemnly reproving her for her worldly state of mind. 'Remember that there is no one in this world whose life is indispensable to the scheme of it. Try to think more humbly of yourself, my poor friend, less regretfully of the world you are hurrying from. Fix your eyes on the heavenly prospect. Try to join with me more heartily in the prayers for the dying.'

She listened to them, making no response, with slow tears falling from shut lids to pillow. ''Tain't for myself I'm a-pinin', 'tis for Depper,' she said, the parson being gone.

'All the same, Car'line,' Mrs Brome said, sharply admonishing, 'I'd marmar a ward now and agin for myself, as the reverend ha' been advisin' of ye, if I was you. Depper he can look arter hisself; his time for prayin' ain't, so ter say, come yet. Yours is. I should like to hear a "Lord help me," now and agin from yer lips, when I tarn ye in the bed. I don't think but what yu'd be the better for it, pore critter. Your time's a-gettin' short, and 'tis best ter go resigned.'

'I cud go resigned if 'tweren't for Depper,' the dying woman made her moan.

'I can't think what he'll du all alone in th' house and me gone!' she often whimpered. 'A man can't fend for 'isself, like a woman can. They ha'n't the know ter du it. Depper, he ain't no better'n a child about makin' the kettle bile, and sechlike. It'll go hard, me bein' put out o' the way, wi' Depper.'

'Sarve 'm right,' Mrs Brome always stoically said. 'He ha' been a bad man to you, Car'line. I don' know whu should speak to that if you and me don't, bor.'

'He ha'n't so much as laid a finger on me since I was ill,' Car'line said, making what defence for the absent man she could.

'All the same, when you're a-feelin' wholly low agin, jes' you say to yourself, "Th' Lord help me!" 'Tis only dacent, you a dyin' woman, to do it. When ye ha'n't got the strength ter say it, I'll go on my knees and say it for ye, come to that, Car'line,' the notorious wrongdoer promised.

They sent for Depper to the White Hart to come home and see his wife die.

'I ain't, so to say, narvish, bein' alone with 'er, and would as lief see the pore sufferin' critter draw her las' breath as not, but I hold 'tis dacent for man and wife to be together, come to th' finish; an' so I ha' sent for ye,' Mrs Brome told him.

Depper shed as many tears over his old woman as would have been expected from the best husband in the world; and Car'line let her dying gaze rest on him with as much affection, perhaps, as if he had indeed been that ideal person.

'There'll be money a-comin' in from th' club,' were almost her last words to him. She was speaking of the burial-club, into which she had always contrived to pay the necessary weekly pence; she knew it to be the surest consolation she could offer him.

Depper had made arrangements already for the payment of the eleven pounds from the burial-club; he had drunk a pint or two extra, daily, for the last week, the innkeeper being willing to trust him, in consideration of the expected windfall. The excitement of this handling of sudden wealth, and the dying of his wife, and the extra drink combined, completely upset his mental equilibrium. In the first moments of his widower-hood he was prostrate with emotion.

Dragged downstairs by the strong arm of Dinah Brome, he subsided into the chair on the hearth, opposite that for ever empty one of his old woman's; and with elbows on knees and head on hand he hiccoughed and moaned and wept aloud.

Above, Dinah Brome and that old woman who had a reputation in Dulditch for the laying-out of corpses, decked the poor cold body in such warmth of white flannelette, and such garniture of snipped-out frilling as, alive, Car'line Kittle could never have hoped to attain to.

These last duties achieved, Dinah descended, her arms full of blankets and pillows, no longer necessary above. These, with much banging and shaking, she spread upon the downstairs couch, indicating to the still weeping Depper it was there he was expected to pass the night.

'Bor, you may well blubber!' she said to him, with a kind of comfortable scorn of him and his sorrow. 'You 'ont ketch me a-dryin' yer tears for ye, and so I tell ye flat. A crule husban' yu ha' been as any woman ever had. If ever there was a wife who was kep' short, and used hard, that was *yer* wife, Depper, my man! Bad you ha' been to her that's gone to 'er account, in all ways; who should know that better'n me, I'll ask ye? An' if at las' 'tis come home to ye, sarve ye wholly right. Tha's all the comfort ye'll get from me, bor.'

'Stop along of me!' Depper cried, as, her work being finished, she moved to the door. ''Tain't right as I should be left here alone; and me feelin' that low, and a'most dazed with affliction.'

'Tha's how you've a right to feel,' the stern woman said, unmoved by his tears.

'I keep a-thinkin' of wha's layin' up above theer, Dinah.'

'Pity you di'n't think on 'er more in 'er lifetime.'

''Tain't natural as I should be left wholly alone with a dead woman. 'Tain't a natural thing, I'm a-sayin', for me to du, Dinah, ter pass the night alone along o' my old missus's corp.'

'Bor, 'tain't the fust onnat'ral thing you ha' done i' your life,' Mrs Brome said; and went out and shut the door.

An hour or so later Depper opened it, and going hurriedly past the intervening cottages, knocked stealthily upon the door of Dinah Brome.

She looked out upon him presently from her bedroom window, her dark, crinkled hair rough from the pillow, a shawl pulled over her nightgown.

'Whu's that a-distarbin' o' me, as ha'n't had a night's rest for a week, at this time o' night?' she demanded sharply.

'It's me; Depper,' the man's voice answered, whisperingly. 'Le' me in, Dinah. I daren't be alone along of 'er no longer. I ha' only got you, Dinah, now my old woman's gone! Le' me in!'

'You're a rum un ter call yerself a man and a husban' – you are!' Dinah Brome ejaculated; but she came downstairs and opened her door.

A DULDITCH ANGEL

'SHE lived by my side a matter o' sixty yare, and she niver so much as laid a straw i' my path,' said old Angel to me, speaking of the wife he had just buried.

He was a little old man, blue-eyed, white-haired, apple-cheeked. He was dressed in the Sunday suit which had distinguished him, perhaps, from the time when he went courting the paragon he lamented: a long worn velveteen coat adorned with brass buttons, a tall hat, decorated with a hat-band now, worn at the back of his head. Under one arm he carried a huge green umbrella, under the other a heavy stick. Outside his own gate he never ventured without these implements of offence and defence; he brought both to church as regularly as he brought his Bible and Prayer-book. I never remember to have seen him use either.

There may have been in former years weather 'big' enough to warrant him in mounting the green umbrella, but he speaks of present-day downfalls cheerfully as 'a m'isture,' and lets the rain beat upon his round, rosy face, and pour off the battered brim of his tall hat, keeping his gingham safely under his arm the while. Perhaps he shrinks from seeming to claim a superiority over the other men, who have no spare cash for such trivialities as umbrellas, and who adopt no protection from the storm than an old artificial manure sack flung over their shoulders. Perhaps he fears lest the rain should injure the dear possession. It is never unfolded, neither is his stick used for support.

Old Angel lived at the extremity of the parish in a little one-storied cottage, planted all alone behind a long strip of garden, where marigolds and the dark columbine, tall white lilies, and the old York and Lancaster rose grew among the gooseberry and currant bushes. For Angel was, as will be seen, a man of sentiment and encouraged the beautiful.

The garden boasted also a very old greengage tree, the pride of old Angel's heart.

With his umbrella and his stick tucked away under his arms, he would toddle up to the Rectory in the early spring to solicit orders for the fruit. It was an unceasing satisfaction to him – a satisfaction, however, which he politely strove to conceal – that there was not a greengage tree in all the Rectory garden.

'I thought as how I'd be betimes wi' ye for th' gages,' he would say; 'I thought as how I'd give ye fust chancet. I ha' heared tell as th' Rev'rend is agraable to th' fruit; and I think, ef so be as my mem'ry don't mislade me, ye ha'nt a gage i' yer orn gaarden?'

We always hastened to confirm this point and to lament the fact.

'Maybe 'tis made up to ye,' he would continue, as one who was loath to press an advantage. 'Theer be a fine bully' (bullace tree) 'I know i' th' orchard; for one day we was a-talkin' matters over, th' Rev'rend and me, and he telled me so hisself. He di'nt patronomise th' bully like th' gages, from what he let onto me. Howsever, there be a good show t' year – th' tree be a picter for blow, and ef so be as th' kerstels' (clusters) 'set, yer may reckon I'll be able to 'blige ye. An' ef so be as I kin, my dear wumman, you may be sure I wull.'

The time of blossom is the only time of triumph for old Angel, for the harvest of the tree is apt to be sadly disappointing. We at the Rectory have had to make up to him for the deficiency of the measure we had ordered by unmeasured praise of the quality of the fruit.

''Tis a good gage,' the old fellow would admit dispassionately, looking mournfully upon the pint or so of the plums – the entire crop – he was transferring from his basket to our own, 'and th' Rev'rend is agraable to th' fruit, I know. The bully be a useful sorter plum, but he ain't to comparison in tastiness to th' gage.'

The tears ran down his cheeks as he talked about the old wife he had just laid in the churchyard. It was of her goodness to him alone he spoke; but for years we in Dulditch had witnessed his patience, his tenderness, his unfailing devotion to the peevish and afflicted old woman whose loss he now artlessly mourned.

She was, it had seemed to us, a troublesome, unlovable patient, fractious, ungrateful, indocile. In the last years of her life she had been imbecile as well as incurably afflicted in other ways. As gently and as wisely as a good mother waits on her stricken child did the old husband wait upon his wife. There were no near neighbours, and those from a distance who had lent a helping hand soon tired of the unremunerative office. He made no protest or complaint; cheerfully and alone he laboured on.

A young man rejoices over his bride, wondering at her beauty, waiting on her whims, indulging her caprices, worshipping her with heart and eye; and the world smiles indulgent at the pretty sight. Over such a devotion as this of the ignorant old pauper husband to his unlovely, ungracious old wife it has seemed to me that the angels themselves might smile, well pleased.

'I'll tell ye how't be,' he said, with his little half-childish chuckle, one day when I had been moved to express to him my appreciation of his untiring care and tenderness; 'I'll tell ye th' wuds I used to say to my old wumman in our young time, when her and me, happen, di'n't allust think alike, as, happen, men and wummen sometimes don't, "Meery" I'd say, "Meery," (these hare be th' wuds), "theer's on'y one thing to be put down to yar favour, Meery, bor," I'd say, "and that be – I love yer."'

He nodded his head triumphantly at this reminiscence. 'Tha's how't be, ye see, wi' Meery and me,' he cried in concluding the matter – 'Tha's how't be.'

About his poverty, any more than about his trials with his invalid wife, he never complained. He was neither ungrateful for kindness nor avaricious of benefits. He was incapable of grudging what fell to another's share or was given to another's necessity. More than once he refused the little money-help that could be offered him.

'Kape it yerself, my dare wumman,' he said, his stiff fingers closing mine upon the coin in my hand. 'Ye'll maybe want it as much as me. I ha' heered tell as how money's skeerse up to th' Rect'ry, and th' Rev'rend he don't look no matters hisself. Come sickness, tha's expensive, as ye'll find, mayhap. Kape 't yerself and thenk 'e.'

For any little service he does accept, the white lilies, and red and white striped roses of his garden pay a pretty toll. So sure as a can of broth, a medicine-bottle filled with wine, is despatched to him, so surely does old Angel present himself with the floral tribute gathered from among the gooseberry bushes. In payment for the old night-shirt from the Rector's stock, given him to be buried in, he insisted on bequeathing me the lavender-bush from beside his door.

The last garment which shall drape their mortal bodies is always a matter of import to the poor. It was with much reluctance that old Angel confided to me the fact that the shirt which had been set aside for his own burial had been taken to deck the body of his wife; she, during the irresponsible condition of the last few years of her life, having 'made a hand o' th' shift' she had provided for the occasion.

The lavender-bush was especially precious to her husband, as 'Meery' had set it and had always 'favoured' the plant. He had 'strowed' her body with the flowers when she lay in her coffin, he told me.

Angel had been born and bred a Primitive Methodist, but seceded from that body twenty years or so before his death and came over to the Church, the reason he gave being that he wished to 'set under' a gentleman.

'Why, him as prache at chapel bain't no better nor me,' he used to say, with fine contempt. 'Wha's th' good o' his settin' hisself up ter mandate ter me. Gi' me a preacher as kin look down on yer, high and haughty-like, to hold forth. I don't, so to say, set no store by none o' them smiley and similiar' (familiar) 'ones.'

He was an out-and-out Conservative, although he never knew it, and was always on the side of the moneyed classes and of authority.

'Them as ha' th' proputty is them as oughter rule,' he said. ''Tis for th' quality to ha' th' haughtiness, and for we to ha' th' manners. Manners don't cost nowt, as I tell 'em, and a man'll be a sight o' time a-wearin' up 's hat by touchin' on it. As fur a-settin' up ter be akal' (equal) 'alonger th' gentry and sech like – why 't can't niver be done – niver! Theer be them, sure enow, and hare be we, and us can't imitate ter say as we be o' th' same pattern. Why, even in heaven, bless th' Lord, theer be the angels and the archangels, and ef so be as I ha' to chuse when I git theer, I think, happen, 't'll be th' lessest o' th' two I make ch'ice on.'

Such views would not meet with approval in the 'White Hart' sanded kitchen, or even in Littleproud's shop, but old Angel was not a frequenter of either place.

He was one of the rector's staunchest upholders, although his favourite form of defence, when put down in black and white, appears somewhat of the lukewarm order, and his praise seems to some of us unnecessarily faint.

'That he's a p'or critter I bain't a denyin',' he would say dispassionately, 'but them as know tell ter me there ain't much ch'ice among 'em. An' ef so be as we ha'n't got much ter boast on, we must be thankful for no wuss. Th' Rev'rend – yew kin see he've got book-larnin', by the wacant look on 'im, and I'm one for heerin' them as ha' book-larnin' hold forth. Ef so be as yew ha'n't th' ondeerstandin' for 't

– 'tis wallable all th' same. I ha'n't naught to say agin th' Rev'rend, considerin' his capacity o' life.'

It is said that the greatest compliment a man can pay his wife is to take another after her death. The number of wives who wish to have the admiration of their husbands so expressed is probably small. Be that as it may, it is certain that old Angel, who had loved and sincerely mourned his mate, lost no time in trying to replace her. He was specially attracted to our own faithful and invaluable domestic through the coincidence of her bearing the Christian name of the deceased Mrs Angel. On the day that he called to arrange with the rector the hour for the burying he made an offer of himself, hand and heart, stick, umbrella, and two-and-sixpence a week, to our Mary while he waited in the kitchen.

We were a little shocked at such precipitancy, but we soon learnt that even this was not his first *affaire*, he having already proposed matrimony to Susannah Chaney, the widow woman who had been summoned to lay Mary Angel forth.

Our Mary always refused to believe that she herself was not the widower's first choice, and she stoutly discredited Mrs Chaney's report. For although Mary had treated the old man's proposal with the savagest contempt, the report that another had seen fit to refuse him filled her with fury.

'Oh, dessay!' she said with fine disdain, and dashing the crockery about, as is her reprehensible habit when her temper is disturbed. 'Refuged on 'm, have she? Oh, dessay! What Sesanner! Ketch 'er at it!'

But Mary's anger could not alter facts, and the fact is well authenticated that within the six weeks following his wife's death old Angel made as many as a dozen offers of marriage. Among women of all ages, from eighteen years to eighty, he sought a mate, and I, for my part, think it a great pity he could not find one. He was a cheerful, chirpy, companionable little old man, and he found his solitary fate very hard to bear. In marrying I believe that he was chiefly anxious to find a companion to whom he might chatter incessantly of the defunct Mary. He had treasured up in his mind, to produce on the shortest notice, a store of the perfectly pointless remarks to which she, in the sixty years of their married life, had given utterance, and of the entirely unremarkable replies they had called forth. But the attitude of the peasant mind is not critical; it is only the oft-told tale that finds favour, and there always seems to be a preference for the one that has neither end, nor beginning, nor life, nor favour. I do not think that the second

Mrs Angel, if she had ever existed, would have understood that she should have been bored to death by such reminiscences.

His cottage stood away by itself in a very lonely part of Dulditch, quite half a mile from any other habitation. Unless the old man shouldered stick and umbrella and came 'uptown way' in search of society, he might go for weeks without seeing a soul to speak to. He had grown so old as to be very much a child again in many ways, and he had a child's fear of being alone.

Interminable those long summer days must have seemed to him, no particular work falling to his hand to do. The gooseberries and currants picked, the pea- and bean-stalks – their produce all gathered and eaten – pulled up, the garden – for the greater part laid out in rows of potatoes – required just now no attention. But the habit of a lifetime cannot be abandoned when there is no longer any call for its performance, and old Angel still arose when the day was in its earliest hazy freshness. Hours before it was time for his breakfast he had completed those small household jobs which were all he had to look forward to for the day's occupation. From the time he broke his fast – from eight o'clock in the morning till eight at night, when he locked his house door and went to bed – time must have hung wearily on his hands. How he lingered over taking up the one root of potatoes which yielded enough for his dinner! What a business he made of washing, and peeling, and putting in the pot! After that there was only to watch the potatoes boil, and to turn them bodily into the big yellow basin in the centre of the table – the basin which for sixty years had been wont to hold a double share.

He ate his portion with tears now, and many gurgling noises, and little clicks of emotion, but having eaten invariably felt strong and perky again, and would place his tall hat on his little white head – he always wore the rector's left-off hats, which were sizes too large for him – and saunter jauntily down to the garden gate to look out for moving incidents of the road, and to intercept the passer-by.

He made a practice of hailing all the carts that passed by means of his uplifted stick. Now and again a driver would obey the summons and would let his pony crop the grass by the roadside, or pull at the long branches of the honeysuckle and blackberry bramble trailing over the fence, while he exchanged a word or two on the state of the weather and the crops with the lonely old man. On rare occasions the present of a lettuce for his tea, or some sticks of rhubarb for his 'old woman to put down', would tempt a passer-by to enter the gate, to wander down the narrow garden path, bounded by the currant and gooseberry bushes, to stand and stare with old Angel at the 'inion' bed, to contemplate the long rows of potatoes, and to hear the history of every row – which went in at the time observed by universal custom, and which was the result of the wild experiment of 'Febbiwary plantin'.'

The days that the old man toddled down to report himself to the relieving officer and to receive his dole of money and of bread were red-letter days in his calendar. Waiting about among the old widows collected for the same purpose he offered himself wildly, right and left, in matrimony, as did that gallant knight Sir John Dureley in days of yore at Windsor.

'Tain't good for man to be alone,' he reminded me when I spoke to him on the subject. 'Theer's jobs a man weren't never meant to 'complish in his capacity o' life; and th' time hang wonnderful heavy. I bain't a complainin', my dare wumman; for th' Lord He ha' made th' sasons, and the sun knoweth his a'goin' down. But my nights du fare ter'ble long now there bain't Meery no more to wait on.'

I noticed that he had aged a great deal in a very little time, and that his cheerful perkiness had ceased to be a habit and was only assumed on occasion.

One morning he appeared at the Rectory carrying a little parcel tied in a cabbage leaf, as well as the umbrella and stick beneath his arm.

'I thought, happen, I'd make sure as yer had yer bush,' he said as he untied the string of this parcel; 'there's no accountin' for how matters'll be at th' garden arter I'm gone. Th' incomer he, mayhap, 'll want ter stick ter th' lavender. As long as Meery planted on't I don't fare i' the mind to dig it up – not i' my time. Tha's where she wushed th' bush ter be, stan' ter rayson, else why'd th' wumman plant it theer? An' ef so be as Meery bain't hare to spake fur 'erself, I don't keer to cross her wushes, that laid alongside o' me fur sixty yare. So I ha' tuk slips o' th' bush, and I think y'll stan' a chancet o' raisin' on 'em. And ef so be as my time's come, I kin fare aisy ye ha'n't been chated out o' yer lavender.'

He said, in answer to inquiry, that he was feeling 'no matters' that morning, and that he fancied 'mayhap' the Lord had need of him, and that his time was about come. 'My po'r Meery, she be gone,' he sighed, wiping the back of his little horny red hand across mouth and nose, 'and I reckon as I'm ter foller.'

He had caught a 'chronic cold' the night before, he said, 't'rough slapin' wi' th' windy open.' Reminded that the heat of the summer was

44

over and that the year had suddenly turned very cold, he admitted his imprudence.

''Twere th' furst frost o' th' yare,' he acknowledged sadly. 'Th' daylies i' Littleproud's gaarden be all black and limpsy-laved this mornin', and the mar'go's and snapdragons is dead. 'Twere strikin' cold. But theer was raysons,' he added mysteriously, with a bewildered trouble in his moist blue eyes. Touching me confidentially on the arm, he repeated the phrase in a whisper: 'Theer was raysons, my dare wumman, why I ope'd the windy.'

He went away carrying the 'chronic' cold and the familiar stick and umbrella, and I thought that the little old man looked smaller than ever – strangely shrunken and dwindled.

It was Amelia Sprite, the woman who once a week 'rid th' old chap up,' who a few days later volunteered to enlighten me on the subject of the 'raysons'. Amelia is a gossiping, foolish woman, not at all a favourite of mine. She hailed me as I hurried past her door – her manner is always entirely wanting in respectfulness. I find it advisable to avoid conversation with her as much as possible.

'Ye've heerd as po'r old man Angel is harnted?' she called. 'He be, howsomdever, sure enough,' she added with curt insistence when I indignantly repudiated the notion. ''Tis old Meery a worritin' on 'm again, most like. She allust were a onsat'sfied, restless old critter. I take it more'n likelies she 'ont lay quiet i' th' graveyaard.'

Amelia treated my angrily remonstrant remarks as if she had not heard them.

'She be allust a flappin' across 's faace sure as th' dark come on and he crape into 's bed,' she continued. 'Th' po'r old chap, he's all on a trimble when's time come ter lay down. I ha' left 'm of a muck-swat when I ha' closed th' door on 'm. 'Tis old Meery, sure 's eggs; I tell'd 'm so from th' fust; and he don't imitate ter deny as how 't be.'

I tried to point out to Amelia the wickedness of putting such ideas into the head of old Angel, who had been so good to his wife and who still so loved her memory.

'He bain't so fond o' havin' on 'er floppin' about over 's faace for all that, I kin tell yer,' Amelia called after me defiantly, as I walked indignantly away.

There is no real harm in the woman, only she is made so that she must 'run on,' the neighbours say. She has worked much mischief by her ignorant tongue. Her 'running on' in the present case had certainly a disastrous result.

The old man sat and shivered over his fire; all the cheerfulness gone out of him for ever; a stricken look on his face. He received all that was said to him deferentially and did not attempt any argument, but it was easy to see that his belief in the supernaturalness of his experience was not shaken.

'Tain't till I'm abed and th' light out,' he said dejectedly, 'then she begin a whirrin' and a swoopin' and a flappin'.'

'Why do you call it – this thing of your imagination – she?'

The watery blue eyes were shifted from mine, and he did not answer.

'Oh, Angel! You that spoke to me with such beautiful faith of the heavenly home to which your wife had gone!'

He gave the hand that was laid on his a trembling pressure.

'Maybe I was i' tew much 'f a hurry,' he said timidly. 'Maybe she weren't gone so much 'f a suddint. Mayhap she be a waitin' fur me!'

'Don't lie in darkness. Keep your candle burning for tonight.'

He evidently thought me crazy to make such a suggestion.

'My dare wumman, 'twould gutter down 'n a jiffy in th' draught from th' open windy.'

'Shut your window. Your bed is directly beneath it – you might as well lie in the open air.'

'I kape i' open agin she may take i' in 'er hed to go out by the windy,' he explained. 'I lave th' sneck o' th' door undone for th' same rayson.'

Small wonder he had a cold, small wonder the 'rattlin' on his chest was, as he said, 'terrufic'!

'Put out your hand and catch the thing,' I counselled him. 'It is either a bird or it is nothing. I incline to think it is a bird.'

''Tain't nayther,' he said with resigned wretchedness. ''Tis a sight tew big for ayther o' them. 'Tis my po'r Meery herself, I make no doubt.'

''Tis a bat,' our Guy said, laughing, when he heard the tale.

'A bat! My dear Guy, he describes a thing of as much size and importance as an eagle. He couldn't possibly have mistaken anything like a bat for his Mary!'

'Ten to one 'tis a bat,' Guy persisted. The boy is very fond of his own opinions. He is bound to be, as they are always right, he says. ''Tis a bat that hides in some corner in the daytime and flies about at night. Be sure you tell him 'tis a bat, sir,' he said to his father, who was standing hat in hand ready to depart, in obedience to a wish old Angel had expressed to see 'th' Rev'rend' and to take the sacrament.

The rector forgot the pocket communion service and presently came back for it. Five minutes later we heard his step in the hall again, and Mary put her head in at the door to tell us that the master could not remember if it was old Angel who wished to communicate, or Martha Brown's brother (commonly called among us Fitz-Brown because he is subject to fits), who was lying ill of a 'twinsy' at the other end of the parish.

'The dear old shepherd!' Guy said, laughing a little sadly as he watched the bent figure of my brother disappearing for the third time through the Rectory gate; 'he is always so sadly "mixed" about his sheep.'

When I lay down in my own comfortable bed that night and put out the light, my thoughts wandered to old Angel at the far end of the village. The solitary old man, ill, and haunted by his ignorant fears! By dwelling on them, his loneliness and his terror oppressed me. The night was inky black, a dreary length of uninhabited road and a thick plantation of dark firs, full of melancholy noises and ugly possibilities, separated him from any human help. Then wind was abroad, I heard it sweeping through the trees in the garden; it came tearing round the corner of the house; the blind over my window stirred and rustled; a creeper tapped, like a peremptory finger, against the pane; I began to feel old Angel's terror as a very real thing.

'Put out your hand and lay hold of whatever it is that hovers over your face,' I had said; I who cannot repress a shudder if an 'arwriggle,' as Mary calls an earwig, crawls upon my dress, and who screamed aloud the other evening when a midsummer daw dashed itself in the dark against my face. Dare I, twenty years younger than the feeble old man, nurtured in no superstitious terrors, strong of body and fairly sane – dare I put out my hand in the dark and grasp at any felt but unseen, mysterious presence?

How terrible, when one's mind dwells on them, are the sufferings of the poor! How horrible, above all, is the enforced solitariness of the very old! To be ill and quite alone; in terror – terror of an exaggerated kind it must have been, which could have reduced cheery, pleasant old Angel to his present physical condition, and put that look of trouble in his serene blue eyes – quite alone; thirsty – as the human soul must always be for sympathy, companionship, comfort – longing for the touch of a friendly voice – always alone!

Something might have been done for him if I had realised all this quite in the same way before. I might have induced old Skipper, his rheumatics being temporarily better, to hobble down on his crutches

47

and share the horrors of the night with the other old man. Skipper was a soldier once, and is reported to be afraid of nothing. Perhaps 'Dummy' Borrett, who, being stone deaf, can't have been frightened by the story of the 'harntin',' would, for a consideration, have sat at the bedside.

As it was, I pictured the old blue and white checked curtains of the four-poster swaying in the night wind, the poor shivering figure upon the bed, cowering, waiting for that mysterious swirling of the air which would come surely at last, that swoop of something huge, shadowy, awful across his face. The poor defenceless, kindly old man, suffering the agonies of a terror which nothing earthly, surely, could call forth. The unseen presence is lifted. There comes another rush through the air, another swirl and swoop, nearer to his face this time.

My own hair had begun to creep with horror. I kindled the light again and took up a Book which lies always by my bedside, wherewith to exorcise the spirit of terror.

The next day happened to be that of the weekly 'redding-up', at which Amelia Sprite officiated. The gale of the previous night was still blowing when 'Meelyer' reached the old man's cottage. The door, 'unsnecked' for the egress of 'Meery', was blowing noisily to and fro; the blue and white cotton curtains of the four-poster were tossing wildly in the wind from the wide-open lattice. Old Angel was lying upon the bed, still and dead.

The toothless mouth, the one visible eye, were wide open, giving a look of terror to the face. Over the other eye and over part of the sunken cheek something black was lying, which on closer inspection proved to be a bat.

Before she discovered the nature of the object, Meelyer, with the touch of disgust, had twitched the shrivelled-looking patch off the face. For a moment or two it fluttered feebly on the floor till Meelyer's heavy foot put an end to its existence.

Guy had been right as usual. 'Did you tell the poor old fellow his ghost was only a bat, sir?' he asked of his father.

But the rector had forgotten. A circumstance the more curious as he now recalled the fact that while reading and praying with old Angel he had observed a bat clinging to the top of the bed among the curtains.

'Bat or no bat, 'twere Meery,' Meelyer Sprite said. ''Twere old Meery, safe enough. And I jemmed my fut on 'er, thank th' Lord.'

RATS!

ALICK is digging the rose-bed in the Old Master's garden. The duties of Alick are multifarious. He cleans the knives and boots, fills the coal-hods, feeds the pigs, helps in the stable, pumps the water for the maids. He is nineteen years of age, and receives a stipend of eight shillings a week. He is of a rather torpid disposition, but there is in his mind a lively anxiety so to order the performance of his services that they should not be worth more to his employers than the sum paid for them. He is tall, with hard-shining, expressionless eyes, and an ever-open mouth.

His attention is very easily diverted from the work in hand; and as he slowly drives his spade into the heavy earth of the half-dug rose-bed, it is attracted by a little group of young men and maidens passing through the gardens – girls, sportsman-like and trim, in skirts short to the ankle, tweed hats, golf coats; men in breeches and belted jackets; one of them holds a bag in his hand, one carries a gun upon his shoulder; a couple of little fox-terriers are at their heels. Perceiving the youth with the spade to be staring at them with his glassy eyes, they stop, and explain to him that they are there by permission of the Old Master for a morning's ratting on his premises.

'You've got a quantity of rats about, in these old stacks and buildings, I suppose?' one of the party says to him.

'Dessay,' says Alick, applying the back of his hand to his nose, and staring ahead.

'Can you show us where they principally lie?'

'No.'

'You can't?'

'They're all abeaout.'

'But mostly in the stables, cow-houses, granaries?'

'Mostly i' th' hidges,' Alick vouchsafes. 'The banks down the Sandy Lane's raddled with them.'

'Really! And where is Sandy Lane, then?'

'Acrost theer!' If Alick's eyes could have been eloquent of anything, it would surely have been of a surprised contempt for a person who did not know the whereabouts of Sandy Lane! 'T'rough th' clover layer and the turmit field, and athwart th' ploughed land, and a corner of Widder's Midder.'

'Widow's Meadow? That's interesting. Why is it called Widow's Meadow?'

Alick, who accepted his facts and never troubled about the whys and wherefores of more curious minds, simply stared.

'You think we should have more luck in Sandy Lane than in the stackyard, for instance? The Old Master said something about the piggeries –'

'Theer might be a chancet one, here and theer; but i' th' Sandy Lane theer's a sight of 'em.'

'Bring your spade and come with us.'

But he had his 'wark ter du,' Alick said, and struck his spade in the earth with great force to show that he was no trifler. Having got so far, however, he paused, and, great foot on spade, watched the retreating party making for Sandy Lane. He did not smile to himself, nor sigh, nor give vent to any sentiment he might have had in regard to them; he simply looked, with vacant stare and lopping mouth, till he could see them no more, then spat upon his hands and went on slowly digging.

The party of young people had a very pleasant morning in Sandy Lane, which they worked in business-like fashion from end to end. They did not get on to any rats, but were not perhaps the less happy. The youngest girl, who wore her hair still in tails, had a secret terror of seeing one killed, and preferred to watch the wriggling undulations of the ferrets safe within their bag in her brother's hand to seeing them disappear into holes, where you never knew what might happen! The elder ladies, armed with murderous sticks, were quite ready to give account of any rats which ran in their direction. But then, the young men who handled the ferrets and carried the guns were not *their* brothers, and ratting was not the only sport they had come out to play.

The brown ploughed lands and forsaken harvest fields lay serene that morning beneath a sun robbed of his power to torment. The air was kind and the heavens azure. The scant leaves of the beech, the elm, the oak, golden and lemon-coloured and bronze against the blue, detached themselves regretfully from the parent branch and silently floated down to join the majority lying moist and shining on the roadside grass.

The little group of young people sat to eat their lunch on the light soil of the bank beneath the Scotch firs; and they decided that November was the rippingest month of the year in which to have a meal out-of-doors. How jolly the coral-red berries were in the hedges – jollier even than the jolly little roses had been. How simply too sweet was the plaintive note of the chaffinch, and the 'chittering' of the little birds in the thorn. A robin, hopping ever nearer, bore them company while they stayed, and in the finish they stayed, and in the finish they stilled their laughing and chatter in order not to abash him when he came to their feet to pick up the crumbs they tossed him.

And when the air had grown more chill, and the light of the short afternoon had begun to fade from the sky, in an old thatched bullock shelter which they passed on their way home, they did have the satisfaction of killing a rat. They held it up to Alick in his rose-bed as they passed him, going through the garden.

'We didn't see *one* in your Sandy Lane,' they called to him.

'Mayhap you skeered 'em away,' Alick suggested; and growled after them the information already vouchsafed, that the banks was raddled with 'em.

Then he withdrew his spade, wiped it, and walked away, for his day's work was done.

But before he betook himself homeward, he repaired to a certain building, a sort of antechamber to the piggeries, where stood a huge open boiler in which meal was mixed for the pigs. The place was already in darkness, and, as Alick opened the door, letting in a tempered light, there was a hurry and a scuttle, and forms shadowy and noisome sprang from the brim of the boiler and disappeared; and something secret and loathly ran over Alick's boots.

To the sides of the copper remnants of the pigs' last meal were hanging. Having dislodged these portions and massed them at the bottom, Alick withdrew the stick which had served as escape-ladder for the rats he had disturbed, and went on his way to home and supper.

In the morning he arose an hour before his usual time, and made his way to the same building, lantern in hand.

In that receptacle which had held the pigs' meal, and from which all means of egress had been taken, what a struggling, seething mass of noxious vermin was there! What a noise of scratching upon the smooth sides, of scrabbling, scrambling, squeaking, shrieking! Into what a miniature inferno was the copper converted!

Alick set his lantern where its dim light could fall upon that ugly, writhing mass, and gazed into the pit of destruction with staring, expressionless eyes and lopping mouth. Then he fetched a heavily knobbed stick he had procured for the purpose, and set to work.

Alick was not at all interested in the great war of rat-extermination raging in his native county; he had not even heard of the bubonic plague; but he had been told on the previous day that a prize of a penny had been offered for every rat murdered on the premises. And when the Old Master had finished his breakfast, and was ready to sally forth his leisurely rounds that morning, he was waylaid by Alick, who proceeded to drag from his pockets the blood-stained trophy of one hundred and seven rats' tails, for which he demanded immediate payment.

BEN PITCHER'S ELLY

HAIR as golden as sunlit corn; a skin of roses – red and white; eyes blue like the May-day sky, bright and clear and sweet – Ben Pitcher's Elly.

So attractive-looking and winning a child was she that some in Dulditch were for keeping her at school after she had passed the fifth standard, and having her trained as pupil-teacher. But there is an annual new baby in Elly's home; the mother wanted help; Elly must be sacrificed.

Her education completed, therefore, we came upon her henceforth, a coarse brown apron reaching from neck to heels tied about her short, broad figure, her bare arms gleaming as she dashed the water from her brush, scrubbing with noisy energy the red-tiled floor of the living room, washing down the bricks outside the cottage door. We met her, one heavy baby weighing upon her arm, another toddling at her skirts, taking the air in the vicinity of her home.

Ben Pitcher and his eldest boy work on the Brightlands Farm. His cottage stands in a field away from the rest of the village, and looks out upon the Brightlands orchard.

A favourite spot with all the little Pitchers is the orchard, and many a beating did Elly get through her predilection for the place. It held greater attraction for her and her little charges than the speedwells, blue as their eyes, the golden cowslips, the white dead-nettle, about which the bees made such a humming in that favoured locality. The Pitchers' family is fond of apple-dumpling, apple-pie, apple raw, and apple baked; and it is foolishly credulous of Pitcher himself to believe that all the fruit consumed at his table comes off the one not too fertile apple tree in his own back garden.

Yet now and again the owners of the orchard complain. Now and again the neighbours tell tales. Now and again the farm servants, on some blustering autumn day, a linen basket swung between them, their caps awry, their hair blown into their eyes, come laughing and galloping over the meadows to pick up the windfalls in the orchard. Then, sad to say, although the apples are nearly fit to gather, although the gale has lasted all night, they find none. On occasions such as these Elly is always beaten.

He is a tall, silent, dark man, hollow of cheek, sharp-featured, Elly's father, and both she and her mother hold him in greater dread than anything in earth or hell or heaven. Both deceive him and play into each other's hands.

Those constantly recurring babies (there are seven younger than Elly, and there is one boy older than herself) keep the Pitchers' establishment a very poor one. There is a constant effort to make the twelve or thirteen shillings stretch from one pay-day to the next.

With the assistance of our Mary, who knows the ins and outs of many such poor households, I have tried to parcel out the little income to the best advantage. I am told that I must allow to the man, his wife, his five eldest children half a stone of flour each a week. A shilling must always be laid aside for rent; at least sixpence for keeping up the club money. Coal, oil, candles, little groceries must be bought. The head of the family is always a smoker, and he keeps back a shilling a week for tobacco and beer. A piece of meat has to be provided at least once a day for the father and the working son. With what remains shoe-leather and raiment must be supplied for eleven persons.

In the Pitchers' case the eldest boy earns his three shillings and sixpence a week, which goes into the general fund; but he must be better fed and better shod than those who can stay at home, and costs at present as much as he earns. Then there is the extra money at harvest time; but extra food has to be found also, beer must be supplied, if it is nothing more than the watery decoction brewed at home. In the case of a wet, long harvest all profit disappears. Also there are the heavily wet days of winter when no field work can be done. The farmer, poor struggling wretch, is glad to save the day's wage and dismisses his labourers to their homes. A few such days, and there are bound to be several in the year, soon neutralise the poor advantages of the harvest.

'How is it done?' I ask of Mary. 'How does this outwardly patient great army of workers, almost silent so far as any utterance of theirs reaches the outer world, struggle on, decently accoutred, apparently fairly nourished, in a measure holding their own?'

'Some on 'em do it by denyin' of theirselves,' Mary tells me, 'and some on 'em by a gettin' inter debt.'

Mary's solution of the problem does not strike me as particularly happy, but for all my efforts I can find none of my own.

Week out, week in, on such tables as that of the Pitcher family no meat appears, with the exception of that apportioned to the two bread-winners; little but bread and cheese and potatoes, and those apples which Elly shakes down from the orchard trees.

It was a nasty implement, that with which Ben Pitcher corrected the failings of his daughter, but it was handy too – the belt he wore to strap his coarse trousers about his waist. It was a belt that was in the army once, like the grey great-coat he put on over his sleeved jacket on Sundays, and it was ornamented with clasps and buckles, which raised ugly lumps on Elly's head and cut her bare arms and shoulders. And Elly was not built in the heroic mould at all; she maddened her father to greater exertions by yelling lustily before her punishment began. The cottage stands in a lonely spot, and there was no one but the mother to hear Elly's cries, to comfort her when she ran in, bruised and beside herself with rage and hate and terror, to fling herself face downward on the bit of carpet before the fire.

Small wonder that mother and child connived at deceiving this husband and father, at once so passionate and so sullen.

In all ways they deceived him. Elly's mother, despite the dragging upon her of the constant babies, is a pretty woman still. She is wonderful to relate, light-hearted too; and although her figure is no more, her skin is almost as pink and white as Elly's. Her hair was once like Elly's too, and for all its careless keeping and rough treatment is of a pretty colour still, and breaks into little roughened waves about her forehead as does Elly's own.

When Elly and she, shutting up two or three of the older children in the cottage and carrying a couple of babies with them, tramped the six miles to Runwich to visit the old father and mother of Mrs Pitcher living in that town, Elly knew that three times out of four she did not catch a glimpse of the aged grandparents. She sat all day long with her mother and the babies in the long kitchen of the 'King's Head.' The outing did not cost Elly's mother a ha'penny. There was no stint of old and new friends, frequenters of the place, to treat the bright-faced woman and the fair-faced child. Sometimes they came home with money in their pockets.

Ben Pitcher knew nothing of all this. Elly kept the mother's secrets. Later the mother kept Elly's.

To the Pitchers' cottage there was but one sleeping-room. In this husband, wife, and eight children slept together, the littlest in the big bed with father and mother; three of the next sized with Elly on the rickety iron bedstead pulled across the foot of the larger bed; the boy had for his separate accommodation a shake-down against the wall.

Of this shocking state of things Mrs Robinson, at the Brightlands Farm, spoke to Sir Thomas, her husband's landlord. Sir Thomas is a bachelor, not deriving sufficient money from his estate – all Dulditch belongs to him – to afford a wife. It is a pity, he being made for the love of women and children – honourable, unselfish, manly, gentle. He, rendered miserable by the recital, could not sleep of nights in his own not too luxurious apartment in the London chambers to which 'hard times' have banished him. On his estate, impoverished as it is, there must not be such a crying scandal. He resolved to give up his last remaining extravagance, his annual six weeks' fishing in Norway, in order that funds might be supplied for the necessary alterations.

So the order went forth that on Sir Thomas's estate a second and third chamber be added to all those cottages at present having only one.

Then was there excitement in the family of the Pitchers. A constant racket of conversation and exchange of rough compliment passing between the two bricklayers engaged upon the Pitchers' cottage and Elly's mother, who is a match with her tongue for a dozen such. Meanwhile a youth of seventeen – the 'slab,' as he is called – passed his spare moments in flinging stones and lumps of hard mortar at the daughter of the house when she appeared; in 'chivvying' her round corners when she ran away; in calling out to her epithets no softer than his chosen missiles in return for the chaff to which she treated him.

Very attractive was this horseplay to Elly, and it lasted on and on over several weeks – months even – for the boy's masters were no more expeditious nor constant to the work in hand than the rest of their kind. So friendly did the boy and girl become in their rough, uncouth way that when at last the bricklayers' work was done and they were gone for good, and the painters and glaziers set to work in their places, Elly's spirits were gone too. She showed no inclination, as her mother once did, to enter upon friendly relations with the quieter and more respectable workmen who, for a time, hung about the cottage.

'Eller hev finely got on,' the village women say, talking her over; 'grown a'most a wumman, th' mawther hev.'

She was but sixteen, but she looked older all at once, and carried a quiet and sensible tongue in her head instead of that pert and foolish one with which she used to make herself enemies among her kind.

Presently Elly tired at the wash-tub and fainted among the dirty water as she was scrubbing the floor. Then there came a day when she went on foot with her mother to a town ten miles distant, where the bricklayers, who besides building another chamber to her home had made such an epoch in Elly Pitcher's life, were at work.

It was on the evening of their return, Elly sitting listless and weary in the chimney corner, her head fallen against the wall, that Mrs Pitcher broached to her husband a scheme for sending the girl to service at last.

'O' course! Ha'n't I allust said it? An' oughter ha' gone suner. She be on'y a duin' yer wark hare. Du yer good to be a duin' on it yerself.'

'She be a gettin' a right big gal,' the mother acquiesces. 'She'll be a duin' harself good and a larnin' harself, as I tell her.'

She gives a glance of wistful encouragement at Elly, who, however, begins to cry hopelessly.

'I sholl miss the baby and my little brawthers,' she says, and sobs and snivels, so drearily that her father with a warning scowl on his face begins to unbuckle his trouser-strap.

So, in a week or two Elly went away. A place was found for her in that public-house at Runwich with which she was already familiar. She wrote miserable letters home to her 'dere father and mother,' sending many kisses to the baby and the 'little brawthers,' and complaining – safe away from the strap with the leather buckle – of the hardships of the place, of the tiredness of her legs, of how her hands are chapped and her feet swell, of how the whole work of the house is put on her, of how she longs to be at home again.

'Send me a flower, O Dere father and mother, ef tis only a Dasy out of the grarse. I fare so to long to look at somthin from dulditch,' one of the letters concludes.

The poor little 'brawthers' missed their sister sadly, for Elly, by no means neglectful of the salutary rod, yet had all the small hearts in her possession. The baby but one grew up quite bandy-legged through having to be put too early upon his feet. There was no one so quick as Elly at seeing birds' nests, so expert at cowslip balls and daisy chains, so successful with the whistles and pop-guns made from the 'hilder' branch. Spring was robbed of half its pleasures for the little Pitchers that year. Mother, too, had grown so 'short' with them all, and the children saw her more than once 'making a face' and crying quite openly into the wash-tub; and now and again as she knelt upon the hearth, splash would come a great tear upon the potatoes she was peeling for supper.

She has the 'neuralisy awful in her hid,' she tells the father apologetically, and gets small comfort from that quarter.

One summer evening, when the sweet dusk had fallen and the scent of the lime trees was heavy in the air, when the children had been long abed, and the snores of the master of the house could be heard as far as the little garden gate, against which Mrs Pitcher, on the look out for a chance gossip with a passing neighbour, leaned, Elly, poor child, came home.

So fagged and weary was she with the walk, so worn out and exhausted, that before she could complete her story – broken and disjointed, it is true, but in the telling of which not one word, alas! was needed – she had fallen asleep upon the bank on which she had sunk down.

She was put to bed in that second chamber, the building of which had cost her so dear, and the father goes to his work in the morning unawares, for the wife, lying weeping out the hours beside him, dares not tell him that his daughter has come back.

However, in such houses secrets cannot long be kept, and when he returns for his midday meal he is confronted by Elly, her blue eyes wide with terror of him, as she sits on the stool in the chimney corner.

'What air yu back for till yu was guv' lave?' he demands of her, stopping with a suspicious scowl upon the threshold.

'I come becos I had tu, faather,' Elly says, with a pitiful twitching of the lips; her voice is thick with fear. She dares not turn away her eyes from him to look at her mother, but stealthily puts out a shaking little red hand and clutches at the skirt of her mother's dress.

'Har missus hev tret 'er shameful,' the mother explains in nervous haste, and stands in front of Elly dishing up the dinner.

Plunging wildly with a fork into the saucepan over the fire, she proceeds to fill a large yellow basin waiting on the fender in readiness with the sloppy 'light' dumplings – composed of flour, water, and baking powder simply – which are to form the meal.

But with a by no means gentle movement Ben Pitcher thrusts her on one side, and with a lowering light in his eyes confronts his daughter.

'D—— yer! ha' yu been a bad hussy?' he demands fiercely. 'Answer me true – or, by God! I'll cut th' life out on yer.'

And Elly, shivering, white-lipped, answers:

'Oh, faather – I hev.'

At that a wail went up from the little 'brawthers' seated round the table – from the bandy-legged youngest but one, who had been given a hot dumpling into his hands to keep him quiet, from the baby in its cradle kicking bare red heels in the air and sucking at its guttapercha tube. For without a word the father began to busy himself with the belt that was around his waist.

At the sight the mother, bold beyond precedent, flung herself upon him.

'Ben – for God's sake – yer'll du murder, man! – for God's sake!' she cried.

She clung to him, trying to imprison the cruel right arm, but despite his daily diet of dumpling and potatoes the man had strength in that hour of his fury and savagely flung her off.

Yet when he reached his victim his arm was mercifully stayed, for the girl, who had not uttered a sound, had fallen sideways against the wall, and was lying there white and senseless, the terrified blue eyes closed.

The father stood and looked at her for a long minute; then, with words on his lips crueller than the cruel belt, turned away and sat down to the table.

When a man is in a constant condition of unsatisfied hunger it will not do – if the heavens fall – to neglect a chance of eating. The dumplings, depend on it, were bitter enough that day in Ben Pitcher's mouth, but eat he must in order to be able to place them again tomorrow for self, wife, and children upon the board.

The mother dared not stop in her duties of the table to show any attention to the unconscious Elly. But before the meal was over the girl had revived and was taken with strong shivering, which she strove vainly to repress by hugging herself tightly in her locked arms and pressing against the wall. Her teeth chattered loudly in her mouth. The 'little brawthers' regarded her open-mouthed, and Bandy-legs, leaning, dumpling in fist, against his sister's knee, gave a burst of delighted laughter, evidently thinking it an entertainment arranged for his benefit.

Ben, having concluded his repast, pulled forward over his brow the hat he always wore at the back of his head in the house, and pushing his chair from the table with a grating noise, got up and went to the door. There he paused for a minute, looking out beneath the blue fields of heaven over the sleepy summer land. Nothing of the peace and the sweetness of the sweet and peaceful spot and hour were in Ben Pitcher's heart. Presently he turned his head back into the cottage-room and looked at the girl. She was shaking still with such violence that the rickety chair on which she sat rocked noisily with her.

'Don't le' me find yu hare, in home o' mine, when I come back ter-night – du I'll kill yer,' he said. Said it savagely, but convincingly too, with the tone of a man who quite possibly might keep his word.

Then he went.

So, on that same afternoon, when the heat of the day was at its height, Elly, loudly sobbing, said good-byes to babies and little brawthers, to mother, giving the baby refreshment at the open door, her face made up like the face of a little child for weeping, after the artless manner of the poor, her tears falling on her bare bosom.

Poor Mrs Pitcher was fagged out with emotion and the day's work; the kitchen had still to be 'redd up,' and there was the evening meal to see to, and the home-coming of her lord and master to attend. She could not accompany Elly even half a mile of her weary way, but she looked after the girl's short, broad figure yearningly as she went, the mother's eyes all but blinded with the tears she was too much occupied to wipe away.

Across the fields poor Elly journeyed to the workhouse.

The sorrel pats against her weary feet as she goes, the hem of her pink cotton dress fans away the dandelion-down by the grassy roadway. What a road for such young feet to travel! What a burden of terror and of sorrow for such baby shoulders to bear! For if in the eyes of the law, which permits her father to turn her from his door at the age of sixteen, Elly is a responsible person, morally she is but an infant still. No bird, with its 'little life of bush and brier,' should have been more joyous of spirit and condition than she.

Elly has lived all her life among people who hold the workhouse to be an earthly hell, who loathe and dread its officers, laws, and institutions as we should loathe and dread the devil, the brimstone, and the unquenchable fire – if we for one instant believed in them. She has, added to the terrors and shames which are familiar to the situation, private shames and terrors of her own. She is, besides, unutterably weary and sick with painful bodily weakness.

Let us leave the child to perform that drear journey alone. Who cares to imagine the terrors of such a miserable pilgrimage?

⇥✶⇤

When, six weeks later, Elly Pitcher retraced her steps along the same road, she carried in her arms her baby of three weeks old. White and pinched and emaciated she looked, her steps uncertain and wavering from weakness, the light, miserable bundle she carried weighing like lead in her arms.

A few yards she dragged along the weary way, and giddy, trembling, sat down to rest; then, rising with painful effort, dragged a few feet more. After hours of such painful resting, such cruel toiling, reached the cottage door once more.

The little 'brawthers' were still at school at hour, the mother was standing at the wash-tub. As Elly's figure darkened the door Mrs Pitcher looked up, and the women gazed into each other's eyes.

Elly does not utter a sound, but the mother, recoiling for a moment, with a cry rushes forward, pulls the child almost violently from the girl's arms, and turns away sobbing wildly as she rocks the baby on her own breast.

Elly's voice is hollow, all the childish ring of it gone.

'Mother, I cou'n't stop theer. I tried, but I cou'n't,' she said. 'Yu mus' kape th' baby, mother. I'll wark and pay yer for it. She'll du as yar baby du. She's so wake, she 'ont take much. Kape her out o' faather's waay – don't let 'm strap her – not yit. She's sech a little un – yit.'

She had come in and was sat down, and the mother, regarding her with woful eyes, had placed food before her.

'I bain't hungry and I 'ont stop, 'cause o' faather,' Elly says, and, staggering, gets to her feet again.

'Wheer be yu a goin' i' that plight, gal?' the mother asks, fretful and helpless, and is told that Elly is bound for her old place at the 'King's Head.'

'Missus – she's a hard un, but I warked; and she said as how she'd maybe take me on agin when the baby was born. I ha'n't nowheers else to go, and I'm a goin' theer,' Elly concludes.

Before she leaves she comes forward and takes the miserable white-looking atom of humanity she has added to an already over-teeming population into her arms, and kisses the little pinched face.

'Mother, ha' yer seen – him?' she asks.

Not so much as a 'glint' on him, the mother declares, although she has tramped many a mile in search. As a matter of fact the 'slab,' scenting trouble ahead, had given up the brick-laying profession for that of arms and had 'listed, and was already on his way to India. No help to be expected from that quarter.

Not a word was said to Ben Pitcher on the subject of the new addition to his family. Perhaps he deemed it wise to take no notice and to treat the little workhouse descendant of his line as if it had not existed. Perhaps, in the fulness of his quiver, he had really lost count of the number of arrows allotted to his share. He said nothing.

The offspring of the immature girl-mother did not thrive. Whereas the lawful inhabitants of the cottage, they who by paternal right claimed their share of bed and board, were round-cheeked, bright and pleasant-looking, the alien remained ever feeble and flaccid of limb, white and unattractive. It may be that the weight of its young mother's woe and terror was indelibly stamped upon her unborn child; it may be that it felt in its melancholy little spirit the shadow of its birthplace, of its nameless and shameful condition; or it may be (as is more likely) that the requirements of Mrs Pitcher's own baby restricted the allowances of Mrs Pitcher's grandchild. Certain it was that the contrast of the two children nourished at one breast was a striking one.

From being ashamed that flesh and blood of hers should be so puny, and diseased, and unlovely, the grandmother grew to feel a positive pride in the child's diminutiveness and feeble condition. The 'quality' interested themselves. The 'missus,' as she was called in the Pitcher family, that is the wife of Mr Robinson at the Brightlands Farm, having exhausted her own specifics, insisted on driving Mrs Pitcher and the baby into Runwich to see the doctor there, being privately of opinion that the grandmother – no better than she should be – was starving the child. Her daughters – 'the young ladies' – for whom Elly had always found the earliest violets in return for a left-off dress, a ribbon for her hat (they were Elly's age and older, but in the school-room still), knitted little under-shirts and woollen petticoats for Elly's baby because its tiny hands and feet were always cold. Now and then a sympathising person sent a shilling for the benefit of the dwarfed, unwholesome child; a donation which, thanks to the close reasoning of Mrs Pitcher, arguing that what was for her own support and nourishment must be to the advantage of Elly's child, was generally laid out at the 'White Hart' in draught stout.

If it could but die! the tender-hearted women say, looking upon the miserable little atom of humanity. If it would please God to take it! But it does not please Him. By the loss of beautiful, cherished daughters, chief pride and comfort of idolising hearts, by the death of promising, healthful sons on whom high hopes are built, whose future stretched all golden before them, heads are bowed and homes are desolate. The deformed sickly workhouse child clings to its small thread of life and pines on.

Presently it is a year old. And while the babe, a few months older, runs, catching at chairs and tables and mother's gown with chubby, clutching fingers; will make his escape from the brick floor, which is his natural playground, to the garden where the marigolds, with whose dew-drenched leaves he loves to play, grow wild beneath the currant bushes; the unhappy alien lies ever on its back upon the top of the chest of drawers where is its bed. Its thin, wearying little voice, night and day, is hardly hushed. Its face is white and moist and pinched; its little in-drawn lips are blue; it lies always with one shrunken foot and leg twisted the wrong way.

It is not claimed for Mrs Pitcher that she was a faultless person. On the contrary, it is hinted among the neighbours that she has not always been faithful to her husband. It is certain that she tells lies and loves a glass. Yet is she a good-natured and kind-hearted woman; beyond the neglect of ignorance, and the bad usage consequent on a poverty of resource, her grandchild has little to complain of. Even when the weekly payments cease, as presently they do – when Elly goes without a word from the 'King's Head' at Runwich, leaving no address – the baby is still kept fairly whole and clean, gets the morsel of bread, which, its supply of milk having ceased, is all that it consumes.

It is an evil day in its wretched history when Elly again appears upon the scene.

She comes, a girl of only seventeen still, but with all trace of youth gone from eye and voice – comes with a brazen face, a hardened glance; with a loose red handkerchief twisted about her neck; with a dusty straw hat, looking as if it had roofed many a villainous head, pulled upon her sunny hair; with a thread of yellow beads about her throat, and a large white apron girt about her waist.

She brings some cheap tins and skewers in her hands, and standing in the open cottage doorway, with a burst of musicless laughter, asks her astonished parent what she will buy. There is a travelling-van hung round with doormats, with saucepans, with common earthenware, upon the open green space before the orchard where Elly used to steal the apples. She steals other things by right of profession now, having joined herself to the rascally-looking, middle-aged proprietor of the above itinerant establishment.

He has taken Elly to supply the place of the last woman who called herself his wife. There are half a dozen small children who play in the dust of the road, unwashed, unkempt, half-dressed. Another, of which Elly is to be the mother, will soon be added to the stock.

Elly is not afraid of her father now, alas! She stands, arms akimbo, on the steps of her caravan and watches him as he goes slouching to his evening meal.

At a word from his wife he comes to the door of the cottage, looks across to the green, and is greeted by a burst of laughter from the girl.

With the finger of scorn she points him out to the pock-marked scoundrel with the earrings who is her mate. The owner of herself and the caravan acknowledge this species of introduction by a volley of abusive language addressed to Elly herself and her father impartially.

The girl does not care. That poor woman whose successor she is, died from ill-treatment, and this Elly knows. But he has not begun to beat her yet.

Ben Pitcher is not a man to be laughed at with impunity. A word to his master 'up to the house' brings Mr Robinson, who hates gipsies as Betsy Trotwood hated donkeys, upon the scene. He did not forget in a hurry the volley of oaths with which the pock-marked gentleman of the earrings received his order to depart, nor the string of abusive slang (happily as Dutch to his simple ears) with which Elly, from the vantage-ground of the caravan, greeted that old master to whom, with a nervous recollection of apples misappropriated, she had been used to curtsey.

Before they started – they prepared for departure as the darkness of the summer night came on – Elly's mother came across, weeping, with the grandchild in her arms. Ben had turned it out of doors.

The grandmother kissed the poor waif passionately, with many tears, before she left it; lay and wept all night, her own children sleeping around her, for the poor outcast journeying away from her under the stars.

But what is in the small bundle of whining humanity to Elly?

When, in the first blush of morning, the caravan came to anchor again, the owner, having walked at his horses' heads all night, unharnessed the tired beasts, hobbled them for their search for a well-earned breakfast on the short, springy turf of the heath, and went to fling himself, all dressed as he was, upon his bed. To find yet another occupant of his already overcrowded couch was not a pleasant surprise to him. Elly had to explain the newcomer's presence there as best she could.

She was rewarded by her first experience of the weight of that heavy hand which had beat the life out of the other woman.

The greater part of the long summer day Elly spent sitting at a distance from the caravan, the babe, whose wailing no instinct or experience taught her to hush, in her lap.

All about are little hillocks of wild thyme. She crushes the plant with her elbows as she leans back, and the warm, still air is sweet with its fragrance. There is not a breath to stir the harebells growing in a big patch beyond her feet. The sky above is as blue as they.

So still she sits, the little rabbits, bright-eyed and wary, look out at her from the prickly covert of the furze bushes, only half afraid. A sorry sight they see: a disfigured face with bruised cheek and cut and swollen lip; great eyes that, looking out sullenly from under the battered, wicked hat, keep a watch upon the movements of the ear-ringed man going about the daily business of the caravan without Elly's assistance.

When the shades of evening begin to fall once more, and the baby rabbits, grown bolder, scud across the flowers at her feet, and she sees in the movements about the caravan the well-known signs of an early departure, a deep fear seizes upon Elly. She is half dead with faintness, having tasted no food all day; she is distracted by the incessant moaning of the child upon her lap.

She hates that cause of all her woe. Why does it lie there, miserably wringing from side to side its thin blue lips? What binds her to such hideous companionship? What is the child to her?

She had had untiring patience with those dragging babies of her mother's, beneath whose burden her own growth had been stunted; she had loved and wept for the 'little brawthers'; but it seemed as if all that girlish tenderness of heart had left her with its innocency. Nothing but hardness was in her breast to-night – that and a desperate anxiety not to be left behind.

The eldest of the vagrant children, brown of face, white-haired, was sent to bring in the hobbled horses. She watched each led across the uneven ground, its reluctance met by kicks and blows of the small tyrant of seven summers who had it in charge. She laid the baby beneath the little hillock of wild thyme and, breathless, rose to her knees – rose to her feet, trembling with eagerness, sick with fear. Would he go and leave her so?

He had knocked her about cruelly that morning; he had had no thought of the child she was soon to bear to him, but had half killed her in his stupid, brutal rage, but would he leave her so?

The sun had set. The eastern sky was glorious in crimson and gold, the heavens above her head were flushed through their pearly tints by a divine rosiness. The horses' heads were turned to the west. She put her hands above her straining eyes and looked and looked, then called the man's name with hoarse anxiety.

'John, John, I'm hare! Don't lave me, John.'

But there was no strength in the weakly voice. In the noise of departure it was drowned. The children tumbled one after the other into the caravan, the man at the leader's head cut the air with his whip; with a strain and a jolt the creaking, cumbrous machine started.

Her hands still shading her eyes, Elly followed, stumbling over the ant-heaps, the hillocks of moss and wild thyme, the prickly gorse catching at the hem of her dress.

An hour later the man, having occasion to stop his horses, becomes aware of the broad, short figure in the white apron and the battered hat trudging behind.

'You here?' he asks, his speech illumined by the interspersal of many oaths. 'And where is your —— brat?'

'I ha' left it. Yu said as how I worn't to bring it.'

He looked at her, scowling upon her beneath the starlight, and caught her roughly by the arm.

'You ha'n't made a hand on 't, d—n you?' he asks suspiciously.

She is almost sinking from exhaustion, but she looks him straight in the face. 'I ha'n't hurt a hair of its head, so help me God,' she says. 'I di'n't want it. It worn't nawthin' ter me. A woman tuk it. John, I'm a'most starved.'

She ends with a sob, and he lets her climb up into the caravan. When she has found herself food and a drink of tea from the pot which is always on the stove, she sinks upon the bed and falls into a heavy, dreamless slumber.

When they find the miserable baby its misery has ceased at last, for it is dead upon its bed of wild thyme, its moaning quiet for ever.

And the next night Elly passes in prison, having been arrested, on the borders of the town to which the caravan was making its way, on a charge of child murder.

DORA O' THE RINGOLETS

'I WISH I c'd du my ringolets same as yu kin, mother. When I carl 'em over my fingers they don't hang o' this here fashion down my back, but go all of a womble-like; not half s' pretty.'

'Tha's 'cause ye twist 'em wrong way, back'ards round yer fingers,' the faint voice from the bed made answer. 'Yu ha' got to larn to du 'em, Dora, don't, yer'll miss me cruel when I'm gone.'

The dying woman was propped on a couple of pillows of more or less soiled appearance; these were raised to the required height by means of a folded flannel petticoat and dingy woollen frock, worn through all the twelve years of her married life, but now to be worn no more. On the man's coat, spread for extra warmth over the thin counterpane, lay a broken comb and brush. Over her fingers, distorted by hard work, but pale from sickness and languid with coming death, the mother twisted the locks, vigorously waving, richly gilded, and dragged them in shining, curled lengths over the child's shoulders.

Because of the extreme weakness of the hands the process was a laborious one. A heavier pallor was upon the face, a cold moisture upon the sunken brow, when it was accomplished.

'I'll kape on while I kin – I don' know as I shall ha' the strength much longer, Dora.'

The child twitched her curls from the fingers that lay heavily upon them and turned on her mother fiercely. 'Yu ha' got ter du 'em, then!' she cried. She glared upon the faint head slipped sideways on the pillow. 'Yu ha'n't got ter put none o' them parts on, du I'll let ye ter know.'

Her eyes were suddenly wide and brilliant with tears; the fading sight of the mother was dazzled by the yellow shine of them and of the richly-coloured hair. 'My pretty gal!' she breathed; 'my pretty Dora! I ha'n't got no strength, bor.'

'I'll let yer ter know!' Dora cried with fury. 'I'll hull yer pillars away, and let yer hid go flop, if ye say yer ha'n't got no strength. I'll let yer ter know!'

She stopped, because the sobs which had been stormily rising choked her. She seized in her red little hands the pillow beneath her mother's head. No word of remonstrance was spoken, the faded eyes gazing wearily upon the child held no reproof.

'What d'ye look at me, that mander, for? Why don't ye ketch me a lump o' the hid?' the child cried fiercely; then gave way to the suppressed sobbing. 'Oh, mother, yu ain't a-dyin'? Yu ain't a-dyin' yit?'

She flung her own head on the soiled pillow; all the crisply waving, long ringlets flew over the mother's sunken chest; one fell across her parched lips. She moistened them with her tongue, and made a feeble motion of kissing. A tear slid slowly down her cheek.

'Not yit, my pretty gal,' she whispered. 'Mother ain't a-goin' ter lave yer yit.'

'Promus! Yer ain't a-tellin' no lies? Yer'll stop along of me till I kin carl my ringolets myself. I ha' got ter have 'em carled, and there ain't no one else to du 'em for me.'

The mother promised.

'There's Jim and Jack – they don't want ye, mother. Their hairs is short. They kin play hop-stock i' th' middeer, alonger th' other boys.

Both on 'em kin put their own collars on. There's on'y me, what have carls, that'll want yer so. Mother! Mother!'

'Don't I kape on a-tellin' of yer I ain't a-goin'.'

There was no time to sob for long on the mother's pillow. Dora was due at school. She wiped her crimsoned cheeks upon the corner of the sheet, stood up and put her sunburnt sailor-hat upon the carefully curled hair. She was neatly dressed in a brown woollen frock nearly covered by a white, lace-trimmed overall; she wore brown stockings and brown shoes. The mother watched her to the door with yearning eyes.

'My pretty gal!' she said.

The neighbour who waited on her in moments spared from her own household labours came in. She held a cup of paste made from cornflour in her hand, and stirred the mixture invitingly.

'It's time yu had suffin' inside of yer, Mis' Green,' she said. 'Yu ha'n't tasted wittels since that mossel o' bread-an'-butter yu fancied las' night.'

She put a spoonful of the food, stirred over a smoky fire, to the parched lips.

'I'd suner, a sight, have a drink o' water,' the sick woman said. 'There ain't nothin' I fare ter crave 'cept water now.'

'There ain't no nouragement in water, Mis' Green. Take this here, instids,' the neighbour said firmly.

Two spoonfuls were swallowed with difficulty.

'Come! Tha's as ter should be! That comfort ye, Mis' Green, bor?'

The faint eyes looked solemnly in the healthy, stolid face above her. 'There's nothin' don't comfort me, Mis' Barrett.'

'An' why's the raisen?' the neighbour reprovingly demanded. 'Because yu're a-dyin' Mis' Green, and yu don't give mind tu it. I ha' been by other deathbeds – the Lord reward me for it, as 'tis ter be expected He will – and I ha'n't never seed a Christian woman so sot agin goin' as yu are.'

The reluctant one shut her eyes wearily; the dropped lids trembled for a minute, then were raised upon the same hard face.

'She don' look like a labourer's gal, Dora don't,' she said faintly. 'She ha'n't got th' mander o' them sort o' truck.'

'What then, Mis' Green?' the neighbour inquired, stern with the consciousness of her own large family of 'truck'. The supposed superiority of Dora of the ringolets hurt her maternal pride and raised a storm of righteous anger in her breast.

Mrs Green did not explain; the discoloured lids fell again waveringly over the dim eyes, the upper lip was drawn back showing the gums above the teeth.

It was the mere skeleton of a woman who lay there. She had suffered long and intensely; no one could look upon her now and doubt that the hour of discharge was very near. The woman standing above her reasoned that if a word of reproof or advice was to be given there was not much time to lose. Often, from open door to open door (for the pair inhabited a double dwelling), often, across the garden fence, she had called aloud her opinion of her neighbour's goings on; she would seize the opportunity to give it once again.

'And why ain't yer Dora like a labourer's gal, then?' she demanded, shrilly accusing. 'Oh, Mis' Green! Don't yu, a-layin' there o' your deathbed, know right well the why and the wherefore? Ha'n't yu borrered right and left, ha'n't you got inter debt high and low, to put a hape o' finery on yer mawther's back? Ha'n't yu moiled yerself, an' yu a dyin' woman, over her hid o' hair? Put her i' my Gladus's clo'es, an' see what yer Dora 'ud look like. Har, wi' her coloured shues, an' all!'

'They was giv' her,' the dying woman faintly protested. 'Her Uncle William sent them brown uns along of her brown hat wi' th' welwet bow.'

'Now, ain't yu a-lyin', Mis' Green, as yu lay there o' yer deathbed? Them tales may ha' flung dust i' th' eyes o' yer old man, them i' my hid is too sharp for no sech a story. Di'n't I see th' name o' "Bunn o' Wotton" on th' bag th' hat come out of? An' don't yer brother Willum live i' London, and ha'n't he got seven of's own to look arter? Ter think as I sh'd come ter pass ter say sich wards, an' yu a-layin' there a-dyin'! Ain't yer ashamed o' yerself, Mis' Green. I'm a-askin' of yer th' question; ain't yer ashamed o' yerself?'

'No, an' ain't,' said Mrs Green, feebly whispering.

Beneath the flickering, bruised-looking lids, tears slowly oozed. The neighbour felt for a pocket-handkerchief under the pillow, and wiped them away.

'Fact o' th' matter, Mis' Green,' she inflexibly pursued her subject, 'yu ha' made a raglar idle o' that gal; yu ha' put a sight o' finery on 'er back, an' stuffed 'er hid wi' notions; an' wha's a-goin' ter become on 'er when you're gone?'

'I was a-wonderin',' the dying woman said, 's'posin' as I was willin' to speer this here parple gownd o' mine, rolled onder my pillar – I was a-woinderin', Mis' Barrett, ef so bein' as yu'd ondertake ter carl my gal's ringolets, now an' agin, for 'er?'

'No,' the other said, spiritedly, nobly proof against the magnitude of the bribe. 'That'd go agin my conscience, Mis' Green. I'm sorrer ter be a denyin' of yer, but yer mawther's hid o' hair I ha'n't niver approved on; I can't ondertake it, an' so, I say, straight forrerd, at oncet.'

The face so 'accustomed to refusings' did not change, no flush of resentment relieved its waxen pallor or lightened its fading eyes. ''Tis th' last thing I'm a-askin' of yer,' the poor woman said, weakly. 'Try as I kin, I can't live much longer. 'Tis on'y nat'ral I should think o' Dora an' th' child'en.'

'Yu think a sight too much on 'em, bor! 'Tis time yu give 'em up. Yu lay o' yer deathbed, Mis' Green, an' yu a mis'rable sinner; can't you put up a prayer to ask th' Lord ter have marcy on yer?'

'No,' said Mrs Green.

' "No" – an' why not?'

''Cos I don' keer.'

'Don' keer, Mis' Green?'

'No, Mis' Barrett, so's, He look arter Dora an' th' child'en, I don't keer what He du ter me.'

'Mother!'

No answer, but a quiver of drooping lids.

'Mother!'

At the sharp terror of the voice the lids lifted themselves and fell again.

'Yu ain't a-dyin', mother?'

''Course I ain't.'

'Yer promussed! Yer said yer warn't a-dyin'!'

'An' I ain't.'

'Then don' kape a-lookin' o' that mander. Lay hold o' th' comb an' du my ringolets.'

The comb was thrust within cold fingers which did not close upon it.

'If so bein' yer don't set ter wark and comb 'em out I'll shake ye. I'll shake ye, mother, du yer hare? Du yer hare, mother? Th' bell's gone, an' how'm I ter go ter school an' my ringolets not carled?'

They were not curled that morning, however, for at the sound of the child's angry, frightened voice Mrs Barrett came running upstairs and seized her and dragged her from the room.

'Yer baggige, yu! Ter spake i' that mander to a dyin' woman!'

'She ain't a-dyin', then,' the child screamed as she was thrust from the house. 'She ain't a-dyin', an' I want my ringolets carled.'

Once, when Dora had announced in the hearing of a pupil-teacher that she was the prettiest girl in the school: 'You ain't, then,' the older girl had told her. 'You are not pretty at all, Dora, but exactly like your brother Jim.'

'Jim's ugly! You're a-tazin' of me!' Dora had fiercely cried.

'If you hadn't your curls you'd be Jim over again,' the teacher had persisted.

She was a tempestuous little animal. She had flown to her mother with the horrid insinuation, had sobbed and screamed, and kicked the innocent, ugly Jim. If she had not her curls!

But she had them. Even this morning, when for the first time she must appear in school without having them freshly curled, the consciousness of their weight upon her shoulders was a comfort to the child. As well as she could without disarranging the set of it, she smoothed each long curl into order as she walked along. The sun of autumn shone, lying like a benediction upon the land whose fruits were gathered; among the hips and haws in the hedges the birds, their family cares all over, sang lightsomely, with vacant hearts. Happiness was in the air. Perhaps someone would say how the curls were, to-day. Perhaps, as once, blessedly, before had happened, a lady riding slowly along the green wayside might pull up her horse to inquire whose little girl she was, to give her sixpence, to ask how much she would take for her beautiful curls.

Ah, with what joy on that happy morning Dora had galloped home to give the account to her mother! The sixpence had gone to buy the blue ribbon Dora wore among her locks on Sundays; but how the mother had cheered up! She had seemed almost well for half an hour that evening, and Dora had told the tale again and again!

'I was a-walkin' along, like this here, not a thinkin' a mite o' my ringolets, an' I see th' woman on th' horse keep a-smilin'. So I made my manners, an' she pulled up 'r horse. "Whu's a little gal be yu?" she say; "an' where did you git yer lovely hair?"'

Her mother had eaten two bits of bread-and-butter, that evening, and had drunk the tea Dora all alone had made her. How happy it had been! Perhaps it would all happen again.

Morning school over, she was putting on her hat among a struggling mass of children anxious to get into the open, where there was a great blue vault to shout under, and stones to shy, when the schoolmistress from the empty class-room called her back. The woman stood by her silently for a minute, one hand on the child's shoulder, the other moving thoughtfully over the shining fell of hair.

'Don't shout and play with the others to-day, Dora,' she said at length. 'Wait till they clear off, and then go right home.'

'Yes, tacher.'

The schoolmistress waited for another minute, smoothing the curls.

'You're only right a little girl, Dora, but you're the only one. You must try to be good, and look after poor little Jack and Jim, and your father – and be a comfort.'

'Yes, tacher.' Dora took courage beneath the caressing hand: 'I like to be a comfit to mother best,' she vouchsafed, brightly daring.

'But your mother...' the governess said, then stopped and turned away her head; she could not bring herself to tell the child the news of the mother she had heard that morning, since school began.

So Dora went, sedately for the first few steps, afterwards with a happy rush, the curls dancing on her shoulders.

'Yer mother is a-dyin', she 'ont be here long; you must try to be a better gal'; how often of late had that phrase offended her ears! She had met such announcements with a fury of denial, with storms of tears. She had rushed to her mother with wild reproach and complaint. 'Why don't ye tell 'm yu ain't a-dyin', stids o' layin' there, that mander? They're allust a-tazin' of me.'

To-day no one had said the hated words; and mother would like to hear how teacher had 'kep' her at her side, and coaxed her hair. 'I ha'n't niver seed her du that to Gladus, nor none on 'em,' she would say, and would remind her mother how these less fortunate girls had not her 'hid o' hair.'

So, her steps quickened with joyful anticipation, she came running across the meadow in which was her home.

'Here come Dora,' Mrs Barrett, who had been busy in Mrs Green's room, said to the neighbour who had helped her. Both women peeped through the lowered blind. 'She'll come poundin' upstairs to her mother. There ain't no kapin' of 'r away; and a nice how-d'ye-do there'll be!'

The elder boy, Jim, whose ugly little face Dora's was said to resemble, was standing against the gate of the neglected garden. He did not shout at her, nor throw a stone at her, in the fashion of his usual greeting, but pulled open the rickety gate as she came up.

'Mother's dead,' he whispered, and looked at her with curiosity.

71

'She ain't, then,' Dora said. He drew his head back to avoid the blow she aimed at it, and shut the gate after her.

Jack, an ugly urchin of five, the youngest of the family, was sitting on the doorstep, hammering with the iron-shod heel of his heavy boot a hazel nut he had found on his way home. The nut, instead of cracking, was being driven deep into the moist earth. He did not desist from his employment, or lift his head.

'Father's gone for mother's corffin,' he said.

The howl he gave when Dora knocked him off the step brought Mrs Barrett upon the scene. She pulled the girl off the fallen Jack with a gentler touch than usual.

'You come along upstairs, along o' me,' she said.

There was not only the coffin to be ordered in Wotton, but suits of black for himself and children, besides the joint of meat to be cooked for the meal after the funeral. Mr Green did not hurry over his purchases, but went about them with the leisurely attentiveness of one anxious to do the right thing, but unaccustomed to the business of making bargains.

His wages had been 'made a hand on,' lately; there had been brandy and 'sech-like' to buy for the missus; the neighbour to pay, leaving little more than enough for bread for the rest of them. But now, with this burying money –! The new-made widower enjoyed the hitherto undreamed-of experience of knowing that he might put in for a glass at every public-house he passed, and not exhaust it.

He treated himself to a tin of salmon to have with his supper, when he got back to Dulditch. While his wife had been well and about, she had been wont at rare intervals to supply such a 'ralish' to the evening meal. Having the means to indulge himself, his thoughts had at once travelled to the luxury.

Yet, arrived at home, he had had too much beer to be very hungry, and the thought of the dead wife, up there, just beyond the ceiling, destroyed what little pleasure the feast might have held.

'Happen she'd been alive, she'd maybe ha' picked a mossel,' he said to himself.

That she could be totally indifferent to the delicacy, even although dead and fairly started on her heavenward journeying, was a bewildering fact his dull brain could scarcely grasp. He got up from the table, and taking the unshaded lamp, walked heavy upstairs to look upon this marvel – his wife who was no more.

He was a stolid creature, but was shaken enough to give a sharp growl of fear when, from the other side of the rigid form upon the bed, a head was lifted.

'Hello!' he called. 'Hello! What yu a-doin' here? Now then! Come out o' that, young warmint; don't, I'll hide ye.'

The figure lying by the dead woman slipped to the ground. It wore a brown frock and a crumpled white overall trimmed with lace.

'Hello!' the man said again. He looked stupidly at his little daughter, then pulled aside the sheet which covered his wife.

In the waxen face, with lids still half-open above the dull eyes, with lips drawn back to show the gums, was little change. Beneath the chin a large white bow of coarse muslin had been tied. It was designed to hide thinness of the throat, but gave, besides, a dreadful air of smartness to the poor corpse. Above the sunken chest the arms were crossed, but, over them, and over the thin hands, in a burning, shining mass of resplendent colour lay – The husband held the lamp nearer, and bent his dull, red face to peer closer at the scattered heap – the miracle of bronze and red, red living gold. 'Hello!' he said again, then moved the lamp to let its light shine on his daughter's face, and stared at her.

'Hello!'

'I ha'n't got no one now to carl my ringolets,' the child sobbed, her voice rising high in the scale of rebellious misery; 'my ringolets ain't no good to me no more. I ha' cut 'em off; mother, she kin have 'em. They ain't no good ter me.'

The glare of the lamp held awry was upon the broad red face of the girl with the streaming, yellow eyes, with the unevenly cropped head.

'I thought yu was the boy Jim,' her father said.

THE WITCH OF DULDITCH

THE woman who is confidently accused by her neighbours of having formed a compact with the Evil One, and of having until the day of her death exercised her supernatural powers with the devilish malignity natural to her tribe, was far removed in appearance from the popular conception of a witch.

She was a quiet, inoffensive-looking person, with a pale, smooth skin, light, rather prominent eyes, and scant, fair hair, brushed plainly behind her ears, and twisted into a small but protuberant knot at the back of her large head. She was married in her fortieth year; and it was on the occasion of her wedding that she was first openly accredited with the evil reputation which stuck to her through the rest of her life.

For some twenty years before her marriage Queenie Mask lived in our parish in the capacity of housekeeper to Mr George Ganders, called among us 'Gentleman George' – the epithet not having been applied to him so much on account of the graces of his person or the refinement of his mind, as for the fact that he is the lucky possessor of property bringing him in twenty pounds a year; such annuity removing far from him the necessity of stooping to earn his daily bread.

Rose Cottage, in which Mr Ganders and his housekeeper lived alone, stands a dozen yards back from the line of cottages bordering the grass-edged road. In the heater-shaped front garden – wide as the cottage itself at the top, narrow as the gate which opens out from it at the base – a couple of large standard roses flourish: a giant of battle, crimson-hued, and the pink-petalled 'maiden's blush.' Up their stems convolvulus and sweet pea are always carefully trained, and the land around them is sweet with self-sown mignonette. Over the front of the cottage itself a small-flowering, dark red rose grows and blows luxuriantly.

Inside, in the perpetual twilight of the small 'keeping-room,' there is a constant smell of apples, crossed at certain times of the year by a stronger smell of onions, mingled with faint odours of lavender and dried rose-leaves, and blended with the pungent fragrance of herbs drying on the tea-tray in the window. The window, by the way, is never opened. Long ago, in the days of Gentleman George's comparative youth, it had been fastened with a couple of nails to cure it of rattling when the wind blew, and the nails have not been withdrawn. Strong smells Mr Ganders does not object to, but a 'flap' of air is an abomination to him. His garden is as sheltered as a room – his room is as close as a box.

In the drawers of the large press entirely filling one side of the room separate species of apples are kept; the key of each drawer is in Gentleman George's pocket.

In Queenie's day it was as much as her place was worth to touch those keys, to finger the contents of those drawers. She was a woman, honest to the backbone, who would not have robbed her master of the value of a split pea, yet was she guarded from temptation and watched by him as if she had been a seven-times-convicted thief. It was he who weighed out the flour for the daily dumpling; who, with his own 'shut-

74

knife,' pared and cored the apples, lest there should be undue waste; who counted the potatoes he put into the pot.

It was the interest of his life, this strict guard exercised over his household goods. The pride of his life was that on every day of the three hundred and sixty-five he was enabled to produce from the pocket of his coat (smelling like a cider-press) an apple for himself and one for Queenie.

A tiny orchard was at the back of Rose Cottage; the trees therein had been arranged with a view to apples all the year round, and nobly the intention was fulfilled. No hands but Gentleman George's own were allowed to touch the product of his trees. He kept a suspicious eye on Queenie in the autumn gales, and was always on the spot to catch the windfalls. He gathered the apples himself, stored them himself, was careful to turn each one as it lay in its nest of straw every day with his own fingers. His talk was ever of 'Norfolk biffens,' of 'Rollands,' of Ribstone pippins,' of 'Pearmains.' If two or three of the codlings went rotten, or a 'Dr Harvey' had to be thrown away, the fact afforded master and servant after-supper conversation for a month.

But there was no talk in Rose Cottage when once the shades of night came on, for Queenie would not talk in the dark, and Gentleman George did not 'hold with' the expense of candle or lamp when there was no work to be done. So by eight o'clock in the autumn evenings, and by seven in the winter, the doors were fastened, the remnant of the fire in the grate carefully damped, and the household retired to rest. Yet did Gentleman George, not a heavy sleeper himself, greatly grudge the hours wasted by his housekeeper in repose. On baking mornings – those momentous weekly events when seven loaves of bread were cooked and an apple-roll made – Queenie was up before the dawn. On the fortnightly occasion when Gentleman George's two shirts and the less important items of the family linen were washed, the poor soul was bending over her tub by four o'clock of the summer morning, the master sitting beside her and keeping a keen eye on the soap. Then there were the brewing days, when a gallon and a half of the liquor facetiously termed among us 'guide-ye-right' – because with any amount of it on board you are said to be able to pursue a straight path – was brewed, an occurrence which necessitated a rising in the small hours of the morning. In a word, at those times of the year when the sun rose early enough to save Mr Ganders's candles, Queenie was rarely allowed to press her pillow after daybreak.

But she was a meek and exemplary woman, and never complained. For all those twenty years she had no holiday, as Gentleman George objected to gadding; for nearly all that time she had not set eyes on one of her own relations, as they lived in a neighbouring parish, and Gentleman George was averse to visitors. Such a life had made of the naturally quiet and retiring woman a very silent and timid one. Of the experiences of her past life, of those kin of hers, whom she had not forgotten, although the longing to see them had probably left her, she may have thought as she darned her master's grey woollen stockings, or put yet another patch in his much-mended flannel shirt, sitting on the doorstep, to catch the last light of day, or sitting on the fender, the blaze of the fire on her work. She was a faithful soul, not one easily to forget, and her thoughts of these things may have been long and deep, but she kept them to herself. Gentleman George was not a person inviting confidences from the most effusive; and other companion had she none.

The hospitalities of Rose Cottage never extended beyond the entertaining of a passer-by with a few minutes' gossip at the gate. The only refreshment the master of the establishment ever offered to his kind was an apple pulled from the coat pocket where a few of those delicacies always lurked. He prided himself on his reserve in these matters. He interfered in no one's business, he wanted 'no interfarin' ' in his, he declared. Friends meant money, he was fond of saying. If you shook a hand, sooner or later it was in your pocket. If every man would keep his door shut, and his mouth shut, and his pocket shut, all the world might be as prosperous and as individually satisfactory as Gentleman George himself. Whereas now 'all the world' slouched past to the ale-house, where wages were spent and foolishness talked, or toiled home from labour in the fields to bare cupboards and overcrowded beds. And why? asked the astute bachelor from the safe security of his own position, his rose trees, his apple orchard, his twenty pounds a year at his back – looking out upon the world of fools beyond his gate. Because each man having in evil moment opened his door to a woman, a crowd of children had come in. A rural philosopher is Mr George Ganders; somewhat blear-eyed in appearance, a fringe of white whisker, thick locks of iron-grey hair, surmounted by a very broken-down black felt hat, framing a florid, sheepish face; attired always in a manner befitting his title to gentility in a suit which once had been black – a suit honourably distinguished among those clay-hued garments worn by the neighbours he could afford to despise.

Queenie had a profound admiration of the wordly-wiseness of her master. She accepted his dicta on all such matters, not even conceiving the possibility of dissenting from them. But she looked rather wistfully at the prematurely aged women from the cottages on either side and over the way who came to their doors in the mornings to watch their children toddling off to school, or shaded their eyes from the rays of the setting sun, looking out for husbands and big sons coming home from work. Often she saved that apple, polished to shininess by her master's red pocket handkerchief, his daily offering to her merit, and bestowed it secretly on a neighbour's child.

Within sight of Rose Cottage, if you stand by the gate and look past the cottages to the left of you, past the ugly red-brick chapel of which our Dissenters are so proud – having at their own expense lately rebuilt it of glaring brick, with large shining windows, with all available crudity of material and architecture – past the small plantation of spruce and larch, where the nightingale is always first heard in Dulditch, is the small thirty-acre farm called Brummles. The name is a corruption, it is supposed, of 'Broomhills,' most of the land now under cultivation having been, within the memory of the oldest inhabitant, waste land, growing broom and heather. The reclaiming those thirty acres has been a mistake, the present tenant declares, and certainly they yield starvation crops.

'God A'mighty knowed best,' this gentleman is heard to say, shaking his head. 'Ef He went and planted fuzz bushes 'twer a sign th' sile wor'n't suited to corn. Ef He up and called a fiel' "Good-for-nothin' fiel",' 'twor a goin' agin' Prov'dence to look for good to come out on't.'

Here is he, he will continue, 'Benjymun Squorl' (only the rector, who prides himself on his nicety of pronunciation – 'his finneckin' talk,' his parishioners term it – persists in addressing Mr Squorl by his rightful patronymic of Squirrel), 'had been fule enough to run agin Prov'dence – which yer might as well bash yer hid agin a brick wall as done it – and hung these hare tree-and-thutty acres o' rubbage about 's neck!' As the 'refuge' (refuse) 'o' the 'arth,' he is wont to say he regards the farm which he rents. 'Ay – come to that – th' refugest o' th' refuge!'

Besides his unsatisfactory holding, poor Squorl was troubled with a helpless, good-for-nothing wife. Her one recommendation in sight of the child-ridden neighbours had been that she bore him no children; but perhaps Benjymun, who was of a tender and kindly nature, may have held a different opinion on this point. That she mismanaged his home, made the worst butter in the county, lost all her young chickens, and always had tainted pork in the pickling pot, was common talk. She ended by dying miserably of a cancer in the breast, having given poor Benjymun the miseries of a two years' illness, and left him with a doctor's bill likely to prove a drain upon his resources for the rest of his life.

The duties in attending on her being so disagreeable, and she herself so little of a favourite among them all, the neighbours deserted her in the last stage of her terrible illness, and no nurse could be found. Day and night her husband and herself dressed that ghastly sore, which she all along eagerly displayed with an entire absence of prudery to any stray visitor who could be prevailed on to set foot in her room. Dreadful stories (I have reason, I thank God, to believe exaggerated) of her suffering, said to be 'terrufic,' touching stories of Benjymun's fidelity and attentiveness were extant. How, in addition to his heavy work on the farm (for poor Squorl had a difficulty in finding the money for wages, and was always 'short-handed'), he now had to milk the cow, to make the butter, to clean the kitchen, to do the washing for the poor woman which no one else would undertake, to sit up with her as the end drew on 'o' nights.'

These tales, repeated over hedges as she was hanging out the linen, called from neighbour to neighbour across her garden-gate as she sat on the doorstep sewing of summer evenings, Queenie heard. Her own mother had died of a 'sore' – (it was by that generic title that poor Mary Squorl's dread disease was known among us). She longed to concoct a remedy from the 'comfort' (comfrey) root, which grew in the back garden, but Gentleman George at once vetoed the design. He never had countenanced the establishment of friendly relations with his neighbours, he 'were not goin' to begin with no comfort rutes' to please Queenie.

But Queenie's interest was kept alive, and once or twice she ran out to the gate and stopped the poor husband, hurrying by to make his small purchases at the shop, to whisper timid inquiry about the sufferer.

Then there came a day when she, having been to the mill for her weekly stone of flour, found that she had a quarter of an hour to spare before her master would expect his tea. Screwing up her courage, she hurried on to Brummles, resolved at length to carry out her great desire to speak a kindly word to the poor unfriended creature who was dying as Queenie's own mother had died.

She had never before set foot in the little farmhouse – in worse repair and with no better accommodation than many of the cottages – but she stood on no ceremony now, for she had small time to spare.

Finding the kitchen empty, untidy, desolate, the fire dead in the grate, the remains of the meals of which Benjymun had partaken for days past on the table, she mounted the dark staircase, and, emerging from that steep and tortuous way, found herself at once in the sick-room.

Benjymun was there, sitting on the side of the bed. No fire in the room, although the biting winds of early spring blew up the open stair. But a coldness icier than that of east wind or of frost seemed to smite Queenie in the face as she entered.

'I come to see ef so be as I kin help yer, po'r sufferin' soul!' she said, hurriedly advancing toward the bed.

The woman was lying on her back, her waxen-hued face turned upward; but at the sound of the strange voice – as it seemed, for probably the ears were deaf then to all earthly sound – the skeleton head slowly turned, the hollow eyes fixed themselves with an awful stare upon Queenie's face, and in a minute Benjymun Squorl's wife was dead.

It was a great relief to the widower that in the supreme moment which he had superstitiously dreaded, when the last bodily pang came and the soul of his wife took flight, he was not alone with her. He both thought and talked a great deal of the happy coincidence of Queenie's appearance at the moment of poor Mary's demise.

'She jus' twirled her eyes on her, giv' a gulp – and were gone,' he said many times, telling the tale, using always the same phrase, after the manner of his kind. 'She di'n't seems no matters worse than she'd ha' done for weeks; but she twirled her eyes on ter Queenie and were off.'

Gentleman George of course heard the tale. The woman had been so long a-dying, her sufferings were so great, her death such a relief, that even he could not upbraid Queenie for having made things easy to her.

'She'd ha' been a-lingerin' on Benjy's hands now, mayhap, ef it hadn't been for Queenie a droppin' in,' he said, with some natural pride in his retainer, as the neighbours stopped to talk at his gate. 'Queenie cou'n't du no less, po'r critter. She jes' twirled her eyes, and _'

Gentleman George, repeating the now popular phrase, would brush one hand over the other to illustrate the perfectly easy manner of Mrs Squorl's departure.

On the day of the funeral both he and Queenie stood at the gate to see the little procession pass, and Gentleman George nodded with friendly condescension to the chief mourner as the coffin was carried by. Yes, Queenie here, his housekeeper, this woman at his side, unostentatious as she seemed, and averse from taking any credit to herself, she had had a hand in that matter!

The poor woman was put into the ground on a Saturday, and the next day an event almost unprecedented in the annals of Rose Cottage occurred. Squorl o' Brummles, on his way home from afternoon church, stopping to speak to Mr Ganders, leaning on his garden gate, found that gate opened to him, and was bidden to enter.

The widower came into the stuffy front room, sacred to all the vegetable odours under heaven, and looked around him, marvelling at the combined luxury and comfort of the apartment. Every inch of the brick floor was covered with carpet; curtains shrouded the window. Sunday afternoon was always converted into a festival at Rose Cottage by the appearance of a red and blue checked cloth upon the round table, in the centre of which a dessert dish, green of hue and shaped like a leaf, was placed filled with apples. Two biffens, destined for the delectation of master and housekeeper, were roasting on small pieces of brown paper on the hob. Queenie, stiff and upright in her Sunday dress, occupied the Windsor chair on one side of the hearth; to Mr Ganders himself evidently belonged the other.

The poor widower, sitting there in his brown velveteen coat, a crape band upon his arm and another on the billycock hat, two sizes too large for him, and coming well down over the long ringlets of his iron-grey hair as rusty as the hat, thought of the uneven, unscrubbed bricks of his own front kitchen, of the broken victuals upon the table, of the cold and lonely hearth. His kind are not generally open to impressions, but he felt the contrast like a revelation. He had heard the word 'comfort' without rightly understanding its meaning till now. There had been none in his life. Here, in this breathless little box of a room, was Comfort. And Queenie, sitting prim and upright in her Sunday dress of violet merino, with little stripes of black velvet running round the short skirt and round the tight sleeves from which her red, rough wrists emerged, was its presiding genius.

Benjymun is no more artistic than the rest of us in Dulditch. He does not understand the beauty of proportion, nor delight himself in grace, nor intoxicate his senses in colour. But the way that Queenie Mask's red-braided holland apron sat upon her meagre bust, half covered her full, short skirt, the fashion in which her scant, straight hair was brushed smoothly on either side her high, narrow head and passed behind her wide, white ears, appealed strongly to Benjymun's taste. Looking at her, he pushed the rusty hat a little off his brow as he breathed the warm and heavy air, and uttered a sigh that was partly for his lost wife and partly for Gentleman George's housekeeper.

He did not offer many observations during that visit. The warmth, and the scent of the apples, and the unusual experience of a new idea which had come to him were altogether rather overpowering to Squorl. He felt unusually heavy about the head and a little sick, if the truth must be told.

'Th' p'or soul!' said Queenie, talking him over afterwards with her master; ''tis trouble pas' speech wi' him. Did ye note how he sighed and sighed as ef 's very inside was a-comin' up; and never so much as ope'd 's mouth?'

But if the visitor was not talkative he was in no hurry to depart, and his host, having at length opened his door to his kind, felt a rarely experienced pleasure in showing off his possessions. The various drawers in the oak press were unlocked, and the different kinds of apples lying snugly in their straw exhibited, their several properties of growth, of eating, of keeping discoursed on. The body of the canary, which had hung in the window for a dozen years or more, filling the room with song, and whose death had been the great grief of Gentleman George's life and a real sorrow to Queenie, was shown. Queenie had interred its corse in a moss-filled paper box with a glass lid, having first driven black beads into its head to take the place of eyes. She felt a little bashful pride in having this resourceful dodge pointed out to the widower. A little shelf full of books, which Mr Gander's father had bought for a song at an auction, was inspected.

'They ain't smart 'uns,' their present owner said, with a decent veiling of his natural pride in his possessions. 'They ain't a sight to look on, but them as know tell to me that theer's a won'erful wally set on this here antikity by the gentry.'

He flicked his red handkerchief softly at the volumes suspended by green cord on their little shelf.

'I don't read 'em myself,' the master said with the conscious air of one whose life-business allowed no space for trifling – 'I don't read 'em, but there they be.' He took down a work entitled *The Mariner's Guide: A Treatise on Navigation*, and opened it, showing the charts and hieroglyphics before Benjymun's uncomprehending eyes; shut it again beneath his visitor's nose, and restored the volume to its place between the Rev Samuel Clapham's *Sermons* and the second volume of Bulwer Lytton's *Rienzi*. The other works of which the library was composed

81

were an odd volume of the *Quiver* and a dozen unbound numbers of *All the Year Round*.

Queenie stooped forward to turn the 'beefuns' on the hob.

'Tell Mr Squorl about the Cleopatrick; giv' um th' hist'ry, master,' she said.

''Tis another antikity,' Mr Ganders said, with an affectation of disparagement. ''Tain't on'y th' gentry that keer for sech.'

He fetched from its accustomed nail a small black-framed print which had suffered serious damage from sun and damp before ever it was hung upon the Rose Cottage walls. It was covered with brown and yellow spots, its lines were blurred and faded.

'This here is a French party,' Gentleman George explained, his broad finger-tip on the principal figure. 'That theer little sarpent she've ketched hold on, she's about to swaller it for a merracle. This here young person aside on her she be a-washuppin' o' Cleopatrick. 'Tis a Scripter subjec', and bein' antikity is wallable. 'Twas th' postman, a-callin' to ax me for the faviour of an apple, come ten yare las' Janiwary, as giv' me th' hist'ry.'

Altogether, the bereaved Squorl must have spent a pleasant and an improving afternoon. It was his host himself who had to suggest his departure.

''Tis gittin' for our hour for tea,' the Gentleman said. 'I take my males reg'lar. Queenie, set the kittle bilin', wummun. I'll see Squorl ter th' gate.'

'Good arternune, and thenk ye,' Benjymun said.

It was to Queenie Mask that the departing visitor addressed his thanks, which might have struck his host – who, if he had not exactly stayed him with flagons, had at least comforted him with apples, and had shown him, out of his treasure-house, things new and old – as odd and ungracious in Benjymun.

By ten o'clock the next morning the widower was there again, thus showing greater appreciation of his entertainment than the master of Rose Cottage quite approved. He rattled the locked gate at the end of the heater-shaped garden, and Gentleman George, hearing his name called, went out to him there.

'Mr Ganders, bein' onaisy, I ha' come fur yer adwice,' he said with great gravity. 'Yer a man o' th' warld, wi' book-larnin', and knowin' th' wally o' things, and I'd thenk ye fur yer adwice. My p'or woman's dead; and, bor, I'm lost without her – lost; and tha's th' down fac'. Theer's bakin' day a-comin' on, and th' dairy, to say nothin' o' th' wash – and theer's a sight o' duds i' th' chamber-corner a-waitin' for th' tub – and I'm ter'ble upset i' my mind.'

'I heered,' said Gentleman George, condescending to bring his mind to bear upon his neighbour's trouble, 'the neighbours was a-passin' the word as Meelyer Sprite were a-waitin' on yer.'

'Meelyer's charge is high – sixpence a day and her wittles. A man can't stan' agin it.'

'A wife's chaper and more economical,' Ganders said thoughtfully. 'Wheer theer's housekeepers theer's all mander of expenses – and theer's waste. Though I ha'n't tied myself up thus fur, I bain't a denyin' a wife's economical, Squorl.'

Benjymun's face lightened.

'I ha' tarned my thought in that theer d'rection, I don't gainsay,' he admitted with eagerness, 'and as yu – a man o' th' warld, and allust much thought on i' th' place, and wi' proputty – see northin' agin th' coorse o' my takin' a second wife, I may as well let on as I ha' tarned my eyes on Queenie. I shall be obligated, Mr Ganders, ef yer'll contrive so' I can marry on her at oncet.'

The course of Benjymun's true love did not run smoothly, and his courting was carried on under difficulties; but it came to a speedy and triumphant conclusion for all that.

When once Queenie was aware of the man's intention – and, in spite of the locked gate and the unwinking watch kept upon her, she learnt it somehow very quickly – she contrived to let it be known that she favoured it.

'I ha' allust wished to try my hand at th' dairy wark,' was all she said when her master endeavoured by threats, by coaxings, by tears, by bribery to put her off the project.

She said the same thing to Benjymun on the occasion of the only interview between them.

She said the same on her wedding-day, walking soberly homeward in the violet dress, covered for the occasion by a brown ulster of a very cheap and thin description, white-gloved, a black straw hat with white ribbons on her pale smooth hair. At her side walked Mr Squorl, also white-gloved, in his old brown velveteen, still wearing the band of crape on his arm and on the hat which covered the whole of the back of his iron-grey head, and was, indeed, only prevented by a pair of serviceable ears from extinguishing him.

The wedding was not, in appearance, such a festive occasion as the funeral of a few weeks back. Queenie had invited two of her neighbours to support her through the ceremony, but these ladies had declined, giving no reason. As the new-made wife passed her old home on her husband's arm, these former acquaintances of hers laughed with a jeering note, standing in their doorways. A little farther on one of them caught up a white-haired toddler who had run out into the road and hurried indoors with it.

'Why, Meelyer,' Queenie said, who was fond of children, 'let th' little un be! We shorn't do um no harm!'

But Meelyer pressed the child's head upon her breast and looked back with a gaze at once frightened and vindictive at the bride.

'Likelies I'll lave my Wulfrid i' th' track o' one that ha' th' evil eye,' she muttered as she went.

Gentleman George, leaning upon his little gate, looked after the wedded pair as they passed with an expression of the frankest ill-will.

'Ongrateful wretch!' he said, as his old servant looked up and nodded to him. 'Ongrateful, black-hearted wretch!'

Poor Queenie, walking with the strange man at her side, who was her husband, but with whom she had hardly interchanged a dozen words, could not feel very elated at such a reception by her old friends. She had to keep up her courage by the reflection that her ambition 'to try her hand at the dairy work' was to be satisfied at last.

And the dairy, under the new management, proved a success. 'Queenie werern't niver a mawther to go about things in a halflin' way,' her worst enemies admitted. A new complexion was put upon the uneven, broken bricks in the Brummles kitchen. Washing-day ceased to be a terror, whose misery (in the shape of wet linen flapping about Benjymun's ears and encumbering his dinner-table) no longer extended itself over the whole week. The weekly bake became a pleasurable as well as an eventful occasion. His expenses were cut down, but he had never tasted 'no sech a wittles' as Queenie now set before him, her husband gratefully declared. Queenie was shocked indeed when she learned from Squorl that her predecessor had 'ran him up' at Littleproud's for tinned lobster, tinned salmon, even tinned beef, and such-like 'fancical' articles with which certain weak-minded and idle housekeepers are apt to be tempted.

'Theer ain't no support in them theer ertifeecials,' Benjymun announced, squaring his elbows over his savoury meal of pig's fry, onions, and potatoes.

Queenie, who, in the atmosphere of her husband's approbation, expanded even to the extent of expressing ideas of her own, had advanced the proposition – become proverbial since in Dulditch – that no woman should hold herself fit for wife or housekeeper who could not 'go through a pig.' She was now enabled, four times a year, to prove her own efficiency for such post by this process. From the gouged-out eyes, which went into the swill for the animal's successor, to the tip of its curly tail, which formed an ingredient in the pork-cheese Benjy enjoyed so much for supper, there was not an ounce of waste material.

But, although his wife gave satisfaction to the good man who had so quickly made his choice, outside the doors of Brummles dark things were spoken of Queenie.

She had 'twirled' her eyes on poor Mary Squorl to some purpose! She had bewitched the poor husband! Why was it that everything began to prosper now at Brummles? Why did the pig fat twice as quick as other people's? How came it that the pork was never 'slammacky'? Why did the cow, that had always 'gone dry' half the year, now give a plentiful supply of milk nearly up to the time of calving? Why was the butter, that used to be pale and 'intmenty,' now of the colour of buttercups? Let Queenie explain these matters if she could.

And by-and-by there happened a more wonderful thing still. Brummles boasted no orchard, but in the garden behind the house were one or two very old apple trees, and growing close to the gable-end of the house was a pear tree that in the memory of man had never grown fruit. Behold these trees, in the first spring after Queenie's marriage, each blossoming like a bride!

This was a memorable circumstance in itself; not much short of a 'merracle,' indeed, if one omitted to take into consideration the fact that Queenie, in her spare hours, worked like a man in the back garden, digging there and pruning the old roots of the trees, which had spread themselves wide beneath the rarely troubled soil. But a more significant event was to follow. For the first time since the tenancy of Gentleman George the orchard of Rose Cottage was bare of blossoms!

What proof more conclusive of the power of the evil eye was wanted than this?

If it had been that more was needed, look at Gentleman George himself. Gentleman George, who, having tried and discharged three different housekeepers since Queenie's desertion of him, now chose to dispense with those expensive luxuries altogether, and lived alone, preparing his own meals, making his own bed, sweeping his floor, and weeding his garden in tragic solitude, interrupted only by weekly charring visits from Amelia Sprite!

Sad tales Meelyer had to tell of him. How he wept over the food he could not make to his taste; how he was fearful as a child to be left alone when the house was locked at night; how, by the hour at a time, he hung over his gate and looked towards Brummles, only to rush within doors and hide his head if Queenie appeared, dreading above all else that she should turn the evil eye upon him as she had turned it on his orchard.

Was not all this, coupled with the improvement in Queenie's own position, enough to rouse the wrath of the neighbours?

When the autumn came, and Mrs Squorl, mounted on a rickety ladder, gathered the plentiful crop of apples in her own garden, the women drew round the gate and flung stones at her, so that she had to desist. She said nothing of this to Benjymun, possessing in a really fine degree that '*grand héroïsme muet des âmes fortes*,' which belongs by right to a certain order of woman; but she left the rest of the apples and the abundant produce of the *Bon Chrétien* (The 'Bun crick,' Squorl called it) for her husband to gather. He was a quiet, inoffensive man, but Queenie knew very well the women would not stone Benjymun.

Later, Mr Ganders fell sick, and lay lonely and weeping in his bed. Then Queenie put a pork-cheese and a new-baked loaf and a little currant cake in a basket, and ventured within the precincts of her old home. She was not unobserved. A neighbour, wringing her hands free of soap-suds, called loudly on Meelyer Sprite, washing her own doorstep ('lickin' it over,' Queenie had said to herself contemptuously as she passed), and the pair, entering the house simultaneously with Queenie, dashed into Gentleman George's bedroom, and slammed the door of that apartment in her face.

Then from the bedroom sounds between a howl and a roar arose, in which Queenie easily recognised her old master's voice becoming articulate now and again in the bellowed forth entreaty, 'Kape 'er away from me. Tarn 'er out. T'row 'er into th' roadway. Don't let 'er twirl 'er eyes on me.'

Queenie listened, grown pale, then took her small basket on her arm again, and went back to Brummles.

When Benjymun came in to supper, the meal was ready, the hearth clean swept, the kettle singing pleasantly on the fire, and Queenie herself, very pale, with red-brown rims round her white-lashed eyes, sat sewing at a patch she was putting into his sleeve-waistcoat. Benjymun, happily unobservant, made a remark or two as to the bad state of the land, 'like a pit' from yesterday's rain, and in five minutes after bolting his last mouthful was asleep in his chair, loud snorts breaking the stillness, the aroma from his working clothes and his heavily steaming boots filling the atmosphere.

Mr Ganders having recovered from his illness, made a pilgrimage to Runwich and had an interview with Mrs Hubby – she who is so successful in the treatment of ringworm, of whooping-cough, of sores. Mrs Hubby is an exceedingly fat and red-faced woman, with an iron-grey moustache and a thick voice. She keeps a tiny shop behind a red curtain, ostensibly getting her living out of ointments and washes, and pills which have a great local celebrity, but carrying on at the same time a secret and lucrative occupation, not even guessed at by the clergyman of her parish and the better-class people of the place. Counselled by the resourceful ladies on either side of him, Gentleman George determined to engage the wise woman of Runwich to baffle the Dulditch witch.

He returned from the interview hopeful of the success of the undertaking, but naturally depressed over the parting with the five shillings which had been necessarily sacrificed to the preliminaries.

As the charm proceeded, Mrs Hubby proved herself a perfect horse-leech's daughter in the matter of asking for more. Again and again had Gentleman George to put that unwilling had of his into his breeches' pocket in search of crown pieces. When the day, and the hour, and the minute of Queenie's birth had been given, after Mrs Hubby had on several occasions consulted the stars and concluded other occult ceremonies necessary to the end in view, she conveyed to her employer the intelligence that for the complete overthrow of the enemy a piece of gold, accompanied by three of the longest hairs out of Mrs Squorl's head, was necessary. The gold, in the enthusiasm of his pursuit, Mr Ganders might have contributed, but the scheme must fall through from the impossibility of procuring the necessary hairs out of the witch's shining, smooth locks.

'She be a sight too deep for th' wise wummun,' the neighbours who were in the secret said to each other. 'Tha's a masterpiece, that be, what can hamper old Mrs Hubby.'

Queenie's persecutions were doubled; the children, with whom she longed to make friends, ran from her, shrieking if they were small, howling and pelting her with stones when they were of larger growth. 'Down to Littleproud's' on Saturday evening, where happier women stood, basket on arm, to 'mardle' through the process of 'getting up' their parcels of sugar and cheese and candles, she was let severely alone. Did a death occur in the parish, of pig, of cow, of child, the disaster was laid at her door. The hunted look which her eyes had begun to wear grew more perceptible after each such fatality; her own prosperity, although she worked early and late to attain it, became a shame and a terror to her.

When the story of the consultation with the wise woman of Runwich reached her ears she set her face like a flint. Her old master, he whose home had been her home for twenty years, for whom she had spent the best days of her life, whose interests still – so much had she become in that monotonous time a creature of habit – were to her above and beyond the interests even of Benjymun Squorl, he to have meant her that wrong! He should have his way.

With a trembling hand she unfastened the small protuberant knot of her hair and pulled out a lavish amount, considering the scarcity of the supply, of the shining strands. These she folded in a paper, and, scrawling in her untutored hand her name and his upon the envelope, despatched it to Rose Cottage.

Before nightfall the three long hairs and the necessary gold piece were in the hands of Mrs Hubby of Runwich.

That was a night of bitter frost; the first sharp frost of the year. The unusual cold awoke Benjymun at an unduly early hour, and he found that the place beside him on the pillow was empty. He had a great pride in the energy and cleverness of his wife – or not so much in that perhaps as in the perspicacity which had led him to choose a woman of such parts.

'She's arter sum'at,' he said to himself now, chuckling with swelling satisfaction.

She had got up to inspect the cow who was expecting her calf; or she was getting the copper fire alight, that her washing might be out of the way before her neighbours were astir. He sighed with content as he pulled the patchwork 'twilt' up to his chin, and turned over again on his pillow. With a mate so filled with zeal, so given over to good works, a husband was entitled to a half-hour's extra snooze in such weather.

However, Benjymun himself was no laggard, and when the light of day was beginning to peep in cold streaks through the kitchen lattice he had descended, tallow candle in hand.

The place was tidied for the day, the floor swept, the fire laid ready for lighting, the kettle filled, the table set for breakfast.

Benjymun, in the time of the late Mrs Squorl, had been used to doing these offices after a fashion for himself. He stooped now and thrust the candle between the bars. When the straw, which was the groundwork of the fire, blazed up, suddenly illuminating the room, he saw what he had not observed before, that the breakfast table, graced with its slab of white bacon, its small section of cheese, its pat of butter, its basket of bread, was set for one person alone.

'She've forgot her and me make two,' he said with a slow chuckle. He thought this would be a matter to joke the 'wummun' about on future occasions: on summer evenings when he, lounging against the door-post, watched her weeding the onion-bed, digging up the first mess of potatoes, gathering the broad beans for to-morrow's supper; or on Sunday afternoons when, no stress of work being on their minds, light badinage was not out of place.

Having made sure that the crackling, spluttering fire had really 'caught,' he set the kettle thereon, and blowing out his candle, went forth into the biting coldness, the dark unpleasantness of the morning.

A fringe of icicles was hanging on the brown thatch of the house, on the roofs of the tumbledown farm buildings. Queenie was not in the wash-house; the copper fire was not even lit; she was not in the dairy. It was certain, then, that she must be in the cowshed.

But she was not there. The heifer – to whose purchase-money Queenie had contributed the seven pounds which represented the savings of twenty years in Gentleman George's service – had been milked, and was turned, together with the cow to whose confinement Brummles was anxiously looking forward, into the yard. The animals did not appear to appreciate their release, but stood against the door of the yard with lowered heads, their breath hanging visibly in the air, the grey chill dawn around them, the frost-fringed straw beneath their feet.

When the daylight was a half-hour older, struggling feebly in the chill air against the powers of darkness, Benjymun returned for his breakfast. He expected confidently to find his wife awaiting him. But no sign of her was there, and although he called her loudly, outside and in, there was no answer.

'What in tarnation be th' wummun at?' he said to himself, for the first time uneasy and irritated as well as puzzled. All at once that single cup and saucer on the breakfast-table seemed to convey a message the reverse of jocose. Queenie had never deserted him in this fashion before. There was an element of discomfort in the new departure, if not of anxiety.

He poured the boiling water upon the tea in the earthen pot; and then his eyes, roving uncomfortably around, fell upon the old hat and ulster which, except on Sundays, Queenie always wore abroad, hanging from their accustomed nail upon the door.

Then Queenie was not out of the house after all!

He gazed in slow astonishment at the poor garments, seeing to retain, in their slim outline and the unobtrusiveness of their fashion and colouring, so much of the likeness of their owner. Presently his eyes, slowly travelling downward, fell upon two pairs of boots beneath the press, the only two pairs possessed by his wife, as he well knew.

Tarnation again! She could not have gone out on such a morning in the only other foot-covering she possessed – the old carpet slippers, patched and mended, and only assumed when, the day's work being done, she was at liberty to warm her toes upon the fender.

With a shaking Benjymun pushed his cup away from him and started upstairs to the one bed-chamber. The room was as empty as when he had left it. He pulled away the sheet, depending from tapes, which hung before Queenie's 'violet' frock and her best ulster; he opened the box containing, wrapped in layers of white paper, the hat she had worn upon her wedding morning. All were in their places. Benjymun turned cold with the mystery of the thing as he looked.

She was gone – and she was gone in her stocking-feet, bareheaded!

As he turned slowly – for a numbness seemed to have fallen upon brain and limb – to descend, his outer door was opened and his name called sharply.

'Hi, Squorl, Squorl!'

A small, white-headed boy who worked at Brummles was standing in the kitchen, the door in his hand; his usually florid face was pale, his round blue eyes were wide and unwinking; there had been the sound of disaster in the shrill, high voice.

'Theer's summut wrong at th' roun' pond, maaster,' he cried excitedly; 'I come that waay to wark and I hulled a stone to see ef 'twould beer – and – theer's summut wrong and I dussen't go alo-un.'

Without a word, but with a trembling in his legs and a dreadful feeling of constriction across his chest which turned him sick, Benjymun stumbled out of the little gate, so low that a man could pass his legs over it, across the by-road and the field where the rime frost, which

> 'Enchants the pool
> And makes the cart-ruts beautiful,'

had whitened the grass.

Across the wide meadow, plain in the otherwise trackless expanse, were the marks of two pairs of feet: one those of little Johnnie Lawrence in his hob-nailed boots, the other lighter, less distinct, such as might have been caused, Benjymun knew it, by a woman walking in her stocking-feet.

The farmer ran in such slow, stiff, stumbling fashion as was alone possible to him, the child keeping a little ahead, but ever looking fearfully back to be sure that he was not alone. The small pioneer went on talking excitedly, but without conveying any meaning to Benjymun, whose sense also appeared to be frozen and who could not catch the words.

But when the pond, with its one pollard willow, its fringe of melancholy brown reeds, rattling in the deadly chill of the breeze which suddenly swept across the meadow, was but a few yards ahead, the boy stopped and, turning his face full upon the man who followed, pointed to what lay beneath the willow behind the loudly shivering reeds.

'Yar wummun's drownded,' he cried, shouting the words angrily in his nervous terror; 'be yu deaf that you can't hare me, mister? Queenie's drownded. I knowed 'twere har. I see'd th' colour o' har gownd.'

The child would not touch her. He put his knuckles in his eyes and began to cry dismally when Squorl called to him for help.

'I sholl drame on 'er,' he sobbed. 'I wush I ha'n't hulled the stun – that hit her flop i' th' face. She gi'en me tu eggs for my supper las' night. I wush I ha'n't sin her.'

The pond was but a few feet deep. Only a very determined suicide could have found death there. She (having accomplished the cold journey in her stocking-feet in order that her boots should not be destroyed) must have broken the ice, laid herself down, and deliberately suffocated herself.

Although with Queenie's death the ban was taken off his orchard, and his trees are pink and white as ever in the spring, weighed down with fruit as rosy and golden as of old in the autumn, Gentleman George has never recovered his old health and spirits. He has no relish for his daily apple. He takes no pleasure in his library of 'antikities,' nor in the Cleopatrick on the wall, now that Queenie is no longer there to call on him for the scriptural history of that 'French party.' Meelyer Sprite, who does his washing, rules him with an iron rod in the matter of soap, and refuses to give him an account of the candle-ends. He pities himself extremely.

'Things is all at Harrudge i' th' house,' he says to those passers-by who speak a sympathetic word at his gate, 'and I myself bain't no matters to spake on since that ongrateful wummun tuk and desarted on me.'

Mr Ganders has run down mentally through missing the hand that wound him up to effort. For lack of the accustomed prop he has come neck and heels together in moral and physical collapse; and he 'bain't a patch,' as we say in Dulditch, on the well-brushed, spruce and intellectual Gentleman George of old.

Johnnie Lawrence makes a circuit of half a mile in coming to his work in the dark winter mornings, or returning in the half-lights of the winter afternoons. For Queenie's spirit haunts that shallow pool beneath the pollard willow; her voice can plainly be heard screeching above the sorrowful rattling of the brown reeds.

''Tis well she chuse th' shaller water,' Queenie's old neighbours say. 'The mawther knowed well enough that sech as har 'ud never sink. Har badness 'ud ha' kep' har afloat i' th' deepest ocean-sea.'

HIS FIRST DAY AT THE SEA

THREE farmers' wagons, brave with red and blue paint, drawn up beneath the big elms at the schoolhouse gate. In each a couple of huge horses in their best harness, the early morning sun shining on the brass fittings and ornaments, the little crimson tassels shaking on their sturdy necks. The first wagon is filled as full as it can pack with boys and girls, their eager faces glowing beneath Sunday hats and caps, eyes glittering with expectation; dumb for the most part, too excited to speak.

'Lucy Stubbs, you have got Horace in charge, remember.'

'Yes, Gov'ness.'

'Stanley Arch, take your little sister on your lap. She's being jammed.'

'Yes, Gov'ness.'

'What have I told you about sitting still and keeping your places till you get to the station? All of your answer together.'

A big shout of 'All of us is to set still and kape our places, Gov'ness.'

'Where are your flags, then? Wave 'em! Off you go!'

Not quite yet; for here is Mrs Shildrick, hot and unkempt and breathless, dragging her lop-mouthed, white-faced offspring by the hand, making wild motions to the wagoner in charge of the horses, and shrieking 'Stop!'

'Mrs Shildrick, you know well that none of the children under six are to go to the sea, and that Herbert is only five. You have been told many times that he is not eligible.'

'He's a-goin' for all that. The Squire, he's a-payin'. He never said nothin' about no fiveses and no sixes. He's a-sendin' th' schoolchild'en to th' sea. And my Harbie's a-goin' with the rest.'

'Stan' back, missus,' says the wagoner, who at a sign from 'Gov'ness' has started the horses. Flags wave, children shout, the first wagon moves on, and Mrs Shildrick, more wildly determined than before, attacks the second. In this Governess herself has taken her place.

'Whu are yew to give laws, and say as my po'r little un shan't go?' the angry woman demands. She shakes a threatening hand, becomes abusive even. Governess, apparently no longer aware of her presence, starts on a high note the song in praise of ocean the children have been learning; and that wagon also rolls away.

The third is only three parts full. The children in it are in charge of a young teacher. The curate, who has run up, hatless, wet and wild of hair, a bath towel round his neck, fresh from his morning swim, and a little behindhand, to see the expedition start, is quite unequal to cope with the situation.

'My Harbie is a-comin' in here,' Harbie's mother says; and, making her son into a ball, without more ado pitches him upon the wagon floor. The child, who is bruised in the process but is used to being thrown about, picks himself up and says nothing. It is a peculiarity of Harbie that he never says anything, having had most of his wits knocked out of him in his earliest years, and being as good as dumb.

'You know, Mrs Shildrick, your poor little boy would be a great charge if we sent him. The schoolmistress has already ninety-nine children to look after.'

'Then, wha's one more? My Harbie haven't never sot eyes on th' sea. And I've a mind as he should! B'sides, I'm a-goin' myself. I don't want to be beholden to no gov'ness. I'll see arter 'm.'

'How do you intend to get to the station, Mrs Shildrick?'

'Run by th' side o' th' wagon, if tha's all.'

93

'You'd better ride with Herbert,' the conquered curate says. And Mrs Shildrick, clambering up the wheel, hurls herself down, shaken, battered, but triumphant, with a sounding thump upon its floor as the last wagon moves off.

'Because my Harbie is slow of his tongue and ain't so showy as some of 'em ain't no rayson why he shou'n't set eyes on th' sea,' she remarks, for the benefit of any who might listen.

Into the antecedents of Mrs Shildrick it would not be profitable to enquire. Her conversation is never instructive – indeed, the young teacher thinks it advisable to keep the children singing all the way to the station in order that they may not listen to her talk – her tastes are not refined. She, no more than Harbie, has ever 'sot eyes' on the sea. That she is not influenced by ardent desire to do so is evidenced by the fact that, following in the wake of the school, as the children make their glad way down to the sea, chucking the long-suffering, ineligible one by the hand, she stops with him at the first place of entertainment she comes to. It is a little yard over which an awning is stretched, and in it are set forth tables where saucers of yellow mussels steeped in vinegar are temptingly displayed. Refreshment more suitable for hot and thirsty excursionists is also to be obtained there.

Nor, at night, when 'Gov'ness,' making the roll-call of her charges, in readiness to depart, discovers Mrs Shildrick sitting on the station platform, has that good lady made any nearer acquaintance with the ocean.

Poor 'Gov'ness,' worn out with her labours and responsibilities, has engineered her flock safely through the dangers of the day. Through the first mad rush to the sea – the glistening, glittering blue-and-green-and-gold-and-silver dancing sea – more glorious than anything the children's eyes have yet beheld; and enough of it – enough for all of them! through the perils of cliff-climbing; of seaweed hunting; of paddling, and the dear delight of feeling the caressing waves, hailed with shouts of welcoming laughter, creep over grimy little toes, rise above red ankles, swirl about fat and skinny knees. Through the dangers of over-indulgence in the roast beef and green peas for which they are so enthusiastically prepared. She has had their Sunday trousers and best frocks, of such extreme importance to the poor mother who must save her pennies all the year to buy them, on her mind too. Has had to dissuade Mabel Dodd from her passionate desire to follow the organ-grinder who invites her with such strange words and leers and grimaces to dance to his music; to dog the footsteps of Willy Back, known to be cruel to animals, and always

94

drawn to the spot where the patient goats and donkeys stand in their melancholy ranks.

All these dangers and difficulties overcome, here they all are, red faces freshened by the sea, hair damp with its breezes, treasures of shell and pebble and seaweed grasped in sandy little paws – not so much as a cap or a handkerchief missing! The ninety-and-nine all safe – where is the little lamb outside the flock? Where is Harbie, left in his mother's care?

'Mrs Shildrick, where is Herbert?'

'And tha's the question I was about to ask of yew,' Mrs Shildrick retorts. 'You're th' person in charge o' this here treat. What ha' you done wi' my Harbie?'

The train is to start in five minutes: small time to argue the question of responsibility. 'You must go to the police-station and give notice of the loss of the child, Mrs Shildrick.'

'What! and lose my train? Not me! And who's a-goin' to see to my husban', and give 'm his supper, I'd like to know?'

In order that she might not be persuaded to alter her mind, Mrs Shildrick scrambles into a carriage of the waiting train, and takes her seat there. 'Them that ha' brought the school-child'en here have got to see all of 'em's brought home again,' she declares. 'Not but what Harbie'll tarn up. He's a master one for tarnin' up, Harbie is. There he be!' she excitedly cries, and points to where a flustered-looking group of men and women in black emerge upon the platform, Harbie, in his absurd Sunday suit, his man-of-war cap on his red, lank hair, composed, and silent as usual, dragging behind.

'Harbie!' screams the mother, wildly gesticulating from the train window.

'Harbie!' call the ninety-and-nine, with beckoning hands.

The flustered party in black explain the situation hurriedly to Governess while a porter hustles them into the train, which is about to start.

'We never asked for his company; we never set eyes on 'm before. He been with us all th' day, a-hitchin' hisself on to our party. Drowned? There weren't no fear of his a-gettin' drowned. We han't seen the sea, nor been a-nigh no water. We come to gran'father's fun'ral, and this here little un he hitched hisself on, and come to gran'father's fun'ral too.'

In such fashion it was that Mrs Shildrick's Harbie enjoyed his first day at the sea.

WOLF-CHARLIE

IN a tumble-down cottage at one extreme end of the parish of Dulditch Wolf-Charlie lives. It is one of a couple of cottages in such bad condition that they are held past repairing. Year by year Sir Thomas threatens to pull them down, and year by year, merciful man that he is, holds his hand. For years he has received no rent; for years Wolf-Charlie and his old grandmother, who inhabits the other miserable edifice, have received notice to quit at Michaelmas – a notice always disregarded. In the one cottage the ground floor only is found to be habitable; in the other, by reason of the absence of door and window in the downstairs apartment, the grandmother has been compelled to take up her abode in the upper storey. With the broken panes from the window her great-grandchildren dig in the heaps of dust and rubbish where is their playground. The door was long ago broken up and converted into firewood.

The cottages are approached by a lane too narrow to admit of any vehicle wider than a wheelbarrow. It is a lane which leads only to these poor 'housen', debouching on a melancholy space of grass and nettles growing above brickbats, tiles, broken chimney-pots, refuse of all sorts, which space was once on a time the trim garden plots of the houses. Between the broken bricks of the little paved way before the doors a plentiful crop of sickly fungus grows.

More than once there has been illness among the children caused by impromptu feasts off the unwholesome growth. One child, rendered reckless by stress of hunger and indulging in a surfeit, gave the crown and glory to Wolf-Charlie's history by necessitating an 'inkwitch' in Dulditch.

He is called Wolf-Charlie, I suppose, by reason of the famished look in his melancholy eyes, of the way in which the skin of his lips, drawn tightly over his gums, exposes his great yellow teeth; by reason of the leanness of his flanks, the shaggy, unkempt hair about his head and face, the half fierce, half frightened expression. He is what is called in employers' parlance 'a three-quarter man,' receiving only three-fourths of the wages of the other labourers.

He has the use of his hands and feet; he is not a 'down fool' like 'Silly Solomon,' idiot *par excellence* of the parish, nor a cripple like Dan'l Luck, whose leg the Runwich Hospital authorities deemed it wise to leave dangling from his trunk after his accident, the foot turned the wrong way, so that for the honour of swinging the useless member he has to go on crutches for all his life. Wolf-Charlie is not specially afflicted in any fashion, yet he is in some indefinable way deficient. His fellow-labourers will not 'du' a harvest with him, and no farmer dares employ him to feed his cattle or to plough or drill.

Yet such labour as is entrusted to him he does with unfailing industry and a dogged, dull persistence. When the vapours hang white and ghost-like over the low-lying meadows, he stands all the day knee-deep in water 'ditching'; and he can always be trusted to 'top and tail' the turnips. In the winter, when work on the farm is only to be obtained by the best men, and such hangers-on as Wolf-Charlie are invariably among the first to be paid off, he sits patiently by the wayside breaking the stones of the road; or for a few pence he will trudge the seven miles to Runwich to fetch a sick neighbour's medicine.

His clothes are in rags, showing the poor flesh in many places which custom and comfort have ordained shall be hidden from view; his thin hairy chest is oftener bare than covered; of Sunday clothes he has none. When he sits on the long dank grass of the roadside bank, with his back to the wind and his shoulders pulled to his ears for warmth, and feels in the red and white bundle beside him for the midday meal which is to support him till he can look for his bowl of potatoes at night, he finds nothing but dry bread there. He does not even possess the 'shut-knife' with which etiquette ordains the agricultural labourer shall carve his *al fresco* feast, but he pulls it to pieces, wolf-like, with claws and teeth, looking out with the fierce, yet melancholy gaze over the grey and shivering meadows as he drearily chews his food.

He is in a word the poorest of the poor – a most wretched and pitiable object.

Yet not so poor but that Wolf-Charlie, too, has had his romance. And here it is.

There was, some years ago, a winter longer and more cruel than any in Wolf-Charlie's experience; when a bitter frost bound the land in bands of iron, 'its rigid influence seizing Nature fast'; when the saddened sky looked down on a dead world wrapt in its winding sheet; when for even the valued hands no work could be found; and when the poor 'three-quarter man' was in every sense of the words out in the cold.

The Wolf was not a householder in those days, but shared bed and board with a family in exchange for the five shillings a week he paid them. For a couple of weeks not one of the five shillings was forthcoming.

The winter was hard in degree to all classes of the poor; no man dared to soften his heart toward his comrade; no woman ventured to give away bite or sup from the children's scanty meal.

There came a day when Wolf-Charlie, buckling the strap of his trousers tightly round his empty stomach, turned his back upon that poor table at which for long he had taken his place. The mother was doling out to her half-dozen little children the morning meal of bread soaked in hot water, peppered and salted; of this for the first time she ceased to offer the lodger a share. The poor fellow said no word of remonstrance, of appeal, of farewell even, but turned his back upon the place where his home had been and on the familiar faces, and took his way along a certain road. A road which the agricultural labourer and his wife travel (spiritually) in many a moment of depression and in their bad dreams; a road where surely no flower should grow, where the wayside grass and overhanging leafy trees should wither; a road paved with bitterness and hatred and a burning sense of injury and all evil thoughts and despair – the road to the workhouse.

No flowers were there to mock the passer-by on the morning when Wolf-Charlie sought the cold charities of the dreaded place; but the icy air cut his ill-protected body like a knife, the hard-encrusted snow of the road sounded like iron beneath his unwilling feet.

A taciturn man in company, the Wolf is given to talking a great deal to himself. As he trims the 'roots' for grinding, lops the overhanging branches of the trees, clears a way for the watercourse in the 'dekes,' his lips are always seen to move, and a low muttering issues forth. With such melancholy, indistinct murmurings, fit accompaniment to the vague, only half-comprehended bitterness and aching of his heart, Wolf-Charlie went his way and was swallowed up in the portals of the big whitewashed poorhouse. And in that village where hitherto his work was done he was seen no more.

In the springtime, when, as we are told, 'A young man's fancy lightly turns to thoughts of love,' and turns also, as we know in the case of our present hero, to possible odd jobs, easier to be come at in barley-sowing time and in the lambing season, Wolf-Charlie emerged from his place of retirement – not unaccompanied.

In spite of the warmth, regular food, and better clothing which he enjoyed in the workhouse, want of liberty had told sadly upon him. The strength of his longing and his misery had been too much for the body weakened by other privations, and Wolf-Charlie, who was not a favourite with the master, and whose sullen ways and uncomprehended mutterings made him obnoxious to the other officials, fell seriously ill. In this condition there was allotted him as nurse the woman who now issued with him from captivity.

She was a middle-aged woman, with a red and foolish face, with dust-coloured, dusty hair. She had a wooden leg and six children. She had been an inmate of the workhouse since the birth of her last, which toddled along, dragging on her skirts, a child of four.

So, boldly, Wolf-Charlie reappeared in that world which had not treated him too gently hitherto, bringing with him seven mouths to feed besides that capacious, never-satisfied one of his own. In such patriarchal fashion he made his entry into Dulditch, and, getting employment at the Brightlands Farm, installed himself and his tribe in the cottage above described.

It is probable that the idea of legalising the bond which bound the Wolf to the wooden-legged mother of six emanated from the rector. He found neither of the interested parties loth, and met with no such rebuff on the occasion as that with which Cyprian Crook answered a like appeal.

Crook is the village cobbler, a bad workman and a tipsy one. He does not come to church, and the rectory boots and shoes go to the next village, to be repaired there in the odour of sanctity.

'You don't employ me, why should I employ you?' Crook demanded of the rector, who had urged him to make the lady who resided with him as housekeeper his wife.

On the part of the Wolf and Wooden-leg no difficulties were made; the banns were duly asked, and all went merrily as the proverbial bell, until a report, speedily confirmed, was circulated through the village to the effect that Wooden-leg's husband, the father of the six, was still living, and not only living, but living in the adjoining parish.

Neither intending bride nor bridegroom was at all overcome by the announcement. The woman had known it all along – to the man it apparently made no difference. The idea of marriage having taken hold of their slow imagination, they would not relinquish it. Now that the 'crying' had made them celebrities in the place, they determined to accomplish that which they had publicly pledged themselves to perform. They would be married or perish in the attempt. They finally accomplished their purpose at the Runwich Registry Office. Having made all necessary and false declarations, they tramped off in the sunshine of an early summer morning, the six children, who could not with safety behind, trailing after them.

The bride, arrayed in her one frock – the old lilac print the matron had given her on her leaving the workhouse – hopped along bravely on her sound leg and that wooden substitute which, through use, had grown too short for her, causing her to walk with much pain and caution. The bridegroom, with his shaggy head sunk upon his breast, walked behind her, silent, his hands thrust in those slits in his trousers where his pockets had once been, gaping holes at his knees. So, with one shilling and twopence in hand to furnish forth the wedding feast, they tramped the seven miles.

So, having accomplished their object and expended their fortune, with the calm of satisfied ambition did they presently tramp home again – to the shelter of the filthy room with the empty cupboard, the bare table, the three broken chairs; to the connubial chamber where the big wooden bedstead filled all the space not occupied by the sacks of straw flung in one corner for the accommodation of the elder children. It swarmed with fleas, that gigantic couch; smelt abominably; its four great posts, undraped, used to reach to the ceiling and serve the children for impromptu gymnastic exercises until they were cut down, one at a time, in the first winter and converted into firewood.

On this wretched bed in the fulness of time a baby was born to the Wolf, and then another. Those few shillings which Wooden-leg picked up by gathering acorns for the farmers at sixpence a bushel, by picking stones, by singling beet, were stopped for these events; and at such times the family came dangerously near starvation. No nurse could be found, even if the necessary few shillings could have been scraped together to pay her; the eldest girl, thirteen years of age, was her mother's sole attendant for those few days she could lie beside her miserable baby before, with her hopping, painful gait, she must limp to her labour in the field once more.

As has been said, the Wolf's old grandmother lies bedridden next door. You mount to her room by an open flight of steps arising out of that ruined down-stair room, strewn with plaster falling from walls and ceiling, with the broken bricks kicked up from the floor. The old woman has not been down these steps for years, nor will descend them until she is carried down in her coffin; and because Wooden-leg cannot mount the unprotected, rickety stairway, the eldest girl is told off to wait on 'Gran'mawther.'

Considering that the child is only thirteen years of age, that she has had the worst possible training, and that there is practically no supervision (for when 'Gran'mawther' grumbles from the bed Beatrice thinks it wiser not to hear), the work is done fairly well. A few favoured ones among the uneven boards are scrubbed; the bed-linen – the threadbare blue counterpane, the cobwebby blankets, the yellow sheets

100

– is neatly arranged; the chair and table dusted. When Beatrice is particularly energetic she spits upon the latter and polishes it to a quite cheerful shininess. The little nurse appears on the best of terms with grandmother.

The child receives, by family arrangement, the sum of sixpence weekly for services thus rendered. 'Gran'mawther' is not of a liberal turn of mind and has never been known of her substance to offer her small attendant bite or sup.

But at night when everything is still Beatrice noiselessly mounts the unsteady stairs, gently opens the door of the old woman's room, steals across the rotten boards, and with a deliberate, unwavering little hand robs her grandmother.

The poor old soul has but an allowance of a half-stone of bread, a weekly dole of two shillings and sixpence. Her coffers are not over full, her board is not too luxuriously spread, but to the famished set next door she is a feminine Crœsus, a pampered being enjoying continual festival, diverting to her own selfish indulgence necessaries of life needed by far hungrier people.

The dark, still bright eyes of Gran'mawther open upon Beatrice, watch her as she appropriates the slice of cheese, the tallow candle, the lump of bread, which, with few variations, is the nightly toll she exacts. She watches that little marauder, but she says nothing. There is something uncanny to the imagination in the picture of the dauntless, small depredator at her nightly work, and the old woman, glib enough of tongue in the daylight, lying there, voiceless, to be robbed of her cherished store. It is almost as if that ugly grandchild in her scant and ragged chemise, barefooted, exercised some spell over the aged parent – as if supernatural agencies were at work.

But it is more the spirit of prudence than that of fear which strangles the curses on Gran'mawther's lips. She is entirely at the mercy of this abominable child, this unnatural descendant, who must have the elements of a conscience somewhere about her, as, up to the present, she has stayed her hand and left enough in cupboard to preserve her relation from starvation.

Suppose that, night by night, the thievish imp made a clean sweep of the provender! Suppose, instead of coming with commendable regularity to 'redd up' her granny, she slunk out in the fields to play, and left the poor old soul to die of dirt and neglect?

In submission, it seems, Gran'mawther's chief safety lies. Her only chance of deliverance from such outrage is to give up her wretched bedstead, her round table, her couple of broken-seated chairs; to give up all her pride and her lifelong prejudices, and have herself carried to the workhouse. But Gran'mawther – who prays that she may not live long in loud monotonous petitions, which only cease when Beatrice is in attendance, and which are a sound as familiar to the household next door and as unregarded as the soughing of the wind in the broken chimney – would sooner endure ages of lonely, miserable days, centuries of horror-haunted nights, than face that indignity.

So from year to year the family of which Wolf-Charlie is the head goes on. They are scarcely, one may say, in fortune's power – they never can be poorer than they are; their cupboard is empty even of the skeleton of fear.

Yet often, perhaps, the thought of that other husband whose responsibilities he had taken on his own shoulders may have troubled the Wolf's slow brain. By the irony of fate it happened that this man, who had deserted his wife and children to follow a wandering life, settled for a time in the parish adjoining Dulditch (he had kept clear of the neighbourhood while the parish authorities were interested in his whereabouts). Fortune had smiled upon him and trade had prospered. He had lately started a donkey-cart, and was looked on as a well-to-do person. A buyer of rabbit skins, old bones, rags and papers, a vendor of dried herrings, tapes and cotton.

Often, as Wolf-Charlie sat by the roadside, breaking the stones on the heap before him, this hero would drive past in his pride and arrogance, belabouring his donkey, with not a thought or a look for that other poor bearer of other folks' burdens under the hedge.

The Wolf was not a speculative, nor an inquisitive, nor a ruminative person; his reasoning powers were of the smallest; yet surely in his half-awakened mind, in his twilight consciousness, there must have dwelt thoughts at such times which one would be curious to know.

Once, when the second baby was born – when winter was lying, dark, silent and sullen upon the land, when, tighten the trouser-strap round his shivering body as he might, drag the manure sack he wore as great-coat close as could be about his throat, he must yet suffer dismal pangs of hunger and of cold – these thoughts strove to become articulate.

Stooping over the beet which he was pulling in a field adjoining the road, he heard the well-known sound of the donkey-cart approaching. He stood, arrested in his work, his back bent, the beet he was in the act of pulling in his hand. The wheels of cart or carriage passing along the road never diverted him from his work; even when the traction engine panted slowly by, its fire gleaming redly in the gloom of the thick afternoon, he would not lift his head to look. But the donkey-cart was a different matter.

Presently he raised himself, and with a light of unlimited resolution in his eyes stood erect. The donkey-cart approached, and in the lightness of his heart and triumph of his fortune the owner whistled gaily as he rode along.

Suddenly, swinging the turnip in the air and holding it above his head as a signal, Wolf-Charlie hailed his rival.

'Hi! I say!'

The driver of the donkey-cart paused, looked beyond the hedge, saw the shaggy, ragged figure, the hungry, melancholy eyes, brightened by the unwonted fire of purpose.

'Hi!' the driver called back.

This did not look like a man with money to spare for bootlaces and such-like vain trifles. He did not have the air of a purchaser of red herrings even. The 'hi!' the trader gave was unexpectant, indifferent.

'I ha' got yar wife and child'un,' the Wolf shouted aloud to him.

The driver gazed for a moment at his wretched-looking rival, then turning back to his donkey belaboured it with a heavy stroke across its ribs.

'I don't keer whu th' devil ha' got 'em so long as I ha'n't,' he called out. And so, master of the situation, drove off.

After that rebuff the Wolf made no further effort to detach from himself the burden he had hung about his neck, neither does he make complaint. With an intelligence not much removed from that of the beasts of the field, he is patient and uncomplaining as they.

And the children in some mysterious way seem to thrive on their half rations of bread, cunningly soaked in hot water to make the allowance appear more, their random dessert of hedge berries, wild apples, and the fungus from the doorstep. They are ragged and they are filthy, it is true, but they are not particularly thin or pitiable-looking; they inherit their mother's complexion of brick red; their hair, which one would not care too closely to inspect, seen from a safe distance is a luxuriant growth. Perhaps out of their potsherds, their bits of window-glass, their 'rubbage' heaps, and that most prized and precious plaything, the especial property always of the youngest, a rusty key attached by a filthy string to the half of a pair of scissors, they get as much pleasure as happier-circumstanced children may from a nursery over-crowded with toys.

There is something too melancholy in the history of such sordid lives. One stands aghast for the moment, frightened at the privation which those fashioned like ourselves in outward seeming can bear and live, shrinking from the recital. It is only from such a 'perhaps' as that above we can regain ease of mind and conscience and go on our way comfortably indifferent once more. Perhaps the toys suffice; perhaps, never having had enough to eat, Wolf-Charlie does not understand how bad it is to be hungry; perhaps, educated in the school of hardship, Wooden-leg does not feel pain and weakness and privation as gentler nurtured women must; perhaps their lot, if one could see from the inside, as it were, is a happy one after all.

> 'Poor and content is rich, and rich enough,'

says Shakespeare.

It is comforting to reflect that if Wolf-Charlie is not thoroughly contented, he at any rate does not complain.

THE COUNTRY DOCTOR

'A DAY to be alive in,' Nancie said.

For the Fog-month, the Winter-month, the Snow-month, the Rain-month are over; even the Wind-month is passing away, and Bud-month is almost here.

We see the woods and copses this morning, the village on the low crest of the gently rising ground, the grey church tower, the far-off mill with its white sails – every distant prospect – through the purple haze which painters love to imitate. Upon the tree-tops in the plantation there is a tender shimmer of greenness; illusive, because, drawn closer, you perceive no adequate cause for that verdant promise; the branches are still withered and bare against the blue of the sky. Green is the colour of hope, and that faint glimmering is but the joyful prophecy of good things to come. Near at hand the pussy-willows, all fluffy down, clinging to the branch, are golden in the sunshine; the old clay-pit beyond the hedge is gay with the yellow colt's-foot. Spring is not here – not yet; but one of her bright hours has strayed our way, and the earth smiles at her coming.

'A day to be alive in,' Nancie says.

There is a blessing in the air. As we jog slowly along the green-bordered road that leads from our village to our little country town, we feel the south wind soft and fragrant on our faces. So gentle is the breeze, it hardly shakes the dewdrop from the thorn, and sets the lamb-tails on the nut bushes only delicately a-swing. From the hedge to the left of us, a flock of greenfinches starts, with a sudden sharp chirping, upon the wing, wheels upwards in a green and yellow cloud, and, loudly twittering still, settles in the hedge once more. The gorse bordering each side of the road along which we are travelling, sparsely flowering as yet, is alive with linnets. Loud arguments are carried on by the rooks from their busy parliament in the elm-tops; a robin on a gate, eyeing us as we pass with a glance all bright and unabashed, puts up his tiny mouth and loudly sings.

'A day to be alive in,' Nancie says.

She says it softly, regretfully, accusingly; for she and I are journeying through the waking life around us, to assist at the ceremony which signalises the triumph of Death.

It is the funeral day of one we have loved; and as we drive along, noting with dim eyes the signs of the dead years revival, Nancie, who treasures such mementoes of her friends in her heart, talks to me of the patience, the sweetness, the cheerfulness of one who is no more. Above all of the cheerfulness; that blessed habit of the mind which is as a perpetual sunshine shed around. What dark places grew the lighter for this man's smile; what poor sinking hearts, heavy with pain and grief and fear, his unfailing hopefulness lifted. His bright, courageous voice was as good a tonic for a sick man as the drugs he so sparingly administered. What a friend he was to rich and poor; what a safe, incorruptible confidant for secrets whispered in no other ear; how unwearied, how brave, how uncomplaining.

Of these things, as we drive to the good doctor's burial, we talk; and Nancie, who is a nature-lover, – she to whom the plaintive voice of the new-born lamb makes a special appeal; who knows by heart the songs of the birds, and watches the budding leaf; who is a prey to that 'divine excitement,' the love of flowers, – holds a spite in her heart against these things to-day; because the forces of awakening nature are at work in a world where he will awake no more.

Much of his practice lay in the direction from which we come. Along the road he travelled so often, beneath the burning sun, beneath the wintry stars; through wind and rain, sleet and snow; battling against the elements with that high spirit with which, arrived at his destination, he would battle against the forces of disease and death, pain and the weakness of sinking hearts. At every turn of the winding road it seems to us we meet the familiar figure; impossible to realise that the brave laugh, the hearty voice calling a greeting will be heard no more.

Surely, surely the heartless birds should be mute to-day, Nancie thinks; the sun for a little veil his face!

'All that talent, that energy, that helpfulness destroyed!' she whispers on (it is half to herself she is talking). 'That magnificent material waste! Isn't it senseless? Isn't it cruel?'

The question is put with a sob which is almost angry; for Nancie, who is a religious woman, has been startled out of the habit of her mind by the shock of this man's death. He had but died as hundreds of his profession have done before him, from an illness contracted in performance of his duty; but because he was a young man still, and we loved him, it had come home to us.

But we are not the only people jogging along to that meeting in the churchyard. There pass us on our road, or we pass, vehicles of all sorts, but most of them humble, bearing men and women dressed decently in black. As we draw nearer to the town, the roadside is dotted with scattered wayfarers – women, for the greater part, not many of them clothed in black, being of the poorest, but with some sign of mourning about them, and always bearing in their hands bunch of primroses, bunch of snowdrops, culled in cottage gardens or beneath the wayside hedge, to lay upon a good man's grave. And as we reach the outskirts of the town these wayfarers become groups, become a crowd, all journeying in the same direction.

Arriving at the straggling street of the mean-looking little town, Nancie's accusations burst forth afresh: 'To have finished here!' she cried. 'All those fine qualities which might have enriched the world to have had *this* for their sphere, to have ended – here!'

But the window of every little house we pass in the mean streets is lowered, and every obscure little shop is closed; and in the road before the church and in the churchyard a thick crowd of people has gathered.

⟞✦⟝

'Lord, now lettest Thou Thy servant depart in peace,' chants the choir, slow and sweet and solemn; and down the church and through the churchyard (for no interments are made there now, but at the little new cemetery upon the hill) the flower-laden coffin is borne to the hearse at the gate.

'Never no haughtiness about 'm,' a man standing beside us, with a bit of crape tied round his shabby sleeved-waistcoat, remarks, for the benefit of the crowd. 'Shaked hands wi' me wheriver I met 'm. Blame me! I ha' met 'm as good as t'ree times a week, and he have shaked hands wi' me ivery time.'

A little girl half-hidden in the skirts of her mother begins to cry. 'She's *done*, because she'd wanted to drop her flowers on 's coffin, and she couldn't come nigh enough,' the mother explains. 'Time she lay a-bed six weeks wi' them burns on 'er legs, she got wonnerful set on th' doctor. We han't got no garden, and only this one tulip in a pot in th' winder; but nothin' would suit but she must ha't to-day, for him.'

'There was no one understand my leg as he done, God bless 'm,' an old woman who had hobbled there on a stick declares. ''ntments niver touched it, washes niver touched it; milk poultices, and a drop o' brandy, took inside, is all I iver found to give me aise, and so I telled 'm. He shaked 's hid when he looked at it. "Kape on, poor soul," he say, "wi' the milk and the brandy – the waker the better," he say; and he give me the money to buy a bottle, God bless 'm.'

A consumptive-looking young fellow, hardby, tells in his hollow voice how his wife and he saved up thirty shillings at Christmas to pay off a bill which had been running for four years, and how the doctor had given them ten shillings back again.

A woman in artless, unrestrained sobbing is crying aloud, talking incoherently, for the easing of her heart, of the dead man's goodness to her little boy who had died.

Friends he had in all classes, but his patients were mostly of a class too poor to pay him adequately for his services. Looking upon those tear-stained faces to-day, we decided that he had been paid.

But at last the wreaths are arranged upon the hearse, are piled upon the carts and carriages following; the sun which Nancie had reproached shone upon the flowers, the gentle breeze blew their sweetness in our faces; and, 'sepulchred in such pomp that kings for such a tomb might wish to die,' our good doctor passes for the last time upon his way.

As we drive homeward, no more we speak of the cruelty of Fate, of the remorselessness of Death, of the waste of tenderness and manhood and courage. These things are never wasted.

> 'There never yet was flower fair in vain,
> Nor is a true soul ever born for naught.'

Of him whom we have lost we say no word; but we watch the white-winged plover wheeling upward from the brown ploughed lands in her sounding flight, we listen to the mounted lark singing his divine message amid the clouds. Presently Nancie must get down to gather some violets she espies amid the long grass of a shaggy bank. Mounting again, she holds the little bunch of fragrance against my face.

'Spring isn't here yet, but spring is coming,' she says. ' "God's in His heaven; all's right with the world." '

MITTENS

MITTENS, with Eliza Skipper, and Amber, her son, lived in a little two-roomed cottage, first of the half-dozen such cottages called Barker's Row, in that part od Dulditch known as the Town Street.

Beyond the fact that the houses of the Row had no gardens; that you walked straight from the 'street' into the front rooms; that, across the way, in the window of a similar dwelling, three oranges, strings of liquorice, and a pair of men's grey stockings, were exhibited as a token that there merchandise was carried on, there was nothing strikingly *towny* about the locality. The back doors of the only downstair rooms opened on to wide fields sloping gently upward to an almost unbroken semi-circle of woods beyond. In the summer-time, amid the dust of the road, the yellow-flowered musk came up year by year beneath the brown-red walls; here and there the canariense was twined on strings by the side of front door or lattice window.

Eliza Skipper had been one who had so adorned the exterior of her home; had indulged in the extravagance of a penny packet of Venus's Looking Glass, besides – an annual fond of showing its clean, homely little face beneath such humble walls, and not at all particular about the quality of the soil it grows in.

Eliza, however, died of the black jaundice one spring. Before the time for planting her seeds was here, she had left the familiar region of Barker's Row for the chill hospitality of the churchyard. Then Mittens and Amber lived on alone.

Both were celebrities in their way; for Amber was a cripple and went on crutches, while Mittens – . But everyone in Dulditch knew what Mittens was. Every one, that is, who had ever enjoyed five minutes' talk with Mittens's proud master.

What other pussy-cat in this or any other neighbourhood, had the accomplishments of Mittens, standing alone in the cat-world on the pinnacle won by individual achievement? To begin with she was a big cat, and by erecting herself on her hind-legs could reach the door-latch, which she opened for herself when she wished to go out or in. Among other attainments, Mittens knew the time of day, it was declared, as well as if she had kept a watch in her pocket. Never, day after day, the whole year round, did she fail to walk down the Town Street to welcome her master, heavily swinging along on his crutches, his face one broad grin of delighted expectancy, as he returned for his supper.

'Tis getting' for six o' th' clock. Theer go Mittens,' the neighbours said.

Mittens meant that they should not miss her; for she went with growlings and caterwaulings, her tail waved high in the air. To see her return in a few minutes perched on Amber's shoulders, moving from one to the other of them as he limped along, her sleek body rubbed against his shock head; to see Amber, broadly grinning, all the great yellow teeth in his wide, ugly mouth showing, his black, protuberant eyes twinkling as they moved from side to side, eager for spectators of that performance, was to witness a daily triumph. None so low perhaps to envy Ambrose Skipper his home, with its dirt, its odour, its abject poverty; yet who more innocently content than he when he arrived there, the admirable Mittens on his back, to light his fire, to fill his kettle, to eat his bit of bread and cheese?

It was reported in Dulditch that only for the purpose of boiling it for tea, did Amber ever go through the labour of drawing water from the well. That never had he washed even his hands and face since his mother's death. His cat was nicer in her personal habits, the thorough manner of her ablutions being one of the characteristics nobly distinguishing Mittens.

She would sit opposite Amber on the hearth, in the chair vacated by his mother, and would scrupulously perform her toilette there, each evening, supper being done; the peculiarity distinguishing the ceremony from that favoured by less accomplished cats being, that those parts of her person that she could not reach with her tongue – her ears, the top of her head, the back of her neck – she cleaned with her paw upon which she spat for the purpose.

To tease him, Amber's neighbours would discredit this detail. 'Spit on 'er paws! Go along wi' yer. Don't *yew* spit on yer paws, bor!' would be said to him in derision.

'True as Bob!' Amber would declare, using his accustomed oath. Then, releasing one of his crutches, he would expectorate upon his

109

own dirty palm, would rub a space to paler dirtiness upon his ugly cheek. 'Like this here she done. True as Bob.'

He who continued to scoff would, sooner or later, hear a single loud rap from a crutch-head upon his door; would open it to find Amber grinning on the other side of it; would receive the whispered intimation, 'She's a-doin' of it. Seein's believin' bor; step round and see for yerself.'

Unless he cared to be brutal enough to refuse, the neighbour would presently stand upon the delighted Amber's threshold, watching, while Mittens, in her dirty nest of rags upon her old mistress's chair, loudly spat upon the paw with which she afterwards rubbed her face.

The cripple did not, of course, receive the wages of an able-bodied man, but picked up a living of sorts as poultry man at the Grange Farm; he likewise blew the organ at church on Sundays. Once or twice he had brought home day-old chickens, hatched before the rest of the sitting, and had given the motherless ones into the care of Mittens, who, accepting the trust with perfect comprehension, had lain all day in the sunshine on the doorstep, her body twisted into the similitude of a nest for her charges which she carefully embraced.

Who so exalted as Amber when the description of this achievement was read out to him from one of the Norfolk papers? 'Mittens, the cat of Mr Ambrose Skipper, of Dulditch.' How well it sounded! Amber's great prominent eyes glittered with pleasure. He carried the precious paragraph in the pocket of his ragged waistcoat till it was illegible, then pinned it on the wall beside the mortuary card of his mother.
'The blow is bitter,
The loss severe,' etc. etc.,
the card set forth; the undertaker having thus put into poetic form the grief at his bereavement which Amber had never expressed in his own language.

There had fallen one memorable, scorching day of summer when Mittens could not be found. She had sprung forth when Amber had opened the door to go out to his day's work, and she had not returned. To her master's anxious inquiries none among the neighbours could give a satisfactory reply. She had not been seen, stretched at full length, sunning herself on the doorstep, nor seated with hunched back upon the sill of the cottage window, watching with narrowed yellow eyes the business of the flies upon the pane. Amber, returning to his supper, met no Mittens miauling her accustomed greeting, going forth with arched back and triumphantly waving tail to welcome him.

Until darkness fell he searched for her; the cripple was a favourite with his neighbours, and some of them searched too. The hot noon of the following day found Amber, recklessly absenting himself from his post in the Grange poultry yard, searching still.

'Mitt – Mitt– Mitt – Mitt,' he called with the peculiar chirping noise which had always brought the beast. He swung himself on his crutches across the burning dust of the ploughed fields; the lanes and driftways, the woods and plantations, echoed with the thin cry 'Mitt – Mitt – Mitt,' as he dragged himself, his progress impeded by under-growth of bramble and thorn, beneath their shades.

It was on the brink of a gravel-pit in the midst of a field of barley white for the reapers, that the cry was at last answered by the well-known yowl Amber would have recognised among a thousand cat-calls. Mittens was found.

A cat with whom she was on terms of friendship had been caught in an iron-trap – that brutal survival from the dark ages; a disgrace to a generation that supports societies for the prevention of cruelty, and to a civilisation becoming careful to the borderland of squeamishness in other directions. The trapped creature had dragged the heavy instrument of torture on a broken and mangled leg across the field to the gravel-pit, down which it had tumbled. The trap catching in a thorn-bush, the poor victim had hung suspended there, the scratched and torn side of the pit giving evidence of its agony and its frantic efforts to escape. There, by the side of her friend, Mittens, through the day and the night and on into another day, had sat; unable to help, it is true, but proving herself, thereby, above the reproach of those who could not watch one hour.

And many other attainments Mittens had, and many more prodigies did she perform, of which, although Ambrose never tired of the recital, space forbids the chronicling.

Speculation had been rife in Dulditch as to what would become of Amber, crippled as he was and without other relatives, when his mother died. Mercifully she was spared to him for long, he being well over fifty years old at the time of her death. Beyond the fact that he and his house were dirtier; that his table was never cleared, from one week to the next, of what he called his 'wittles'; that his clothes were in rags; that he wore his shirt and his stockings till they dropped off him, and then wore none; his bereavement apparently made very little difference.

To the inquiry often put to him 'didn't he fare lonesome-like' he ever returned the same reply, 'I *should* fare lonesome, and no mistake, if 't worn't for Mittens.'

The cat filled the place up of his absent mother, truth to say; and if he wished for his parent back, if he missed her from the bed which stood opposite his own in the dark little den of a bedroom, if he wished to reinstate her among the filthy cushions of the chair in which Mittens now sat, he never paid her memory the compliment of saying so.

For ten years after his mother's death, with Mittens taking the place of mother, wife, sister, friend, Amber lived on. His health, never of the best, did not improve under the condition of dirt, bad diet, insufficient clothing. Every few weeks in the tenth year he fell ill, staying in bed, for a few days at a time, in his airless den of a bedroom, Mittens sitting on his chest, faring royally at such times on the charities from farmhouse and Rectory. With the coming on of winter a more serious illness befell.

Night and day he wanted a nurse, but had to depend on the casual help afforded him by neighbours, too busy with their own affairs to do much. The guardian of the parish reported the case. An extra shilling was added to the one-shilling-and-sixpenny dole which supplemented the cripple's earnings. For the sake of the shilling he was now in a position to offer, Becky Bee undertook to do for 'im.

Becky Bee was a widow of not quite irreproachable history, keeping her son's house at t' other ind of Barker's Row. For her the bitter-smelling atmosphere of the public-house, the benches full of men with their glasses in their hands, the loud, ugly laughter, the incredibly stupid talk of unbridled Ignorance setting forth unfettered, unchided, its pernicious misapprehensions and baleful conceptions, had an almost irresistible attraction. With such delights her middle-aged dreams were filled, as are those of the young country-bred girl of different station with the glittering allurements of a society from which she is debarred.

The shilling a week paid her by Amber opened to Becky the gates of Elysium for at least one night in the week. That of Saturday by preference; for then, to add to the other nightly fascinations, Music, 'sphere-descended Maid,' lent her aid to grace the scene. Although the instrument available to give forth her voluptuous swell was only a wheezy accordion played by a blind boy from a neighbouring village, yet hearts grew gayer for the sound, and Becky, frisky matron, stood up to toe and heel it with the rest.

A shilling a week is not first-class pay, but it was all that the services of Becky Bee were worth. Once a week she slopped water on the bricks of Amber's sitting-room, and wrung it into her pail again from a rag of a 'dwile'. When she was so disposed, she ran in and lit a fire at which to heat the soup and milk supplied to him by 'the gentry'. She was attentive to Mittens, Amber always declared when questioned as to her care of himself; but the general condition of things did not improve under her ministrations. The doctor pronounced the state of cottage and patient a disgrace. It began to be said that Amber must go to the workhouse.

Amber's dark, glistening eyes nearly fell from his head at the first mention to him of the project. He would rot in a ditch fust. True as Bob he would! Ef so bein' as he went to th' House what was to become o' Mittens?

His mistress from the Grange, the rector of the parish, pointed out to him the benefits to befall him by the change. The clean bed, the wholesome food, the healthy atmosphere, the companionship, the comparative ease and comfort of such a life. In vain. His answer was always the same – Mittens.

Mittens, missing the daily scraps rescued from the refuse turned out from the Grange kitchen, grew very thin and rakish-looking, her tortoiseshell coat lost its sleekness and soft gloss, her great round cheeks grew peaked, she carried her tail less jauntily elevated than of yore, and almost entirely omitted to spit upon her paws.

At last the state of affairs in the little evil-smelling hut grew such that, instead of the question 'would he go to the workhouse?' the assertion 'go he mus' was made to Amber. His weekly allowance from the Guardians was stopped. There was nothing else to be done. Arrangements were made for him; he must go on the morrow.

'Kin I take Mittens?' the old man asked.

When they told him that of course he could not, he made no moan; but the great tears gathered in the glittering black eyes and ran down the dirty face.

All through the evening he washed his ugly face with those salt drops, sitting in the chair by the scrap of fire, his crutches leaning against the filthy table at his side.

His neighbours came in to condole with him. No word he spoke to them; only sat, his horny hands clasped on his body, his eyes fixed on the now mangy-looking cat on the chair opposite, and silently wept.

He might have enjoyed a feast that night. Soup came from the Rectory; a pudding, slices of meat from the Grange; a tin of new milk. He would take neither bite nor sup.

'I don't care to fancy nothin',' he said, and turned sickly from the food.

Mittens, however, held high revelry.

'The cat'll bust herself. Leave a bit for her breakfus', bor,' Becky advised.

'Let 'er be! She shall ha' 't ter night,' the master persisted.

Becky, unusually assiduous, would have assisted Amber to bed. He refused to go there.

In the course of the evening there came from the Grange a little box for Amber, containing a few luxuries with which to begin his life at th' House.

'They mostly have a basket, or suffin', to kape their few bits o' things in,' Becky explained. 'Yu'll ha' this here box, Amber.'

Amber unfastened the box; looked at the Bible, in large type, the little parcels of biscuits, of tobacco, of peppermint sweets. Looked with lack-lustre eyes, and readjusted the lid.

'She mane well, the missus do,' was all he said.

The kind lady had meant to comfort. She had not even touched the fringe of his distress, which was not for himself at all, but for Mittens.

'You ain't a-goin' to bed, then?' the sedulous Becky finally demanded. Getting no other reply than the slow rolling of Amber's tears, she at length left the old man, sitting over the dying fire, facing a now complacent, well-filled, sleepy Mittens on her chair, the string from the little box sent by the missus in his hand.

The cart provided to convey the cripple to the workhouse was early at Barker's Row. As it drew up to his door Amber appeared there on his crutches. They had some difficulty in hoisting him into the high cart. All the neighbours not already at work came to shake hands with him.

'That fare wholly a shame, poor old beggar; that 't du!' they said to one another. 'Some on 'em surely might ha' kep' a roof over 's hid. Him and Mittens wou'n't ha' ruined 'em, ef so be they'd ha' give 'em their wittles iv'ry day o' their lives.'

In the moment's excitement it was easy to forget that they, themselves, might have done more for the helpless old man.

'Well, fare-ye-well, Amber. Kape yer pecker up, bor. Some on us 'll, mayhap, be a givin' of ye a look, one o' these fine days. Don't yer take on about Mittens. All on us 'll have an eye ter Mittens, Amber, bor.'

But where was Mittens that she had not come to say good-bye to the poor old chap? one of the women wondered.

She passed into the dark little vacant home, but in a moment was at the door again.

'God A'mighty! Come and look at this!' she cried to the rest.

The neighbours all pushed into the little room.

'I heer'd a-knockin', I' th' night,' one of the women remembered.

'To think as how that was the best he could du for the poor old cat!' another said.

For he ha driven a nail with his crutch-head into the smoke-blacked chimneypiece, and with the bit of string which had been tied around the missus's box he had hanged poor Mittens.

A DULDITCH SABBATH

'GOOD crops as ever grew out of the earth,' old Adams said, as he walked with heavy tread and gloomy face over his sodden fields, 'and there they lie – to spoil!'

For a fortnight there had not been a day without rain. The clover-layer was showing green through the cut swaths of barley; about the standing sheaves of wheat and oats, grass and weeds grew tall. For three weeks harvest had been 'about' – eighteen working days. His fourteen men had done, put it altogether, about eight days' work.

Old Adams was a man of a calculating, meditative mind; given, as he walked about his fields, to reduce theories to a practical working value, to set matters, which his brother farmers dully accepted without the trouble of reflection, lumping them vaguely in their minds as material that did not concern them, in a logical order. Not a man of sentiment, perhaps; not quick-witted; but honest with himself as well as other people; holding the opinions of others in decent respect, but with faith in his own reasoning powers left free to combat them.

Thank God, so far, not much harm was done to the corn. Cold winds had accompanied the rain, and kept the ears from sprouting; but today there was a change of temperature: a wind still blew, but it was a warmer wind; since early morning there had been no rain.

Rain at harvest-time was bad, but rain and heat together were the devil, as old Adams put it. In no time the grain in its soaked condition would grow again. Grown corn spelt ruin.

He looked over his broad acres. Only about a fourth of the harvest was got in. Corn cut, and still to be cut, on all sides. The grey brooding eyes of him were wistful in his heavy healthy face: "'Tisn't only the loss to me, but, God in heaven, the pity of it!' he said. 'Food for thousands spoiling; the beautiful, bountiful gifts of Nature useless.'

At noon-time the drizzle, threatening each minute to begin again, had still held off. Old Adams turned his weather eye upon the clouds hanging low, transparent, and ragged at their edges, drifting over the sullen grey of the sky; noted their direction; went home, tapped his weather-glass – risen a point; looked at the weather-cock on the granary roof, visible from his office window. His face lightened; the wind had shifted from west to north.

A labourer passed the window, slouching, hands in his pocket, head heavily hanging, a sack on his shoulders to protect them from the rain. The master tapped sharply upon the pane, and called to him through the open window.

'What about the weather, Barker?'

'Bad weather for such as we, master. Bad weather.'

'We shall have a fine afternoon. There's no carting to be done yet, but you can cut down Dingle's Bre'k.'

Barker cocked a sullen eye skyward without lifting his head. 'There ain't no makin' a good day outer a bad un',' he remarked.

'The men are all at the public-house, I suppose?'

Barker thought it likely. Their time was their own at harvest. There weren't no good in hangin' about, to get wet.

'You are going there, yourself?'

Barker vouchsafed no reply. It was unnecessary. He dragged a hand from his trouser-pocket, dragged it across his lips, restored it to his pocket, and slouched again on his interrupted way.

'Tell them they can set to work to cut the Dingle's Bre'k,' his master called after him.

'Lazy beggars!' old Adams said to himself. He knew well enough that, once settled in the public-house, they would stay there, idle, for the day; that the extra money earned at harvest-time, which should help to pay the rent and buy the children's boots, would be drunk away in the evil-smelling kitchen at the White Hart.

By four o'clock the changed landscape lay smiling under a gladdening sun, the blessed wind still blew, lightly stirring the ears of the standing corn. Old Adams walked among the barley swaths, picking up a handful here and there. The wheat in shocks was all but dry. To-morrow the field could be carted, he said to himself.

Then he looked grimly upon the loaded acres. To-morrow would be Sunday.

He lived alone in the substantial house belonging to the big farm of which his father and grandfather had been tenants before him. He had no wife with whom to talk over a project which stirred in his mind, no grown children whose opinions could weigh with him, to temper his judgments. What he thought it right and well to do he was accustomed to do, being responsible to no man; and that afternoon he decided, if the fine weather continued over the Sunday, to save what corn he could, and to cart on the morrow.

To the White Hart he went, called his men, all more or less drunk by that time, to come out and speak to him by the roadside. There he told them that in view of the harvest having been already so prolonged, and threatening to be ruinous to the men as well as to himself, he had decided to use the Sabbath day as if it were made for men, not men for the Sabbath, and to make, for once, of the Sunday a working-day. At nine o'clock to-morrow morning, therefore, if the weather continued fine, they were to hold themselves ready to cart the wheat on Dingle's Bre'k.

Then he went round to his neighbour-farmers and invited them to follow his example.

His neighbour farmers thought of their wives, their parson, their parson's wife, and refused, to a man.

'You're in the right, Adams,' one man said. 'If there is a God, He can't wish us to go on for ever playing the fool like this in His name; and so I tell my wife. What's a Mosaic law, made, how many thousand years ago, to do with us to-day? I say to her.'

''Tis a wise law,' old Adams made slow answer. 'A beneficent, and a wise law. Keep the Sabbath holy. But He that called Himself the Lord of it was accused of breaking it, remember.'

The other man agreed with his neighbour, who was a better Churchman than he, and knew his Bible. 'Why are we the only ones to stand by and see our property spoil on the seventh day?' he asked. 'Trains run, ships sail, letters are carried, bread is baked, bridge parties are given, public-houses are open –'

He agreed with old Adams, but he thought of his wife, his parson, his parson's wife; cursed the law in spirit, but kept it to the letter.

Bright and clean and cheerful the morning rose. The light breeze still stirred, as with a ringing of fairy rattles in the air, the heavy ears of corn; the warm sun lay like a blessing upn the fields of harvest. Old Adams went out to the yard to see his labourers start according to orders.

Not a man, not a boy was there.

He wasted no time in expressions of surprise and dismay; in his heart he had not expected them. He had decided what to do. He could not single-handed, cart his corn, but, single-handed, he could cut it.

He was called a gentleman farmer; his capital of some seven thousand pounds was invested in his farm; he had never felt himself called on to work with his men, yet he 'knew the ropes' thoroughly; he knew his work, and was not at sixty years of age, afraid of it.

By the time the wives and daughters of his orthodox neighbours had made ready in their best hats and frocks to show themselves in their pews at church, old Adams, driving with sober assurance, his portly frame perched high on the seat of the reaper, was making the first wide circuit of his barley-field. The swishing sound of the knives as they cut through the heavy crop mingled pleasantly with the sound of the bells ringing for morning service. Above his head fleecy dots of clouds lay like lambs on a blue pasture. In the ditch on one side of him as he guided his machine the yellow ragwort and pink willow-herb grew tall and luxuriant. Wild honeysuckle, flinging up strong tendrils above the hedge, proclaimed its sweet presence to his nostrils. It was such a morning when to be alive is to rejoice, when to taste through all the senses the gifts of the Creator of things fair and good is to give thanks with the best members that we have.

By the time the church bells had ceased to ring, the rumour of what old Adams was 'after' had mysteriously circulated; and half the village – that half of it which is at a loose end, and does not know what to do with its leisure till the ale-house is open – had congregated on the other side of the hedge to see him 'a-doin' of it'.

'Kape on long enough an' he'll know what wark is!'

'He's a-doin' of our job for us. Lerrem du ut! I'm wholly agrable.'

'I'll see him an' his mucky corn a-blazin' in hell afore I'll lower myself to wark, of a Sunday.'

''Tain't the deed of a Christ'an man' (an old woman was the speaker now. She was a member of the minute chapel in which her husband, one of old Adams's labourers, occasionally held forth). ''Tis to be hoped the Lord 'ont wisit it on them as take 's wages.'

'A pollutin' the Sabbath, tha's what he's a-doin' of,' her old husband put in, and spat upon the honeysuckle in the hedge.

But, agreeable as was the sight in such eyes, more seductive pleasures were to be had; and presently, old Adams, passing that side of his field next the road where the onlookers had collected, found it empty save for the presence of a boy or two, who flung stones at the spare horses waiting patiently their turn to be harnessed into the machine. The orthodox Sabbath-keeping crowd had betaken themselves to the precincts of the White Hart, and were lounging outside the inn, hanging over gateways and fences, or standing in silent groups in the sunny road, waiting until the opening of the door proclaimed that, divine service being over, all were at liberty to enter the attractive place.

The blazing heat of the afternoon, the peaceful cool of evening, found old Adams steadily driving his reaper round the ten-acre field. As the congregation were filing in for evening service he cut his last thin line of yellow barley. Then, taking his horses home, he fed and watered them, before he went in to the substantial meal of cold meat and beer which his servants, with furtive looks at their sacrilegious master, set before him.

The rector had been at pains that afternoon to dig out from the not very valuable collection of sermons he dished up in their turns as the Sundays came round, a dissertation on Sabbath-breaking. He gave it forth that evening with telling emphasis; even venturing to produce an extempore clause bearing upon the flagrant case of old Adams, and calculated to thrill the ears of those who heard.

'Is there a man among us who, for his own convenience, his own paltry gain, desecrates the Sabbath which we are commanded to keep holy, by working on it? Then, mark him, brethren. No matter how confident in his own strength and hardihood he may be, the hand of God will sooner or later be heavy upon that man; he will go down into the pit, terribly smitten. But upon those who, by turning a deaf ear to the voice of human authority, have shown their scorn of earthly tyranny and have honoured the divine law, blessings of holiness shall rest.'

The scant occupants of the pews heard with satisfaction, wondering in what painful form the wrath of Almighty God would first be visible on old Adams.

But those specially commended, – they who, resolute in the upholding of the sanctity of the Sabbath, had defied 'the voice of human authority,' – did not unfortunately benefit by the oration, or enjoy in prospective the blessings to fall upon them; they being again collected outside the village public-house, waiting for the door to open to them.

As for old Adams – Adams the sacrilegious, – neither did he hear. Pleasantly tired with his day's work; grateful for the strength which had been given him to do it, and for the good meal which he had eaten with such excellent appetite; filled with the blissful consciousness of a duty, in accordance with the rulings of divinely planted reason, accomplished; blessing God for His goodness, and at peace with all the world, he walked to the scene of his unwonted labours, and contemplated with satisfaction his day's work.

'Reason is the life of the law. Nothing is law that is not Reason,' old Adams said to himself, having evolved that dictum from his inner communings, and happily unconscious that he was making a quotation.

The sun had sunk gloriously in a sky rich with promise; the beautiful stillness of a Sabbath peace rested like a benediction upon all; and the barley in Dingle's Bre'k lay in rich swaths upon the shorn field, ready for carting on the morrow.

OLD BILLY KNOCK

OLD Billy Knock stood at the gate of his cottage and watched the cart holding his table and cheers, his bed, his sofy, his frying-pan, saucepan, his two chaney dogs off the chimbleypiece, and his odds and ends of crockery, making its way across the fields which led from his isolated home i' th' low midders, village-ward.

A tall, meagre old man, despite his rheumatism and his seventy-two years, he stood fairly upright still. His hair, clipped close where it grew, iron-grey over lip and chin, was dark and plentiful on his head. In his eyes that followed his receding household goods was something that belied the expression of the lean, grim face; something wistful, regretful, almost ruminative. His hat, worn from the moment he arose from his bed in the morning till he flung it from him to lay his head on his pillow at night, was green with age, battered into shapelessness; his clothes, neither to eye or nose agreeable, were patched out of recognition of the original material; but the scarlet cotton handkerchief he wore loosely tied about his throat, gave him something of a picturesque and gipsy air.

When the cart, sinking behind the gentle slope of grassland two fields distant from where he stood, was lost to sight, the old man turned and made his way back into the empty cottage at his back.

Quite empty; for, among the paraphernalia steadied with ropes upon the inadequate looking cart, Mrs Billy Knock also rode.

He minded, when on the top of just such a cartload, he walking by the horse's head, she had arrived at th' Low Midder Cottage forty years ago, her first baby in her arms, a wild-looking, maturely-developed, black-eyed girl of twenty. She had been free of her tongue even in those days, and had cursed the loneliness of the spot, its distance from shop and from pub, and him for bringing her there, as she had cursed, this morning, with her parting breath. In the interim that wicked tongue of hers had been busy cursing all the time: employers, husband, children, home, Providence, lustily she had cursed them all. To Billy, who was not exactly squeamish but could swear good tidily himself, come to that, the sound in his ears had the inoffensiveness of familiarity. Missing it, more coldly than its emptiness even, the silence of the deserted house struck upon his heart.

Into each of the five rooms of the house he glanced, to make sure, as he explained to himself, nothing worn't forgot. For long he stood in the kitchen, with broken brick floor, blackened plaster-walls; its smoke-grimed rafters, not many inches from his tall head – the living room of everyday life. That it had been a small, and mean, dirty room had never occurred to old Billy, seeing it as Home, and nothing more; the fact of its being such a cramped space became apparent to him for the first time, now that there was nothing to interrupt the view of the few feet from wall to wall.

Six children had been born to him at th' Low Midder Cottage, one, born three months after marriage, had been brought there when they had taken up occupation. Was it possible that nine of them had eaten their meals here, had gathered of evenings round the fire?

If, at any other moment of his life, Billy Knock had been called on to give the dimensions of his living-room, he would have said it was 'tidy-sized'. (He would have used the same words to describe the spaces of Westminster Abbey; of which edifice, however, he had probably never heard.) Now, with a surprised perception of its limitations, he murmured to himself the comment that it fared small.

Yes, it had held them all. The wild, gipsy-blooded, slatternly wife with the first baby; and gradually Jack, and little Emma, Eduth, and Nelly, and Will; and, last of all, Polly, that hadn't been black-eyed and

121

black-haired like the rest, but had favoured Billy Knock's own mother, with a blue eye and light-coloured heer.

He saw her more vividly than the rest, somehow – Polly. He had clouted his wife on the hid on more than one occasion, he remembered, for having chastised the youngest child with her heavy, coarse hand. He, come to think on it, had never lathered Polly with the belt which buckled his trousers – an educational instrument found convenient in the upbringing of the other six.

Strange to recall that Polly was a married woman now, with children of her own. So he and her mother had heared tell, at any rate; for Polly, having been sent into the Shares to sarvice, had never writ nor took no notice of the family at home, since.

He snuffled as he thought of her now, and drew the back of a veined and dark-skinned hand across his nose.

Her mother still cursed and swore when her name was mentioned. 'Ongrateful baggage,' 'Onnateral beggar,' were the mildest epithets applied to Polly's name now. Stories of how Mrs Knock had denied herself, and worked her fingers to the bone to provide the shoes, the gownds, the ap'ons, in which the hussy had been equipped for her start in life, fell glibly from her lips. It was a relief to be able to think of Polly beneath the roof where she had been – although he had never given that name to her, or even been conscious of the fact – his favourite child, without the accompanying torrent of abuse.

The others had all left the parent-nest early in their careers. Polly had been the last to go. Had carried his dinner to him across the fields; had sate by his side beneath the sheltering hedges while he ate it; had stood by the gate, of evenings, to watch for him coming home.

'Gi' me boys!' his wife was always ready to shout; (living so far from humankind, with no fear of passers-by or of listening neighbours, they all shouted, unaware of the fact, when they talked). 'A sight o' good our gals ha' done to us, Billy Knock! And look at our boys. Look at Jack and Will, poor beggars, ache of 'em wi' wives and child'un o' their own, yet allust a half-a-pound o' baccy for you, come Christmas, and a shillin' or so to git their mother a drop o' somethin' to warm 'r inside, for me. Talk o' gals – gi' me boys, I say!'

Jack and Will. Yes; they also were in the Shares. They had tired o' th' land, and gone off. Healthy, brown-faced lads, as like their father as peas in a pod, his wife always assured him. But they had gone off; and they, too, had gone for ever. Not in the thorough manner of the onnateral Polly, however; for, now and again, they returned from the mysterious region of the Shares to the old home, bringing, each, a foreign woman with a strange lingo, and several white, wormy-looking children in their train. Two strange, pallid, haggard men, – bent in the back, shrunken in frame, altered in speech, in habit, in thought, out of recognition, – who, they told old Billy Knock, had been his sons.

It was not of these strangers, but of the healthy, shouting little lads who had helped him with the rabbiting in the plantations, and sat in this squalid kitchen over their meal o' nights, he thought now.

For the last ten years he and his wife had lived alone. It had not been an idyllic *solitude à deux*, although the situation of the warrener's cottage had been idyllic. When the devil wanted to tempt Jesus he led Him to a wilderness. The wide expanse of fenland, of water-meadows, with their wild, luxuriant growth, their green and luscious beauty, into which her cottage was sunk, was but a wilderness to the wife of Billy Knock. The only life that of the birds of the air, and the wild rabbits, regardless of Rose the dog and the ferrets in their cage, scudding from shelter to shelter among the coarse tussocks of the grass beyond her garden gate. What to her were 'the swing of Pleiades,' 'the light of dawn, the reddening of the rose'? What to her the fairy foliage of the nut-bushes in the hedges of spring, the finches singing among the fresh green leaves of the beeches, the scent of the sweet briar-bush by the well, and the November sunsets?

Unable to read, untrained to think, having very little to do, a woman might weary very quickly of the loneliness of the low midder paradise – being of a certain temperament might die of it, even. Keturah Knock did worse than that. She took to walking the three miles over the fields and through driftways to the public-house.

She had always been fond of her glass, and not at all ashamed of the fact; debarred by poverty, the cares of maternity, and the long walk to the White Hart, alone, from indulging.

There had been a day in their lives when Billy, having quarrelled with her in the morning for neglecting to mend his trousers which for weeks had been crying to be patched, had come home at night to find her lying dread-drunk, upon the floor of the kitchen in which he now stood. He remembered how in his savage disgust he had dragged her, on that first occasion, across the garden to the outhouse, and left her lying there. The second, third, fourth time he had so dragged, so left her. Then grown wearied and apathetic, had forborne to take the trouble; had prepared his own supper, gone to his bed; forgetting, in the end, to protest when she, awakened from her stupor, would fling herself beside him.

For five years what a life they had lead, hidden away from the sight of man in the warrener's cottage! A life worse than the life of beasts. What cursing, swearing, fighting, even, there had been.

That had all been over and done with for another five years. For that period a bad leg had mercifully kept Keturah to the house, with no means of procuring the poisonous, adulterated drink she craved. As far as the man was concerned, a kind of rough comfort had taken the place of the hell he had known.

Besides her bad leg Mrs Knock had been troubled of late years with a chronic wheezing upon her chist; a disease for which a certain quack medicine is considered in Dulditch a panacea. It costs half a crown a bottle, and in its purchase a large proportion of Billy Knock's earnings from this time went. The remedy had, however, a less stupefying effect than the public-house beer; and as Mrs Knock was of opinion she could not live without it, it was perhaps money well spent. When the pantry had been emptied of its few cracked dishes and plates, dozens of empty bottles labelled 'Quelch's Magic Lung Repairer' had been disclosed. Keturah was proud of the display as some women of their pearls.

'Look what this here blamed physic ha' cost me!' she called to the man who was loading the cart, and swore blindingly about the cough with which she was afflicted.

Slowly Bill Knock turned his back on that place of memories, and wandered through the tangle of garden. Rags of what had once been clothes put out to dry clung to the gooseberry bushes, too worthless to retrieve; tin boxes that had held pickled salmon of a dangerous brand were scattered among the wall-flowers, the daffodils, the dandelions of the beds. A handleless kitchen shovel lay in old Billy's way as he went down the path. He kicked it listlessly in the act of walking, not with any rancour against it for being there. That heap of rubbish in the corner had been the pig-sty. Never, since Polly, who had tended it, left them, had it sheltered a pig. There was Rose's kennel. The chain, supplemented by a bit of frayed rope, which had held the old dog, trailed from it still.

In those long weeks of Billy's illness in the winter, Keturah had declined to drag her bad leg out, all weathers, to carry the animal's food. The poor brute, straining at her chain, winding in and out of her kennel, had howled and barked, night and day, till her voice failed her, calling upon that rough master of hers, who did not so much as look out to curse her from the door of his dwelling. Instead, had come an emissary from her master's master, who had shot her as she lay, too exhausted even to whine any more, at the door of her kennel, but with her eyes still expectant of him who did not come.

Loud was the snuffle of emotion Billy gave as he looked down at the kennel. He had been a hard master, kicks and short commons had been Rose's daily fare; but he was, it was said of him, a wonnerful man for a dog, for all that. Many predecessors had Rose, until her death he had never been without a dog. He had felt the loss of that companionship among the chief ills which his breakdown and consequent loss of post had brought him.

She had been a nervous, sleek-coated thing, trailing her little body in and out between the heavy boots which had kicked; often he had felt her deprecating muzzle pushed into the hand holding the stick that thrashed her. A word of encouragement, and the soft, kind tongue was licking his grim face. Not from malice had he ever chastised her, but from an ignorance perpetuating itself through generations of such slow wits; an article of faith unquestioned, and adhered to with the tenacity of stupidity: that dogs are made to be half-starved, to be sworn at, to have stones thrown at them.

The garden gate which opened to the fenland at the back was off the hinge; the fence was broken down; from the ferret-cage which stood empty, Keturah had wrenched the door, but yesterday, to feed a fire which was slow to burn.

He'd find a sight o' wark, gettin' things in order, the new chap would, when he come o' Monday. Billy Knock did not pity his successor. Through all his troubles he had not found a weariness while he could keep employed. 'S'long as I kin wark I kin put up wi't,' he had said. He thought grudgingly of the man who would have to get chaos into order.

But even if his rheumatics would permit, he must now relinquish his club-money or remain idle. If he had so much as stirred a finger to help in the flittin' his seven shillin' a week would ha' been took off.

He moved his lean shoulders stiffly in his dirty, clay-coloured jacket. 'How long is this here a-goin' on?' he asked himself. 'Whar am I a-goin' to do wi' myself, yinder, ef so be as all day I'm to set 'side the chimbley-corner, and can't wark?'

The position of his new home directly opposite the village inn held not the attraction for him as for Keturah. He was a sober man. Neither did the prospect of neighbours' society appeal to him. He had never held with a sight o' talk; an assembly of people was a Bedlam to him. It was an unknown life to which he was going. He shrank from it as

125

nervously as if it were a new world he was to inhabit, instead of a two-roomed cottage in his own village street.

He had promised his old woman to make his way after the cart, as soon as he had locked up the house and taken the key to his master. But he could not bring himself to shut the door, to turn his back on his life there. He did it once; started to walk across the fields that rose in a gentle green slope from the squat, one-storeyed, thatched house, which from the distance looked like a gigantic fungus growing there; but his feet lagged cruelly as he dragged them along. Presently they stopped; retraced themselves.

'Fare as I was theer still,' he said to himself, trying to explain the curious feeling he had that all that was best of him was left in the home of his youth and manhood.

It was not until the day, 'apparelled in the celestial light of spring,' was passing, and evening, chill with a slight frost, came on, that he finally left the place, and, the doorkey in his pocket, made his way to his new home. He had had no food since morning, but he was not hungry. 'Them that can't wark, can't ate,' he had said of late at meal-times. He was never hungry now; but he was weak, and as he went his long thin legs shook under him. 'My rheumatiz,' he said, uneasily moving the shoulders to try to shift from their dull, incessant pain.

He had been warned that it was not the rheumatiz alone from which he suffered. The doctor, standing out of earshot of the patient, had made a communication to the wife in an undertone. And Keturah had shouted from kitchen to bedroom, doctor being gone, the intelligence that Billy Knock's last day's wark was done, that his heart was 'fected, and might at any moment stop beating.

'Theer ain't no doubt 'tis 'fected. I could ha' telled him that,' Billy had answered contemptuously.

Once or twice as he walked the weary miles tonight, he thought that the moment had come; that the heart was going to stop.

As he went through the last field where the young barley was pricking, single-leaved, through the dusty soil, he encountered his master, who hailed him as the old man would have passed sullenly on without giving him the sign o' th' day.

'Cleared out?' the master called to him cheerily; and Billy, without turning his face in the other's direction, admitted that he had done so.

'You've lived in the Low Meadow Cottage a long time, Billy?'

'Forty yare, come Lady-day,' Billy grimly said.

'A lot of years, Billy!'

'Several.'

'Thirty years before I came to Dulditch!'

'Ah!' The grimly closed lips, the eyes gazing into a retrospect in which the master had no part, held the old man's bitter unspoken reflection, 'Better folk than you was above ground then!'

'Have you got the key, Billy?'

'I ha' got it.'

The master held out his hand which Billy ignored. 'You shall ha' the key, come Monday,' he said. The fingers in his jacket pocket tightened stiffly upon it; he could not bring himself to part with the key.

He moved on; the master, a young spruce-looking man, who liked the old fellow, in spite of his uncouthness and his surly ways, walked a step by his side.

'How's your health now, Billy?'

'No matters, the wind ha' been a-shiftin'; my rheumatiz is all of a whizzle ter-night.'

'You ought to be at home by the fire.'

'I'm a-goin' theer.' He looked ahead of him with his regretful eyes. 'Ef so be as you kin call it "home",' he added.

'You're still on your club?'

'Ah, I'm on it. Wheer'd I ha' been ef I worn't on it? Parashin' o' want, mayhap. Who's to keer?'

'If you'd had a decent wife, remember, you might have put by a tidy bit of money by now.'

'My missus is as good as other folks's missuses, I take it,' the old man said, and turned an angry shoulder upon the other man. 'I don't lay no blame agin my old woman.'

When he reached the cottage opposite the public-house, he found that Mrs Knock had availed herself of the propinquity of that hostelry, and repaid herself liberally for her enforced abstinence of years. The furniture had been put down, helter-skelter, in the rooms and the little oblong of garden; she herself lay among it, drunk on the dirty floor.

A neighbour, who had been on the look-out for old Billy's coming, found him gazing down with an expressionless face upon the ugly, unwieldy body.

'Me and my neighbour didn't take it on ourselves to touch your goods while things was like this here,' she explained, delicately alluding to Mrs Knock's unconscious condition. 'But now you're here to give us the ward to lend a hand, me and her will put up a bed for ye in no time, Billy.'

The old man declined her offer without a word of thanks, and turned away. 'I don't want no bed, I'll be a-gittin' back,' he said.

'Come in, Billy, and get a bit o' supper alonger me and my old man,' another pitying woman said.

He did not stop in his hurried retreat to consider the invitation. 'I'll be a-gittin' back,' he said again.

The neighbours stood to look after him as he went; the tall, only slightly-stooping figure in the shabby hat, the patched, clay-coloured clothes; the ends of the scarlet handkerchief loosely flying.

'He's in a fine hurry to be gone, and no wonder! Poor old beggar!' they said.

For his footsteps did not lag now; he forgot the wearying ache of arm and shoulder; the load seemed lightened upon the labouring heart. 'I cou'n't ha' stayed theer, nohow,' he kept saying to himself as he hurried along. 'I'll make th' best o' my way back again.'

His weakness, aggravated by the day's fast, increased upon him as he went hastily, stumbling on his way.

'I cou'n't ha' ralished no wittles theer,' he told himself, shaking his head.

Among the worrying noises surging in his head as he hastened on, the pitying neighbour seemed still to be offering him food. 'I'd rayther wait till I git home, bor,' he answered the voice of fancy. 'I shall ralish it more ef I hold out till I git theer.'

' "'Fected"!' he was saying aloud presently. 'I should think 'tis "'fected"! I could ha' telled him that. Ef he was to know how tha's a hammerin' i' my inside, he wou'n't want to be no doctor to know 'twas 'fected.'

'I can't bide, I tell ye,' he made irritable answer to another imagined voice. Following in his footsteps the people were; crowds of them; the whole population from that strange country by the inn where they had wanted him to make his home; they were hurrying after him, asking him to eat, plaguing him to stay. Through the hammering in his chest and the throbbing turmoil in his head, he made out their words with difficulty. He was hampered to keep up the necessary pace, but he urged himself with difficulty on, feeling he must escape them.

'The missus, she'll be a-waitin' supper; and Polly, maybe, 'll be a-hangin' on the gate.'

Perhaps in the end he saw her there, the only little one amongst them who had had the blue eyes of his mother. Perhaps, his journey being done, in spirit he took her hand again, and went once more into the cottage, sunk fungus-like among the verdure, that had been home to him for forty years.

For when Keturah, going the next morning, spite of her bad head and bad leg, to see what had become of that silly old beggar, her husband, and to swear at him for leading her such a dance, found him lying dead in the middle of the last meadow he had had to cross, his face was turned towards the cottage, and there was a smile upon his lips.

DAVID PECK'S LOVE AFFAIR

HE had been married ten years, and he had eight children when his love affair, which caused so much interest in Dulditch, began.

It began by his going home late one night, leaving the under-keeper to watch the brooding hens in the Long Meadow plantation where the pheasants were reared, calling in at the 'White Hart' on his way, and carrying a drop too much from there. He had had a sunstroke at an early period in his career; his head was still a trouble to him at times, and the drop too much was a matter for which he had to suffer. Worse than that, his wife, more rarely his children, had to suffer too.

And it happened that that night, when he reached home an hour before midnight, he found no supper left out for him.

He called his wife's name angrily up the stairs, but if Mrs Peck was not too sound asleep to hear, she at least pretended to be. So up David went, stumbling a little in his heavy boots on the uncarpeted stairs and muttering to himself. A small shadeless lamp was burning on a chair beside the bed, and by its light he looked upon his wife's face.

'Matilda,' he said, with tipsy dignity, 'where's my supper?'

Even when he put his hand upon her shoulder and shook his wife as he repeated the question there came no answer, only the flicker of Matilda's lashes upon her cheeks.

The husband swore an oath at this and called his wife by an ugly name.

'If I'm to have no supper, that should be the master in my own house, I'm blamed if you should lay here and snore,' he said.

With that, and without more ado, he pulled her out of bed, and she, not trying to save herself in any way and still feigning slumber, fell heavily upon the floor. He left her there and went to get his own supper ready; and when he came back to bed she was gone.

She had got into bed with some of the kids in the next room, he told himself, and vowed, with a tipsy pride in his prowess, that each night she served him that trick he'd punish her after the same fashion.

But Matilda Peck had not taken refuge with her children, creeping into their already crowded bed as she had done on other similar occasions. She had dressed herself, had wrapped the baby which slept with her in an old black shawl over its night-shirt, and had gone, in the burning sense of injury and the strength of the anger which possessed her, through the night to her mother's cottage.

'I've had enough of blows and blackguarding from a thankless, beer-drinkin' brute,' she said. 'I'll ha' done with havin' a child a year, and bein' at the mercy of that villain. I'll stop along o' you mother, as you've often arst me. And he can shift for hisself at last.'

The mother was a widow still carrying on the little farm of fifteen acres in which her husband had died, and where Matilda, her only daughter, had been born. She was a woman filled with restless energy, an anxious, prating, uncomfortable woman, who had led her lazy old husband a stirring life, routing him out of existence and into his grave at last, the neighbours said. She had been no friend of David's, even in the days when the young keeper had gone courting Matilda Bush in the long, one-storied farmhouse, not much more than a cottage, to which she had now returned. She had sided with the wife in all disputes which had arisen in her married life; and son-in-law and mother-in-law never met without a quarrel.

On the afternoon of the day following that on which she left him, David Peck, taking easily in his long stride the little barred gate of the garden, appeared before the locked door of the Pound Farm, and in loud tones, banging upon the door with his stick, demanded his wife.

It was early summer time, and the lattice window of the kitchen through which Mrs Peck looked forth upon her husband was wreathed in long branches of the pale monthly rose, which had bloomed in like luxuriant way, framing her face, when, a girl, she had looked out upon the same handsome figure awaiting her there. She took one hurried glance now and shrank away to the shady corner of the room, nervously patting, with her work-worn hand, the back of the baby boy who hung over her shoulder.

'He's here, mother. Here's David,' she said breathlessly whispering.

'Kape your mouth shutt, and kape out o' his way,' commanded the mother.

Receiving no answer to his attack upon the door, David moved to the window. Such a strong big figure blocking out the sunshine! How many a time in the old days Matilda had talked to him as she moved about her work, laughing into the sunburned face looking in upon her as it was looking now.

'Mother, I ha' come for my wife,' he said.

To this the woman made no reply. The baby, hanging over Matilda's shoulder, jumped a little on her arm and crowed delightedly at the sound of the father's voice.

David held up a finger to his wife. 'You come along o' me, and bring our boy along o' you, or I'll break every bone in your skin, my woman,' he said; and she making no reply to that gentle invitation, he picked up a stone from the loose soil at his feet and, standing a few paces off, flung it at the window.

At the sound of the shivering glass and the angry cry from old Mrs Bush, two policemen, lying in ambush there, walked out from the elder bushes at the end of the little garden and took their friend and comrade, David Peck, into custody.

Because of his good looks, his honesty, and other good qualities which, spite of the little surface failings already indicated, he possessed, David was something of a favourite with the better classes. Several locally influential people came forward and said a good word for the man before the magistrates; so that in spite of Matilda's bruises, to which the doctor testified, in spite of, or perhaps because of, the animus of Mrs Bush, the keeper was not sent to prison, only bound over to maintain the peace and dismissed without a fine. But Mrs Peck duly obtained the separation for which she asked, the custody, besides, of the five youngest children and maintenance for them; to the father being committed the charge of the other three.

So Matilda was driven home triumphantly through the little town where the magistrates held their meetings in her mother's donkey-cart, her baby in her arms. David, being treated to drinks by various sympathisers in the hotel bar, made a rush through his companions to see her pass. He lifted his stick high as a signal for the ladies to stop.

'You shall pay for this – both of you,' he called after them.

Mrs Bush shook an angry fist at him, belaboured the ass, and passed on.

'I shall go in peril of my life,' Mrs Peck said to her mother.

Perhaps she, who knew her husband well, was not so timid as she seemed; but the mother, who firmly believed her son-in-law would not stop short of murder, would never allow Matilda to go beyond the precincts of the Pound Farm alone.

Before long the young woman found irksome this watch set upon her goings and comings, appreciative as she must have been of the blessings of a mother's care and protection. When congratulated on the increased comfort of her position, she would remind the neighbours that 'there was alwayst trials wherever you was, and if they weren't of one sort they was of another. Young and old didn't always agree,' she would add. 'The little uns alwayst seemed to be in their gran'mother's way, and the old lady didn't never seem to think as the po'r little boys and girls couldn't never do right.' She never failed, however, to finish up with the remark 'that she was thankful to be out o' David's clutches, for no one couldn't never say how much she'd had to put up with wi' the man, and she for her part weren't a-goin to tell.' She made no specific charges against him, however, and was always decently reserved on the subject of his shortcomings, having a by no means cruel tongue and a temper still unspoilt by ill-usage.

It was otherwise with David. Being released from his wife, it seemed that nothing was too bad for him to say of her. She had mismanaged his house, spoilt his children, wasted his money. 'Twas her love of a pint that had first urged him on to drink. But for her going in bodily fear of his vengeance she would have been unfaithful. She was a lying, idle, worthless slut.

Such wild statements he made for all Dulditch, standing agape and much enjoying the situation, to hear. He had never been so happy and free since his wedding-day as now, he declared. He blessed the day when the Lord had put him in mind to turn the old woman out of bed. He had forbidden the children under his care to go near their mother, and boasted that he had beaten the eldest boy for disobeying orders.

But the children could have told a different tale. They knew their father did not sleep of nights, but wandered about the house, going restlessly from room to room, as if seeking something he never found. They knew that as soon as the early dawn came, and before his duty called him, he went eagerly forth as if escaping from a spot he had come to loathe. What they did not know was that instead of going at once to the young pheasants hatching off in the Long Meadow, to look for eggs in the hedgerow and plantation, or to watch for poachers on the confines of the 'shoot', he walked a mile and a half out of his way to pass the Pound Farm; that arrived there, he did not pass it, but hid among the elder bushes and laburnum trees, in full flower now, to watch a certain window which had been his wife's room as a girl.

Once, as the weeks passed on, he stole out from that odorous shelter and threw a tiny pebble at the window, and softly called his wife's name.

The birds were singing in mighty tumult that morning; every bush was alive with them; in the ivy which covered one end of the house were as many noisy sparrows as leaves. His voice was drowned in the shrill concert, or it refused to obey his will. He had no voice, nor heart, nor hardly any care for life, for missing that which the room, whose window he watched, held.

'Matilda,' he whispered, 'come and speak to me. Say a word to me. Give me one look. You know me, my old woman; you know I would not hurt you.'

But for all the hunger of his heart and the yearning in his eyes, and the hoarse appeal of his voice, no one came to the window. The birds sang in the full dawn, and he turned heavily about him and went on his way.

But a man who does not eat and cannot sleep, and who has lost his interest in the pheasant hatching, and could not be roused to anxiety when the rain, lasting two nights and a day, threatened to swamp the young partridges, is in a bad way. In the public-house it began to be noticed that David's eyes were very wild, although he was quieter in his talk; and the women at the Pound Farm were warned by neighbours, always ready to do anyone a turn, that David had a won'erful desprit' look and that probably murder would be done.

David's employer, running down from London to see how the young birds prospered, was shocked to remark the change in his handsome keeper's face, and how loosely the smart velveteen coat hung on the man's broad shoulder. Something this gentleman learnt of the story – that Peck and his wife had had a disagreement, and that she had left him – and, that being so, was inclined to think the trouble, whatever it had been, over. He made his keeper a present of a five-pound note, and said a word of encouragement as to the better times in store.

'Husban's have a deal to put up with, sir,' Peck volunteered solemnly and with dignity. 'You being a gentleman of the world doubtless knows that conclusion, sir; but what my own troubles are is known to none but me.'

Thanks to his employer's generosity, he looked in oftener at the 'White Hart', and his head became chronically bad. One night the little boy who slept with him was wakened by his father's moans of pain.

'Get up and into your clothes,' David said to his son. 'Run off, hard as you can go, to your mother. Says you to her, "Father's a dyin'; come and see him, mother, afore he die." Tell her she and me have been sweethearts since we was boy and girl at school, and I call on her now to come and see me die.'

The child's little feet flew over the mile and a half of meadow way and lane that made the short cut to Mrs Bush's farm. It was the hour before the darkness is overthrown of the dawn, and he was frightened of gipsies, of horned cattle, of hob-goblins. Arrived at the farmhouse door, he could only sob forth that he was frightened, that his father was dying, that he wanted his mother.

But Mrs Bush knew that her son-in-law had spent the last evening at the public-house.

'He's drunk, the brute!' was all she said; and Matilda, carrying her boy to the warmth and comfort of her own bed, vowed that he should go back no more to such an unnatural father, a man who could send such a little, timid boy for such a distance at such an hour of the night.

But when her own mother had gone back to bed Mrs Peck questioned her boy; and at the tale he told of this new strange father, who never laughed or played with Willy, or cared to hear him read out of his school-books or say his pieces to him any more; who never took his son to help feed the young pheasants, or to hunt up eggs; who ate no dinner, but who sat at the meal with his head bowed upon the table and sometimes cried like quite a little child, Matilda grew very thoughtful and still. Before her mother was 'astir' in the morning she had been to the nearest town for the doctor and sent him on to her husband.

The doctor came upon Mrs Peck, waylaying him as he left the keeper's cottage.

'Drink!' he said significantly; 'he has been drinking heavily. He knows what he has to expect if he does it.'

He had barely slackened his horse's speed as he passed her. 'Don't let him drink, sir,' she called after him. 'Frighten him. Don't let him drink.'

And when it was told to David that his wife had besought the doctor to keep him from drink, he took an oath, to be kept to his dying day, that not a drop of alcohol should again pass his lips.

'My life is a dog's life,' he said to the doctor. 'I han't no wish to prolong my days, but she wished it – she have always wished for me to take the pledge and now I done it.'

'The fact is, Mrs Peck, that poor soft-headed husband of yours is dying of love of you,' the doctor told Matilda, going out of his way to call at the Pound Farm one day. 'Life isn't long enough to bear malice. You'll have to forgive him.'

'Never!' cried Mrs Bush, shaking an excited fist in the doctor's face. 'You seen her bruises, sir; you know the hard time she have with her babies –'

'I think I'm best as I am, sir,' Matilda said quietly; and the doctor acquiesced regretfully.

'To be frank with you, I think you are,' he said. 'But there is David to think of as well as yourself.'

And of David she thought a good deal as she moved about, her child in her arms, in the low-ceilinged, red-bricked kitchen where David had 'come a-courtin' ' in years gone by. She was an industrious woman and a good mother; she would work till late at night – washing, ironing, mending, in order that her children might go spick and span to school in the morning. But although she spent herself willingly for them, it was of David she thought – not so much in these days of the David who was the father of those chubby ones with his eyes and a promise of his strong limbs, but of the young under-keeper of long ago, with one of her own pink rose-buds pulled through his button-hole, who had waylaid her by this meadow path and that, who had always divined her goings and her comings, who had hindered her sadly in her mother's business to talk with her over hedges and across gates in the years gone by.

One night she awoke with the moonlight strong upon her face, her heart beating wildly in her breast, and the sound of her names whispered in her husband's voice in her ear. She sprang from her bed and went to the window. The man she had believed to be upon his sick bed was standing in the moonlight-flooded garden looking up at her. She softly opened the window, and he threw up his arms and called her name.

'For shame, David! Go along home,' she said, trembling and much moved. She leant out of the window in her nightgown and whispered the words, lest her mother in the next room should hear. 'You'll get your death for certain, in these here night dews. Get along home with you, do, David.'

'I'm so lonesome,' he sighed, 'so lonesome, Matilda.' Then the hands he had held out to her dropped upon his face, his shoulders heaved once, twice, slowly, and she knew that he was crying.

She thought she heard her mother stirring in the next room, and she softly closed the window and crept back to bed, where she gathered her baby into her arms and lay till morning, softly weeping, his warm brown head upon her breast.

The man took cold from that midnight escapade and had a relapse.

It was a bleached and shrunken David Peck who, a few weeks later, and as the sweet dusk of the summer night fell, made his way to the little farmhouse where the pink monthly roses blew upon the plaster walls, and the pigs grunted a familiar welcome from their house in the background. He threw a light pebble at a certain window, then drew back a few steps, and hid himself in the elder bushes by the gate.

Soon a woman came warily down the pathway, a woman whose fair hair – the only beauty she had preserved unimpaired from girlhood, although she was still under thirty years of age – was prettily ruffled beneath the black handkerchief she had tied over her head, whose face looked lined and worn and anxious, but whose mouth could smile tenderly, if not mirthfully, still, and whose eyes were steady and kind.

Without a word he drew her by her toil-worn hands into the deeper gloom of the shrubs.

'Now you've got me, what have you to say for yourself?' she asked him, her lips tremulous, her eyes mocking him as he held her before him in silence. 'Surely, surely there's something to be said after all this worritin' of me to come.'

But it seemed that, in articulate speech, nothing was to be said.

'You never was backward wi' your tongue, nor yet always wi' your fists, come to that,' Mrs Peck rallied him with an effort at indifference. 'Now I've come o' purpose to hear what you have got to say you ain't a-going to remain silent for the first time i' your life – sure-ly, sure-*ly*, *sure*-ly!'

But not a word could the ready tongue speak, and the last 'surely' broke in a little laughing sob; for the man's head lay on her shoulder, and she felt him draw his breath painfully in weeping.

There was silence between them after that and what could eloquence have done more?

⸎

For minutes the soft and scented stillness of the night was unbroken, save for the man's sobbing breath as he struggled to composure, and

136

the tender '*hsh-hsh*' of the woman's voice. Then the cottage door opened sharply, and a stream of light was thrown upon the garden path between the tall white phloxes and purple delphiniums of the box-edged borders. Presently Mrs Bush, with angry suspicious voice, called her daughter's name.

The pair in the shade of the elder bushes waited, holding their breath, till the old woman withdrew, till the delphiniums grew black again in the deepening twilight, and the phloxes showed starlike through the gleam. Then the man lifted his head.

'To-morrer!' he said to his wife, holding her close in his strong arms; and 'To-morrer,' she answered.

And when to-morrow came Matilda excused herself and her available children from accompanying her mother and the donkey-cart to do the week's shopping in the market town. At which disappointment of all their hopes and expectations the five lifted up their voices and wept. For was there not the lost delight of the farthing cakes with which to beguile the journey home as they sat, a huddled mass, in the bottom of the cart? Was there not that, now forever to be missed, screw of sweets purchased with the ha'penny change when granny paid the bill? Was it not a thing of enjoyment to sit safely in the cart and to hear their relative belabouring Teddy overhead – Teddy who never moved one sturdy leg the faster for all her whacks? To them in their small experience there was not in the world a richer woman than their grandmother, and it was a proud privilege to see that mighty woman laying in her week's stores with a judgment that never faltered and a princely liberality.

Defrauded of the chief pleasure of their days, they howled rebelliously, and were scarcely reconciled to their disappointment by watching the eager bustle of mother, who went about from place to place collecting all their small belongings. These, finally, the eldest boy had to drag in the go-cart, his smallest but one brother suffocatingly wedged among the bundles, while the mother trudged alongside, her brown-haired baby in her arms, and the rest of her offspring clinging to her skirts.

When grandmother returned with her marketing she found only an empty house and silent rooms. She set her thin lips, with disappointment and bitterness at her heart, as she stalked about the forsaken kitchen getting her solitary tea ready.

'There's no helping a fool,' said grandmother through her close-set lips.

LITTLE BROTHER

I MET the parish nurse hurrying from the cottage in which a baby had, that morning, been born, towards a cottage at the other end of the village where a baby was due to be born, that night.

'All well over!' she said. 'Mrs Hodd going on as nicely as can be expected.'

'She ought to be used to it by now, Nurse! The thirteenth!'

'Well, this one is dead. Born dead.'

'What a mercy!'

But our nurse does not like a case where the baby is born dead.

'Such a beautiful child too!'

'It's more than can be said of the other twelve.'

'How can you tell?' Nurse said. 'Look at their clothes; look at their hair, standing on end; look at the scenes they live in!'

'The Hodds ought to be sent to prison for having thirteen children.'

'Go and tell Hodd himself so. You'll find him, if you go through the farm-yard. In the turnip-house. He slept there, last night; did not come home at all. He always clears out on these occasions. "A good riddance," Mrs Hodd says.'

Mr Hodd answered my greeting by a side-ways chuck of his head, and went on turning the handle of the cutting-machine which a small boy, working with him, replenished with whole turnips. The father of thirteen was a wild, unkempt-looking creature, habited in an outer garment composed of a dirty sack, through the hole cut in the bottom of which his head projected; a tangle of matted red hair met a tangle of matted red beard; a small portion of white cheek beneath the angry-looking blue eyes was the only part of his face uncovered. His arms, thrust through the slits cut in the sides of the sack, were hung about with rags which might once have been sleeves of a grey flannel shirt. Not such a family as the Hodds do we often see in Dulditch, but in the present shortage of labour the farmers are glad to welcome what help they can get.

'So I hear your wife's given birth to a dead baby, Hodd.'

Swish – swish – swish went the knife through the turnips, the neat sections dropping into the basket beneath. Two revolutions of the handle, then a curt, 'So they tell me.'

'Haven't you been home to see your wife?'

'No.' Swish – swish. 'Nor ain't a-goin'.'

'I think you ought to. Mrs Hodd will be wanting to see you.'

Two vicious turns of the handle of the machine which the boy feeds assiduously. Hodd is 'putting his back into it,' this morning!

'She's borne you many children, Hodd.'

'A sight too many!' Swish – swish. 'The place is chuck full of 'em. You stamp on 'em as you walk.'

'They keep you poor, I'm afraid!'

'Ah!' Swish – swish – swish.

'At any rate this poor little one won't have to be fed; you're no worse off than before it came.'

'There'll soon be another,' Hodd grunted, savagely prophetic. 'There's no stoppin' my missus, once she' sot a-goin'.'

The reflection that it was hardly fair to put it all on to Mrs Hodd, this way, I kept to myself.

The little boy, pitching the turnips into the voracious maw of the machine, looked at me brightly. He also was red-headed, he also was attired for the most part in a sack. He was the eldest hope of the Hodd family, helping his father in the hour between morning and afternoon school.

'Him and me –,' a nod in the direction of his parent, 'have got to make a box tonight, when we laves off work,' he said. 'Mother, she've sent ward by Nurse we've got to make a box to put little brother in.'

'Ah, poor little one!'

'Then him and me,' a chuck of his chin at the parent Hodd, 'is a-goin' to carry 'm to the corner of the chech-yard where there ain't no blessin'.'

'Now then! Git on wi' them turmits, boy.' In his pleasurable anticipation of the jaunt before him, the boy had stopped in his work. But he at once re-addressed himself to the task of throwing the turnips into the ever-open mouth of the cutter, where they bobbed about merrily for a moment or two before settling into position for the knives to slice.

'Well, good morning, Hodd,' I said. 'I shall go to see your wife and the poor baby before it is put in the box.'

Swish. Swish. Swish.

In the kitchen I passed through on my way upstairs, a pair of Hodds, of too tender an age to be at school, were seated on a sack – again a sack! – spread before the fire, and were playing with a large battered doll. Mrs Hodd, above, lay in her big squalid bed, alone.

'Have you no one to wait on you?'

'Blesh you, yes! There's the gal Maude.' Maude was the twelve years old daughter. 'Nonly she've gone on a narrand now, to let the parson's folk know as I'm brought to bed, and to ask for a drop o' soup, and a packet o' gro'ts, and a few nouraging matters o' that sort. For I've got to have life kep' in me somehow, I s'pose. And if parson's folk don't do it I don't know who should.'

'So the poor baby is dead, this time, Mrs Hodd!'

Mrs Hodd wrung her nose round to the middle of her cheek with a loud snuffle, tears streamed from her blue eyes. (All the Hodd family have red hair and blue eyes; so adorned themselves, and having started on a family thus endowed, Mr and Mrs Hodd had never paused to alter the pattern.)

'That fare hard,' she gurgled, 'to go t'rough it all, and then to lose 'em.'

'But you have so many, Mrs Hodd. This little one could well be spared. Hodd thinks as I do.'

'Ah! Hodd, he han't a mother's heart!'

'I am sure it is all you can do to feed and clothe the twelve.'

'Clothe? I don't clothe 'em. I look after their insides. No one can't say as my child'en look starved. If parson's folk want to see 'em clothed they must do it theirselves. My job's their insides, I take it.'

'I should like to see the poor baby, Mrs Hodd. I hear it was a very fine child.'

'Mine allers is!' Mrs Hodd testified. 'A crop o' heer he'd got all over his poll like golden suverins. My little uns, they're all that plased wi' their little brother! A fine hollerin' there'll be when he's took off to the buryin'.'

'Where is he? Look, I've brought a few flowers to lay upon his tiny coffin.'

Mrs Hodd, without lifting her tousled head, cast a glance of enquiry round the almost bare room. Near the door a rude bed had been made by spreading a towel over a frowsy pillow laid on two chairs.

'Ain't he theer?' the woman asked, her eyes upon the chairs.

'Nothing's there, Mrs Hodd.'

'Randolph!' Mrs Hodd screamed with startling abruptness. ''Vangeline! Come you here, this minute; don't I'll warm yer jackets for ye when I git yer.'

'Pray do not excite yourself,' I cried, alarmed. 'If you want the children who are in the kitchen I will fetch them for you.'

The tiny children on the filthy hearth were too much engrossed with their play to be aware of me, standing to watch. They were striving to draw over the rigid legs of the doll the grey calico nightgown of which they were stripping it when I saw them last. Their fat dirty little hands trembled with their eagerness to accomplish this feat. The mite who had the toy on her knees rocked herself maternally, and gave chirrups of encouragement as she worked.

'Theer! put ickle arms in! Put in ickle arms!'

Failing in every effort to insert the arms, she decided to dispense with that formality; pulling the awful nightgown over the shoulders she knotted it at the back of a little red head.

Then she turned the battered doll on its back and I saw that it was the dead baby.

Evangeline and Randolph pushed their grubby fingers into the open mouth, and tried to force them into the sunken eyes, in order to raise the lids.

'Wake up! Wake up, ickle brudder!' they said.

When I had rescued the desecrated body, and borne it to its poor bier in the mother's room, I spoke a word to Mrs Hodd which she resented.

'Time is long for sech little uns, when t'others 're at school and I'm laid by,' she said. 'Other folkes' child'en have a toy, now and then, to kape 'em out o' mischief. My little uns han't. He've kep' 'em quite (quiet) for hours, the po'r baby have; and I'll lay a crown they han't done no harm to their little brother.'

THE GAL LA'RENCES

YEARS ago, when our little Margaret was with us still, she startled my absent thought to attention one day by the remark that she considered Hannah and Rhoda Lawrence the happiest women she had ever known.

'The very happiest in the world,' the child repeated, smelling at the bouquet of auriculas, wallflowers, and lemon-thyme she had gathered from the little strips of flower-garden which border the tiny path before the 'gal La'rences' ' door. In reply to my surprised inquiry, she explained that their supreme bliss, to her thinking, lay in the fact that each of them had the happiness to possess a child of her own and neither had the affliction of a husband.

The circumstance which seemed so felicitous to Margaret was not, it need scarcely be said, of a nature to make life unduly smooth and easy for the two principally concerned. Each, at intervals of several years, had gone from service to the workhouse; each had brought from thence her babe to her parents' home, and had gone out to service again – to a lower, less reputable service, where mistresses were not particular about the antecedents of their servants so long as each could do the work of three women of fairer record.

On the death of their parents, dying of a fever in one week, the sisters, girls of twenty and twenty-two, came home, service being no longer possible to them, as their children must be looked after. To bury the father and mother, to pay the doctor's bill, every penny of that collection of silver and pence – the paternal savings of many years confided to the earthenware tea-pot on the mantel-piece – had to go, besides what could be dispensed with of the scanty furniture the cottage contained.

The little girl, Becky, by this time five years of age, was sent all day to school, and to set the sisters free for the only labour obtainable, the year-old boy was, at the cost of a shilling a week, put out to daily nursing. Little 'Becker,' despatched with her slice of bread and dripping, bread and treacle, dry bread, according to the state of the exchequer, her little bottle of cold tea for her midday meal, was no worse off than the rest of her school-fellows. But it is to be feared that the infantile 'Biller,' relinquished to the tender mercies of Happy (christened Hephzibah) Hunter, must have gone through some trying vicissitudes. After he had fallen among the hot cinders beneath the grate for the third time, Rhoda insisted on having his petticoats pinned to those of his nurse, so that if Happy did fall asleep as soon as she sat down with her charge over the fire the danger to Biller might be minimised. With her own hands the mother erected a guard across the 't'reshol' of the Hunter door to restrain the wanderings of the venturesome Biller, who, while Happy went about her domestic affairs, had twice been rescued from beneath the feet of horses passing on the road. Biller's soft and hairless head was always swelled in some new direction through being brought into contact with hard and immovable objects; his arms were ever varicoloured from bruises, his legs were covered with scratches. Yet Happy, who was deaf and blind and without a roof to her mouth, was glad to earn the shilling a week, and Rhoda could find no one else willing to tend the child.

Their children being all day long off their hands, the 'gal La'rences,' as they are still called in spite of their sixty years and more, went to work upon the land. Week after week, year out, year in, from sunrise to sunset during the winter months, from six to six through the golden summer days, those two trudged off when work was to be had. Insufficiently clad, half fed, they set themselves to labour for which no woman's frame is fitted in order that the boy and girl, poor nameless little mortals with their heritage of shame, should be kept alive; in order that the rent of the wretched house in which their father and mother had lived for thirty years should be paid; in order that they who had covered themselves with a disgrace which, according to our charitable code, there is no washing away, should not stoop to that worse disgrace from the 'gal La'rences' ' point of view – the disgrace of asking for alms.

It never entered the heads of these two women, any more than the head of little Margaret herself, that they, in giving birth to their boy and girl, had committed sin of which they should repent. Her offspring of shame has been to each woman the flower and crown of her life, the bright spot in her existence. The cup she has had to drink has been bitter enough; its one sweet drop has been mother-love. The boy and girl have grown to man and womanhood now; they are in middle life indeed, with the premature look of age upon them which characterises the very poor. Not an especially well-favoured couple, nor very gracious in bearing. One wonders, was all that love and labour lavished in vain? Would the world have been no worse place – better even, with so many mouths less to feed, so much room to spare for healthier, more promising members of the universal brotherhood – had those two babes of Hannah and Rhoda Lawrence been left to perish?

No question of this kind, thank God, troubles the feeble woman crouching over her fire, the busy woman at her ironing-board.

To the simple thinking of the gal La'rences, and compared with the semi-starvation of earlier days, the sisters live in affluence now. Their spotless, wholesome cottage is as a palace to the swarming grandchildren, offspring of the married cousins – that big-headed, small-limbed race, whose heated complexions and scaly skins render them of but small attractiveness in stranger eyes. Every meal partaken at the grandmothers' table is a feast. To sit on Sunday afternoons on the shiny chairs ranged round the walls, with an apple off the one apple tree in the garden and perhaps a chestnut apiece to hold in their hands, is a privilege which it would be terrible to forfeit. It is Hannah who presents the new pinafores; Rhoda whose hands, tortured by rheumatism, 'blow up' as big as her head in her efforts to keep little stockings and elbows free from holes. That one among them whose turn it is to dine with the gal La'rences 'come Sunday' is regarded for the time as the most enviable of mankind. There is no room for uncertainty about the fare; the unchanging Sabbath-day repast, laid forth on the white, coarse cloth of the little round table, is the same year after year: a tiny joint of cold baked pork, a large rice pudding in a yellow pie-dish, a basin of hot potatoes, and a wedge of cheese.

It isn't so much what there is to eat which fascinates the little visitor, perhaps, fills him with such unspeakable longing in anticipation, such rapture in enjoyment; it is the order, the cleanliness, the sweet propriety of all which appeal so strongly to the small grandchild. To see the black-handled knife and fork laid beside each willow-pattern plate, the white cup and saucer with the small blue flower (the gal La'rences always indulge in tea for the Sunday dinner); to admire the glass salt-cellar, the knitted mat adorning the plate which holds the loaf; to smell the wallflowers in their jar among the precious ornaments on the side-table; to catch glimpses through the open door of the neat little flower-borders, the buttercup meadows, and blue fields of sky beyond – these are the things, after all, which make the Sunday festival memorable.

The boy 'Biller' was little more than eighteen years of age when it was discovered to be advisable to marry him as soon as might be to his cousin of twenty-three.

'They'd been allus brought up, and slep' together as little uns – 'twere on'y nat'ral like,' Rhoda says indulgently, telling the tale of the marriage. 'It all come of Becker a-comin' home for the Whissun holidays. Biller, he'd growed 's w'uskers since she went awaay two yeer agone, and when she set eyes on 'm she set a-laughin'. That wos how it were – she set a-laughin'.'

The explanation, which seems to be somehow deficient, is quite satisfactory to Rhoda. In talking to such simple people, the discrepancy between the picture in the mind's eye and its verbal exposition is very observable. It arises perhaps from a frequent talking over of facts in a small circle where the details are already known. It is probable that by an inhabitant of Dulditch a lively and lengthy history of courtship and marriage is at once unfolded by the allusion to the time when 'Becker set a-laughin'.'

But the consequence of this early marriage of Becker, who could never keep her places, and the boy who had not received 'man's wage' long enough to have saved from his earnings was that the young couple had to go into debt to furnish their house, and have remained in difficulties to the present time.

The pair, struggling in extremest poverty, are given to look with a grudging eye upon the comforts of Hannah and Rhoda. Such spotless cleanliness has very much the air of luxury to Becky, worn out with an apparently hopeless washing of eight children and a continual scrubbing of an always fresh 'drabbled' floor. Of that table of ornaments, presented principally by the 'Rober'son child'un,' for whose parents Hannah works – tiny baskets, in which sweeties had once been packed, empty chocolate boxes, sixpenny ornaments bought from the gipsy at the door, cracked wine-glasses – Becky is proud while resenting the splendid effect. With her house full of children she acknowledges that such elegancies would be inappropriate, even if attainable—there is barely room for the chairs to seat the numerous progeny in the over-crowded place; but the female soul longs after the ornaments of life, and the treasures are looked at with admiration, but askance.

It is matter of complaint between husband and wife that 'mothers' could do more than is done for them all. Yet in this forbearance the women still consider their children, as they have always done. They have their own old age to provide for, the not distant time when the one working member of the little partnership can work no more. Their children are faultless, the most beautiful, wise, and affectionate of their species, but it will not do to 'come on' Biller and Becker in a few years to support their respective mothers. The pleasure of helping son and daughter in their necessity is perhaps the greatest the women could experience; but it must not be indulged in, any more than those other pleasures of life which Rhoda and Hannah, did they give the matter a thought, must acknowledge they had known only to decline.

Should it come to pass that the maintenance of their mothers must fall upon Becker and Biller, the bread so eaten would be the bitterest of all the bitter bread the 'gal La'rences' had eaten, would be washed down with the saltest tears. Had they not under their eyes the case of half a dozen old men and women, for whose support sons and daughters, compelled thereto by the parish, were contributing their hard-earned, ill-spared, dearly-grudged shillings? Was there not old Marthy Brown, for instance, whose eldest born, living only five miles off, had refused to see his mother for twenty years, so incensed was he at having to sacrifice a tithe of his income to maintain her? Was there not poor old Skipper, continuing, to his sorrow and dismay, hale and hearty at nearly ninety years of age, spite of the wrong he was doing his children by keeping out of his grave?

'What! Yu bain't dead yit?' is the usual filial greeting to which the poor old fellow is accustomed.

'Well, I were the same to my faather,' Skipper admits, mumbling the matter over to himself at his scant and lonely fireside – he does not complain.

But, rather than share the fate of Skipper and old Marthy, Hannah and Rhoda turn niggards to the clamorous horde about them, and store their hard-earned shillings with greediest care.

Another case they remember too: that of Shadrach Allen – he whose three sons, living in a distant county, were summoned to Dulditch to attend their father's death-bed. Shady, poor lonely old man, cheered up at the sight of those middle-aged boys of his whom he had not seen for a dozen years. The presence of those heavy, altered faces did him more good than 'a hape' of medicine had done; the illness took a favourable turn. The doctor when he came laughed good-naturedly over his patient's improved condition, rallied the old man on having taken them all in, his medical adviser above the rest, and declared that Shady was 'good enough man still to see out half the young uns.'

His laugh was not echoed by the solemn-looking sons sitting in their Sunday clothes around the bed. The old man had been a burden on them for a good many years. They had come a 'matter o' tew hunder' mile to see father die; 'twould be middlin' awk'ard' if he failed to do what was expected of him.

But Shadrach did not fail. The sons took care he did not. They quietly ignored the doctor's altered tone; they did not recognise the improved condition of their parent. 'He'd allust thort he'd git over this bout,' the old man cheerfully declared. "Twere along o' their bein' so good to 'm he'd made shift to drag along so far; and, please th' Lord, he'd git t'rough th' summer that allust aised his corf and set 'm up wonnerful.' The sons paid no heed to 'sech-like mardlin' '; their faces discouraged all hopefulness; they spoke to him only on the subject of his demise. They reminded him that they had procured a fortnight's holiday, thinking that that would see the finish of all things; they hoped the 'p'or old man 'ud be out of mus'ry' before that time, please the Lord.

It was those sons of Shadrach, who had 'holp' him with contributions of a shilling a week each for much longer than was agreeable to them, who nursed him to death. Their devotion was edifying in the extreme, and the neighbours all declared them to be 'wonnerful 'fectionate young chaps'. They would not let him put so much as an arm upon the coverlet, but kept the 'twilt' pulled tight under Shady's nose; one or other of them was always employed in tucking it in tightly around him. They declined the proffered services of the next-door women to 'shiffen' the old man in his bed, declaring ''twould be a sin to onsettle po'r old faather in 's last hours.' It was not Shady who benefited by the port wine and the soup sent from the Rectory. 'Th' old chap were past nourishin',' they said, and for days they persisted in giving him cold water out of a teaspoon as his only refreshment, other members of the family having taken that unstimulating beverage alone for the last days of their lives.

Well, they had 'kep' ' him in comfort while he lived, had 'holp' him through his dying illness, and they closed his eyes when he died. Many times Shady had assured them from his strict retirement beneath the sheet that they had been the best of sons to him; and they conscientiously acquiesced in the statement. By hurrying the burying a little they were even enabled to follow the old man to his grave and to superintend the selling of his sticks of furniture before their fortnight's leave was up.

The doctor was a little surprised to find a corpse instead of a recovery on his next visit. He was somewhat abashed before the triumph of the sons, who 'had seen death writ in 's faace from th' fust,' they said. 'We nivver had no other thort but that he were a goin'. We waited on 'm hand and fut, but we nivver, so to say, had no hope.'

The man of medicine had thought otherwise, certainly; he had thought that by careful nursing and strict attention to his directions –. But it was not the first time the parish doctor had been mistaken by a good many. A few hours would bring about great changes, he admitted, and one could not give the close attention to the paupers' cases that perhaps they needed.

By that time the doctor's gig had whirled him to another 'pauper case,' and Shady's name was struck off his list and forgotten.

But Rhoda and Hannah Lawrence had no desire to be nursed out of existence in this attentive way, even by Billy and Becky.

''Tis nat'ral,' they say, 'natural th' young uns sh'ud feel th' old uns a barden.' They are sorry for the parents, but they do not condemn the children. ''Tis but nat'ral.'

And so most anxiously they apply themselves to the increasing of their little hoard. If good luck attend them and 'th' Lord plaase,' there

147

is always the 'chancet' that they may not survive the time when Hannah is too old to work. Then the son and the daughter will reap the benefit of those savings, a thought stimulating to yet further effort.

Hannah, what with her heaters and her starch and the difficulties with the bosoms of 'the master's' shirts, is too much engaged for sustained conversation. But Rhoda, crouching over the bright fire, her swollen and cramped hands lying idle perforce in her lilac apron, is 'allust fit ter mardle, and allust wor,' the sister declares, and adds that she bain't a sayin' as how Rhoda were one o' them golderin' ones tha's allust a runnin' on; on'y companiony and agraable-like.'

So Rhoda, while you will sit to listen, is glad to talk; and her favourite theme is of the days of their extremest poverty, when 'bread and groshery was dare, and Becker and Biller wos little uns.' She tells the story simply enough, with smiles rather than tears; with no thought that it is a tale of heroism – that she is revealing the history of a constancy and a courage of the highest and a devotion which is beyond praise and without reward. She tells it because, sitting there, racked with pain, crippled, a fixture in the chimney corner, she is proud to remember that she was once, as she says, 'as good a man as Hannah.' That she, too, morning after morning, turned out in the darkness, the biting wind and sleet to the day's work. That although, being a woman, she only earned sixpence a day, work as she might, she could yet fill a tumbril as quickly as the best man on the farm, could weed the 'mangles,' gather stones, top and tail the 'turmits' as well as he.

'Th' maaster he complain sometimes there bain't no women nowadays to wark i' th' fiel's; but though the young uns is *nicer* than they wos in my day, 'tis maybe for the best,' Hannah says, and glances at Rhoda's crippled limbs. 'There's women that can stand such a life,' she adds, with a sharp shake of the garment she is about to iron, 'but then there's also women that can't.'

When Becky was about five years old luck seemed suddenly about to change for the gal La'rences – only seemed, alas! And about this chapter of their simple history, opening so brightly and ending only in disappointment and woe, no word is said in Hannah's presence. Rhoda watches her opportunity, waiting till the elder sister goes into the little garden to collect the collars and small articles hanging out on the gooseberry bushes to bleach, or into the little inner kitchen to attend to the bread 'doin' ' in the 'bak'us.' The crippled sister gives you the story with her hand on your knee, her face pushed forward, in a hurried and husky whisper.

'He wor a stiddy, hard-warkin', 'dustrious chap, and he cast 's eyes on Hennah. He spoke her fair enough, and said as how he wanted a wife, and he ha'n't no 'bjections to me a livin' 'long on 'em nor yet to th' child'un. His mother, she were a foul-mouthed old mawther, and she come a mobbin'. "I want nothin' to du wi' yu, Mis' Butters," Hennah she up and say tu her, "nor yet wi' none o' th' bilin' on yer, 'cept Jabez; an' I reckon he know 's own mind and want none o' yar interfarin' ".' Hennah she'd got chakes like a pe'ny i' them days and eyes like sloes, and there weren't none on 'em that dust take no lib'ties wi' Hennah; and Jabez, he' set 's heart on her.

'He were a-gettin' o' things comf'table for 's home, and Hennah she'd been cried i' th' chech, and 'twere i' th' haymakin' time. Me and Hennah, we wos a rakin' side by side 'twere i' Rober'son's cherry-tree piece (Hennah she ha'n't niver so much named the name o' that theer field up till this day) – and th' sun were molten hot. I were a'most done up. I looked at Hennah. "Bor," I say, "how yu du swat." "I du," she say; "th' drops be a fallin' off on me like rain. Tha's bad for the men a mowin'," she say; and I knew as she were a thinkin' o' Jabez, for he were a fiery-hidded chap – like all th' Butters – wi' a short neck, and he felt th' hate won'erful.'

'An' someone come a runnin' – 'twere a p'or du-nothin' mawther that ha' left the parush now, and right glad I were when she went, for the sight on 'er allust giv' Hennah a turn arter that day. She flung up her hand and kep' a callin' su'thin' acrost the swaths o' hay.

'We cou'n't make nothin' on 'er, and she kep' a callin' still. Hennah she hulled down her rake and went up ter th' wumman. Then she come back and set a rakin' oncet more. "Wha's come ter th' mawther?" I say tu 'er. "Bor, he's dead," she say. "Jabez ha' fell down dead i' th' hayfield."'

'Hennah she tuk 't wonerful quite-like. Like a sorft fule as I were I set a blubberin', but Hennah she di'n't imitate to make no complaint. "That fare as ef I'd allust knowed it," she say. "I ban't one o' them to make a piece o' wark."'

'Yet Hennah weren't never th' same wumman arter that day's wark,' Rhoda assures you. And then, perhaps, Hannah returns to the front kitchen and the ironing board, and Rhoda, to get as far as possible from that scene of the summer hay-making, plunges into a description of beet-pulling 'mid the snows and slush and sleet of winter.

'We used ter pull our pett'coats 'twin our legs trouser-fashion,' Rhoda goes on, 'and fine and mucky our stockin's got by night-time;

and we allust had ter wash 'em out for th' mornin', for we'd on'y a pair o' white uns apiece. An' then ol' master – we'd played along o' him when 'e wos a buoy, and he allust tuk notus 'f me and Hennah – he gi'en us aich a pair o' butes. Wellinghams, he called 'em, and they was the usefullest iver yu see, for they come right up o' th' leg; and ef so be as yu ha'n't a pair o' stockin's on no one weren't th' wiser.'

Then Hannah, engaged in testing a red-hot iron by holding it within half an inch of her cheek, declares with perceptible bitterness that Rhoda 'shou'n't tell about them theer butes,' and adds, as she brings the heater forcibly down upon its work, 'We shou'n't nivver ha' had 'em ef so be as I'd ha' had my way.'

Whereat Rhoda chuckles and explains that Hannah is always 's'naisty' on that subject, being of opinion that on that cold and rainy morning when 'th' master' called over the hedge to know why Rhoda and Hannah hadn't got their buskins on, Rhoda, wet to the knees, standing among the drenched leaves of the turnips, should have answered with prevarication. She should, Hannah maintained, have perished ('paraged,' she called it) sooner than 'let on' that of buskins they had none.

''Twere like askin' o' th' man to give 'em,' Hannah says with fierceness.

'But I wanted 'm ter give 'em,' says Rhoda simply.

At which Hannah brings down her heater with force upon the sleeve of the nightdress lying spread before her. It is a kind of protest against Rhoda's view of the subject. She has gone over the whole story so often in the last thirty years, there is no good in repeating her arguments; only –.

'Hennah, she were allust won'erful proud,' Rhoda goes on, with visible pride of her own in that quality of 'Hennah's'. And she tells how, in the harvest field, when 'th' 'levenses and fourses' came round, and the labourers' wives and children would bring their meals into the field, and the men, sitting in the midst of their own and their neighbours' families, would enjoy the extra delicacies appropriate to the occasion – the mild home-brew, the wedge of 'mate dumplin',' the harvest cake – Hannah would ostentatiously set forth her slice of cheese upon the red handkerchief spread upon her knees, 'as grand as the rest on 'em.'

''Twere for show on'y,' Rhoda says, chuckling, and it lasted all through the harvest month. 'Th' chase were for show only, and so 's none cou'n't pity us with our slice o' bread, or think as we was forced to it.'

A white glass bottle of cold tea was also carried out day after day for appearance sake, the cold water which served them to slake their thirst disguising its tell-tale hue in a black bottle.

Hannah laughs a little shamedly over the reminiscence, bending the dark head, into which no line of white has come as yet, above the ironing-box upon which she is pressing with both hands.

'I di'n't want no hape o' talk,' she explains. 'They'd ha' been orferin' me their wittles; an' they'd ha' choked me.'

Rhoda presently goes on to speak of one especial night when things had come to the worst. A week or so before a sister had died, leaving a child of six years old with no prospect before it but the workhouse. No 'flesh and blood' of the gal La'rences had been 'beholden' to the parish as yet; and without any hesitation, with no debate on ways and means, no question as to how the extra mouth was to be fed, such as must have agitated people less desperately poor, they walked one evening, work being done, to the parish where the mother had died and fetched the orphan home.

. It was as much as they could do to keep life in the four of them without this added burden, for flour was half a crown a stone in those days, and if they worked every day of the week, which through stress of weather and other drawbacks they could not always do, there was only six shillings to take at the end of it. Out of this a shilling must be laid aside for rent and a shilling for the services of Happy Hunter, whose watery eyes used to gleam with delight for her part when she received the magnificent sum.

'I tell ye,' Hannah says, 'I was allust er'table in them times; but my wust tempered days wos pay-days. I were that worritted to know how to make it go th' fuddest.'

But this especial evening was not that of pay-day, and things looked more than usually hopeless. The last slices of bread had been sent in the children's dinner-bags to school; the two sisters had had nothing but some raw turnip, eaten in the field, to stay their hunger since morning.

'We must git suffin' somehow to put inter our insides ternight,' Rhoda said, as they walked home through the winter evening's dusk.

But for once Hannah despaired. ('She were th' strongest, but she were allust th' downest-hearted,' Rhoda explains.) 'We'd best ha' done with it, and give 't up,' she declared. 'Howsomdever I telled her we worn't sech downpins as that come tu yit,' Rhoda continues. 'We'd done to th' best o' our know, and now th' Lord 'ud ha' to help us. I dussen't say so to Hennah, but I'd up and arst Him tu, time we wos i' th' fiel'. For I'd been a tarnin' matters over, and I seen that, whether Hennah liked it or no, we must ha' help, ef so be as th' child'un worn't ter parage. An' when we got in, what d' yer think we see? A half-sack o' taters shot agin the wall, and as much as a peck o' bewtiful inions, and a bushel or more o' apples! 'Twere a present from th' folk up to th' Hall, a neighbour telled us, to all them cottages as hadn't no gaarden.

' "Worn't I right?" I say to Hennah. "I telled ye suffin' 'ud turn up, and here be half a sack o' taters!'

'But Hennah, she were snaisty still: she were allust grudgin' agin anythin' she ha'n't, so to say, warked for.

' "A sight o' good taters be without no saucepun to bile 'em in!" she say.'

'For our one was past mendin', at las', and we'd gi'en it awaay to a neighbour to mess up her chickens' food in, on'y the day afore.

'"I 'on't let on we ha'n't no saucepun. I 'on't ha no borrerin'," Hennah, she say. And so the end on 't were we biled th' taters i' th' kittle; and I don't know as iver I tasted none better biled, nayther.'

And after supper Hannah, who was never a hand at thanking people, put the littles to bed and scrubbed the floor, and 'redd up' the kitchen, while Rhoda walked the couple of miles to the Hall to thank 'th' laady' for her gift. And 'th' laady,' who was Sir Thomas's mother, 'without no haughtiness about her,' came out of a room where 'singin' and musickin' were going on bewtiful,' and spoke to Rhoda herself, and ordered her a 'glass of wind' and a slice of cake, and told her that out of some dozen families to whom like presents had been distributed among the cottagers, she had been the only one who had been gracious enough to say a word of thanks. After which she asked many questions and seemed interested in the answers; and she insisted on Rhoda taking home the remainder of the cake for the children, with some tea and sugar and a tin of rich soup for herself. 'And a nice how-d'ye-du there were with Hennah for my a takin' of 'em!' Rhoda chuckles.

But the worst of the troubles of the 'gal La'rences' were over after that night, for the Hall lady 'tuk notus' of them and gave them sewing work to do – not very particular jobs at first, their hands being so stiff, and not enough of it to allow them to give up their field work. Many and many a night did Hannah, the day's work being done, sit sewing until the hour came round to begin the work of another day, Rhoda having been decoyed to her night's rest by the promise that Hannah would soon join her. But the women grew in favour with the Squire's wife, and presently the field labour was given up and the hard struggle was over.

They never, however, 'tuk kindly ter th' sewin', bein' used to active employment,' and the Hall lady being dead, and Rhoda fallen rheumatic, Hannah was glad to take the washing at Rober'son's, which she keeps to the present day.

The 'Rober'son child'un' had most of them been born since she was there, and she'd seen some of them grow up and go out into the world, but she is 'fond of 'em all,' she tells you and 'th' child'un is fond of me. As fur Rhoda – they'd allust come ter Rhoda in all mander o' little troubles – there'd allust been child'un in Rhoda's life, she were so wonnerful set on 'em.'

Rhoda admits the soft impeachment and counts up her treasures for your benefit.

'Fust there wos Becker and Biller and po'r Arnust' (the dead sister's child). 'He, po'r chap, had fell orf th' shaffs of a cart th' fust year he warked o' th' farm – an' he so proud o' arnin' his little wage – and were brought in with 's hid a mash and 's inside a gushin' out 'f 's body. Then there was the Rober'sons, bless their little hearts, and now th' gran'child'un that sometimes fared th' darest and most engagin' o' th' lot.'

'Ef 'tweren't for me she'd allust have 'em messin' about,' Hannah declares. 'They smudder th' floor wi' their mucky butes, and allust a fingerin' and a fidgettin' – makin' a sight o' wark.'

'Better so than to be as bad off as Sam Uttridge,' Rhoda avers.

If you have not already heard the interesting history of Sam Uttridge, Rhoda will tell you that the gentleman in question is a nephew of theirs, who, being in every other way prosperous and commendable, labours under the extreme disadvantage in Rhoda's eyes of having been married for fourteen years to a wife who has not borne him a child.

Rhoda has on this account the deepest compassion for Mr Uttridge (his name, by the way, is Etheridge, but that does not make his case better or worse), the utmost contempt for his better half.

'To call herself a wumman! I wonder what she think women are made fur?' Rhoda cries, for she takes a very simple view of the great woman question which, unknown to her, is agitating so many superior minds, and she is happy in the proud consciousness of having fulfilled to her entire satisfaction her own mission.

If you inquire into Mrs Sam Uttridge's antecedents, you will hear that the lady is an 'orficer's' daughter, and on pursuing inquiries you will learn that in the 'gal La'rence's' vocabulary an 'orficer's daughter is not the child of a gentleman in the army or the navy, as might naturally have occurred to you, but of one whose occupation ('writin' and figgerin' and seck-like') lies in an office.

Was Margaret right, I wonder, and are these two women, crouching by the fire, toiling at the wash-tub, to be envied after all?

To me who write, to you who read, such a history is one of unrelieved misery, we say. But are we happier after all? We have loftier aspirations, higher ideals, nobler ambitions. But do we realise, can we attain them? We can only be successful in that which we put before us as the object to be accomplished. We can but have the thing we long for. In a world so filled with disappointment, where failure is for the many and success for the very few; where desire is so constantly baffled and hopes drop off before fruition; where thwarted ambition embitters the heart, and shattered illusions leave the eyes that beheld them darkened for ever; where the cravings of the soul seem given us only to be denied; where, grasping the thing we long for, we find it broken and ruined in our hands – in such a world surely the 'gal La'rences' may esteem themselves blest.

For the one simple duty of their lives they fulfilled, the one uncomplicated desire of their hearts they attained to.

And, for that Biller and Becker – the unlovely, the loutish, the ungracious, and uncouth, whose births were shameful, whose personalities are disagreeable, whose histories are squalid – are born into the world, and are in their own obscure way holding their own there, the two women nightly give thanks and are ready at any moment to sing their *Nunc Dimittis*.

SOME OF THE SHIPWRECKED

'The voyage balked, the course disputed, lost,
I yield my ships to Thee.'

Buns for the old ladies, an ounce of tobacco each for the men, a toy or two for the children. A small outlay for such a large return of smiles, of thanks, of interest, of the quickening of stolid faces! Humiliated by the disproportionate gratitude they evoked, we saw distribution made of these poor offerings.

Of children in all that big workhouse – the poorhouse of the union of twenty-five country parishes – there was but one of an age to understand toys: a Tot of three years who sat in silence and an unnatural quietude on the settle by the fire in that brightest of all the wards, where curtains hang at the windows and matting is on the floor, and a bunch of daffodils in a jug upon the table – the ward devoted to the old women. The child's mother, a girl of eighteen, had died last night in giving birth to her second child. The Tot, as soon as a home could be found for her, would be boarded out with a family willing for three shillings a week to undertake the charge, and so mercifully would escape the unwholesome influences of a workhouse rearing. In the meantime, planted on the settle between the two old women, she sat in a silence and a patience, which seemed never to be broken and waited for the mother who would never come again.

She had not been educated in the use of toys, and turned away her head in fear and dislike of the woolly dog with the pink ribbon and the bell about the neck which we would have presented to her. The old woman beside her, with a wrinkled, cheerful face, bright eyes, and the high-pitched voice of second childhood, proved far more of a baby than she. She pounced upon the dog with the most infantile delight, coaxed it, chattered to it, hugged it to her withered old breast, while the rest, wiser and less happy, looked on uncomprehending.

At a word from the matron a singular-looking creature, bent chin and knees together, her plentiful beard and moustache beneath the frilled white cap giving her an uncanny look, her large lack-lustre eyes gazing into vacuity, got up and mechanically turned her twisted back upon us to show us the extent of her misfortune.

On the other side of the fire an alert old woman, stone deaf, pointed insistently to an unframed cabinet photograph on the mantelshelf. It was the portrait of her granddaughter in Canada, who had sent to the unknown granny in England the picture which had found the poor old relative in the workhouse. Altogether impossible, so deaf was she, to make the old woman understand our felicitations on the possession of a descendant of so much elegance. When she, with whispered chatterings quite unintelligible, pointed to the portrait, we could only point to it too, and smile and nod our heads, and at her invitation shake hands right jovially, and smile and nod and point again.

Of the child – child of a child-mother, with the care of all the ages stamped upon its still, wan little face – no one took any notice. One of us having children of her own, held out her arms to her; but the Tot turned from the uncomprehended caresses as she had turned from the unproved delights of a toy. For a second her baby-mouth drooped and trembled, the wide, sad eyes grew larger with tears that did not fall; but the lips quivered back into sedateness again, the sad eyes turned from us as if our pitiful gaze were distasteful; and with her tiny hands laid upon her lap we left her, waiting with the patience so heart-breaking to witness for the mother who did not come – the Tot with all the troubles of life before her among the aged women whose troubles had ended – here.

⁓✼⁓

'There are two men, ladies, who will not be allowed to take the tobacco,' the master said, as he led us down a corridor, through which we emerged into a triangular bricked-in yard.

Here the spring sun shone palely upon a half dozen men of all ages, poor units of the 'brutish, measureless, human undergrowth,' who sat idly upon a bench beneath a high wall. A handsome young man, shivering in consumption, looked up, hollow-eyed, as we passed, torn unwillingly from the contemplation of his own misery; then turned again his darkling, miserable gaze upon the gravel at his feet. A big man beside him, in whose watery gaze and swollen and discoloured features could be read the history of his degradation, arose and struck an attitude as we passed by. He hastily shifted his stick into his left hand, and raising his right to heaven, burst forth in loud and husky voice into verse.

The consumptive hunched his rounded shoulders, shivering strongly in the sunshine; the villainous-looking ruffian on the other side of him, who had come straight from prison to workhouse, laughed, spat upon the gravel, and turned away his head; the master going on before us, casting a careless accustomed eye upon the spectacle, barely halted in his walk. With his moist eye regarding us from the corner, and his trembling hand raised to heaven, the drunkard spouted on.

Compelled to follow to follow the master's impatient steps, we left him after a third verse; but as we went, the rich husky tones rolled after us, pursuing us through an empty, paved courtyard and down another corridor. On comparing notes we found that only the refrain of the verses had lingered in our memories, a refrain he gave with unctuous utterance and a display of tremendous feeling, the extended hand shaking above him, the dim eyes leaving our faces to appeal with watery emotion to the skies.

'Oh, mother, dear mother, look down on your boy!'

God, what a sight for a mother in heaven to see! What a depraved, ruined, degraded image of a boy!

We recognised at a glance, arrived at the old men's ward, one of the two refractory inmates who were to be punished by the withholding of the ounce of tobacco – a big-headed cripple, with a fierce yet cunning and an evil face. He used his crutch for attack as often as for support, and had belaboured with it the head of a porter on that very morning – an Ishmael, whose crutch as well as his hand was against every man's. Him we knew at once the notoriously black sheep of that mirky flock.

By his side sat an old man of eighty, grey-headed, but with colour still in his eyes, and its pristine auburn still lingering here and there in his long moustache and beard. He rose as we entered, and doffing the cap which, although they sat over the fire, all wore, bowed low, and with an old-fashioned grace bade us welcome to that poor abode.

In our ashamed and shrinking ears the master announced in triumphant phrase the munificent donation of an ounce of tobacco apiece which the ladies present had bestowed on the inmates.

At this tremendous intelligence the old man with an unabashed but simple courtesy bowed his thanks.

'There are two,' proceeded the master, 'who for refractory conduct will not be allowed to take the tobacco. You, Fred,' to the lowering hero of the crutch, who lifted his fist and shook it in the master's face; 'you, Winton,' to the old man of the grey and auburn beard and sweeping moustache.

Winton stood, cap in hand, dismay and disappointment written legibly on the handsome features of his fine old face. 'I hope you will see your way to alter that decision, sir,' he said, a quavering note of appeal in his voice.

The master shook his head. 'Break the rules and you've got to suffer like the rest, you know, Winton,' he said.

Once again with his courtly bow Winton proffered his humble request that the master would be lenient; and once again he was refused.

We went to him and took his hand and sat down at his side.

'We are so sorry,' we said. 'We will come again with more tobacco – much more – when – when you are not under a cloud.'

He was visibly depressed. 'I thank you, ladies,' he said. 'And if you never come again, I thank you on the part of my comrades here. It was a matter – a little foolish matter of feeling the cold too keenly. My age,' he explained, with an apologetic smile that was full of sweetness. 'In the early morning I feel a great chilliness around my body. I was tempted to appropriate a jersey I saw at hand as well as my own jersey. I folded it across my body, and it seemed to comfort me –'

'And when we asked if you'd got it, you said you hadn't, you know, Winton,' the master reminded him.

Winton smiled at this, his sweet deprecating smile. 'Ah, well!' he sighed, and waved his hand as one who should admit and smilingly grieve over the lapses common to humanity and put them from the mind.

'Tell us! How came you here?' we asked him, with a surprised curiosity, for in every accent of the man was refinement, in every feature of the ivory-white face, in the shape of the thin long hands and tapering fingers, was written the history of gentle birth.

He mistook or he evaded our question. 'I am quite happy here,' he said. 'I have nothing to complain of. My comrades' – here he looked round upon the faces of his companions, vacant with only half-awakened intellect, sodden with the squalor and hopelessness of life, blighted with evil passion, scarred in the long and useless struggle to avoid the fate which had now befallen, lifeless with the stolid resignation for which another name is despair – 'my companions sometimes complain. They have their different ways of looking at things – the heart knoweth its own bitterness, ladies, and to every man his own burden. As for me, I thank God, and I am content.'

A man who had sat leaning forward gazing stupidly at the fire here turned his head and looked at us. 'He's a scholard,' he said with a surly nod of his head in Winton's direction, and turned back to the fire again.

'Come, give the ladies a taste of your Latin, Winton,' the master said. 'You and the chaplain can gabble one against another fast enough at times. Let's hear you do it now.'

Whereupon Winton arose and stood before us, docilely, as if he were again a boy at school, and in a perfectly modulated voice, and lifting his bowed head, began –

'Eheu! Fugaces Posthume, Posthume
Labuntur anni ...'

The man who had spoken before turned round again; he perhaps felt something of a proprietary pride in this accomplished gentleman who called him comrade. 'He had the name of "the yeller boy" because of his gold and the colour of his hair,' he said in a hoarse whisper across the Latin verse. 'He've run through his quarter of a million of money, he have!'

Undisturbed by the interruption, the old man stood before us, his hands locked behind his bent back in the attitude of the schoolboy who had so stood before his master's desk – how many years ago! – and spouted on –

'...nec pieta moram
Rugis and instanti senectae
Afferet, indomitaeque morti!'

'It is quite true,' the master said in our ears. 'There are people in the neighbourhood, I've been told, who know something of his history; but he don't know it. He'll talk about his school days and the years since he came here; the rest is wiped out – a blank.'

'Thank you for your Latin, but tell us something of yourself,' we said to him again.

'I thank you. I am very comfortable here. All are good to me. I have nothing to complain of,' again he said.

We looked at the kindly old eyes with a reminiscence of the blue of morning skies still lingering in them. Had he forgotten, we wondered, or did he choose not to remember?

'He have fine tales of his schule days,' the man with a pride in him said, turning round again. 'He were a youngster for mischief, he were!'

''Twas to the Grammar School at Bury I went,' the old man said. 'As if 'twere yesterday I remember the day, and 'twas seventy years ago this April. Many a caning I had, for I was a merry boy, up to my pranks – many a caning -'

'And you remember all that, and have forgotten all the rest – the long years when you were rich and gay and had wife and children, perhaps?'

For, finding this shipwrecked stranger of a manner so foreign to the place, it was not strange, perhaps, that we longed to hear of the fair commencement of that voyage which had ended so disastrously, of that long-continued strife of storm and tempest which had finally cast him here, 'all lost except a little life,' bare and defenceless on the pitiless hearts of men.

He answered our graceless persistency with the old formula: 'I am very comfortable, I thank you, ladies; quite content.'

When we had taken leave of him and reached the door, he followed and stayed us with a gentle hand. 'My memory is treacherous,' he said, and touched the high forehead over which the grey hair fell in picturesque profusion. 'Sometimes even the Latin escapes me. But there is one word I never forget, and that is the word Amo, I love.'

159

As we went through the paved courtyard again a deal coffin was carried across.

'There is no one in it,' the master said, as we stopped, startled. 'They are taking it to the dead-house for the body of the girl who died last night.'

That 'heavenly' death which provides for all had found and welcomed this lost, unhappy child. She had got well 'out of the scrape of being alive and poor.' And,

'Praise, praise, praise,' we said.

'For the sure enwinding arms of cool-enfolding death.'

But we thought of the Tot seated between the two old women on the settle, waiting with the patience so foreign to happy childhood, for the mother who would never come again.

A DULDITCH ROSE

WITHOUT a word in anyone's ear Rosa Weeks started off one morning from her lonely cottage in Dulditch. With her thin lips tight-drawn, and the eyes, set deep in her sharp brown face, very bright and determined, she walked through the heat of a summer noon the four miles to the workhouse, and returning, brought with her the few weeks old orphan baby of which one of her sons had been the father.

'No child o' my flesh and blood shorn't be a work'us brat – not while I live, it shorn't – ef I starve for it,' said Rosa Weeks.

So for her dead George's boy, in her old age, Rosa took up the burden of her youth again, going with half rations that the child might have bread, tearing up her poor stock of linen to make him clothes. The allowance she had from the parish – the weekly two shillings and half-stone of flour – was not sufficient to support the child as well as herself. Milk must be bought for the child. Therefore she bent her stiff back and strained her old limbs to labour again – to field work when she could get the work to do, to stone-picking, to acorn-gathering, when that was not to be obtained. A fierce old Ruth, she quarrelled and swore and fought among the gleaners once more, grabbing her own share and that of others where she could get it – for the sake 'o' th' buoy.'

'Th' buoy' the while, together with the sticks she had collected on the way, lying in the old green go-cart which had been the cradle of all her children; beneath him the bottle of cold tea, the slice of bread intended for refreshment in the pauses of labour.

When 'th' buoy' was unusually refractory, a neighbour's larger baby would be hired at the price of her 'wittles' and a ha'penny a day to 'shug' the green go-cart while Rose worked near by. For the boy, even at the earliest age, would never lie staring placidly at the sky overhead when he awoke, as would the more satisfactory babies of the class, but would kick and shout, and clamber up the side of the cart, and get wrong things into his mouth, and generally make his presence felt. It was the sun and the wind beating early and late upon his uncovered face which, added to his originally swarthy complexion and coal-black hair, gave him such a gipsy look perhaps. That, and the wandering glance of his wild dark eyes and the fashion of the garments in which Rosa clothed his early years.

It was a sight to make one laugh, or weep, to see little 'Jarge' Weeks toddling off to school in his nondescript array. His tiny trousers made out of an old black and white large-checked shawl, which had for about forty years adorned Rosa's own shoulders; his coat fashioned from her dark green petticoat and cut in accordance with the exigencies of the petticoat shape; his hat of the same material as his trousers.

When Jarge attained to years of discernment he fought against that cap, taking pains to lose it in all sorts of irrecoverable places. But the parish of Dulditch could not hide the mongrel head-gear. It was as the actions of the just, which are said to survive and flourish under the most unkindly circumstances. It was like the ointment of the right hand which bewrayeth itself. Poor Jarge's abhorred millinery was, times beyond number, rescued and restored to him. It was stoned from the highest tree, picked out from the deepest 'pit,' sifted from the widest dust-bin. Grown desperate, the owner and a co-conspirator poked it under a 'hape o' quicks' in one of 'Rober'son's' fields, to which, having secreted a box of matches, they proceeded to set fire. But ill-luck attended this bold stroke also. The farmer appearing on the scene before the weeds were well alight, the delinquents scampered off, one only being recognised by the cap beneath the 'quick' heaps. Poor Jarge went hungry, bruised, and sore to bed that night, thrashed, in addition to the many promiscuous thrashings which daily fell to his share, by particular request of the tyrant Rober'son.

When his troubles with his cap were past – for in a world given over to decay even Gran'mother Weeks' confections succumb at last – trouble was by no means ended for Jarge. Trouble and 'th' buoy' were akin from birth, it seemed – trouble and restlessness and mischief.

It was he that stoned the ducks and chickens in the Brightlands farmyard (who was discovered in that act, rather, for everybody stoned them – to 'hull a ston' and lame th' old gander,' or to break the wing 'o' th' old yiller hin,' being considered by the youth of the neighbourhood a legitimate pastime and a praiseworthy attention to their employer's poultry); who ran the colts in the Fen; who infuriated the hitherto pacifically inclined bull 'i' Rober'son's midder' till that animal, declining apparently to tackle his lawful prey, turned his unwelcome attention upon Betty Barker, going, can in hand, up to the farm for the 'skim milk' which was her portion. The bull put down his head and bellowed so alarmingly at Betty that that comfortable old body must needs take to her heels and run, an exercise which brought on her 'heart's disease' badly, compelling her to sit for an hour in the farm kitchen to have her courage revived and her palpitations lessened by doses of plum cake and beer. On her return journey she was accompanied by two sturdy champions, who, with sticks and stones and pitchforks, so infuriated the bull that he showed fight in earnest, and had to have a ring put through his nose, with a yard of chain dangling from it, at last.

It was Jarge who was the refractory boy of the school; who was always kept in for his own fault and that of other children during play and dinner hours; who threw a book in the mistress's face. It was he who took live mice in his trousers' pockets to church; whom the outraged clerk dragged up by the ear and set in the centre of the chancel steps, an awful warning to the congregation – some other boy having laughed aloud. It was Jarge – profane young rascal to whom nothing was sacred – who, coming upon the rector's little daughter gathering a lapful of the cuckoo flowers that whitened the lush herbage bordering the 'dekes i' th' waater midder,' chased that fleet-footed little maid homeward, catching her at last by the pollard-alder at the gate. The child struggled and fought and scratched in his arms. 'Yu air a little buty, yu air, and I *wull* kiss yer,' Jarge declared, which feat he finally accomplished; and not all little Margaret's entreaties, nor all her tears, nor her passionate agonies of remorse, could save Jarge's skin from a hiding for that exploit.

For it was as that sweet time of year when 'once more the Heavenly Power makes all things new,' when the white thorn is at its prime, and the cuckoo is shouting in the woods; and Margaret's big brother, home from his first term at college, was lying flat on his back at no great distance from the alder, staring up to the fleecy white clouds sailing over the blue. It was the vigorous arm of the parson's son that saw to the dusting of master Jarge's jacket on that occasion.

'It wasn't that I minded his kissing so much,' Margaret sobbingly informed her avenger when the beating was over and she and her brother had turned their backs on the offender, lying stretched at his full length beneath the alder, his arms above his neck, his face buried deep in the grass; 'it was that his jacket smelt so funnily.'

That patchwork, queer-fashioned little jacket of his was always coming into contact with the correcting rod. Rosa's 'buoy' was the 'scorge' of the parish, it was allowed on all sides, and heavily the 'scorge' was 'scorged' – without that improvement accruing from such drastic measures as Solomon has led us to expect. The wicked light did not die out of Jarge's wandering black eyes, nor did his 'anticking' cease.

It was out of respect for his grandmother alone that 'Rober'son up to the faarm' hired the youth, on his leaving school, at the wage of three shillings a week, to 'plough and to sow, to reap and to mow, and to be a farmer's boy.' All the neighbours remarked that better days were coming for Rosa at last, and that Jarge would now have a 'chancet' of making a 'man i' th' warld.'

But only disaster followed this propitious commencement. Jarge jammed the tips of his fingers in the cake-crusher, broke his ankle through dangling his legs among the machinery of the chaff-cutter, was caught in the act of stealing eggs in the waggon lodge. On one occasion, being entrusted with a gun for the frightening of crows in the young barley, he carried it home, and in the dusk of the spring evening discharged it through the keyhole of his grandmother's neighbour's door. And thereby did Jarge set fire to the shawl which hung over that door to keep the draught out, and frighten old Maundy Harper till her 'inside was all of a trimble,' as she declared. Furthermore, having been enrolled a member of the Juvenile Band of Hope – thanks to the attraction of a teetotal tea in the schoolroom – it was Jarge who was brought home on the same evening dead drunk, and laid at his grandmother's door. 'Meelyer Sprite's Arnest' had 'dared him' to drink the mixture which had wrought his undoing, he explained later on. To do what he was dared to do was the beginning and end of Jarge's creed of honour.

Through all, although Rosa had set her face grimly, and laid on lustily with tongue and stick, she did not lose her love for 'th' buoy' nor her faith in him; she did not hesitate to chastise him heavily for every crime, authentic or otherwise, laid to his charge, but she made a mortal enemy of that one who carried in such reports to her. Her life must have been but an uneasy one through all those years, for, the urchin once out of sight, she never could have known an instant's peace.

Every day as the time for his return from school, from play, from work, came round, Rosa, a shawl flung over her head to protect it from the rain, a brown hand held before her eyes to shield them from the sun, would stand at the garden gate looking anxiously up and down the road. Her lips would be always moving, for Rosa has the bad habit of talking to herself. Ten to one in passing her you would catch amid her whispered mutterings some word about 'th' buoy.'

For th' buoy's sake she fought against all the ills that attack old women – against feebleness, weariness, illness even.

Once, in the days when that historic cap and the small trousers of the large check were newly-fashioned, Rosa was smitten by her old enemy the 'browntitus,' and a more than usually serious illness laid her low. It seemed to those who looked in upon her, 'to du the p'or ol' mawther a han's tarn' as she lay upon her bed, that she must succumb. They impressed that fact upon her after the unvarying fashion of such bedside comforters.

'Rose, bor – p'or ol' dare, yer a-dyin'; yer hour's come, bor. Don't set yerself agin it, nor fly i' th' Lord's faace.'

Rosa flung up a touzled grey head from the pillow; her nightshirt, torn open at the throat to assist the difficult breathing, showed all the lean brown bosom; her fury gave her strength.

'I ain't a-dyin',' she cried fiercely. 'Th' Lord! – what d'ye think the Lord's arter, then, to taak me when th' buoy's a wantin' on me ivery tarn. Whu's to see arter th' buoy, ef so be as I'm tuk? Darn yer – I 'on't die, I tell yer I 'on't!'

And she didn't.

Jarge, grown tall enough, it was, who used to thrash his grandmother, the neighbours said, paying back all those chastisements of his boyhood with interest. It was allowed on his behalf that, much as he owed the old woman, he had 'a sight' to put up with. For, originally a clean and tidy body enough, her sight failing her as time went on, dirt accumulated apace in Rosa's once wholesome little domain. On floors and walls and furniture and clothing it accumulated, and became mixed with the food, and encrusted on the saucepan and frying-pan, and ingrained in the sheets and table-cloths.

In spite of the corrective chastisements from Jarge, the sight grew worse instead of better, the dirt increased, so that the shirt laid out for 'th' buoy' against he wished to 'shiffen hisself' of a Sunday morning was as black as that he 't'rew off' on the Saturday night; so that the bacon dumpling prepared for the young man's principal meal, made in a dirty basin, boiled in a filthy cloth, served on a table-cloth which had been used by mistake to wipe the floor, was not exactly an appetising meal.

Small wonder if such food had a bad effect on Jarge's temper as well as his stomach. But he was kind to his grandmother too, getting up to wait on her at night if she was restless, or her cough was bad; except for occasional outbreaks of temper, putting up with her sharp tongue and her villainous cooking with more patience than a good many better men might have shown.

Meanwhile his character as a labourer, as a member of a peaceful and law-abiding community, did not improve. He was dismissed from 'Rober'son's,' taken on, dismissed again. Having some real or fancied cause of complaint against his fellow-workman, Ben Pitcher, he waylaid the man one night as he returned from the 'White Hart,' where both had been drinking, tripped him up, kicked him into insensibility, and left him by the side of the road. Then, having at last made Dulditch too hot to hold him, Jarge took himself off, and for years none of us knew his whereabouts or what had become of him.

Rough attempts were made on all sides to console the grandmother. She was 'well rid o' bad rubbage,' she was told. 'Th' buoy were allust a mucky chap,' who would come to the 'gallers as sure as nothin'.' But Rosa was but a 'snaisty' old woman even in her sorrow, and did not make polite replies to her Job's comforters.

'They wos all agin th' buoy,' she muttered to herself, sitting in the loneliness of her now nearly total blindness, nose and knees together over her little scrap of fire, that tiny chair which had been little Jarge's, and Jarge's father's before him, pulled up close to her side. 'All agin 'm! an' kep' a pesterin' o' me wi' all mander o' lies. But th' buoy were a good buoy, that he wor! He were gone awaay to git wark, but he'd come back, sure enough. Th' buoy'ud come back!'

We heard rumours in the course of time that Jarge had enlisted. But it was not till after several years that there came a letter from him in India to his grandmother, telling how he was sick of a fever, but was going to kill the 'niggers' when he was well enough; and how, that pleasant duty being accomplished, he should come back to see the old lady once more.

The letter was full of the terms of endearment and the pious phrasing inevitable in the letters of the poor – was, in fact, a 'butiful letter,' as the neighbours all agreed. Many a score times it was read to Rose, who, when no one with learning enough for the task was by, strained her own nearly blind eyes over the worn and crumpled paper – Rose, who never had read a written word in her life! – restoring it always to that place between her soiled dress and her dirty stays where, since her blindness, all her treasures had accumulated.

'He's a good buoy, and I allust knowed it,' she muttered as she folded the precious missive in her trembling brown hands. 'Folks was agin 'm, but he's a good buoy, an' he's a comin' back.'

Meanwhile Rosa, her house and all that was in it growing dirtier and dirtier, the attention of the relieving officer was called to the state of things. There came a Tuesday morning when, instead of her two shillings and her half-stone of flour, she received that dreaded official invitation which is conveyed in 'an order for the house.'

Then arose in that corner of Dulditch a commotion, the like of which has not been heard before. 'Old Rose to go to th' work'us. Rose Weeks that had warked her fingers to th' bone, p'or old mawther, while she'd eyes left in 'r hid ter see. 'Twore a shame – a cryin' shame!' the other old women said, watching the relieving officer cross the road to Rosa's cottage, being very careful he did not overhear.

This official is cordially disliked and feared in Dulditch, for he has not a gentle or conciliatory manner, and those in receipt of relief credit him with a power he does not possess, putting down every unpopular measure of those in authority to the account of this agent. Go where he may, this red-faced, loud-voiced servant of the guardians is not regarded as exactly a favourite; but wherever his not very pleasant duty may have called him, to the performance of whatever ungrateful task, he could not have been assailed with more violent and reprehensible language than that with which Rosa greeted him now. She, for one, had no fear of him. Of what in all her sturdy struggle for life had that unflinching soul of hers been afraid?

Powley is a big and burly man, but he beat a hasty retreat from that dirty cottage. Rosa, stumbling over the threshold, pursued him down the little path between the gooseberry bushes, pouring forth a stream of language which would not have disgraced the mouth of the proverbial trooper.

Rosa would not go to the workhouse; she would die of starvation, she would rot in a ditch before she was dragged there! We all knew it well. All her life she had talked of the extreme measures to which she would resort sooner than become a 'porpoise.' As year by year the hated fate had seemed to loom nearer and nearer her resolution had strengthened. And now, added to all that natural and acquired distaste, was this further consideration: if she was not at the cottage, waiting there for him, what, when at length he came home, was to become of 'th' buoy'?

For the present, at any rate, the necessity against which Rosa has set her face is averted. The magnificent allowance from a grateful country, proud to help all brave, independent souls to carry on the fight of existence in the best of all possible worlds, is graciously continued. Nay, in that great country's regard for the well-being of an aged daughter of the soil, even an extra shilling a week has been provided wherewith to reward those neighbours who assist Rosa in her efforts to prevent the dirt, in which she lives, moves, and has her being, from quite overpowering her.

And Rosa quarrels with and swears at those neighbours who 'come a-meddlin' along o' her.' She loudly accuses them of robbing her linen-chest and her larder. They are poor enough to, those good women, but the slice of perspiring yellow cheese upon which the sugar and the candle-dripping are impartially spilt, the dirty wisps of nightcaps, and the yellow-hued rags appropriate to various uses, could hardly tempt the poorest.

Meelyer Sprite, in spite of a strong desire on her part to annex the weekly shilling, had to relinquish the post of 'redder-up' for Rosa, or murder would have been done.

'Meelyer were allust a light-fingered mawther,' Rosa says, talking her over dispassionately now that she has successfully routed the lady in question. 'Bor, I niver could abide 'er, th' best o' times. I'd a sight suner be smuddered wi' muck than ha' that hussy imitatin' to fye out my plaaces for me.'

So the neighbours 'lend a han',' as they say among them, and, like all work that belongs to no one in particular, the business is not very well done. From Powley, great in dread authority, threats now and again come.

'You'd be best in the "House," old lady,' he calls out to her, not unkindly, stopping his gig for a moment at her door on a Tuesday morning. 'I shall have to get you an order for the "House".'

Rosa, rage in her sightless eyes, comes, stumbling in her haste, to the door, shakes a threatening fist in the direction of the voice, and curses the relieving officer, loud and deep. Powley, safe in his gig, gives a chuck to the reins lying on his knee and laughs as he rides away.

Yet if she does not go to the workhouse what in saddest earnest is to become of Rosa? She is no longer able to pick up the sticks over which she and her neighbour Maundy have been wont to quarrel so bitterly. Maundy's stack grows bigger and bigger; she is queen of the situation at last. But Rosa's coal bill, although she puts on each atom of fuel grudgingly with the fingers with which she is mixing her flour or breaking bread, cripples her resources. She cannot see to glean the ears of corn; she can no longer earn a sixpence by going an 'arrand' for a neighbour, nor by tending a neighbour's child. Starve as she does, she cannot pinch her stomach enough to make up the three pounds needed for rent 'come' Michaelmas Day. If she can't pay rent she must turn out. Where to go? The shadow of that hated inevitable refuge of the worthy and the worthless agricultural poor draws nearer and nearer upon Rosa's horizon every day.

But Rosa herself has no fear. 'Wild horses 'on't drag me theer' is all she says; repeats, perhaps, when pressed about her plans for the future, that she can 'allust die in a ditch.'

So we pass her, standing at her cottage gate – the staunch old soul who has made her brave fight and who is not beaten yet. She is not of those whose 'feet and head come together in life's pilgrimage'; her slight, skinny figure is still upright as a dart. The grey hair, with its untidy, crooked parting, is blown away from the dark, sharp face with its thousand wrinkles. The brown eyes are sightless, but they are bright still, and turn with an eager watchfulness down the tree-shadowed road – the road that leads past the school. Those same eyes used to gaze anxiously down that chequered path of sunshine and of shade in the days when Jarge was the bad boy of the village.

She is waiting for him still.

Oh, Jarge, Jarge in India! When the shades of night come on and give you pause in that occupation of 'nigger' slaying, with which in Dulditch we believe you to be so fully engaged – Jarge, the truant, the liar, the incorrigible, the hopeless – do you never, as you lie upon that bed you have made for yourself, tossing, fevered and sleepless, in the sweltering night, do you never see that road with the shadow of the palm-leaved chestnut branches moving over the sunlight; do you never see that withered, small figure waiting, patient, faithful, undoubting, by the cottage gate, muttering incessantly to herself of 'th' buoy' so long in coming?

⊰✴⊱

Since the above was written that question of Workhouse versus Death in a Ditch has, in Rosa Weeks' case, been settled by an Agent who arranges such-like difficult matters for us now and again.

Rosa made desperate efforts, but she must have failed. Heroically she pinched that poor old body of hers, denying it the warmth and food it needed, but that enormous sum of three pounds needed against Michaelmas Day could never have been saved by such means. She must have failed, but that 'Heavenly Death' which provides for all saved her that bitter defeat.

The battle she fought all through her long life is over for Rosa, thank God. She stands no longer at the garden gate; the door of the cottage she loved is locked; the key will be given to her landlord together with what had been secured for Rosa's rent when on the eleventh of October he comes to claim his dues. The women who undressed her when she was dead found the little screw of shillings and pence tied to her filthy stays.

So God rest you, Rosa Weeks! Not realising how hard the struggle was, you fought a brave fight. Never once naming the name of duty to yourself, your duty was nobly done. Against your name may be written the words 'mortua est,' which, being interpreted, may be taken to mean in your case, Rosa, that your work being nobly done, you have earned your discharge.

THE FAMILY OF WOODMAN HARPER

IN one of a row of tidy, red-brick cottages adjoining the village inn Maundy Harper lives with her granddaughter Marthy.

The inn is picturesque, with irregular roof, with diamond-paned windows, above the tops of whose low blinds geranium and fuchsia blossoms show. The square of garden ground appertaining does not join the inn, but is beyond the grass-grown yard where the few passing customers tie their horses, where the dogs' kennels are, behind hedges too tall for any flowers but the aspiring sunflower and hollyhock to peep above; but the fragrance of wallflower, of carnation, of mignonette betrays its whereabouts to the passer-by, the innkeeper being a lover of flowers and skilful in their rearing.

Fifty yards farther on, on the opposite side of the road, is the village shop, where the trades of butcher, baker, chemist, grocer, draper, boot and shoe maker are combined by one Theophilus

Littleproud, who is licensed to sell tobacco besides, and is agent for various kinds of tea, and who is not at all incommoded by the gigantic nature of his undertakings, nor unduly cramped in the ten feet square space at the disposal of himself, his customers, and his merchandise. Built on to the shop is the tiny store-house and the dwelling-house, gabled, with thatched roof and ivy-covered walls, and beyond these lie the orchard and the fields on the outskirts of Rober'son's farm.

A few acres of land, tilled for him at odd hours by customers desirous of wiping off their scores, are rented by the landlord of the 'White Hart.' A portion of the field immediately opposite the inn has been fenced in by a stout wooden rail. Here the young men and hobbledehoys of the village sit, and against it the elders lounge when their day's work is done.

Because of its situation in the centre of the commercial interests of Dulditch, this spot is spoken of there as 'up-town.' Small messengers to Littleproud's, carrying the maternal order for cheese, soap, candles, a small propitiatory coin towards payment of the standing account clasped in their hot palms, are bidden not to 'l'iter up-town.' Edith, Gartrood, Beetruss, found in lively conversation with the frequenters of the spot, 'jammin' about up-town,' get the rough side of their fathers' tongues.

Among the best looking, best conducted, and most promising of the young men wont to kick their heels on the railing in the midst of the gay distractions of this alluring spot was 'Robbud,' son of Woodman Harper. Of Woodman's seven children, of whom Robbud is the youngest, not one has turned out badly. The parents are chapel-goers, have 'got religion,' but the idea of giving thanks where thanks are customarily considered to be due for this mercy has not entered the good people's heads. It is because of the superior nature of their children's up-bringing, Maundy, who is a great talker on her own affairs, informs you in her own language.

It is because she, their mother, 'ha'n't had no sorft lubberly ways wi' 'em, but ha' naggled at 'em to keep 'em straight, and ha'n't encouraged no antickin', for her part.' And because their father 'niver made no bones about it, nayther, but ha' larruped 'em whenever he was i' the mind to 't.' It is because of these parental customs that the Woodman's boys have done so well.

'And now, bless th' Lord, He have rewarded us for it!' Maundy says. She is a plump and pretty and comfortable-looking old body of seventy and more, and she sits upright in her chintz-covered chair in a chimney corner, fenced in by curtains composed of all materials, patterns, and colours to shield her from the free ingress of air through a door badly hung on the 'jimmers' and shrinking away from the 't'rushold.' 'He ha' rewarded us,' she says. And 'Woodman,' the big, red-faced old man opposite, with the pinched nose and the dragged-down, peevish lip and watery blue eyes, gives a grunt of acquiescence.

Maundy apologises for her husband's glum demeanour. He has a delicacy about speaking in the presence of 'the quality,' it appears. She herself is not troubled with any such foolish diffidence. Without the smallest encouragement she gives you particulars of all her many illnesses, with detailed accounts of her seven confinements. You learn with which son she had a 'hard time,' with which daughter an easy 'gettin'-up.' If you heard all of this yesterday, she tells it to you over again to-day, using identical phrases; and will enter on the same theme in the same words to-morrow if you give her the chance.

She tells you, too, how Bill, 'up to Lunnon,' her eldest, with thirteen children of his own, never forgets his duty to his parents, but always remembers to send her a quarter of a pound of tea 'come' Christmas, together with two ounces of tobacco for his father. How 'Arnest i' the shares' and 'Harbart over to Brummagum' make shift to allow her and her old man a shilling a week 'atween 'em' for house rent. How Jabez, who was a 'butiful writer,' always wrote home two letters a year, and never 'missed of 'em,' till he got mixed up in the machine he was tending in his professional capacity, and was cut in pieces.

And then she comes to Robbud, the Benjamin of her heart, who is first team-man 'up to' Rober'son's farm; who has 'never giv' her an onkind word, nor so much as tarned his tongue in 's hid to s' faather all the thutty years he ha' been born.'

Recalled by this to a sense of his responsibilities as parent, the old man on the opposite side of the hearth gets up and, fetching his stick, hobbles out. Looking about him with his weak, blear eyes, he discovers the object on his accustomed perch, poisoning the evening air, sweet from the mingled odours of the 'White Hart' garden, with the fumes of the villainous tobacco he smokes, a couple of hobbledehoys by his side.

'Hare be yar old man, Bob,' one of these boon companions says, giving his neighbour a slow drive in the ribs with his elbow.

Robbud smokes on with composure and in silence; his placid blue eyes watch the old man, with angry mutterings, cross the road. Standing before his son, Woodman animadverts in no measured terms upon the hulking form of his offspring, upon the tobacco he smokes, upon his companions, upon the hands that rest in shameful idleness upon his knees. The men at his side laugh and jeer; Robbud listens in submissive silence, his ruminative eyes upon his father's face.

'Be them peas sticked i' th' gaarden?' the old man firmly demands, pointing with a trembling stick to the narrow strip of land running toward the wheat-field at the back of his cottage.

'I done 'em las' night,' says Rob patiently, sucking at his pipe.

'Ha' yer stowed away them faggits I ligged home this arternune?'

This also, it appears, Robbud has done in the half-hour before supper previous to giving himself over to 'up-town' dissipations.

'Then,' with savage triumph, 'yer ha'n't drawed yer mother no waater, for I seen th' empty buckets a standin' by th' t'rushold as I come by. Don't sit a laggerin' theer, yer great idle hulk; go and fetch yer mother her waater.'

With that, pointing authoritatively with his shaking stick to the well standing before the row of cottages, and common to them all, the woodman hobbles off.

'Crack that old fule o' th' nut, and ha' done wi' 'm,' one of the hobbledehoys advises.

'Oh, ah!' Robbud says in good-tempered derision of his friend's advice. Slowly he puts his offending short pipe in his pocket, spits with much thoughtfulness, having previously contemplated the chosen spot for some instants, at the grass between his knees, and, shuffling from his perch, follows his father across the road, and proceeds to do his bidding, strong, manly-looking fellow that he is, as docilely as a child.

He has been a hard and untiring taskmaster to the lot of them, wife as well as sons, has Woodman Harper.

Robbud, with stolid good humour, interposes that broad, strong frame of his between the rageful old man and the pretty, comfortable mother many a time still, although Woodman is getting on for eighty years of age.

'He've passed his 'llotted time,' the neighbours say, with small indulgence for the crusty old man. 'When th' Lord 'll be plased to take 'm nobody 'on't fret.'

'Po'r harmless old critter, le'r 'm be!' says Bob, the strong and patient.

⚜

On a day when the brazen faces of the sunflowers showed with native effrontery above the broad, brown-green hedge of the inn garden, and within that fragrant inclosure mignonette and marigold ran riot, disdaining their box-edged boundaries, when the field behind the Harpers' cottage was a blaze of 'poppy-mingled, green-eared corn,'

172

and in the field across the road the 'dim-eyed, curious bee' was busy among the white clover blossom, Maundy Harper stopped me as I sauntered by.

There is something unfamiliar in her pleasant, plump face, but Maundy's accustomed 'bedience, her unfailing greeting, 'Servant, miss,' is made with her habitual decorum.

'Miss, my Robbud is a-dyin', and he's wishful to say good-bye to ye,' she says, making the astounding announcement with an admirable calm.

Dismayed, I stare speechless into the pretty old face, its crisp waves of white hair tucked away beneath the frilled net cap, the cap itself surmounted by the small dark shawl without which, summer and winter, Maundy never appears, then hurriedly I enter the cottage.

Old Woodman, sitting drearily on the edge of the well, his hands clasped on the stick between his knees, looks up at me miserably with the bleared blue eyes, but says nothing as I pass.

Against the window, beneath the short red blind, which makes for the passer-by such a cheery illumination at night when the Harpers' little lamp is lit behind it, and by the oak table with the carved legs which had belonged to generations of Harpers, Robbud is sitting.

He is arrayed in his Sunday suit, honouring his dying day as a holiday, and on his big feet are his Sunday boots, unlaced. The best suit is not moulded to the sturdy figure yet, and does not show Bob Harper at his best, but even in that stiff and unlovely disguise one cannot help seeing what a fine specimen the young man is of his class. I myself – an elderly maiden lady, who never, even at the more propitious seasons of my life, concerned myself with the constituents of masculine beauty and who am now arrived at an age and a condition when such considerations are out of place – even I am conscious of looking with admiration at the big curly head of the man, at the dark, weather-stained face, out of which the patient, honest eyes gleam bluely, at the broad shoulders.

Dying – he? Reassured, I smile at the idea.

'What has come to you, Robert? Your mother tells me you are not feeling well to-day.'

He puts out his big, horny hand; there is a look of great solemnity in his eyes.

'I'm a dyin', miss – dyin' – tha's what I'm a doin',' he says.

'But why – of what?'

He presses his crossed hands upon his broad chest.

'It is hare my mis'ry lay – right hare!' he says; then, clutching at his neck-handkerchief and his shirt, tears them open, and with a gesture of despair flings his arms upon the table before him and drops his head upon them.

Turning to the mother, I suggest her sending at once for the doctor.

'Miss, we ha' sent. We ha'n't stopped at no expense, but ha' hired Littleproud's dickey-cart. Dan'l Luck have druv orf at six this mornin'. Th' dickey and him's back a matter o' t'ree hour an' more, but not a glint ha' we caught o' th' doctor. I doubt as he'll be tew late.'

Robert, sitting at the table, hopelessly moved his bowed-down head.

'Tew late!' he echoed. 'I'm done for, miss; my mis'ry's great.'

'His mis'ry's great,' his mother repeated.

'If his chest is sore,' I said, irritated by his mother's almost cheerful resignation, 'you had better rub his chest; you had better put on a poultice – you –'

Robert, with the tragic gesture so new to him, stretched out his hand as if to silence me. He rose to his feet and with a heavy, uneven tread began to pace up and down the little space between the window and the door.

'He's on th' club, bless 'm!' his mother said as she watched him. 'He's a gettin' his eight shillun' a week. He've nothin' so fur to trouble 's mind – my po'r boy ha'n't.'

'Theer's th' bur'al club too, mother,' Bob reminded her hoarsely, blundering up and down the room.

She sighed, and wiped her eyes and nose with the duster she always kept for that purpose lying in the chimney corner.

'Yes, theer's the bur'al club, bless th' Lord!' she acquiesced. 'Theer'll be enough and to spare. Don't yer worrit yerself about none o' them mortial consarns, Robbud.'

I learnt on inquiry that the club doctor had been visited two days ago, Robbud 'farin' so wonnerful p'orly.' He had walked the six miles to Runwich after work was done. There he had had two of his wisdom teeth pulled out, the doctor having discovered for himself that that was where the poor fellow's 'mis'ry' lay. On his homeward journey, after partaking of refreshment at the Runwich Hotel, Robbud had lost his way. According to his own account he had wandered all night in a wood where the trees and the undergrowth had been so thick he had choked for want of air, and where creepers, 'ground-ivory and

174

blackberry brummles,' had caught him round the t'roat and held down his feet till at last he was dead beat and couldn't stir.

'He were delurious,' the old mother said, with an explanatory nod. 'I tell'd um from th' fust he were delurious. We know well theer's a bit of a spinney, but theer ain't, so to say, a wood near nor by. He were all of a muck wi' moss and laves and rubbage when he come home, same as if he'd passed 's night of a deke i' th' roadside.'

Reassured as to Robert's condition, but a little shocked by the mental picture called up of that pattern son sleeping off the effects of the Runwich 'King's Head' brandy and incurring a cold on his chest in a ditch by the wayside, I left the Harpers' cottage.

In the afternoon of the same day, having to pass that way again, I found Maundy standing sentinel against the door. She lifted her hands, palm outward, as though to ward off my approach.

'Go yer ways,' she said, with a composed solemnity. 'Go yer ways, and let us wark orf our trouble alone. 'Tis th' doctor's orders that no one come anigh us. 'Tis th' dip'thary, miss.'

I had not perhaps too much respect for the opinion of a doctor who mistook, even in its earlier stages diphtheria for toothache, and I took no heed of his warning.

'Robbud 'on't heer nothin' o' goin' ter bed,' Maundy told me when I stood by her side. 'He niver were a contrairy boy to 's faather and me in 's life afore. Howsomdever now theer ain't no a-gettin' of um to 's bed.'

Behind her, through the open door, I could see Woodman Harper seated on the edge of a chair and leaning forward upon his stick. There came a heavy, shuffling step upon the brick floor, and Robbud passed him by.

The old man lifted his head and looked up at his son, the water thick in his eyes, the painful drops trickling slowly down the wrinkled channels of his red cheeks.

'Go to bed, my dare,' the father said, with a sob now and again between the words – 'go to y'r bed, Robbud. 'Tain't nat'ral, my son, that a man should die out of 's bed.'

Robert shuffled past him without a word, with a face livid now beneath the sun and weather stain, with traces on it, in the broad glare of day, of an agony past expression.

With a sweeping motion of his arms, to remove his mother and me from his path, he stumbled past, and dragged his heavy, unlaced boots over the yards of roadway that led to the inn.

Following him, fearfully we saw him enter the long, sour-smelling room, which, with its sanded floor, big table of discoloured deal, its high settles by the fireside, and its dozen chairs ranged round the dirty walls, holds such an irresistible attraction for the male population of Dulditch. The half-dozen men, sitting with their heads against the wall and their feet scraping the floor beneath their chairs, turned slow eyes of inquiry upon the figure of Robbud entering, so unfamiliar in its holiday attire on a working day, in its wild eyes full of suffering, in its drooping shoulders and stumbling gait.

In a voice that was terrible to hear he asked for drink – 'Ale; gi' me ale, for th' love o' God.'

Beer was brought him; but when he tried to drink, the sight was sad to see, for the liquor refused to go down his throat, but returned, streaming over him from mouth and nose.

'Blame me if iver I seen the like o' that!' the landlord said, a small, half-starved looking man with beady, black eyes, looking round upon his seated guests. 'An' 'twere Bullard's best!'

. With a look of despair Robbud dropped the pint mug he was holding; it split into a dozen pieces on the floor. Without a word he turned away. But having reached the door – fallen upon it, rather – he stopped there and looked back.

The rough men sitting there, gazing with dull eyes, open-mouthed; the loquacious little landlord who resented the poverty of his customers as a wrong personal to himself – these the woodman's son had known for all his life. The ugly bare room with its familiar stale odours, its small window blocked with plants, the clay-coloured walls – a picture from the *Illustrated News* of the entry of Princess Alexandra into London and a five-years-old coloured almanac their only adornment – Robbud looked round solemnly upon it all. Vaguely he knew that there were in the world places of greater splendour than this, of larger political import, of livelier entertainment. He had never desired to see them. He knew that there were men who had made themselves great names, of whom the world thought highly – had he not himself seen Joseph Arch in the flesh at Runwich 'come tew yare ago'?

But 'what is the British Empire to Battersea'? What interest for poor Robbud had these phantoms of great people? They were not so real to him as were Daniel and Job and Samuel, about whom he read 'Sunday evenin's' in the Bible at home. Of what importance all they could have told him in comparison with the ''orsepittle' experiences of Dan'l Luck, of which one never tired to hear; with the unsatisfactory domestic arrangements maintaining in Ben Pitcher's home; with the bits of gossip gleaned during the day by Littleproud "cross to th' shop,' and retailed by him bit by bit at night over his beer in the inn kitchen?

'Good-bye,' Robbud said hoarsely, and waved his arms with a rough but tragic gesture of farewell. 'Good-bye to ye, mates – an' feer-ye-well.'

He shuffled heavily out into the road again, tumbled over the threshold of his own door and past the miserable old father weeping still, still calling upon the son, never refractory before, to go to bed.

Maundy, following closely, laid a hand on the bent, broad shoulder.

'Don't ye mind what yer faather's a sayin'? Go to bed at oncet, my boy – du!' she said.

With a feeble push she guided him towards the door which opened out of the room upon the dark and crooked stairs.

Docile as ever, the poor fellow followed the motion of the guiding hand. We heard his difficult, halting progress upward, his great boots catching with a hollow sound at each stair. We drew a breath of relief as the chamber floor was gained. There was a couple of shuffling steps upon the bare boards overhead and then a heavy fall.

His mother and I made a rush for the stairs, but the old man, flinging away with his stick, without which for years he had not walked, was before us. When we reached the room (emphatically 'the' room; there was but that, and Robbud had lain for all his life on a bed drawn across the foot of that of his father and mother) we found Woodman Harper sitting on the floor holding upon his breast the head of his dead son.

Robbud had been popular in Dulditch – 'a wonnerful quite chap' was universally said of him (this, locally, is high praise) – and everyone was sorry for the poor old mother. It was held to be a pity Robbud had died without a 'draught of medicine,' that he had not been given a 'chancet.'

But the poor are very easily reconciled to the inevitable; each one finds his own private wrongs and troubles sufficient for his 'soon choked mind,' and a club doctor is a powerful person. If you don't approve of his treatment or acquiesce in his death certificates it is wiser to say nothing about it. The women agreed it was a pity his mother hadn't tied 'a bit o' tar-line round her son's t'roat.' That remedy had cured Meelyer Sprite's youngest o' the 'whoopin' corf,' and might, it was thought, have been efficacious in this instance. But Maundy –

177

'poor old mawther!' – was, they supposed, 'duzzy-like' with grief, and 'niver so much as thought on 't.'

As for Maundy herself, she to whom her boy had been so good, hardly any diminution of her cheerfulness is to be observed in her. Religion is to the woodman's wife a very real thing. Her literal exposition of the text makes her sound even a little blasphemous at times. She is so confident of her own intimate acquaintance with the workings of the mind of the Creator, of His alacrity in taking any hint communicated in the long prayers she makes for the readjustment of her own affairs. She has such an unshaken belief in the streets and the gates of gold and of pearl; of the silver wings and the harp that await her beyond the blue of the sky. Even the undying worm and the unquenchable flame, the portion of the greater part of her neighbours, whose names she glibly gives you, do not subdue her cheerful optimism with regard to her own future and that of her kin.

Robbud had been 'a good-livin'' boy. 'He had niver so much as tarned 's tongue in 's teeth agin his faather, who had been wonnerful erritatin' and snasty wi' th' boy.' He had saved 'ten pound,' which with the money from the 'bur'al club' would keep his parents in comfort for years, 'and th' Lord had took um to glory and giv' um his reward.'

'She've a terrufic sperrit, Maundy have,' the neighbours say in humble admiration. 'She du kape up, and no mistake. Robbud, he were a wonnerful quite sort of a chap; and he right analysed' (idolised) 'his mother.'

For all her cheerfulness it is to be supposed that Maundy misses the big, docile young fellow who used to fall asleep in his chair over the fire on winter evenings and would wake up and talk to her when 'faather' was gone to bed. Going out to draw her pails of water at the well – so cool and pretty, with hart's tongue growing up to the very brink and shining through the darkening, narrowing shaft as far as eye can reach – she casts a wistful eye, perhaps, upon that 'up-town' railing, where the young men of Dulditch still sit, their pipes in their mouths. They smoke and spit, laugh and make their rough, witless jokes, as if there were no such thing as parting or death in the world.

For some time after Bob Harper's death one or other of the hobbledehoys would slip ashamedly off the rail, and, shambling across the road, would draw the old woman's water. But there was always something a little shamefaced in the action; one of those left behind, with some allusion to the 'sorftness' displayed by Harbart or Tim or Horus, would set the rest 'a-sniggerin'.'

It was the dread of ridicule rather than hardness of heart which robbed the old woman of that welcome 'hand's tarn' long ago.

Maundy accepted the service and does without it with the same happy content which characterises her. Never has her optimism been known to fail.

Last winter I found her confined to her bed with a sprained ankle, a bruised back, a shoulder-bone out of joint. She had slipped and fallen over the 't'rushold' of the door one frosty morning. It is not a light matter for an old woman of close on eighty years to sustain such a shock. However, 'it might have been worse,' I said, using the time-honoured formula which presents itself naturally to the harassed mind when nothing more cheering remains to be said.

'It might have been worse, Maundy.'

'Why, tha's what I tell my Marthy,' the old woman says eagerly (Marthy is a grandchild who waits on her since her husband's death). 'Why, Marthy, bor, I say, I might ha' broke my spettacles!'

So with her round old face, rosy beneath its pretty snow-white hair, with her brown 'winsy' frock hanging in thick pleats from her waist, with her black shawl tied over her cap, and her red cloak on her shoulders, the bright old woman goes in all weathers at a slow trot down the chestnut-shaded road to the churchyard. Every day of her life she stands beneath the chestnuts that shadow the church wall, and looks over at her boy's grave.

It is a nameless grave, no headstone marks the spot, but as the year grows apace 'from flower to flower' every homely blossom that blows in the little garden behind the cottage is carried there. At the time of the poor fellow's death a porcelain wreath reposing on a bright green stand and protected by a glass case was sent from London by a girl in service there, upon whom Robbud, before she left Dulditch, was said to have been 'sweet.' If the poor girl thinks of her lover's grave as decorated by her gift, she is happy in her ignorance. The porcelain abomination is not upon the grave by any means. It lies shrouded in a spotted red and white pocket-handkerchief under Maundy Harper's bed.

'That might ha' got broke i' th' chachyud,' Maundy says complacently; 'there's allust mischerful boys abaout. Onder my bed I ha' got my eye on 't, and so 've Marthy, and when th' Lord have tuk me to glory, why, theer 't 'll be.'

⚜

Old Woodman lies beside his youngest born now. He never spared him, child or boy or man, but chastened him ever with hard blows and

179

harder words, with scowling looks and low mutterings of accusation and reproof, so that 'why Bob di'n't go clane orf's nut wi' um' was often subject of wonder among Bob's friends. Yet, being gone, the father fretted himself into his grave for the son he had not seemed to love.

Silent he sat 'i' th' chimbley-corner,' the unnoticed tears rolling slowly down his crimson cheeks, which seemed to get redder and more inflamed from such painful weeping; only grunted replies to his wife's exhortations to patience, and rejoicing, only grunted amens to her prayers of thanksgiving; grew, time going on, weaker and weaker from no apparent cause.

He took no share in the gossip of Dulditch; cheered hardly perceptibly when the time for the Christmas gifts came round; showed no longer interest even in the faggot-stack in Betty Barker's garden, the ever-increasing dimensions of which had hitherto filled the Harper household with envy and wild suspicion. Maundy's husband was woodman, or had been – he had privileges still. All the world was at liberty to inquire into the history of the Harper faggot-stack. But Betty's – that was a different 'pair o' butes.'

There was one thing that roused him to the last from his apathetic misery. From the sound of all other vehicles passing his cottage door he knew the sound of the doctor's gig. While he could crawl he would drag himself to the window, would shake a trembling, impotent fist at the lounging figure of the doctor, his upright, liveried servant beside him, as the gig flashed by. Poor doctor, lolling unconscious, knowing not even of the existence of the enraged old man, of the threatening, trembling fist of him whose son had died without a 'chancet.' He is such a pleasant-spoken, affable old gentleman. He is a doctor of the old school – of the days before hygiene and its laws became so familiar in our mouths, before surgery had made such giant strides. He may have made mistakes in his professional career, but the younger medical men of his neighbourhood are careful to say what a sound old practitioner he is, and to say it with very solemn faces; and the public speaks of the big fortune he has made. It would shock him to hear the ugly word old Woodman mutters as the high gig flashes by. When it is gone the old man totters back to his weeping and his chimney-corner again.

A few more months for Woodman to sit in that 'chimbley' corner, to sit on the brink of the well before the cottage door, to sit beneath the shadow of his beloved faggot-stack, the familiar scent of the dry wood in his nostrils, the big white blossoms of the 'hilder' tree between him and the blue of the sky, weeping, always weeping for the son that was gone. Beyond the eloquence of the silent tears, beyond that shaking fist, that muttered ugly word, he said nothing; but his grief was there for all the world to see. It is only the 'quality' who regard the necessity to disguise what they feel. Open grief may be numbered among the few luxuries of the uncultured poor.

A few weeks, during which Woodman lay upon his bed, Maundy waiting upon him cheerfully enough, not concealing from herself or him the approaching end – dwelling upon the details, indeed, with a ghastly candour known only at such humble bedsides.

'We ha' clapped a hot brick to 's feet, po'r old dare,' she would say; 'but, bless ye, miss, his feet's past the know of any brick to warm – not if yer made it as red hot as Dan'l Luck did for 's mother, and barnt th' po'r critter's big toe orf, and she never so much as aweer on't. See how hampered he is wi' 's breathun', and th' cold's a-mountin' now.'

She was constantly putting a hand beneath the bedclothes to report to her husband how high the chills of death had risen.

I will not say that Maundy was disappointed when, as happened many times, the warmth came back to poor Woodman's weary limbs again, but she would not admit it as any sign of hopefulness.

''Tis on'y a puttin' orf, po'r dare, and I don't let um set 's mind on 't. Du yer mind how 's finger nails is a tarnin' black, bor? Ef I ain't mistook morti'cation's set in, bless the Lord!'

Woodman listened to it all, consented to make a show of his finger and toe nails with admirable patience. All his 'err'tability' seemed to have left him with Robert's death. The blue watery eyes followed the comfortable form of his wife wistfully as she moved about. He had been a 'difficult' husband, but it seemed he felt the coming parting far more than she. The cheerful temperament of Maundy Harper is not consistent with depth of feeling; beneath the gloom and bad temper of the old man love and faithfulness had dwelt.

There came at length a day when his dead son's name was perpetually on Woodman's lips; and someone thought of putting a black, villainous libel in the shape of a portrait of the poor young fellow, taken by a travelling photographer, into the stiff and feeble hands. His eyes were dim – he could not see the picture, but he crossed his hands upon it as it lay upon his breast and seemed content.

Passing the Harpers' cottage on the evening of that day, I see Elijah (Eliza) Slapp emerging, and I know at once what has occurred.

Elijah is a miserable, half-starved looking little woman, living by herself in a house that is no better than a pigsty. She has of late years

181

developed on her cheek a sore of a cancerous description. It is in the hope of curing this sore that she haunts the chambers of the newly dead. The stroke of a corpse's hand upon the diseased cheek is said to hold a mysterious healing power. Such a remedy costs less than the doctor's, and one naturally has more faith in it.

Before those crooked fingers of the Woodman should stiffen upon the picture on his breast Elijah has been coaxing them to stroke her cheek.

A DULDITCH COURTING

IT is a good ten years ago that Marthy Milch came to live in Dulditch with her widowed grandmother, Maundy Harper. She was then a particularly neat-looking person of eighteen summers. She wore, and still wears, her smooth hair scraped from her face and twisted tightly into a drab-coloured button at the back of her sleek head. Her complexion is of a purplish crimson, and she suffers from a habitual roughness of skin. Her eyes, planted flush with her high cheek-bones and her flat forehead, are pale of hue, and as expressionless as dead fishes in stagnant pools. She possessed a trim figure in those early days, and her dress was then, as now, of exemplary neatness and simplicity. Her skirt was worn too short to become draggled with dust or frayed at the hem. However hard she worked, a hair of her head was never seen awry; in winter storm or summer blow the drab button was as unaffected as though it were nailed to a wooden head.

Such as she is, the eyes of her grandmother delight in Marthy. The old woman herself, at eighty years of age, wrapped in her short red cloak, with plump pink cheeks, snowy hair, eyes bright and blue peering over the top of her glasses, is a far more pleasing object to the eyes. But of this she is modestly unconscious; and her admiration for Marthy's 'nateness' is beyond all bounds.

Old Maundy has a pride of her own, very appropriate and pleasant to note – her pride of race and of place: the peasant pride of England, which seems to be dying out with the old generation. The outward sign of this feeling in Maundy shows itself chiefly in her insistence on the beautiful fitness of things, on what is 'becomin',' as she puts it, in her 'staation o' life.' The immediate outcome of such insistence is to be seen in her own sweet manner and in her perfect taste. Other women may give their offspring fine names, which are more suitable to the curled and titled darlings of cheap literature than to tow-headed urchins whose highest ambition must be to earn a bare existence by the sweat of their brows; the children, grandchildren, aye, and great-grandchildren of Maundy Harper's family are Meery, Marthy, 'Lizbeth, Robbud, John, and Jeems. 'Them high-fliers is for the gintry,' the old woman says. ''Tain't becomin' in us to taake no sech a liberties.' Similarly, no branch of the Harper family has permitted to its female members the vanity of a 'fringe.' The contempt of our fine old lady for such decoration is unbounded. She stands at her window and apostrophises the Brightlands Farm servants as they pass for their Sunday outing.

'Set o' tousle-hidded mawthers!' she mutters. 'Yew ha' been up all night a-draggin' yar hids t'rough a fuzz bush, ha' ye? Yew'd better ha' sat up a-mendin' th' hale o' yer stockin'.' Neighbours may go shabby themselves and empty-bellied to turn out 'their baggages' with smart hats and long-tailed gowns 'come Sunday,' but Maundy ordains that Marthy shall make her best brown frock do for three summers; and shall go without feather and flowers and frippery, so that every day of her life she may contrive to be decently shod and cleanly attired. Marthy is allowed 'none o' them low, upstartly ways' of passing her betters on the road with a nod, or her head turned away to avoid even the courtesy of a nod. She is to 'make her manners' all round, irrespective of private like or dislike of her own.

The grandmother shows her many times, bending her own stiff old knees for the purpose, how to come to a sudden halt when members of the 'quality' draw nigh, how to 'bob' to them with due effect, and a respectfully toned 'Servant, sir,' or 'Servant, ma'am,' and to pass on.

With the unquestioning obedience which the younger generation showed to the patriarchs of old, Marthy obeys the old woman's every behest. Those small enjoyments in which the other young people of the village may indulge she does not taste. Wistful at heart, it may be, although in the fish-like eyes is no expression, she looks out at the girls and boys sauntering by in their Sunday best; and listens to the calling voices and the loud laughter in which she has no share. Standing behind the pots of geranium and fuchsia which adorn the window-sill, and looking above the short red blind, half covering the window, she can see the young men sitting on the 'up-town' railing over the way. Grandmother Harper remembers very well when her youngest born, her Robert, sat there also, swinging his legs, on summer evenings. The memory of age is so treacherous – looking up swiftly she sometimes expects to see him sitting there still. Now and then a matron or a maid comes by, plants her elbows on the rail, leans there to gossip among the men for a while, or, passing on the other side, calls a shrill word or two in their direction as she goes. These distractions are not for Marthy, but she does not dream of complaint.

Each of the cottages in the 'up-town' lot has a long strip of garden at the back. In the strip where her grandmother's potatoes and onions grow, Marthy may walk at cool of evening, may pick the gooseberries for to-morrow's dumplings, may sit on the doorstep to shell the peas with which she has filled her lilac apron. The Harpers are chapel-folk, and to chapel, attired always in her brown alpaca, white silk scarf at her red throat, white cotton gloves on her red hands for summer weather, short black jacket for winter wear, Marthy goes every Sunday afternoon. There is another service in the evening, but Marthy stays in at that time to keep Gran'mawther company, and to read the Bible to her as Robert used to do; and to talk over with her the fashion of a new hat, or the colour of a new gown which the old woman's sharp eyes had noted at chapel that afternoon.

'Better to be a good-livin' gal than to dress up in fine clo'es,' Gran'mawther says, and Marthy assents with complete self-approval.

She is emphatically a 'good-livin' gal'; she knows it herself, and she is recognised as such among the chapel community. At the annual tea-drinking Marthy comes honourably out of her retirement, and is the chosen assistant of Mrs Field, the miller's wife, the miller himself being the great patron of the chapel. Marthy helps to pour out the tea and to cut the cakes and the bread-and-butter with red, cracked hands. And when the meal is over it is Marthy who leads off the subsequent mild entertainment with a recitation, delivered in a particularly hoarse and monotonous voice.

Probably no one present understands a word she says; Marthy makes no effort after distinctness of utterance. She would think it derogatory to the occasion to speak out clearly in a manner easy to comprehend – just as if one were talking to Gran'mawther over the fire at home. She stands up, crimson-faced, smooth-haired, in her brown dress, the white gloves leaving visible a deep-hued streak of wrist, her arms held stiffly away from her sides, her serviceable boots showing beneath the full, short skirt, and says her 'piece' entirely to her own satisfaction.

'She's a good-livin' gal,' her friends in the audience say to one another, as Marthy, with a thud which sounds like the fall of a sack of potatoes, drops off the platform.

'She's won'erful clane-lookin', Marthy be,' one of them adds. 'She ha' got it in her to make some fine, stiddy young chap a rare good wife.'

But Marthy lives in Dulditch for ten years before any love affair threatens to disturb the even tenor of her days. The neighbours' daughters go to service, or get married, or drift away. It comes to pass that Marthy is the only unmarried woman in the parish of the mature age of twenty-eight. The flight of time has stolen away the youthful fulness of figure, but it has not toned down her complexion, or smoothed her skin, or added any brightness to her eyes. Except in the judgment of the most partial, Marthy Milch can never be found to be a beauty. But *'ce sont les femmes laides qui font les grandes passions,'* and at length 'the time and the place and the loved one' came, happily 'altogether' for Marthy.

It was the year that old Bill Nobbs' daughter D'isy died up i' th' shares'; she who had kept her brother's house and worked beside him in the factory in those vague regions. She had stayed away from work to help a neighbour whose children were dying one after another of scarlet fever. The fever killed D'isy too in the finish, leaving Horace with the cares of the home the sister had helped him to establish, and with no housekeeper.

The parents of 'Horus and D'isy' are chapel folk, and in thinking over the lonely and helpless condition of their son – for D'isy was well known to have been the better man of the two – they naturally turned their thoughts upon Marthy in the brown alpaca – the good-livin' gal.

With August Horace came to Dulditch for his fortnight's holiday – a very lean and sallow and strengthless-looking young man, for he too had taken the fever, as he had always from infancy taken any complaint that came within catching reach of him. On the first Sunday afternoon he accompanied Marthy and Gran'mawther to their home when chapel was over. He got no farther than the 't'reshol' o' th' door' on that occasion, for, as Mrs Harper subsequently explained with glee, 'Marthy and me never give sech a thing a thought as th' consarn that were i' th' young chap's mind.

'Marthy, she g'en 'm th' sale o' th' day when we comed out o' chapel, and arter that she ha'n't a word more to say to 'im, Marthy ha'n't – a-goin' on i' front on us, and me a-kaping up th' intercourse. Marthy, she ain't never a talkative one, but she ha' got it in 'er – oh, she ha' got it in her, ha' Marthy.

'Arter that, twice i' th' wake, Marthy, she say ter me, "Gran'mawther," she say, "that theer Nobbs from the shares ha' gone

185

by. He looked i' th' windy," she say. "He were a-lookin' for you, I reckon, Gran'mawther."'

For Marthy stood in great reverence of the old lady's conversational powers. It seemed quite natural to her that any young man who had drunk of the nectar of Gran'mawther's eloquence should thirst for that beverage again. When Horus looked up with a sickly grin at the red face above the geraniums in the window, Marthy stared stolidly back at him. That it had been her personal attractions rather than the graces of Mrs Harper's conversation which had drawn the young man twice from the other extremity of the parish and led him to pass the 'up-town housen' never entered the good girl's head.

At the end of the week he knocked at old Maundy's door, and at her invitation sauntered in, sat for an hour by the fire, which, summer and winter, burnt small and bright in the spotless grate.

'Time hang heavy o' yer hands now, I reckon,' Gran'mawther said to him, looking at him with kindly, bright blue eyes shining above the spectacles. Marthy was out doing a day's washing for a neighbour, and the old lady had all the talk. 'I ha' heerd my old man say there's a harder wark than the wark of a warkin' daay, and tha's th' puttin' awaay o' time of a hollerday.'

She had all the talk. Mr Horus Nobbs was a dejected young man; even the desire to possess the good-livin' Marthy did not brisk him up. In honour of the occasion he had donned the black suit in which he had followed his sister to her grave, and he was wearing a large claret-and-white quilled dahlia pulled through his button-hole. He was evidently unequal to further exertions.

When he was going away he remembered to mention Marthy's name. His mother had told him that she was a good liver, he remarked; and he had heared as how she said her pieces won'erful at th' tea-drinkin'. This was an accomplishment which would be won'erful charin' of winter evenin's, he thought, and he left a message to the effect that Marthy was to take tea alonger his mother on the ensuing Sunday afternoon.

'Me?' said Marthy on her return, opening the fish-like orbs and breathing hard when this invitation was repeated to her. 'What do he want alonger me, Gran'mawther?' And presently, 'Am I a-goin', then?' she asked.

She was getting on for thirty years of age, but she would not have dreamed of deciding such a question as this for herself.

The excitement of a ceremonial such as that in store for her had never stirred Marthy's pulses before. True, she often 'tuk' her meals in company with those families in whose homes she helped at the wash-tub, but the formality of an invitation gave a different complexion to a tea-drinking, and Marthy during the intervening days was lost in pleasurable anticipation. But her stock of phrases was small; she did not often employ more than one for any given subject.

'What *du* he want alonger me, then?' was the only expression she gave to the curiosity and the ferment of delight which disturbed her being.

'He's arter a-kapin' comp'ny wi' ye, bor,' was invariably the grandmother's arch reply; to which Marthy, with a wide smile threatening to split the hard red cheeks, would respond with a playful, 'Git along wi' ye, Gran'mawther,' a repartee never failing to delight the cheerful octogenarian.

With no outward sign of the emotion which filled her, Marthy sat in her seat at chapel 'come Sunday arternune.' In the usual brown dress she sat beside Gran'mawther, the white scarf tied in a nigger bow beneath her chin, the straw hat with its summer trimming of white ribbon pulled modestly over her eyes, a couple of sprigs of wallflower clasped in the white-gloved hands in her lap.

The family of Nobbs sat on the bench immediately in front of her. Marthy, who was a head taller than he, looked down upon the smooth hair – made odorous with much oiling – of the young man; she admired the fine texture of the black coat, with the elegantly-sloping shoulders, the short waist, the long cuffs. The scent of the wallflower clasped close in her hot hand assailed the nostril of Horus Nobbs.

Gran'mawther has to walk home with her short, unsteady steps, her green umbrella – large enough to shelter a family, the companion of half a lifetime, in her arms – alone. Marthy had got the old lady's tea ready on the oak table beneath the geraniums in the window, even to the cutting and spreading of the slice of bread which formed that light refection, the kettle was boiling away on its hook over the little fire. The roads were dusty and hot – fatiguing to such weary old feet – and Maundy stood in need of refreshment. Yet her heart was not with her beloved teapot on this occasion. It was away with Marthy sitting at the hospitable board of the Nobbs', the arm of the sickly-looking, narrow-chested Horus around her stiff waist.

To be in such a situation had never occurred to Marthy before, but she was not unacquainted with the etiquette of the occasion, and she submitted with a good grace. There was nothing compromising in the position; an arm around your waist committed you to nothing. An

187

unmarried woman accepting an invitation to tea, an unannexed male being of the party, expected an arm to encircle her.

The father and mother of Horus looked on with solemn satisfaction. Tea was delayed for some time by the length of the grace which Nobbs senior said over it. Before the meal was half done he burst forth into audible praying again. He was not reckoned to have that gift of 'sending up' a prayer possessed by others of the chapel community, being eloquent principally of gaspings and moanings, with now and then, to fix the attention, a loud and startling calling on the name of God. The poverty of his matter was, however, atoned for by the quality of his devotion and the frequency and length of his prayers. At all seasons, seeming to pick by preference upon those of greatest inconvenience to his hearers, he burst forth. Horus's mother, a meek woman, wearing a black patch where an eye should have been – it had been smashed into a jelly one night, prior to his conversion, by Mr Nobbs – helped along the stammering oration with sighs and moans, tactfully introduced to fill in the gaps. Her husband was converted. He had sat on the stool of repentance in view of the congregation through two chapel meetings to testify to the fact; but if she had failed in the above wifely duty it is possible she might not have kept whole bones in her skin. For 'Old man Nobbs,' who is a shoemaker and pig-sticker by trade, is in his domestic relations exceedingly short of temper, and handy with his fists.

It was the wife who had desired the red-cheeked Marthy for her son's helpmate.

'Horus ain't strong – a corfin' and a spittin' half 's time t'rough,' she said to her husband. 'He'll, maybe, want some'un to narse 'm t'rough another illness sune, and I don't fancy his a pickin' up none o' them theer hussies from the shares. Marthy, she's a good liver, and she ha' got religion.'

And so it was with his mother's entire approval – at her suggestion, indeed – that Horus, the prayers being over, invited the visitor to take a walk with him.

'I reckon I'll be a-walkin' home to Gran'mawther's,' Marthy said. 'Th' road's free; I s'pose yew can come along wi' me, ef so be's yew wush tew.'

So she put on her sensible straw hat and tied her scarf beneath her chin, pulled on her fresh-washed gloves, and sallied forth into the sweet summer evening with Horus Nobbs. Along the white road, lying between the trim thorn fences, they went; through the narrow green lane, with its straggling hedges of sweet-briar, honeysuckle, and blackberry nearly meeting above their heads; across the broad fields where the barley and wheat, fast whitening to harvest, waved breast-high as they passed.

And during that walk, the short cut to Marthy's home, the amorous Horus, as Mrs Harper was afterwards proud and pleased to record, 'oped all 's mind.'

Marthy could not be said to possess that intimate knowledge of him which young women are advised to acquire of the men they promise to marry. She had walked home with him once from chapel; she had seen him twice pass her window; she had looked down on the top of his head through the 'discourse'; she had sat in his embrace through tea. Yet Marthy was by no means afraid; and it is probable that she was not running more than the average risks. It is said that the women who pride themselves on knowing the men they marry sometimes find themselves mistaken.

No doubts and trepidations on the subject came to agitate the simple mind of Marthy Milch. That a man could be other than he seemed was a proposition too complex for her intellect to grasp. He belonged to chapel-folk, he had got religion, his father held forth beautiful, he had good clothes to his back, and a house over his head 'i' th' shares.' What could maiden desire more?

'Gran'mawther, th' young chap ha' axed me to walk along on 'im, and I ha' said 'm yes,' she said when she had bidden good-night to Horus at the house door.

Even Marthy herself, at this unlooked-for acquisition of a lover, was not more exultant than Gran'mawther.

'Ef so be as the feller had come a coortin' th' ole fule herself she cou'n't ha' made more 'f a piece of wark,' the neighbours remarked with indignation one to another. 'She be es pleased wi' that theer coortin' es an old hin wi' 'n egg,' they declared.

For there are those among the neighbours who remember that Maundy was not lenient to her own children in their sweethearting days. There was no weakness about her then.

But the details of that love affair after which the old woman hungered and thirsted, and which Marthy, on the wriggle and the broad grin, related to her, sheep-faced, she gave out again, unashamed, to anyone who would listen. And when Horus had departed to his home in the 'shares' and was compelled to express his love and devotion to his 'good liver' through the medium of pen and paper alone, and when Marthy turned suddenly shy over his letters and refused to show them, Gran'mawther was capable of discovering their hiding-place and mastering their contents.

'Th' young chap were a bewtiful inditer of letters,' she told the neighbours. 'Marthy she say to me, "Gran'mawther," she say, "don't he indite 's letters bewtiful?" "Marthy," I say, "he *dew*."'

'Gran'mawther, whatever will yew dew when I'm i' th' shares,' Marthy asked now and again; but Maundy was too engrossed with childish delight in the present to look ahead. Her exuberant enjoyment of the fact that her Marthy had at length been sought in marriage was a ludicrous or a pathetic thing according to the eyes that looked at it.

'To think as how he should ha' seen Marthy a-sittin' in chapel, wi' no sich a thought as him in 'er hid, and should ha' set 's heart on her at oncet!' she cried triumphantly.

Whole sentences she learnt by heart out of those flimsy sheets of love letters which Marthy hid in the pages of her Bible. Marthy did not enjoy the love-making at first hand half so much, spelling out the endearing terms from the letters. But to have Gran'mawther slyly repeating the phrases while the pair sat opposite to each other on either side of the spotless hearth, the kettle on its hook in the chimney singing between them – this was sweet in Marthy's ears.

'My own dare lovin' Marthy,' the old woman would quote with a pleased cackle. 'Own dare lovin'! Them's the wards, bain't they, Marthy? Oh, bor, depend on't he love yer like's life.'

Each evening the same question would arise: 'Whativer 'll yew dew when I'm i' th' shares?' But Gran'mawther not only did not know, but did not seem at all to care. Let her see her Marthy bound to the young man that loved her as his life – her mind would not carry the old woman beyond that event. It was she who hurried matters on. What was there to wait for? Horus wanted a housekeeper, and Marthy, with the exception of the wedding gown, had all things ready for the marriage. The bride-elect was not the kind of ill-brought-up young person whom such a crisis should find unprepared. Under her bed, in the chamber above, was a marble-papered box containing all her dowry. So many grey calico night-gowns, so many pairs of knitted stockings, so many sheets and pudding-cloths and pocket-handkerchiefs. Covered by a sheet on her bed lay the patchwork counterpane which she had begun the first year she had come to live with Gran'mawther. The rug, made of snips of cloth knitted together with string, which half covered the brick floor below stairs, was only finished last month, and was Marthy's own. In one corner of the box was as much as thirty shillings, which the frugal girl had put by, saved from the sixpence a day earned at neighbours' wash-tubs.

With this sum in its screw of paper between her glove and her hot palm, Marthy walked into Runwich to purchase the wedding outfit. Over one article of the trousseau she and Gran'mawther came near to a falling out than they had done in any time of the ten years they had lived together.

The wedding-gown, of a lighter shade of brown than the time-honoured Sunday frock, was approved, as was also the round hat of white straw, trimmed with white ribbon. But the young lady who had supplied these articles to Marthy, and who had learnt that they were to be worn at her wedding, had persuaded the girl to buy a bit of white tulle for a veil to be worn on the occasion. The effect to be anticipated had been shown to Marthy over the young lady's own face. Everyone who is married must wear a veil, the young lady had said; and, besides, it was so becoming to the complexion.

'Taake ut awaay,' the old Grannie had cried, with righteous wrath. 'I'll ha' no sech a rubbage i' my fam'ly. Ef so be as you bain't never married, yew sha'n't go dressed up i' no falls out o' my house, Marthy. They ain't becomin' to our staation o' life.'

Poor Marthy, with a recollection of the dark eyes and the pale skin of the young lady of the shop shining softly through the tulle, had felt that the 'fall' was not a small thing to relinquish. She kept it folded in a neat square beneath the white straw hat, for Gran'mawther luckily had not insisted that the piece of finery should be given out of her keeping.

'It'll dew to t'row over yer fust baby's faace when yew carry it along to the namin', Marthy,' she said.

'Yes, Gran'mawther,' Marthy had answered, dutifully; and she looked at the yard of tulle with a new interest.

There was positively nothing to wait for. The banns were put up. Owing to the fact that Marthy had given the name of the street in which the young man lived instead of that of the town where he worked – an error only discovered after the banns had been called two Sundays – they were put up five times. The wedding-day was fixed, the butcher spoken to about the 'bit o' mate' Marthy wished to provide for the entertainment of the wedding guests, and for which she was prepared to pay with what was left of the thirty shillings. It was arranged that she should be married in the early morning and travel back, immediately after the ceremony, to that vague region in the 'shares' from henceforth to be her home.

Gran'mawther ordained that any of the 'mate' and the currant cake which should be left over from the feast should accompany bride and bridegroom, to be consumed on their arrival at 't'other ind.'

Everything had been thought of, talked over, planned out a hundred times. Gran'mawther was to lose what was dearest to her in the world, the very prop and stay of her existence, but she appeared quite unable to realise the fact. Marthy, the stolid, red-cheeked, the fish-eyed, was carried away by the old soul's enthusiasm. The village pronounced the pair a 'couple o' fules – the old mawther the wust o' th' pair on 'em.'

'What d' they know on 'm?' was asked indignantly. 'A pore shamblin' chap, wi', maybe, a wife a'riddy at t'other ind.'

'Wheer was Marthy's mother – wheer was Mar' Ann, that allurst had th' name for a sens'ble body – what was she a doin' on to let her gal run her hid at sech a pace o' tomfulery?' was loudly asked.

Marthy's mother was waiting till the pig died.

She lived fifteen miles from Dulditch. She had made a vow in early youth never to trust herself to the dangers of the rail; to hire a horse and cart cost money. On her rare visits to Dulditch she walked both ways, resting herself in her mother's house for a week between the journeys, she being a woman of small physical strength, although possessed of a power of will dangerous to thwart, and a nervous energy which was a terror to those belonging to her.

How was she to spare a week away from home while there was the pig to feed, while its killing had to be arranged and its curing attended to?

Due notice had been sent her of Marthy's approaching marriage. 'Wait till I come,' had been the gist of her reply. 'When the pig die, the Lord bein' with me and giving of me strength, I'm a comin'.'

The last bit of fat meat being in the pickle-jar, she came – a little, wiry, dark woman, with a sharp face and restless bright eyes, and an irritated expression. All the pleasant, foolish repetition of Horus's endearing phrases, all the silly sentiment for which the old woman had developed such a taste, were relinquished when Mar' Ann arrived.

'Mar' Ann's a nailer for sure,' the neighbours said approvingly. 'She oughter ha' come along afore.'

Being come, she let her relations know it. She told her mother in no measured terms what she thought of her. She stormed at Marthy, staring, helpless and gasping. She went down town and made havoc of one-eyed Mrs Nobbs, and bounced out of the house in the midst of Mr Nobbs' prayers. She came to the Rectory and attacked the innocent man who had read the banns, flourishing her umbrella, thumping her fist on his table. The poor Gran'mawther, frightened out of position on her own hearth, took to her bed. 'She allurst had been afeared o' Mar' Ann,' the neighbours said, looking on with approbation. 'Mar' Ann sh'u'd ha' come suner.' The poor old soul's plea that she had wanted to see Marthy settled before she died, and that the pair loved each other like their lives, had no weight against the cruel commonsense of the younger woman. Marthy herself was incapable of standing up for a minute against her mother's wrath. She stared helplessly at the little termagant, screeching in her shrill voice, twisting angrily about the peaceful red-bricked room where she and Gran'mawther had loved to talk about Horus. The tears slid over the narrow lids and rolled over the rough cheeks, the chin quivered.

'I ha' bought th' weddin' gound, mother,' was all she ever said in deprecation of the cruel sentence pronounced on her hopes.

When at length Mar' Ann departed she left ruin and desolation behind her.

The grandmother crept back to her place by hearth, and Marthy sat before her as of old, and the kettle sang between, but everything was altered.

'I ha' writ to 'm, Gran'mawther,' Marthy said with dull resignation; 'I ha' oped my mind to 'm and told 'm all.'

'I hope as how you writ kind and lovin', Marthy, and azed 's pain as fur as poss'ble, pore dare young chap.'

''Tis for me to 'pol'gise – I know that,' Marthy said. It was a word she had picked up somewhere: the use of it seemed to comfort her a little. 'I know as 'tis me ter 'pol'gise.'

'Mother were afeared o' th' risk ter yer clo'es, bor,' Gran'mawther reminded her faintly. ''Twere only nat'ral mother should be narvish about yer clo'es, Marthy.'

'She were,' Marthy assented, looking at the fire. 'She sayed as how I might die wi' th' fust child up i' them thur shares, and then who was to see who got my box o' clo'es, mother sayed. Some o' them truck at th' fact'ry might ha' it for all we could tell, she sayed.'

Gran'mawther sighed: 'She were allust wonnerful filled wi' sense, Mar' Ann were,' she said despondingly. 'But th' pore young chap he loved ye like 's life, Marthy.'

'I sha'n't like none but mother to ha' my box o' clo'es, all the same,' Marthy said despondently. 'That 'on't du ter run no risks. But I know, as far as matters stand 'twixt him and me, 'tis me that ha' got ter 'pol'gise.'

The wedding gown is put out of the way, folded in newspapers in the box beneath the bed, together with the square of tulle which was to have covered the 'fust baby's' face. Marthy works on steadily and stolidly as of yore; wrings out the neighbours' washing, 'reds up' the neighbours' floors, walks beside Gran'mawther to chapel, walks home with the sprigs of wallflower in her hand, and sits down to tea beneath the red-curtained window. Her face is as rough and as crimson as ever, her eyes, even with her cheeks and brow, as void of light. She eats with good appetite, sleeps soundly after her hard day's work, is as docile and as amenable to Gran'mawther's rule as before. Whether she thinks of Horus 'over in the shares,' and of how his arm once lay around her waist, whether she gives a thought to the baby who should have worn the yard of tulle on 'namin' day,' who can say? As far as speech is a vehicle for thought, Marthy might have been born dumb.

'Marthy, bor, he loved yer like 's life,' Gran'mawther still remembers to say sometimes; to which Marthy, gazing upon the fire, makes the unfailing response that she knows 'tis for her to 'pol'gise, and that she cou'n't ha' held wi' none but mother gettin' her box o' clo'es.

Gentleman George Ganders, whose opinion is much respected in Dulditch, and who is held to have a natural intuition with regard to legal matters, says that, her banns having been put up, Marthy Milch is the lawful, 'bounden' wife of Horus Nobbs. He says that being cried in church is all but 'ekals' to being tied there. That, did 'Horus, over in the shares,' wish to claim his wife in Dulditch, he could do so, and no consideration of 'clo'es,' no tempestuous, tyrannical mother could avail to keep the pair apart.

These words of wisdom, repeated now and again in her ears, are of a nature to stir and to trouble the heart of the good-livin', patient Marthy, standing with her crimson face bent above the reek of the neighbours' wash-tubs, the steam curling about her sleek, drab-coloured head.

THE LOST HOUSEN

ON the high road, a couple of miles from the village of Dulditch, but yet within the boundary of that parish, in the midst of a plot of garden ground all waste and uncultivated, the ruins of the two cottages stand which were known to the countryside by the above designation. The position of the 'Lost Housen' is very lonely and remote from any dwelling. They are divided by the acre and a half of ground in which they stand from the wood which runs at the back and on one side of them; on the other side is an osier-bed, and beyond that the river; in front runs the road, from which a straggling, untrimmed hedge all but hides them.

Some forty years ago on the same site stood the turnpike lodge, and the place is still believed to be haunted by the ghost of the gate-keeper, brutally murdered in his bed by a tramp in the midst of the silence and darkness of a winter night. His body, dragged round the osier-bed, was found next morning in the river, too shallow even at that time of year to conceal the ugly crime.

For years after the last toll had been paid on the Runwich Road, the gate removed, and the lodge fallen to decay, the site remained unoccupied, owing to the loneliness of the situation, to the dampness of the surroundings, to the spirit of the murdered lodge-keeper hovering where the vapours lingered among the shivering osiers or rising mist-like from the river.

It was not until old Ambrose Crouch, the Dulditch blacksmith, died, leaving his few pounds of savings between his two sons, that the building of the two hideous cottages, which at present occupy the position of the old toll-house, was begun.

The tale goes that the blacksmith, having enjoyed several years of married life without issue, and being anxious for a couple of strong sons to help him in his trade and to save the wages of journeymen, made a bargain with the Almighty (whose name was familiar in his mouth more in cursing than in prayer) that if He would give him a pair of male children, Ambrose for his part would see to it that they bore respectively the longest and shortest names in the Bible. When, within the year, Mrs Crouch presented her husband with twin boys, those poor unconscious infants were accordingly burdened with the names of Og and Maher-shalal-hash-baz to carry through life.

Thus cruelly handicapped from the beginning, the race of life run by the two sons, for whom old Ambrose, after his ignorant and superstitious fashion, had prayed, was far from being a creditable one. Only Og, after all, helped his father to beat the sparks from the glowing iron in the forge, to shoe the cart-horses, lifting huge, unflinching hoofs for the operation, standing patient on the little green before the blacksmith's door. For anger in the Crouch family was apt to wax as hot and as dangerous as the great bars the men handled so unconcernedly amid the leaping flames, and words of rage and cursing

195

sounded often above the ringing blows of the hammer on the anvil; and Maher – it was by this comparatively insignificant appellation that the owner of the formidable baptismal title was known in Dulditch – who was of a quiet and timid disposition, slipped away from the paternal roof one evening and did not return.

He only went as far as the next village, where he addressed himself to the profession of bricklaying, the noise and the heat of the blacksmith's work being repugnant to him; but it was very seldom afterwards that his father set eyes on the still, white face, the strange-looking blue eyes, the sleek, black hair of his truant son.

In those days the rural population was more averse even than at present from movement. Among the more old-fashioned of them one hears continually still of sons who for twenty years have not seen mothers living a few parishes distant; of sisters within walking distance who never meet. A man who lives within a hundred yards of the workhouse was overtaken the other day by the doctor of that institution, who, knowing the pedestrian, pulled up to ask him why, on working day, he was attired in his Sunday suit, and whither he was bound with such a determined gait.

'I'm a goin' to see faather,' the man said. ''Tis a matter o' twenty year come th' thutty-fust o' next month sin' I sot eyes on th' old chap last. He be a gettin' along i' yares now; and me and my missus ha' set a wonderin' how 'e fare. So I ha' tuk a holiday and rid myself up, and I be a goin' to make my moind aisy by a glint on 'm at last.'

The doctor, having sympathised with the somewhat tardy filial anxiety, offered a seat in his gig to help the pilgrim on his road, an honour the pilgrim, however, declined; and, with evident surprise that the whereabouts of 'faather' was not universally known, pointed across the way to the big white poor-house, intimating that unlovely edifice as his destination.

He had lived within a stone's-throw of the miserable old pauper father for a score of years without feeling the impulse to cross the road to see him.

So Ambrose Crouch had only the one son and the wife to curse at, to batter with hard words and cruel blows. The mother was a woman slow of tongue, with eyes like Maher's, dull and blue as his, and with the same still gaze. How she aroused her husband's fury is not known; it is said that she never attempted retaliation. As for Og, he also seemed to be cowed by the fierce old man, and took his brother's portion of oaths and stripes as well as those due to himself with apparent resignation.

But the day came when the weakness of old age and illness robbed the tyrant of his power, and then did Og and his mother show of what material they were made.

'Th' po'r ol' chap were a bad ol' warmint, but he were th' best o' th' lot, arter all,' the neighbours said, and said truthfully. For his sins he suffered terribly now. There was never a blow that was not paid back to him with interest; he was starved; he was terrified; he was tortured. He escaped from his bed once at noonday, and, in his nightshirt, ran about the village imploring the neighbours to take care of him and protect him. Old Brose Crouch was more terrifying in his frantic dread and in that scant attire than ever he had been in the height of his splendid strength and his unrestrained passion, cursing and swearing and wielding his mighty hammer at the forge. The women hid away from him, doors were slammed in his face.

Finally he was captured by wife and son and taken back to his bed again. Og pushed him homeward in a wheelbarrow, abashed and beaten, the poor old bare legs dangling helpless. The woman stalked before, silent, her thin lips drawn inward, the great pale blue eyes gazing into vacuity, by no means discomposed at forming one in such a procession.

Life was strong in the miserable old man. Starvation, exposure, illtreatment of all kinds failed to kill him. He was found lying insensible upon the snow in his front garden early one morning. His head was cut and bruised, his arm and leg were broken; yet even then he did not die at once, but lived long enough to swear before witnesses that he had fallen from his window in his sleep, and that his son, who had ever treated him with kindness and attention, had had no hand in the disaster.

But the nearest neighbours had heard a cry for mercy in the night; there were signs of a struggle in the bedroom. The village people, excited by the presence of the police among them and athirst for a tragedy, insisted that Og Crouch should at once be taken to Runwich Gaol and hanged there. To their intense disappointment the culprit got off with a six months' imprisonment for assault, the father protesting his son's innocence to the last, dying – fortunately for him – just before that son's release.

Those cottages the blacksmith and the bricklayer undertook to erect with some of their father's savings were long in the building. The men were suspicious of interference in the work, and from foundation stone to topmost bricks in the chimney did everything themselves. Consequently in architectural design, in beauty, and in finish the 'lost housen' left much to be desired. Before paint or paper or whitewash was put on the walls, the brothers, tired of the expense of lodgings, had moved into that cottage which they meant to occupy, and amid the squalid confusion of the miserable place had installed their mother to keep house.

Perhaps it was not to be expected that such a trio should live in peace. It was soon abundantly evident which one among them meant to be master. On the shoulders of Og, it seemed, his father's mantle had fallen. He swore at and beat his mother, cursed and fought his brother to his heart's content. The fear that Jemima Crouch had never shown of her husband she exhibited in a marked degree now of her son. She had seen him grow from childhood to middle age; she knew so much of him, she knew nothing that was not terrible. In her dread of Og Jemima drew near to the son who was so like herself in outward seeming – possessing the same tall, stooping figure, the same air of stillness and reserve upon the white, well-featured face, the same blue eyes, which never lit up, but gazed with their indescribable look into space.

If Maher sympathised with his mother's fears, or felt them on his own account, is not known. He was sparing of speech to an extraordinary degree, and his attitude was ever that of defence rather than defiance. He received what Og dealt out to him in food and fisticuffs, although his own share in the little patrimony had been equal with his brother's, and in spite of the fact that, physically, he was better made and far stronger, with long arms and enormously hands, which were quite equal to the task of retaliation.

Having once settled down in the miserable half-finished place, through whose single-brick walls the wet oozed and the wind blew, Og delayed to enter upon the finishing touches which should have made the home habitable. He guarded the remnant of the money carefully, carrying it on his own person night and day. They could live very well without paint on the 'win-skirtin'' and the 'windies,' he declared. What was the good of whitewash or wall-paper while the 'chimney' smoked, as he put it forcibly, 'like hell'? Jemima, who had been used to a particularly neat and, for her class, even luxurious home in her husband's time, groaned with rheumatism and shivered with ague all the winter through. What Maher could do without outlay of capital for materials he did, but surreptitiously and in a half-hearted way. He cut wedges of wood to stop the rattling of the windows, and daubed a trowelful of mortar over the chinks in the chimney through which the smoke poured. But the effort needed to bring the outer door into closer connection with the doorstep was apparently too great for him, and in the work of cultivating the garden he never got further than spitting meditatively upon the soil over the spade upon which he leant.

Since the money had come into their possession the idea of adding to it by earning a day's wage had been abandoned by both the brothers. Og, who, as has been said, carried the purse, spent his days at the nearest public-house, where he drank himself ever into a savager, more brutal condition; while Maher sat silent with his silent mother, or roamed about the miserable place with his hands in his pockets, making a melancholy survey of its deficiencies.

Then Og fell ill, the cold and the damp telling first on him, apparently the strongest of the three. He began with bronchitis and went on to inflammation of the lungs and to 'ammonia'; and being a hard drinker upon whom the necessary stimulants took no effect, he lay very quickly at death's door.

On the fifth day, when the doctor came out of the bedroom, where a paraffin lamp, sending forth a most abominable stench, burnt day and night in a feeble struggle against the damp and chill of the place, he stopped to speak to Maher, sitting idle and alone in the living-room, his hands in his trousers pockets, his long legs, reaching nearly to the opposite wall, stretched before him, his blue eyes fixed vacantly.

'This brother of yours is in a very critical state, my man,' the doctor said, pausing in the act of screwing his clinical thermomether into its case. 'His temperature is a hundred and seven this morning. If that temperature be maintained till evening he will die.'

Maher's eyes wandered slowly to the doctor's face and fixed themselves there for a long minute before he spoke.

'And if 't don't?' he asked at length.

'If the temperature declines, and the little strength the man at present has is maintained, there is a chance for him – he may recover. The next few hours will decide. I am sorry to tell you that in my opinion he is far more likely to die – and that quickly – than to live.'

The young man said nothing. His eyes continued to be fixed on the doctor's face. There was something disagreeably fascinating in that long silent stare. What an odd-looking figure the man was, with his white complexion and in his white workman's dress! There was no play of expression in the face; the features were as emotionless and as still as those of a dead man.

'That old woman always gives me the creeps,' the doctor said to himself with irritation, thinking of Jemima Crouch, sitting silent, gaunt, and upright by the bedside; 'her son is as bad.'

'I ha' heared the folk let on,' said Maher, speaking slowly, with his hushed and far-off voice, 'as how when a man lay at th' p'int o' death – his breath, which in an or'nary way he live by, a lavin' on 'm – I ha' heared say at them times the breath 'f a livin' human critter brathed into 's nost'ils and down 's tr'ut – ef so be as sech can be found as 'll go t'rough with 'casion – 'ull bring that feller-suff'rer back from 's mortial plight.'

Maher's rare speech was slow and difficult, and by the time he had reached the end of it the doctor had put away his thermometer, had buttoned his great-coat, had settled his hat on his head.

'And what,' he asked as he drew on his driving gloves, 'what do you suppose your patient would be doing while you were whistling into his nostrils and blowing down his windpipe?'

'What?' Maher asked, having paused to watch the other button his gloves and turn to depart.

The doctor turned round upon him, the outer door in hand.

'Why, he'd be kicking the bucket, my good fellow,' the cheerful doctor said with a laugh. 'By the time you'd cured your man he'd be as dead as Moses.'

Then he went, and Maher sat for long hours over the smoky fire, and gazed and gazed at the opposite wall.

At night Mrs Crouch always gave up her post in the sick-room to Maher, she repairing to her own bed for a few hours' rest. The mother and son stood for a few minutes over the fire before going their several ways.

'How du 'e fare?' Maher asked.

'Better,' she answered. 'To my thinkin' he ain't i' th' chechyud yit. He be a goin' to live.'

Maher's jaw fell open, his dull, mournful eyes widened; he said nothing, but gazed stupidly upon his mother. She, for her part, gave her report with nothing of that trembling joy with which a mother might be expected to welcome her son back from the grave.

'He be asleep,' she said, 'and his breathin's reg'lar. The pantin' and the ruttlin' on his chist 's left 'm. So 've the burnin' faver left 'm. He's all of a sweat.'

She sat down, with a groan for her aching bones, in the chair Maher had vacated, and her strange eyes fixed themselves miserably upon the hot wood-ashes in the grate. Og objected to the expenditure for coal, and they burnt what bits of wood they found about the place.

''Tis all to begin over again,' she said, whispering the words to the fire, leaning forward over folded arms. 'He's managing' (manageable) 'in 's ways now, t'rough his wakeness, but give 'm 's strength, and we've a worse devil among us agin than iver 's father were – a cru'ler, selfiger, dartier-mouthed devil.'

'Th' doctor let on as he were a goin',' Maher reminded her slowly.

'Ah!' she said. A quavering, long-drawn 'Ah!' that expressed a great deal – her contempt of the doctor's opinion, her better knowledge of her son's condition among other things.

'We shall ha' to give 'm back the money agin,' Maher said reflectively.

She only nodded at the fire, rocking herself to and fro over her folded arms.

Maher contemplated her in one of his long silences.

'We han't done it yit,' he said at length with more than usual emphasis. 'Maybe we shorn't ha' to du it arter all.'

With that he turned away from his mother, and walked with something of decision in his shambling step into the adjoining room to take up his watch over the invalid.

Before the doctor started on his rounds on the following morning he received a message to the effect that his presence was not needed at the 'Lost Housen,' Og Crouch having died in the night. The man of medicine had left direction with Mrs Crouch that, in this too probable termination of the case, word should be sent him, as the cottage was out of his way; and he now signed the death certificate with a light heart and an easy conscience. He had a patient to see at a distance of fifteen miles in the opposite direction, and the weather was particularly bad that morning, so that the good man was glad to shorten his rounds.

'That shambling half idiot, his brother, didn't try his famous recipe for putting breath into his respiratory organs, I suppose?' he inquired jocosely of the messenger, the Dulditch carpenter, who had already measured the big blacksmith for his coffin, and who had volunteered to let the doctor know of the death. The man did not understand the allusion, and had it explained to him amid much chuckling on the doctor's part.

By night all Dulditch knew the story – how Maher Crouch had tried to save his brother's life by breathing down the dying man's throat.

The experiment had been tried before in the memory of one or two of the villagers, not with success in any case, it seemed.

Gentleman George Ganders was full of information on the point for the benefit of the neighbours who passed his gate, his housekeeper

Queenie Mask's mother's uncle having been operated on in like fashion when at his last extremity. Gentleman George related the occurrence with bated breath, for a 'cur'ous thing had happened on the 'casion, as Queenie, who was a "quite" body and didn't want no pace o' work made, had let on – a won'erful cur'ous thing.' The dying uncle, Jabez by name, so it was told in the family, had rejected the breath so liberally offered in his hour of need, and had breathed his own 'sperrit' down Uncle Thomas's t'rut, the consequence being that Uncle Thomas had never been 'hisself agin' in any sense of the word, Jabez's 'sperrit,' after a sharp contest with the former inhabitant of the body, having at length 'hulled out th' sperrit' of Thomas. So that the living man grew, even in outward form, the 'moral' of the dead brother; and when asked, in the doubt of his identity naturally engendered in the family's mind, which of the two he was, had always unhesitatingly responded 'Jabez'.

'Th' wumman Queenie don't want no hape o' talk made on 't, as that happ'd 'n har own fam'ly; but that were the long and th' short on 't as she gi'en th' account to me. An' I take it 'tis a wonnerful p'or look on for Maher, accordin',' Mr Ganders said.

After such a precedent it is not very surprising that in Dulditch great interest was felt in the case of Maher Crouch, and a curiosity doomed to remain unsatisfied. Those who caught a sight of the man reported him as looking whiter than ever, which was not satisfactory to the prevalent expectation, for Og had inherited the ruddy complexion of his father. But all admitted that he had a 'wonnerful cur'ous look' about the eyes. Asked to describe the look, they said it was 'kind o' wild like.' Now as Og had been always spoken of as a 'wild chap' since his father's death, it was decided that 'Og's sperrit was looking out of Maher's eyes,' and the rustic mind was gratified.

Those who had seen Maher had penetrated to that miserable living-room where he and his mother sat silent over the fire at the mercy of the volumes of smoke that poured down the chimney; of the wind that blew in by cranny and crevice and whirled about them; of the rain that flowed under the door, and ran down the inside of the window, and trickled from the walls. For, in the light of day Maher Crouch never again stirred abroad. When the shades of night came on, his long figure, white and ghost-like in his bricklayer's jacket, might be seen sometimes, creeping about among the mists that rose from the osier bed, wandering around the uncultivated space that was to have been the garden of the brothers' domain. At the sound of a passing foot-fall, at the approach of wheels, he would, even in the darkness, hurry away to hide; for the silent unsociable ways of the man had, since his brother's death, developed into a determined shunning of his kind.

What sort of life the mother and son led together was only a matter of conjecture in Dulditch. Mrs Crouch, who had been 'wonnerful shut-up and quite-like' always, and had made no friends among her neighbours, was shyer than ever of acquaintances, and had acquired since her son's death a nervous and suspicious manner, which those few people who succeeded in getting speech of her greatly resented. It is held to be mannerly in Dulditch for a woman to be as open-minded in her trouble as her joy. She should have no secret recesses in her mind – all the chambers should be thrown open, frankly and confidingly, to the friendly inquisition. There is nothing found so efficacious to ease the heartache as the popular expedient of having half a dozen women in to talk the matter over. One who refuses this form of consolation sows a grudge against her in the breast of her more generous-minded sister.

So it came to pass that in time the inhabitants of the 'Lost Housen' were regarded as an unneighbourly, ill-conditioned couple, and were left to their own silent and secret devices.

No one quite knew when Maher Crouch disappeared from the scene. It was rumoured that the mother was living alone before it was definitely ascertained that her son had left her. And even when the fact became established, no one could make out to his satisfaction where or why the man was gone. That their life together had been most miserable all firmly believed; but there was division on the point of whether he or she had been the 'ill-condition'est.' Nothing more wretched than the white, scared face of the mother could have been imagined till the wild, ashen face of the son had been seen. A man that never smoked 'a pipe o' baccy,' leaning over his own or his neighbour's fence, nor took 'a mug o' ale, sociable-like,' in the 'White Hart' kitchen; a woman who had no answer to give when a neighbour 'passed the time o' day,' but who scuttled away from her kind as dumb and as wild as a frightened rabbit – who should say which was the least human of these?

So Maher at length crept away, leaving the mother, very old now, crippled with rheumatism and with a chronic asthma, quite alone. To all questions addressed to her she vouchsafed the briefest answer, or, when it pleased her, none at all. She did not know where he was gone, she did not know what he was doing, she did not know if he was ever coming back. As to whether she was sorry to be without him, whether she was afraid to live in such a solitary place alone, whether he had gone away in consequence of any unpleasantness, if he had left her enough money to live on, if he had treated her with kindness while with her – on these points when questioned she was absolutely silent.

It was impossible to get on with the woman, so 'onmannerly' was she; and the people, who through curiosity or kindness had valiantly made friendly advances, drew back and left her alone once more.

For years she lived so; alone with her memories of the past, with whatever secrets her life held. By the look of her face uncommonly ugly some of her reminiscences must have been.

As time went on her rheumatism grew worse, so that, by-and-by, she was quite disabled, and lay on her bed groaning and sometimes shrieking with pain. And in the daytime the little daughter of her nearest neighbour waited on her, 'riddin' up' her house, cooking her little food, rubbing her poor limbs with the horse-oils upon which the Dulditch people pin their faith for the 'rheumatics.' But when these duties were fulfilled (with that zeal and discretion to be expected of eleven years) the little maid would scamper off home. She was the eldest of nine, and her parents were among the poorest in the parish – glad enough of the 'shillin' a week and her wittles,' for which Dora, night and morning, walked the long distance between the 'Lost Housen' and her home. But for forty times that sum they would not force the child to sleep in the evil-looking place, falling quickly to decay and ruin through bad building and neglect, where the ghost of the murdered toll-gate keeper still stalked uneasily amid the river fog and the mists.

So that long before the shades of night fell upon the 'Lost Housen' Jemima Crouch was left alone.

For a year Dora walked to and from the cottages. Through evenings and mornings, making three hundred and sixty-five days, she trod the 'joyless fields' of winter, or waded through the same fields 'waist-deep in meadow sweet' in the lovelier half of the year. She made her short cut through the woods from 'faather's' to 'Mis' Crouch's' when the bright leaves of the chestnut, the fierce, copper-hued leaves of the beech, the lemon-yellow leaves of the elm and the maple were falling softly about her ears with a sound as of pattering rain. She came through the woodland path in the early spring when those glorious-toned leaves lay a moist, smelling, rotting mass beneath her feet, and when the buds on the boughs overhead were aching to open:

'Ere a leaf was on a bush,
In the time before the thrush
Had thought about her nest.'

Through the rigours and delights of the year, then, little Dora ran the half-mile homeward, or walked to the scene of her day's labours with lagging feet. For she had a childish, exaggerated dread of the woman upon whom she waited, lying helpless on the bed, regarding the little maid with her wide, staring eyes, or shrieking horribly upon the stillness in her unbearable pain. There had been days in the early part of her service when the child, going her unwilling errand, had heard those shrieks in the distance and had cowered away in the wood, or hidden among the osiers for hours before she had found courage to go on. There had been foggy afternoons in winter when the mists floating up from the river in the form of a murdered toll-keeper's ghost had pursued the child to the very door of home. Awful experiences of unknown terrors, incommunicable sufferings burdening Dora's mind went to the earning of that shilling which was of so much value to the family comfort.

At last there came a day in winter when Dora, trembling, crying, distraught with fear, appeared in her home circle an hour before her appointed time. She had only an unintelligible tale to tell, and no one could satisfactorily determine why she was so frightened.

There had been a noise in the uninhabited one of the 'Lost Housen' of someone moving about there. In the broad light of day, and at first, the child had not been frightened, had even, it seems, offered to Mrs Crouch to discover who or what had taken up abode there, but had been forbidden to stir from the bedside. It was apparently the undisguised terror of Mrs Crouch herself which had communicated itself to her small attendant, increasing in the imaginative but ignorant mind of the latter to a perfect frenzy of fear of that hidden something moving about on the other side of the thin wall.

Something was there that breathed like the bull 'i' Rober'son's midder,' Dora said; that stumbled about the floor and fell against the wall like 'granfaather when 'e were in drink of a Sat'd'y night'; that was yet more awful a thousand times than the infuriated, bellowing bull or the intoxicated grandparent.

All through the long day the child had supported her terror of the hidden thing, cowering away from the dividing wall that at any moment might open to disclose a sight too awful for little girls to see and live. But when, as time went on, the pale woman on the bed, who had forgotten her pain in her fear, or who had managed to repress all the usual cries, intimated to Dora in a strained and agonised whisper that she dared not be left, that the child must promise for the love of God not to leave her as usual, but to stay at her side all night, for that she was afraid, horribly afraid; when she had clutched at the little hand and arm and had insisted, almost voiceless, but horribly, fearfully impressive, in the hoarse, painful whisper of extremest fear, that not for a moment must she be left alone with what was behind the wall; then the child with a wild cry had pulled herself from the woman's clutches, and, without waiting to look for hat or jacket, had flown from the house and torn homeward as if all the fiends of the bottomless pit had been behind her.

Dora was put to bed, her teeth chattering as with ague, and she screamed all night through at intervals, and muttered in her dreams; and in the morning, to her thankful relief, was found to be too feverish and headachy to start on her usual day's work.

It was Dora's mother, therefore, who on pushing open the door of the ill-fated house discovered the horrid sequel of the unknown terror of the day before.

Upon the bed, scratching and tearing at the air with distorted skeleton fingers, lay Mis' Crouch, the silence she had kept for so many years broken hideously at last by ceaseless babble of maniacal raving. Opposite her bed, hanging from a nail in the wall, was a thing terrible to look upon: the hidden horror of yesterday made visible for the destruction of the senses.

Dora's mother with one wild glance assured herself that what Mrs Crouch was addressing in hoarse confidential whisper, or in loud frenzied entreaty, was not, as she had at first thought, the last year's scarecrow out of the patch of wheat behind her own back door, cruelly maltreated, and hung up to frighten the sick woman. That it was indeed and in truth the dead body of Maher Crouch, who had hanged himself there before his mother's eyes. Then, having with desperate effort summoned strength of mind to slam the door upon the ugly sight, she ran as far as the 'White Hart' (where brandy was at hand to recover her) and fainted on the doorstep.

The villagers, who came in a crowd to cut the suicide down, noticed that the rotten wall had given way in several places under the weight of Maher before he had at length found means of firmly fixing the nail upon which to strangle himself. Unpleasant to imagine the sight which must have taken place before the helpless mother's eyes! It was said in Dulditch, where people do not at all shrink from attributing crime or awarding judgment, that the woman's sin must indeed have been great, seeing that her punishment was so terrible.

It is not quite certain if it was from the desire to justify the Power which had so heavily smitten J'mima Crouch, or if it was from the revelations of her own disjointed but incessant ravings that the theory which now maintains about the family was formed. The basis in either case is unsound, for the self-accusations of a maniac cannot be accepted as evidence, and upon perfectly innocent people very heavy misfortunes daily fall.

However the truth may be, it is now held in Dulditch as a fact, undoubted and unalterable as the fact that the world was created in seven days and that Jonah existed for a period in the belly of a whale, that Jemima Crouch assisted her son Og in the attempt to slay his father, and afterwards urged on Maher to murder his brother, and was punished by having to witness the protracted death struggles of the latter, hanging himself with some difficulty before her eyes.

She is very old now, and passes her days in a ward of the pauper lunatic asylum, lying always helpless on her back. But from the way in which her eyes (full of the horror for which perhaps they had kept themselves vacant of expression so long) fix themselves on the white bare wall, and her twisted fingers scratch the air, it is evident she still sees the starting eyes, the protruded, horrid tongue, the blue, hideous face of the son always hanging himself before her.

The 'Lost Housen' are lost indeed now. It is little more than a heap of rubbish which marks the place where they stood.

A MAN AND A DREAM

John Worker desisted from his task of breaking stones on the road, and lifted up his head to follow with his eyes the big motor which flew noiselessly by.

Seated on his coat, folded upon the damp, coarse grass of the wayside, before the self-same heap of stones, he had watched the self-same motor go forth in the morning. Seven hours ago, it bore Mr Felix Fortune and the half-dozen healthy, hearty, prosperous- or aristocratic-looking men who made up his shooting party to and from the outlying covers on the estate. In the seven hours the sportsmen had laughed and talked, had argued and joked and chaffed and whispered; had shot their birds, and eaten their lunch; then shot their birds again, sitting luxuriously to do it, their loaders at their backs. And now, filled with the consciousness of time well and profitably passed, pleasantly tired without having endured the fag of exertion, their memory stored with incidents of the day to discuss over their wine at night, they were being whirled home again.

John Worker had been in the same position chip-chipping all the time. No: there had been a pause for dinner, drawn from the red bundle his wife had slung upon his arm at starting, before the dawn, that morning. A slice of bread, upon which was kept steady, with a black-nailed thumb a slice of fat bacon; a wedge from an apple dumpling; to be washed down with a drink from a bottle filled with weak cold tea. After the meal a few whiffs from a small black pipe, held dangerously close, so short its stem had grown, to John Worker's nose. The coat which had formed his cushion, having been slung over his shoulders while he rested from his labours, was folded and put beneath him again; and once more it was chip-chip at the stones. Chip-chip. Endlessly chip-chip.

'There's that poor devil still tapping at his stones,' Felix Fortune said, as the motor flashed past the solitary figure. The stone-heap, the whirling road, the huddled figure of the man were of the same monotonous earth-colour, in the light which had begun to wane. Trees and hedges were black and leafless and wet; the scene was inexpressibly dreary.

No one paid any heed to the idle remark: the speaker had not expected them to do so. Two of the 'guns' were talking over news which had been wired to one of them that afternoon – disturbing news which had to do with railways and threatened strikes; two of the rest were mildly wrangling about a disputed number of pheasants which had fallen in a certain small plantation. Tom Grix was laughing as usual, Everton and Tuke were as usual making silly old jokes. Felix Fortune, who was the owner of the car, the owner of the beautiful, stately house he called his shooting-box, which the car approached, was laughing and arguing and joking too. Only, in the midst, he had made the unnoticed remark about the man who broke stones by the road.

'Fine doings!' John Worker said to himself.

The hours of labour were over. He lifted his stiff limbs from the position they had held all day, and made his preparations for departure. As he thrust his arms into the damp sleeves of his coat, his eyes followed the motor on its way through the park, and were on it still in the distance as it stopped before the doors of an abode which represented to the stone-breaker the last word in splendour and luxury.

He knew no more of the life inside such a home than he knew of heaven.

The lights in all the many windows of the great house showed that fires were lit in every room. 'They'll likelies have a wash afore they set down to their wittles,' John Worker said to himself in a feeble attempt to realize it all. He imagined, probably, a repast of boiled beef and turnips, with plum pudding to follow, such as he had enjoyed recently at the 'trate' on Coronation day. 'Wittles such as them, with plenty of bread and beer, and a pipe to foller, would suit me werry well to-night,' he said.

However, being of a fairly contented disposition, he did not the less relish his piece of fat pork and mess of cold potatoes which, his long walk home through the dank, chill air of evening over and his cottage reached, his wife set before him for his evening meal. He ceased to occupy his torpid mind with difficult guesses as to what life must be like to a man who had such 'wittles' as he had pictured every night, and with a woman like Lady Margery Fortune – strange to John Worker's experience of the sex as a visitant from another world – to put it on his plate.

But, oddly enough, that patient, earth-coloured figure of the man who all day long had sat tap-tapping upon the stones had impressed itself upon the imagination of Felix Fortune. As he joined in the talk and laughter going on in the luxuriously appointed hall where tea was being served, he followed with his mind's eye the tired labourer wending his way through the shades of evening to his home. A man to whom he was chatting made some witty rejoinder to a remark of his; he laughed aloud, and as he did so: 'He is there now. Home. The door of his hut is opening ——' he said to himself.

On a lounge, deep, wide, superbly commodious and ease-giving, screened a little from the rest of the hall by a wall of tall chrysanthemums topped with great blossoms of gold and bronze and dull pink, three or four girls were sitting, their heads close together. The master of the house, sauntering, teacup in hand, made his way round the wall of flowers, and appeared before them. Of what were they talking, he asked, which kept them so quiet and subdued, with such rapt faces?

'Margaret was telling us about dreams,' one said; 'but now that you are come, we will talk of something more important.'

'Aren't dreams important?' he asked.

209

'*You* don't think so, Mr Fortune!' they challenged him.

For what had he to do with dreams? The man of action, of bargain-driving, of opportunity making and seizing; the man who, by force of mind, intelligence, will, character, had made at five-and-forty years of age an immense fortune – off his own bat, too, as his friends said of him. The man whose business success was colossal. Who by sheer strength of will, by dint of knowing what he wanted and courageously going for it, spite of all obstacles, had in love also been supremely victorious. Who had married the woman he had set his heart on; the woman most men envied him; who had brought him, beside her aristocratic beauty, and that something of mien and of bearing which it is said only a long line of ancestors can give, a high, courageous spirit, an alert and clever brain, a boundless ambition for him whom the world might have thought beneath her. A woman who knew how to spend the money he made, and spent it in a way that told; a way that moved the man she had married surely up, and up, and up the ladder she saw it was good for him to climb.

What had he to do with dreams? A man at whose daily history the finger of calumny could not point; in whose circumstances it was impossible to indicate one particular in which good fortune had failed him, or in which he could reasonably desire a difference. Life had given him so much, he had nothing left to dream of.

She, who was the eldest of the little group behind the chrysanthemums, who had started that subject of the mystery of dreams which had enchained the attention of the rest, looked thoughtfully upon the man who stood smiling indulgently before them, and some such thoughts were in her mind.

'Mr Fortune never dreams,' she said.

'Never dream? Not I? Indeed and indeed I do, thank God.'

'Oh, Mr Fortune! Do tell us what about!' the other girls cried.

'Is it that you are dragging your limbs up the face of a horrible precipice, and come to an impassable projecting shelf you haven't got the strength to reach?'

'Is it that, while everyone else has to come down stairs step by step, you glide from top to bottom without effort? What a delightful sensation it is! How proud I always am of myself in that dream!'

'Is it that you are wearing your pyjamas in the daytime, Mr Fortune, instead of putting on your coat and – other things, you know –'

'Or that your teeth have fallen out?'

'Or your hair fallen off?'

'Oh, when you come to think of it, how beastly dreams are! Hardly ever do you get a nice one. I wish I could sell mine, as that girl did in the story.'

'I wouldn't sell my dream for a million pounds,' Felix Fortune said.

'Mr Fortune! How interesting! Do tell us what it is. Yes, do, now! Is it always the same?'

'Always.'

'How ripping that is! And do you have it every single night?'

'I always hope for it every night. It doesn't always come. If it did -!'

'If it did – what?'

'Nothing. Only I wish it would.'

'Lady Margery! Lady Margery! do come here!' One of the girls had peeped round the screen of the chrysanthemums and called to Felix Fortune's wife.

She came – a slim, tall figure, elegant in soft drapings of purple silk bordered with gold embroideries – and stood at her husband's side.

'Lady Margery, *what* is Mr Fortune's beautiful dream? We are dying to know. Do tell us.'

'His beautiful dream? Ask him. How should I know?'

'He has a dream worth a million pounds. Always the same; and he has it every single night.'

'No,' Felix Fortune corrected, 'I told you no. If it came every night it would be worth twenty millions.'

'But do tell us what it is! Why don't you make haste? Lady Margery, make him tell us.'

Lady Margery turned her face upon her husband with a little questioning surprise: 'Why don't you tell your silly old dream, Felix?' she reproved him.

He only laughed, and shook his head, and went away with his teacup, leaving the subject to be forgotten.

But that one among the girls who carried 'the love-born name of Margaret,' and had the sweet and pensive face appropriate to those who are privileged to be so called, did not forget.

When, a month or so later, she found herself by Felix Fortune's side in his wife's box at the Opera, she had not forgotten. It was a gala night. Royalty was present, and representatives of most families renowned, or noble, or wealthy in the land. In the interval between the acts Fortune pointed out to his young guest, to whom such a scene was unfamiliar, here and there the owner of a name which had made itself famous. Among these was the world-known name of the man who had entered the box, and was sitting, familiarly chatting, at his wife's side.

'What a lot of beautiful women!' Margaret said, looking round. 'And I think Lady Margery the most beautiful here.'

He assented quietly, with the calm pride of possession. 'I agree with you,' he said. 'I always think her the most beautiful.'

'Her life and yours must be perfect; like a dream,' the girl said, and turned her eyes with a pondering look upon his face.

A life so full of energy, of enterprise, of action as his, must leave, on a face ever so impassive, some marks of the ravages of these forces; lines graven upon brow, and about mouth and eyes, must reveal in unguarded moments something of the strain of seldom-relaxed effort, telling a history that the attentive eye may read.

'Do you still have *your* dream, by the way?' she asked him softly. 'The dream you told us of at Claydoring – the dream which was worth a million pounds?'

He smiled, sighing a little, folding his arms across his chest. 'I still have it, thank God.'

'I remember you thanked God for it before.'

'Yes.'

'Tell it me.'

Her voice was low, and full, and winning; the voice of a woman to whom confidences are never denied. So he obeyed her.

'I dream,' he began – then paused for a minute, glancing round upon the brilliant scene: the fair faces, the white arms and necks, the dazzling jewels, the gay uniforms, the profusion of flowers. 'I dream of something quite different from all this. You would not be interested. Why should I tell you?'

'Tell me,' she said again, in the voice which never was denied; and he told her.

'I dream that I am a day-labourer, returning from my work. I don't know at what I have laboured, – the dream, often as it comes to me, never shows me that, – but I am very tired; physically – only physically. I dream I am returning to my hut, the day's work over. At whatever I have worked, the sense that I have laboured well is with me. With an overwhelming sense of thankfulness that it is home I have gained, I open the door. There, in the little brick-floored room, always the same, – ah, how I love the thought of it! – the table, pulled to the hearth, is spread for the evening meal. Such a poor meal – bread and cheese, I think, and that only. At the fire my wife is standing, her back to me; but I know that she is my wife, and that she has been listening for my coming. She lifts a singing kettle from the coals, and pours water into the teapot warming on the hearth. She turns to me then, and I see her face. She is a sturdily built peasant woman, and has a plain, middle-aged, peasant face – a face I have never seen except in my dream. It welcomes me –'

He paused upon the word, and Margaret felt that he looked with inward vision upon the scene of his dream and on the welcoming face.

'That is all,' he said, arousing himself to smile upon her. 'That's my million-pound dream! Not much when it's put into words, is it? But the peace of it! the peace of it! The blessed, blessed peace of it!'

Margaret was silent, watching his face.

A minute, and he turned upon her. 'But you don't understand?' he said.

'Indeed and indeed I do.'

And he was sure that she understood.

'You will laugh at me –?'

But he knew that she would not laugh.

LEVENSES

THE first day of harvest. The sun hot upon the field where the reaper is noisily cutting its broad pathway through the corn. The shadow of the hedge and the two great elms by the gate is thrown black upon the stubble. Within the shade a group of women are seated in the tidy white aprons and with the generally cleaned-up appearance exacted by rural custom at the time of year and the hour when the noontide meal is due. Beside them, in the long dry grass of the bank, where the lavender-coloured scabious, the small scarlet poppy, the slender, wiry mouse-ear sway on their long stalks, the baskets are standing which contain the 'levenses' for the workers in the field.

''Tain't on'y a heavy time for th' men. 'Tis th' wives as bear th' brunt of it,' one of the women was saying. 'I ha' left my gal, Ireen, to drag th' coach wi' th' little uns and the heaviest o' th' things. She ain't on'y twelve, come Janivary, but she ha' got th' strength o' t'ree o' me.'

'You're lucky as you ha'n't only one man to perwide for, tro' th' harvest, Mrs Drake,' the woman who sat beside her remarked.

'I ain't none so sure,' Mrs Drake made answer. 'If so be as you've got t'ree of 'em, Mis' Browne, you ha' th' wages o' t'ree to dale with, remember. And a matter o' fourteen poun', I reckon, a-comin' in at th' ind o' th' harvest.'

'Wait, bor, till yours is growed up like mine – for the two boys is as hungry as th' man – and see what they kin ate! – Here come yer Ireen, Mis' Drake, wi' Ronald and th' lessest little boy i' th' cart. Min' th' gate-pos', Ireen,' she screamed, as the child in question appeared upon the scene.

'What a keerless little mawther you be!' her mother scolded the new-comer. 'You as near as nothin' tarned th' coach over by the pos'. What for d'ye imitate runnin' when th' two little uns is behind ye?'

Ireen, white-haired, red and round and shining of face, was seen to be excited. 'Bobby Wapple, he ha' fell down i' th' midder, a-bringin' his father's wittles,' she was shouting as she approached, tugging at the long handle of the green-painted go-cart, in which lay two children asleep beneath a bottle, a drinking mug, and a basket of provisions. 'He's a-hollerin' like a good un, and th' drink's spilt inter 'is basket.'

'Well, I never!' the women said in a chorus, and stared, pleasantly stirred, upon Ireen. Some children seated by their mothers scampered to their feet and flew off to the scene of disaster.

'Kin I go back and pick up th' pieces, and help Bobby Wapple?' the little girl asked.

'No, and can't!' the mother promptly announced. 'You stop along o' me, and kape a-jogglin' the cart wi' the little uns.'

'Theer! the cutter's stopped!' another voice cried. 'Here come th' men. They'll be riddy for a drink, I'll lay my life on it.'

The labourers came, slouching heavily over the golden stubble. They picked up their discarded coats and neck-handkerchiefs from the bank, donning them, or making of them pillows for their heads as they lay down, sprawling beside their wives. One, a neglected-looking man of forty, with a dark and miserable face, a dirty wisp that had once been a necktie, and once been scarlet, binding his torn shirt about his gaunt throat, stood for a minute looking over the group.

'Wheer's my Bobby?' he asked.

'He've fell and broke th' bottle into 's basket,' Ireen, anxious to deliver the intelligence, panted out.

'Oh!' He spoke with the soured, dejected air of one habituated to, but not resigned to, the buffets of Fortune, and removing himself from rest, sat down upon the warm grass amid the gently stirring flowers of the bank. There, his face turned in the direction in which Bobby should come, he waited; while the slices of harvest cake, the slices of bread and cheese, the mugs of drink were dealt out to the luckier men.

'Sarve 'm right,' Mrs Drake, with her mouth full, was remarking to Mrs Browne. 'Set a little un o' nine yare old to order his wittles, and to kerry 'em! Why don't the man git a woman to do for 'm, and live dacent-like?'

'Tom ha' had enough o' women,' one of the men said. 'Th' one he'd got runned 'm inter debt, and left 'm to help hisself, poor beggar.'

'A matter of eight months ago come the fif' o' September 'tis since Charlotte bust up with 'm and took herself off. A fine time him and Bobby ha' had iver since! And him that proud and shut up he ha'n't niver asked no neighbour to do 'm a hand's tarn.'

One of the younger men got up and carried a mug of beer to him who sat alone. He accepted, and drank it in silence, still looking towards the gate through which Bobby should come.

The child appeared at length, but not alone.

'My word!' said Mrs Drake, staring with all her eyes.

'If that ain't Charlotte, I'm a dead woman!' said Mrs Browne. 'You may bet your life the hussy have come back!'

The woman to whose skirts Bobby Wapple was clinging passed without any recognition the group of old neighbours and acquaintances on the bank. So set were her eyes and thoughts on the lonely figure beyond, it is possible she did not even see them. She stood before him for a minute, and watched his dark, lean face turn yellow beneath the tan. His mouth dropped open, his eyes stared. But he said nothing, and without a word she slipped to the place beside him on the bank. Bobby, with an anxious look at his father, settled down upon the skirt of her dress.

'Wheer's my wittles?' the father demanded of the boy, who began to whimper.

'I bruk th' bottle, daddy. They're sp'ilt.'

'Is they all sp'ilt?'

'Oh, Tom!' the woman said pitifully. 'I looked i' th' basket. There weren't nothin' but dry bread theer.'

''Tis on dry bread him and me ha' lived for a matter of eight months – thanks to you,' the man said. He turned and looked at her with fierce reproach. 'You runned me up bills I thought was paid, to a matter o' fi' pound. Fi' pound! You ruined me; and then you tarned your back, and cut and run; and left him and me to fend for oursel's. And we ha' nigh starved, le' me tell you. A fine mother and wife you be! What are ye a-doin' of here? Who axed ye to come? I swore I'd let my tongue rot out afore I axed ye; and I wull. What are ye a-doin' of?'

215

'I thought as you and Bobby 'ud be muddled i' th' harvest time. I felt as if I'd got to come and lend!' she said, and trembled where she sat.

'I never axed ye?'

'No.' He had a grudging and surly manner, but so miserable a look that she could not but be gentle with him.

'Fi' pound!' he repeated. 'A matter of fi' pound.'

'Theer was the doctor's bill when I was ill i' th' winter; and th' bill that hadn't never been paid when our little Gladys was born. That got me behind-hand, Tom, and I cou'n't never catch up agin. And then theer was you on yer club for two months wi' your sprained back, and not so much, by four shillin's a week, comin' in; and you that hard, Tom, I was afeared to tell ye. So, mother say, "Lave 'm, and come home"; and I took my Gladys and went. I thought as how you'd come after me, Tom —'

'You might ha' knowed me better,' Tom said. 'I swore as th' tongue should rot i' my mouth.' He paused, raised the mug to his lips, loudly gulped down the beer.

She looked at him, sideways, as he drank: at his thin, hungry face; his ragged clothes. She lifted the neglected and weeping little boy into her lap, and began to cry.

'Tom,' she said, 'I went because I was afraid. But I haven't been happy without you and Bobby. I don't believe as you and him ha' been happy without me.'

He put down the empty mug upon his knee; he looked out at the still uncut expanse of corn: the gold of it grew dim, grew black, was blotted out; the coarse hand he dragged across his wet lip shook.

There was a stir among the group farther down the bank. Ireen had started to bump her go-cart across the meadow to her home; the rest of the children made off to play in the dust of the road, to climb the gate, to hang over the sides of the ditch where the water ran in a tiny stream beneath the tall cresses; the women still sat down to talk over their empty baskets; the men slouched off heavily again to their work.

'Tom!' the woman said, and touched Tom Wapple's ragged sleeve.

'The fi' pound is paid off. Me and Bobby well-nigh starved to do it,' he said. 'You kin stop and bring my fourses i' th' arternune, if ye like.'

THE CONSERVATIVE VAN (January 1910)

WE saw a Conservative Van on the Green as we drove by, to-day; so to-night, after supper, when the children were in bed, Nancie and I strolled round that way to hear what was taking place. We stood in the black shadow of the elms, at one corner of the Green; and in our dark clothes, Nancie with a shawl over her head, were unobserved.

A sprinkling of voters had paused, on their way from supper to the public-house, to hear 'what the chap on t'other side had to say for hisself.' They were of the Radical persuasion, to a man; an unfriendly, but generally inarticulate, community.

Scarcely a promising audience. The light from the blazing lamp hanging from the roof of the car fell on slouching figures, on stolid, uninterested faces, or faces whose stiff features had settled into an expression of jeering incredulity. Not ambitious, individually, of refuting the arguments of the speaker on the steps of the caravan by anything more convincing than a boo-ing groan, an ear-grating g-r-r-r, or a contemptuous, loud spitting upon the grass, the meeting yet had its spokesman. Cutty Twiss, the village loafer, who by reason of his being rarely in work had the more time to devote to political controversy, had nominated himself to that post.

'During the last twenty-five years more than two millions acres under wheat, and two million acres under barley and vegetables, have gone out of cultivation,' the speaker was shouting; swiftly he chalked up the numbers on the blackboard hung beside him under the glaring lamp. 'Now, what is it that has made a desert of the rural places, my friends? Tell me that.'

'Pheasants,' called a voice somewhere in the little crowd.

'And the gents from Lon'on that can pay the lan'lord more for his land turned into game preserves than what the farmer kin afford,' from Cutty Twiss in his rasping voice.

'Where are the farmers who used to employ labour on these waste thousands of acres?' went on the shouting orator, bent on making his point.

'Gone to hell. What do we keer wheer they be?'

'Where are the labourers and their wives and children, that depended for their living on the ruined farmers?'

'Arnin' better wages in the towns, mister.'

'What, my friends, if in this county of your own, this agricultural county of Norfolk – where there are still' (so many) 'acres' – the

217

blackboard and chalk again – 'under cultivation, giving you employment, putting bread into your mouths – what if, under the present government, with the advantages given to the foreign producer, the heavy taxation, the burdens on the land, these acres go out of cultivation –?'

'Lerrem go out!' in a snarl from Cutty; seconded by a sympathetic grunting from the crowd.

'What if your farmers are ruined?'

'A d—d good thing!'

'Lay deown!' A boy on his stomach on the grass, digging his toes into the damp sod, was evidently in favour of fair play, and wished to discourage the heckling of the speaker by Cutty Twiss, the loafer.

The orator for the first time turned his attention to his only articulate opponent. He assumed a more genial, more colloquial tone, and flung out an extended hand at Cutty. 'You, my friend over there,' he said – 'my *little* friend' – (Cutty, in spite of the droop and the slouch of him, stood head and shoulders above his neighbours, and this epithet was received with a crackle of appreciative laughter), 'I am going to put a few questions to you. Do you know on which side your bread is buttered, little friend?'

Cutty lifted a hanging head for a momentary malign glance at the speaker, and dropped it again: 'Such as me can't afford none. We eat our bread without butter, mister.'

'I'm coming to that. One moment. I'm going to show you how you can all butter your bread. But you said something just now, I think, about the men and women who had left the rural districts earning more wages in the towns –'

'I say it again. I –'

'Wait, my friend – my modest little friend! Look at this.' Once more the hand that held the chalk flung millions on the blackboard. 'Now, how many is that, sir? That is the number of unemployed in the towns to which your rural population is drifting. Come, read the figures out to your companions. Such an accomplished little gentleman can read, I am sure –'

'Not your writin', mister. I weren't teached like that when I went to schule.'

'He can't read, the poor little gentleman! But we will make allowances for him, my friends. You, yourselves, can read the millions which represent the number of starving, and half-starving, unemployed in our towns. *Under Free Trade*, mind you! Now, with Tariff Reform –'

218

A prolonged growling 'Yah!' from the crowd, a momentary lifting of Cutty's down-dropped head. 'We'll have none of it, mister. We want our food chape.'

'Cheap, you foolish little man? But what does cheapness mean to you? It means *cheap labour*; low wages; unemployment; hunger – or at least insufficient food for your children.'

The faces in the semicircle – those dimly seen at its two extremities, and those on which the dazzling light from the caravan shone – turned and looked expectantly upon their champion.

'You'll never get no chance to prove what your d—d Tariff Reform 'ud do, mister,' he shouted. 'You duss'n't try it, in this country. 'Tis more than your lives is warth.'

'We don't want no tax put on corn,' a mild voice was heard to object; and we saw that Giles, the shepherd, had joined the group. His smock was tucked up to allow the insertion of his hands in his trousers' pockets, and to witness to the fact that he was off duty, his delicate-featured, vacant face was in shade, his pale eyes were raised with timid appeal to the face of the man on the caravan steps. 'Bread's dear enough for our missusses to pay for now, sir.'

The alert orator threw out an arresting hand: 'Who promised you the large and the cheap loaf, my friend? Tell me that.'

No answer.

'Have you got it? – Come! Have you got it?'

'That ain't the fault o' no gov'n'ments,' the meek voice asserted. 'Wet harvests is the wark o' God A'mighty, sir.'

'We don't want no furriners stopped sendin' in their corn.' It was Cutty who croaked the interruption.

'My man, they'll have to send it in! What else – unless they eat it themselves, or make fuel of it, or cease to grow it – can they do with it?'

'We 'on't have no taxes on our food.'

'Won't you? Would it surprise you to hear that your food is already taxed, to the tune of thirteen millions a year?' The quick hand flew to the blackboard, and 13,000,000 appeared there as by magic. 'Why are we now paying more for many articles of food than we were, only ten years ago? Why – ?'

But Cutty had strung himself up to a supreme effort. 'Mister,' he said, tense with the ponderous endeavour to put into words a sentence he had partially mastered from the pages of his weekly newspaper, 'you ha' been free wi' th' questions you ha' brought forrard, I'm a-goin' to put one to yew: What tariff did Jarminy place agin imported flour in the year 1874?'

A hush of awe fell upon the assembly at that portentous utterance. The man on the caravan waited with an air of listening attention.

'– And what tariff agin it have Jarminy got now?'

'Come, neow! Tha's a good tidy one for ye,' an exultant, hoarse voice cried.

The shepherd, who was nearest to us of the little crowd, gave a chuckle of admiration. 'You ha' flummoxed 'm theer, Cutty bor!' He turned his meek old face to the man on the caravan steps. 'I doubt as how my neighbour have wholly flummuxed you, sir,' he said.

'One moment!' pleaded the orator brightly. 'I will answer your question in one moment. But tell me first – tell me first, what was the population of Germany in 1874, as against the population of to-day?'

'Go on, Cutty. Tell 'm that!' the boy on his stomach jeered.

Every eye turned to look at Cutty, staring open-mouthed at his questioner.

'By your reply, my little friend, we shall arrive at the progressive consumption of flour; and –'

There fell a minute of heavy silence, during which the meeting sorrowfully realised the astounding fact that their representative had not the required information at his finger-tips. Then the gruff voice of Cutty was heard growling out an evasion.

'I'm a-askin' of *yew* for information, I ain't a-givin' none,' he said.

But the night airs were chilly, and Nancie had had enough, so we slipped away. As we went, the rasping tones of the village politician followed us.

'Oh, lay deown!' Nancie said in irritated imitation of the boy who sprawled upon the grass.

'He won't,' I said. 'And all the chalking up of millions, the arguments of common sense, the marshalling of irrefutable facts are of no avail to make him. Nor any orator, nor smart Conservative van with its lamp a-shining. Blatant, mischievous, ignorant, he is the oracle of the public-house. It is Cutty Twiss who has the ear of Dulditch.'

THE SUNDAY AFTER (January 1910)

THE Sunday after our election. Calm after storm has fallen upon Dulditch. Snow has fallen there too, in the night; and when we arise

220

this morning we find our village, after all the red-hot passions of the last few days, lying in a kind of visible peace.

We have been actively hating each other for the past week; familiar names have been spoken with naughty adjectives attached; neighbours have sworn at each other from doorstep to doorstep; their women have wrangled as they drew water from the well, or hung wet linen on the line in adjacent gardens; children, freed from school, have flung mud (literally) in each other's faces, have cuffed and scratched and kicked. Men have been against masters – having been taught to regard them as their natural enemies, they have even seized the licence of the moment to 'let on' that they do so, – against teachers, against order and authority. Class hatred, which goes decently veiled at other times, has shown its ugly face, and stalked, dangerous, cruel, and destructive in our midst.

But it is all done with now; and here is the Sabbath; and upon the scene of strife the snow has fallen. The air is frosty but very still, the sun is shining, the bells are ringing for church. Down the village street, over the yet unsullied snow, a pheasant in his gorgeous plumage struts, unafraid.

A sheepish desire to recall what has been said in the heat of argument, to blot out from the mind what has been done amiss, may be noted in the demeanour of the some-time antagonists, talking in a group at the four crossways, or gathering in the public-house kitchen when service is over. Little Tory and little Radical sit side by side in the Sunday-school, not even wearing their colours any longer. Jarge and Jim, between whom a not all unsanguinary fight has been, talk together amiably from doorstep to doorstep.

'Now 'tis all over, and can't du no harm,' Jarge says confidentially to Jim, 'theer's suffin' I should like wery well to ask: What *is* this here tariff reform theer ha' been sech a creation piece o' wark about?'

'The ins and outs of it I don't wholly know,' says Jim, modestly, to Jarge. 'But as I understand the matter, it have suffin' to du wi' th' runnin' o' these here trams and cars and wehicles, i' th' Lon'on streets.'

'Is that how ter be?' Jarge says. He accepts the explanation without demur, but in the silence which follows he wonders, perhaps, why he should have been so keen on such a matter.

Mrs Jarge and Mrs Jim, who have slanged each other mercilessly all the week, walk to church together in the evening.

'Whichever of 'em have got in, I don't s'pose 'twill make a hape o' diff'rence to us,' says Mrs Jim, who is a pessimist. 'They talk high when they're on th' platform – they ha' got ter *du* it, I say.'

'They *kin* talk anyhow!' comments Mrs Jarge with admiration. ''Tis wholly amusin' to hearken how they du spit it out.'

Among the men in their Sunday coats, gathered in the bare public-house kitchen, there is much good-humoured banter of a man called John, a sturdy little red-cheeked man in a velveteen sleeved waistcoat, who sits looking slyly into his pint mug with a grin on his face.

'Ye rid i' th' motor, didn't ye, John bor?'

'Ay,' says John. 'T'other side ain't a-goin' ter have all th' fun, I says to myself, and we a-waitin' till night for our old wan. I ha' rid in a wan afore, I says, but in one o' them theer motors I ha'n't rid. "Will you sweer as you're a-goin' to wote Tory," says they to me.'

'An' you sweered, John?'

There is a shout of laughter at the slow grimace which twists John's stiff countenance into a wink of assent.

'An' you woted Tory?'

'I ain't a-sayin' one way or t'other,' John replies with caution. 'But, if so be 'twas as you're a-sayin', I ain't th' only one what rid in a motor, wi' Tory colours a-flyin', that woted diff'runt from how he'd sweered to.'

Two young men are talking together in the doorway of the inn: 'I was wholly took aback when I heered t'other side's man was in. How come you fust to hear on't, Bill?' one asked of the other.

''Twas like this here,' said Bill. 'Me and my mate was on th' stack – we was a-t'roshin', that day. We heared a hullabaloo. "'Tis th' child'en out o' school, a chairin'," says Joe to me. We could see 'm all a-scamperin' acrost th' field to th' farm. "All of 'em's a-chairin'," says I. "Our man's in!" I set a-hollerin'. "Hold yer row," says Teddy Brown, him as drive th' engine, a-callin' th' ward up to us. "*Our* side's in," says he; "and if 'ter be, I'm danged if I don't stand ye a pint o' beer, a-piece."'

'So you was tore 'twixt yer pint and yer politics, Bill?'

Bill grins. 'I got my pint,' he says. 'If so be as t'other chap got in, I don't know as I should ha' got more.'

Presently old Giles, the shepherd, stands among them. Not smart in Sunday clothes like the rest, but in gaiters, and smock, and battered hat. A meditative man, with a refined and gentle face, having mixed little with his kind, but looked on at the ways of sheep for a lifetime. Of life, of the world, of man, he has little knowledge, but every sheep in his flock he knows; its outward appearance, its dispositions, its character, its history; and he talks these over with his old dog Rose, keeping watch beside him over the fold.

He is not often seen in the gathering at the White Hart; but, once in a while, he leaves his sheep peacefully feeding, and crosses the fields, as now, to seek the haunts of men.

He listens to the talk with lips dropped apart, and eyes round and clear and blue, for all his seventy years.

'How about these here Jarmins?' he asks, at length. 'If so be as they're a-comin', as folks tell, whar are we a-goin' ter *du* with 'em?'

'You arst that question t'other night, o' th' labour chap what was a-holdin' forth in th' parush room, Giles bor,' one of the men reminded him. 'What did he make answer? "If the Jarmins knock at my door," he say, "I shall arst 'em to walk in. What ha' we got to *luse*?" he say, "No land, no money. If so be as th' Jarmins like ter come – let' em!" he say.'

A young man, the son of the village carpenter, who had not spoken hitherto, springs up at that with a sudden fire in his eye. 'That man ought to ha' been shot!' he cries. 'He should ha' been shot for a traitor! I'd like to ha' done it myself.'

But they hush him quickly; the election is over; where is the use of hot words and quarrelling now?

The shepherd has finished his pint; he wipes his mouth with the back of his hand, and coaxes the drops from the ragged growth of hair, mingled white and yellow, beneath his chin. 'Tha's the question I ha' got to ask,' he repeats, as much to himself as the company at large; 'Whar are we a-goin' ter *du* with 'em?'

Then he goes out. At the door his dog is lying in the light snow, waiting for his master. Together they make their way in a bee-line across the fields to the fold, leaving in the whiteness of the snow a track of large black ovals accompanied by small black rounds, showing where Rose has followed in her master's steps.

What a scene of peace it is! What a heavenly quiet is over all! The broad, rolling fields in their unstained maiden white, the dark plantation. A light powdering of snow lies on the black plumes of the towering pines, lies on the low thorn hedges, a sprinkling of it is on the sand-grey, heavy fleeces of the sheep. They are busy crunching the turnips the shepherd and his 'page' have dug out of the snow that morning. The otherwise perfect silence is broken by the sound, and by the nimble stirring of the birds in the hedges as they move from twig to twig, dislodging the feathery snow particles, which make, on the attentive ear, a tinkling as they fall.

The old shepherd stands by the hurdles which enclose his flock, his old dog at his feet. He is one of those who had eschewed the aristocratic motor and gone to the poll in the Radical 'wan.' Since the vote has been his he has recorded it for the Liberals. That he has, on this occasion, departed from that custom is a secret which he has confided to his dog, to his sheep, and to Nature alone.

'I done it agin the Jarmins,' he whispers, looking out with his clear blue eyes to the horizon veiled in a mist as white and luminous as the snow.

He has not understood the arguments for or against. He is a shepherd, and has to think of his flock. The coming of the Jarmins couldn't be good for the sheep.

'I rid i' th' wan, right enough. But I woted agin th' Jarmins,' he says aloud.

BACK TO THE LAND

HE had been a ruddy-faced, healthy-looking lad of eighteen when, a dozen years ago, he had gone away to the 'sheres.' When he returned to his native village last summer, bringing a big and bony wife and a particularly small daughter in his wake, he appeared to have dwindled to half his original size. His once round cheeks had fallen in beneath the sharp cheek-bones; his eyes, grown large and heavy, were sunken in deep sockets; the anatomy of his skull and jaw seemed unnecessarily defined. Never, since he had exchanged the free air of his native county for the close atmosphere of the workshops, in good health, he had of late suffered a long illness. Then, pining for the old and healthier life, he had given up his home, converted his few possessions into cash, and returned, as his vernacular has it, to his nat*ive*. There he took up residence with his father and mother until a separate home could be provided.

The little family came in harvest time, when the labourer's larder is unusually well stocked, when he quaffs almost unlimited beer, when he is hospitably inclined. David Harmer spent the long days in the fields, looking on, in his Sunday clothes, an attenuated figure, oddly foreign to the place, while the harvestmen worked. When the hours for refreshment arrived, and the men, wives, and children gathered beneath the shadowing hedge, sat down, jack-knives in their hands, and with huge appetite to their meals, he took his 'levenses' and 'fourses' with them, feeling the warmth of the sun once more in his bones, filling his weakened lungs with the pure air.

Strength and health came back to him; the look of feverish anxiety left his eyes. His tongue was nimbler than is that member with the dweller in fields alone, and much talk he had of the big black town he came from, with its teeming population and its giant mills; many tales he told of a daily life that was strange and almost inconceivable to his listeners.

Thirty shillings a week he had earned at the work at which he was proficient; his wife had earned fifteen. The mouths of those who heard, undeterred by the circumstance that they were full of food at the time, fell open at these figures. Twelve shillings a week for the most part, and no more, had they on which to bring up their families.

He told of music-halls, of social evenings, of parks in which the band played on Sundays, of free libraries, of workmen's clubs, of a goose won in a lottery at Christmas, of a week's holiday to the sea, for those who liked to contribute to the fund, in the summer.

'Lords and ladies you was, bor,' one of the women, more than a little sceptical of such recitals, commented. 'If such as them was the goin's on – wonder you di'n't stop theer!'

'Tha's whar I tell 'm,' Harman's father chimed in. 'Bein' theer, why not stop theer, Davy?'

'And I make answer, as I done fust day of me retarn,' David answered complacently, 'I ha' coom bock to th' lond.' (He had tacked the northern accent on to his Norfolk dialect, the result being a hybrid pronunciation difficult to reproduce.) 'Ma wife and me and the little un ha' done what we ha' been asked to do by the genelmen in parliament, by the noospapers, by a' th' folk that know summat, and can give it tongue. "Coom bock to th' lond!" they say. "How can we," they say, "entice the wor-r-rker bock to th' lond?" I says to ma wife, "Boock oop, lass. I'm a-goin'." The lass she boocked oop, and here we be.'

'Yes, but bein' got here, whar er you a-goin' to du, Davy bor?'

The question was put not without anxiety. If Davy was taken on again on that farm where his father worked and he had worked as a boy, it stood to reason some one must be discharged to make room for him. The place was over-manned as it was; already a whisper had been around that the master meant to cut down his labour bill. Davy, however, was quite easy in his mind.

'Stan' to reason there's wor-r-rk,' he said, 'or why should we ha' been asked to coom and do it?'

'Wheer are they a-goin' to put their hids to? Tha's what I want to larn,' old Harman often muttered. 'My old woman and me can't harbour 'em for iver; and theer ain't a wacant spot i' th' willage, as I can hear on.'

There was not! Every cottage had its tenants. When Davy came to make serious inquiry, he could not find, in the land to which with such touching confidence he had returned, where to lay his head. Moreover, there was not a farmer in the place who wanted extra labour.

When, harvest being over, and his health re-established, he walked to the neighbouring villages, he found no hope of a job there. Either there were labourers enough already at work, or the farmers shrank from engaging a factory-hand, a poor-looking creature with narrow shoulders and contracted chest; one who had never handled a plough in his life, and had forgotten what he had once known of even a boy's work on a farm.

'Bock to th' lond I've coom, according to what the noospapers and the genelmen advise,' he told them all. He could not get over the feeling that his action in returning had been very praiseworthy.

But they shook their heads, telling him that there were more men in the neighbourhood already than were wanted.

'Fare as if you'd come back to th' land, bor, and th' land hadn't no need of ye,' his father would say to him, night after night, as he returned dispirited from his empty quest.

Peace did not reign in the cottage, where 'the foreign woman,' as they called Davy's big wife from the 'sheres,' and her mother-in-law could not agree. The ways of the old Norfolk wife were not the ways of the dwellers in town. Young Mrs Harman was a clever worker at her own trade, but she did not understand the work of the wash-tub, where she might have helped the elder woman. Her days had been spent in the factory; she had not even the habit of looking after her own child, and only clumsily could patch her husband's trousers. Small as the cottage was, she had been used to a much smaller home, and complained bitterly of the draughts in the big kitchen where now her days were passed.

'I haven't been used to the loike o' thot emptiness,' she would say, waving a great scornful hand at the fields upon which the door opened. 'Give me houses, and summat to look at, I say.'

She was, in fact, afraid of the rolling green spaces, and would beat her three-years-old girl if she strayed beyond the garden gate. So, although there was a child's paradise of green meadow all around, with blackberries on the hedges, and nuts to be had for the gathering in the plantations, the little one played all day on the dust-heap by the back door, disputing with the grandmother's three lean hens the treasures to be found there.

Mother-in-law and daughter-in-law quarrelled fiercely all the day; when evening brought the dispirited young man back from his fruitless search for work, husband and wife quarrelled.

'You and your talk o' the lond!' she stormed at him. 'Give me the clack o' the mills, mun; I'd as soon be i' ma grave as here.'

'I'll gang awa',' at last she declared. 'I'll gang bock to wheer I coom from, and take th' little lass. There's a better livin' theer for her and me. Coom with us, or stay, as you loike.'

He stayed. The standard which he had hoisted he hauled not down. 'Theer's wor-r-r-rk on th' lond for them as coom bock to it,' he persisted, 'else 'tis so much empty clatter they ha' talked.'

It was well to have faith, but hard work to keep his spirits up, as he tramped the country fruitlessly, or watched other men – the men who had stuck to the land from boyhood – at their work. Now and then he was put in for a day when an extra man was wanted for threshing, now and then he walked with the beaters when 'Squire' had a big shoot; but in such desultory employment he felt that his confidence in returning to the land was not receiving the merited reward. In the end he got a job on the road; he had to walk a couple of miles to and from the scene of his labours, and he sat by the roadside all day long to break stones.

It was an occupation affording time for reflection; but Davy's mind, not trained for consecutive thought, was occupied solely by one tremendous fact: 'I ha' been wholly took in,' he would remark to himself as he folded his coat away beneath the dripping hedge, and set to work in the raw morning air upon the little mountain of flints by the roadside. 'I wasn't led to look for th' loike o' this, when I coom bock to th' lond.'

Upon his unaccustomed frame the exposure told cruelly. Soon he gave up stone-breaking for the harder work of coughing away his life by his mother's fireside.

In a few weeks' time she stood in the churchyard, looking into a grave not yet filled in. In her hands she held a porcelain wreath beneath a glass case. It was from Davy's wife and little daughter, and a card within testified to the fact that it was sent 'with sympathy.' At the bottom of the six feet of mother earth was the box which contained all that the cough had left of Davy. Upon it lay the light sifting of sandy soil which had fallen there from the officiating clergyman's hand.

The old woman looked long upon the coffin with a shaking head: 'Bor, you're back to th' land at last,' she said, and her tears fell slowly; 'you came back to th' land more'n you bargained for, Davy bor!'

THE SETTING SUN

IN his worn, earth-coloured smock, crook in hand, and dog at heel, the old shepherd comes, the setting sun upon his face. He mutters to himself, as is the habit of those who live solitary lives, making his way through fields of green wheat and oats, breast-high; through the brown 'summer-lays,' where the young turnips are being chopped out; through a murmuring sea of barley with a silver sheen upon the crests of its waves which will ere long turn to gold. Fair-complexioned, and refined of face he is, and there is something childlike and innocent in the wide gaze of his blue eyes; beneath the smock, elaborately embroidered for him by the wife long dead, his shoulders stoop with age.

What thoughts are in his breast as he turns his back for ever upon the sheep which have been his care, night and day – leaving the ewes on the high meadowlands, the hoggets in the clover-layer, the lambs enjoying the cream of the feed on the second-cream sanfoin – who can tell? He belongs to a class which never consciously indulges in sentiment, which is almost, indeed, without the power of expression. What he feels in his heart he is quite incapable of taking upon his lips.

As he nears the home premises he comes upon the old master leaning over the gate of a field lately fragrant with sweet scents and brave with many-coloured flowers, but from which the last load of hay has been carted.

Giles stops beside him, touches the battered, mouldy-looking hat worn at the back of his head, conveys with a word to Rose, his dog, that his pleasure is to pause there for a while.

'Been to see that all's well, for the last time, Giles?'

'All's well, master. New shepherd, he ha' took's flock i' good order. Le's hope know*ledge*'ll be giv th' man to keep it so, and to sarve ye as well as I ha' sarved ye.'

'He won't serve me for fifty years, Giles.'

Giles shook a wise head: "'Tain't i' th' coorse o' Nater to expec' yew to be speered that time, master. Fifty yare is a sight o' time!'

"'Tis that, Giles.'

'Fifty yare!' Giles repeated, and seemed to muse. 'We ha' give ache other th' best yares of our lives, master. For if so be as we could add another fifty to 'em I reckon they'd be but dwindery, wintry ones, and not like the yares that is passed. Young we was beginnin' o' them times, master. Young!'

'Strange to think on now, Giles.'

'I mind well the fust day I come. Fust wards as iver yew said to me was, "An old yow ha' hulled herself inter th' ditch –" '

'The ditch at the top of the Ten Acre,' supplied the old master, who also, strange to say, remembered.

'Right you are, master. "An old yow ha' hulled herself inter th' ditch," says yew, a-bawlin' th' wards. "Run," says yew, "and pull her out, bor." A-horse-back you was, master, th' little master up i' th' saddle afore ye, and the missus a-walkin' alongside. Leastways, I didn't know as she was th' missus, then. "Whu might that young lady be?" I says to th' boy what acted as my page, fust yare. "There ain't no young lady. That be th' missus," says he, and set a-laughin' to think as how I'd called th' missus a young lady; as how should I know no diff'runt, that had never sot eyes on 'er afore?'

'You knew her, later on, Giles.'

'I knowed her, right well. "Be sure you ha' plenty o' black lambs, Giles," she say to me, "come lambin' time," she say, "for all the black lambs is for me," she say.'

But it was of the 'ship' he was leaving for ever the old shepherd wanted to talk. Of a certain 'crule' lambing time, 'th' crulest ever he'd knowed'; and of one particular night when he had waded through snow to his knees, to tend 'th' yows' and the new-born lambs. 'And yit that yare the yows was the gainest doin', and the lambs th' healthiest iver I'd knowed.' Of the year when the rain fell almost every day without cessation, so that 'the midders was all under water, and the highest land only a slush, and not a dry place to fix the lambyard in the whole farm.' Did the master mind how the hay was all of a white mould afore it could be carted, and how the barley grew again, and rotted as it lay on the ground? 'Th' ship, they suffered crule. There weren't one among the whole flock as wasn't lame. Young master, he come, hand in hand wi' th' missus, one day, inter th' midder where th' twins was tarned out wi' their yows. "Mummy," he say, "look at th' little lambs," he say, "all of 'em a-sayin' their prayers," he say. Forced

229

to laugh I were, and so were th' missus when she heard 'm; for every one o' th' yows and lambs was on their knees, not able to stand.'

The old master was silent, thinking his own thoughts, looking out on the bare field robbed of its flowers.

He came back from his dreaming to hear the old shepherd speaking now of the new one who had taken his place. 'He'll sarve ye well, master. As far as th' young man's know 'll let 'm, he'll sarve ye well; I han't no fare.'

'New servants are not like the old, Giles. But for this old-age pension you would not have left me.'

Giles withdrew a wrinkled hand from the trouser-pocket under his smock to rub a meditative chin, beneath which the whitey fair hair hung in a ragged fringe.

'That mebbe, master. That mebbe. Yit, at seventy and more, a man's wark is done. An' 'tis like this hare: I can't take your wage, and take th' old-age pansion at th' same time. 'Tis agin th' law. "What a fule yew be, bor," my neighbours they say to me. "Take your pansion," they say, "an' let them as can't git it, wark." Fust I tarned a deaf air; daughter-in-law as kape my house, a-naggin' at me at home, and neighbours a-jeerin, abroad. "Was ever sech a sight seed," they say, "as five shillin', come ivery pay-day, a bein' held out to a man and he a-tarnin' his back." So in th' ind I let 'em have their way, though poorer, a sight, I shall be; and I don't say as I couldn't ha' kep on wi' the ship for a yare or so more; and I don't say as I wouldn't better ha' liked to do it. For, I worn't never afeared o' wark, and there ain't none to say as how I were.'

'The younger men are not like you, Giles.'

'Master, you nivver said a truer ward. They ain't.'

'Why? What's come to them?'

'A high stomick is come to 'em. Notions too big for their hids to hold has come to 'em. Wha's yours, ain't yours no longer, master – or shouldn't be – but theirs.'

'Socialism?'

'Tha's th' size on't, master; though 'tis a ward too larned for my tongue. There ain't no content among 'em any more; there ain't no kindness from man to man, nor yit no good feelin' from man to master. Time 'll prove whether they're th' better off for sech a settin' of theirselves agin th' orders o' Nater. But this I say, them as ha' put such contrairiness i' their minds ha' much to answer for.'

'We all have that, Giles; much to answer for.'

'Tha's as mebbe,' Giles assented, not too well pleased. His conscience was clear. He had had th' ship to care for and had done his best by them for fifty years!

With his heavy boot he stirred up Rose, who, her nose resting on her tail, had curled herself up to sleep beside him. 'Fare you well, master.'

'Fare you well, Giles; since the time has come to part.'

'Time! Tha's a master one to do with, Time is, come to think on't! While 'tis hare, 'tis nothin'; you fare to take no reck'nin' of it, and when 'tis gone, blame me, there don't fare to be nothin' left.'

'Nothing left,' the old master echoed.

''Tis wholly so, master! 'Tis wholly so.'

'Shake hands, old friend.'

'That I will, master, though I don't know as in all the fifty yare I ha' sarved ye I ha' shaked hands wi' ye afore. Fifty yare! Yew come a-ridin' inter th' field, a-holdin' little master on front of ye, th' missus – her as I thought was a young lady – a-walkin' alongside, her hand on th' little un's knee – Lor! 'tis like yest'day, i' my mind.'

'God be with you, Giles.'

'Good-bye to ye, master.'

And the old shepherd, his dog close at his heels, goes upon his way, the setting sun upon his face; while the old master, leaning still upon the gate, looks over the empty field from which all the flowers have been mown.

ELLA'S FORTUNE

THE family of Dingle seemed to have been marked by Fate for misfortune; and in the last year of their existence as a family, misfortunes, treading one upon the other's heels, came upon them in battalions.

A smaller but brisker chemist's shop was opened in the High Street of Drowsing, welcomed eagerly by the inhabitants, the establishment of Joseph Dingle having long been conspicuous for its character of being 'out of' all those lip-salves, chilblain specifics, plasters and syrups most in demand by customers subject to the minor ills. Hastened by this event, the failure so long threatened of poor Joseph could be no more retarded.

Then two of the three children died of a fever. A tragedy which, considering the condition of the exchequer, and the hopeless incapacity of the Dingles to feed, to educate, and to place their offspring in the world, might have had its alleviations perhaps. But, perverse and unreasoning creature that she was, their mother wept for them as long and bitterly as if she had infinite leisure to do so, and thousands a year coming in.

She wept indeed, without ceasing, until her baby, which was expected in two months at the time of their death, was born – fortunately dead. Then she, too, died.

Her husband attended her funeral. (Hardly any one else attended it, for she came from a distant county, and if she had any relatives living no one had remembered to let them know.) Then he had come home and had changed his boots (a fact which became of significance in view of after events), and had taken off his watch. This he had left, with a small heap of money from his waistcoat pocket, on the mantelpiece of his bedroom. After which he had gone out and drowned himself.

At least, that was the received and more popular version of his disappearance. Later, there crept in an element of doubt. The river and ponds were dragged – why was not his body found? To his many cronies, talking to them across the counter while other customers stood waiting in the shop, he had told of a younger brother who had run away to sea, had deserted from his ship, and was on the way to make a fortune in America – Africa – Australia. No one was certain of the country, but that detail did not matter. In Drowsing it began to be increasingly believed that Joseph Dingle had left his screaming motherless babe behind, his debts and responsibilities, and was gone to join fortunes with his brother.

It was a fine point to argue over, and a subject which, for a length of time only to be credited by those acquainted with such stagnant neighbourhoods, kept the gossipers at inn bars, and over shop counters, and by tea-tables in back parlours, with food for controversy and speculation.

If the man had been starting on a journey where every asset would have been of importance, why in reason's name had he left his watch and his few half-crowns behind him? Why – get over that if you can! – had he taken off his boots? On the other hand, if he was drowned in the river, tell me why the body hadn't been found? Come now!

But while the fate of poor Joseph Dingle thus remained matter for debate, the fate of Ella, his little eighteen-months-old daughter, was quickly decided.

In order to pave the way for the troubles surely to follow, the chemist had married beneath him – a girl of the servant class. No one belonging to her, even had they been willing to do so, could afford to saddle themselves with the upbringing of a child. The father's people – with the exception of the apocryphal brother in Asia, Africa, or America – were dead or estranged. The workhouse, therefore, was the only shelter offered to Ella; that of pauper was the career apportioned her. The little pile of coins, the proceeds of the sale of watch and of Joseph's new boots, went to help a burdened country with its disbursements for her maintenance. To the workhouse, accordingly, the babe was sent, and upon its charities existed not unhappily for a while.

But it has been mercifully ordained that no workhouse may retain within its walls orphan or deserted children. In accordance with which decree, one cold winter morning, Ella is dressed in new coarse little shirt, her feet and legs – as white, as dimpled, as pretty as if they were the feet and legs of baby princess instead of baby pauper – are stuffed into woollen stockings and stiff leather boots, her protesting arms are pushed through the dark blue sleeves of a thick serge coat; about her round dimpled face a hood of the same material is tightly drawn, hiding all her close-cropped dark hair, its frills flapping over her blue, black-lashed eyes. And Joseph Dingle's daughter is equipped for another start in life.

Mounted on a seat in his car beside the workhouse master, she is driven away from the town in which were her homes of chemist's shop and workhouse. Five miles into the country she is borne to the little village of Dulditch, to the house of a woman who, for the consideration of three shillings (to be increased, on the child attaining the age of ten, to four shillings) a week for board, and a quarterly half-sovereign for clothes, has undertaken to perform towards the orphan girl the duties of a mother.

It had come on to snow during the drive, and the workhouse master, to protect the child, had pulled the rug about her, covering her, face and all. So that when Mrs Gall came to her back-door and looked out with eagerness and anticipation across the green yard in which the blacksmith's forge was situated to the vehicle at the gate, it seemed to her that the little girl she had expected was not there at all. A black disappointment fell upon her.

'What! You've come alone, Mr Francis? Then, ain't I to have her after all?' she called.

Then the workhouse master, saying nothing, descended from his car, and, taking the rolled-up rug in his arms, carried it through the driving snow across the yard, and laid the burden in the woman's arms.

'Is she there, after all? My word, you've taken care of her!' she said. There was something of an almost passionate eagerness in the gesture with which she clasped the little burden. Her eyes shone and her mouth worked. She turned and hurried through a freshly scrubbed little outer kitchen to a large inner one where a bright fire was burning. It was comfortably furnished with spotless table and chairs and dresser; half the wide expanse of red brick was covered with new matting; bright plates and dishes and vessels of tin and copper hung on the pink distempered walls or on the dresser shelves. An ideal kitchen for a cottage home.

'Here, you aren't going to keep rug and all, ma'am!' the workhouse master protested.

He followed her to the fire, and stood for a minute warming his hands and watching while she unfolded the still sleeping child.

Ella, awaking, struggled into a sitting position on the foster mother's knees. She had been used to strange faces, and was not afraid of the honest ugliness of the blacksmith's wife.

The fire pleased her; she tried to stretch her tightly creased arms and legs towards the friendly blaze. Mrs Gall removed the ugly hood with fingers which seemed to tremble with eagerness, disclosing the cropped dark hair. She passed her hand over the little head, and her mouth twitched.

'Mine was a fair girl,' she said. 'This here one's black-hidded.'

'You lost one about that age?' the workhouse master asked.

Mrs Gall nodded, not removing her eyes from the child. 'Just afore her second birthday; ten year ago come Sunday. This here one ain't nothin' so pretty; and I hoped she'd ha' been of her colour. Fair, she was, wi' light-coloured curls.'

'I reckon, and so does my missus, that Dingley is an uncommon pretty child,' Mr Francis said, as though nettled by the disparagement of the goods he had brought. 'You've got no complaint on that score, ma'am.'

'This here little un's eyes is blue, and hers was black as coal, with cheeks like damask. This here one's cheeks is pale.'

'I'd best take her back and change her,' the man said jocosely. He held out a hand to the child in mock invitation. 'Come along back with me, Dingley.'

But Ella, not too young to know when she was well off, turned away from him to the fire and Mrs Gall. 'Take off,' she said, and held up one of her clumsy boots to the blaze.

'She can talk!' the foster mother cried. 'My little un could only splutter, like; spite of our havin' had her tongue cut.' She busied herself unlacing the ugly boot. 'Why, 'tis thick enough for me!' she pityingly grumbled. 'Did ever a body see such a boot for such a foot!'

'Take off,' said Ella again, and held up the other foot.

The workhouse master laughed. 'She's sharp!' he said, and nodded good morning and took himself away.

Mrs Gall, a polite woman as a rule, forgot to respond to the valediction, forgot to pilot him to the door, and even hardly noticed his going. For the thick stocking as well as the clumsy boots had to come off, and the beautiful little feet and ankles must be clasped and warmed and caressed in Mrs Gall's work-roughened hand. A tear trickled down the woman's face as she held them.

'Them feet! They might have been my little un's own,' she said.

'Take off,' commanded Ella, and held up a muffled fist. That too must be released, which, being done, the remembered sensation of the little hand stirring in her own brought a look of something like ecstasy to the woman's plain face.

The blacksmith, crossing the yard in his first breathing-space to look upon the new inmate of his home, heard his wife's voice sunk to a low crooning murmur whose sound took him back a half-score of years. Entering, he found her sitting over the fire, the little newcomer on her knees. The child had fallen asleep while her unrobing was in process, and lay, arms and shoulders, feet and ankles bare, her little dark head pillowed on Mrs John Gall's breast.

'She ha'n't got our Ellen's golden hair, but she have a look of her, John.'

John looked, stooping, hands on knees; his big beard of auburn and grey almost brushing the child's shoulder. Perhaps she had a look of the lost Ellen. Children were very much alike, and ten years is a long time. The memory of Ellen's little face had grown dim to the village blacksmith.

'She have a look of her, John?'

John nodded. 'She'll be company for ye while I'm acrorst th' way,' he said.

For Fate in one matter had been kind to this fragment of Joseph Dingle's family. She had been 'boarded out' in a home where she herself, and not the weekly three shillings and the quarterly ten, was wanted. And where, the little disappointment over the wrong colour of her hair and eyes outlived and forgotten, Ella Dingley became to the Galls as their one ewe-lamb; ate of their meat, drank of their cup, lay in their bosoms, and was unto them as a daughter.

⇒✠⇐

When Ellen Dingley was fourteen years old, the age at which the boarded-out children relieve their country of the burden of maintenance and go out into the world to earn their own living, Mrs Hustler, the wife of the vicar of the parish, proposed that the girl should make her start in life as kitchen-maid at the vicarage. The suggestion was received with scarcely concealed scorn.

'You'll get no more help from the Guardians, you know, Mrs Gall.'

'I'll do without, ma'am. I've took the pay because, her being boarded out, 'twas my due; but when it stop, let it stop. We'll manage. John Gall and me aren't beggars.'

'Still, sooner or later I suppose Ella must earn her living; and it is best for her to begin in a gentleman's kitchen –'

'Ella's own father was a gentleman, hisself, ma'am.'

'Well, hardly, Mrs Gall!'

'Ella's father was a chemister! I reckon as a chemister is among the gentry.' She spoke with a note of defiance, and Mrs Hustler heard in silence with smiles of tolerance. 'Anyone that cast an eye on Ella can see as how she's different.'

'Different, Mrs Gall?'

'Do she look like Amy Leech, or Bessie Hart, or – ?'

'It's because she's so much better dressed, isn't it?'

'I put Ella into no finery.'

'No, no!'

'Never since to me she come have I put a mite o' finery on Ella's back! Let other folk hang their bits o' ribbon in their girls' hair, and put their sham chains round their necks – I don't hold wi't. No one can't say as I ha' messed up Ella with no tawdriness.'

'She has always looked beautifully neat and well cared for; and is dressed as is becoming to her station.'

'I don't know about no station,' the unmollified Mrs Gall declared. 'But this I know, Ella ain't goin' to wear no caps and ap'ons, nor yet come under no missuses.'

In such households as the blacksmith's there is not much reticence, and the conversation with the vicar's wife was repeated several times, verbatim, in Ella's ears.

'Was my father a gentleman?' she asked. The statement had often been made in her presence, but had never apparently carried significance to her mind until now, when she suddenly awakened to interest on the point.

'Ain't I a-tellin' ye so?'

'But what do you say, Daddy?'

Daddy was slower of speech than his wife, but his words when they came were his bond.

Daddy considered a minute or two – a big-chested, powerful man, sitting with rolled-up shirt-sleeves to eat his peas and bacon. 'He were a chemister, sure enough,' he said weightily at length. 'There ain't no doubt but what he were a chemister.' He took a noisy gulp of tea, and went on with greater fluency. 'I mind me as how I once went to 'm with a bit o' hot iron in my eye. Very agreeable he were, and full of his questions about my neighbours, and ivery one in Dulditch. But he never got th' bit o' hot iron out. Misery I were in with it – and him a-talkin'!'

'Then, if my father was a gentleman, I'm a lady,' Ella said. She announced the fact without pride or elation, only as making a statement there was no denying.

'Well, tha's why you ain't goin' out in the world to be no one's servant,' her foster mother had told her.

'I'd like to see where I lived, along of my father what was a gentleman,' the girl said.

Having got the idea into her head, she said it more than once. With the result that on one pleasant summer's afternoon, Mrs Gall, for the modest sum of two shillings and sixpence, having hired the baker's cart, of which George, the blacksmith's assistant, cleaned up and attired in his Sunday suit, was appointed Jehu, the three of them drove the five miles between Dulditch and Drowsing. And all in order that Ella might gaze upon the illustrious spot in which her beginnings were made.

The chemist who had helped to ruin poor Joseph Dingley – amply equipped to perform that office for himself – had, on Dingley's demise, moved into the original shop. It was no longer the dingy, stagnant-looking den, in the house alongside of which Ella had first seen the light. She, who had never been into a town before, was impressed by the mighty bottles of blue and red and yellow fluid in the window, by the plaster statue of the white horse in the fanlight above the door, by the delicious odour of mingled fragrances which greeted her nostrils as she peeped within. The living-house, also, now wore a prosperous, well-to-do look. Lace curtains were elegantly looped with pink ribbons at all the windows; the chemist's name was on a refulgent brass plate on the door.

The child gazed upon it all, standing back in the road by her mother's side, lips apart, eyes shining. 'Ain't it a beautiful place, mother? Think of my father a-living here!' she said, again and again.

'Now you 'on't want to ask no more was your father a gentleman!' the gratified Mrs Gall declared.

She also was proud of the distinguished place. A young lady who had been born in that habitation with the pink-looped curtains called her 'mother,' was as a daughter to her. 'I reckon Mrs Hustler have only got to cast her eyes this way, and we shan't hear no more about no scullery-maid's place!' she said.

'Le's go in, mother,' the girl begged, and pulled upon a yielding arm.

'We kin buy a penner o' cough lozengers for Daddy,' Mrs Gall reminded herself.

Her husband had no cough but was partial to the flavour of the lozengers, she explained to the alert and obliging chemist, weighing and making into a compact parcel the modest purchase. He wore a moustache twisted into stiff points at the ends, had heavily perfumed hair, and was quite the gentleman, as Ella, awe-struck, at once perceived.

'This here young lady was born in this here very place,' Mrs Gall continued, impelled to confide in the agreeable chemist. ''Tis the reason why me and her and George have come to have a look at it, as you may have guessed.'

Thereupon, mildly interested, the chemist inquired the name of the pretty round-cheeked child with the plentifully falling brown hair, the cheeks like roses at dawn, and the eyes blue as moonlit skies.

'Dingley?' he repeated. 'I remember poor Joseph Dingley very well. Anything ever been heard of him?' he asked, confidentially lowering his voice.

'Drownded, sir,' Mrs Gall said. 'Folks as knowed the ins and outs haven't no doubts about it.'

'Ah; *I* doubt it very much,' the chemist said. 'I am of opinion he went off to join his brother, wherever he was, and has probably made a fortune by now. You'll find your name advertised for in the *People's*

Friendly – keep a look out!' he said to Ella with a pleasing raillery. 'What's your Christian name, miss?'

'Ella, sir.'

'Well, Ella Dingley will "hear of something to her advantage" one of these fine days; and there'll be a fortune waiting for her.'

Ella listened, quite credulous, not at all elated or surprised.

'Would that be how we should know of it, sir – an advert*ise*ment in the newspapers?' Mrs Gall asked, eager for instruction on the point.

'That's how 'twould be!' the chemist made answer, with his airy, disengaged manner. 'Watch the newspapers, ma'am. – Shut your eyes,' he said to Ella, and squirted some scent upon her dimpled, pretty cheek before he turned to another customer.

Some of the lily-of-the-valley scent trickled down the cheek to her clothing; Ella carried the aroma about, faintly, for days. The odour of the blacksmith and of George the assistant, always hot and sweating from their toil, even of Mrs Gall's five-year-old woollen dress, worn through the day's work, and laid across the counterpane for additional warmth when John and she were a-bed, was quite other. The delicate fragrance seemed to set her apart as something of a different make from them.

'I'd like always to be made to smell sweet, like this, mother,' she said. 'If I lived in that chemister's shop now, I'd be always a-squirting of the scent-bottle.'

'Well, now you'll remember who you was; and be a good, decent-livin' girl; and hold your head up,' Mrs Gall admonished.

And Ella, always obedient, did hold up her head, but in a gentle, modest way that made her no enemies. And it seemed to Mrs Gall and Daddy that the head thus held grew prettier and prettier every day.

When Ella was fifteen and a pupil-teacher at the school, coming in from a walk with George, the blacksmith's assistant, one Sabbath-day afternoon, she found her mother at her Sunday afternoon occupation of going laboriously through the columns of advertised missing relatives in the pages of the *People's Friendly*. Since that chance word of the agreeable chemist, Mrs Gall had seen to it that the paper was left at her door every week; and she never failed to search it for that fortune which might be coming to Ella.

'S'posin' 'twas there, and we never see it, and thousands was lost to her!' she always said when the blacksmith hinted she was muddling her brain in vain; for she was not much of a scholar.

Tea was already laid; an ample Sabbath-day tea, with cake, and jam-tarts, and meat-rolls, added to the weekly fare. The door to the garden stood open to the sunshine, and the room was fragrant with scent of the pinks which bordered the garden-path leading to the little gate.

'Well, there you be! You ain't in this week,' Mrs Gall said, handing the paper to Ella as she took her own place before the tea-pot.

'I don't know that I want to be,' Ella said. 'I do very well as I am, mother.'

'Yes, my dear. And Daddy and me don't want you no different, and I don't know as George do, nayther.' (George, into whose head it had entered that, when he and she should be fully grown up, he could not do better for himself than one day to marry his master's daughter, scraped his feet on the bricks with a bashful movement and guffawed.) 'But I suppose if you was to find yerself come in for a hape o' money you wouldn't make no objections to it?'

Ella accepted the rebuke and the paper listlessly, and spread the latter on the table between her plate and George's; and while the boy and girl ate their tea, sitting elbows on table, they also conscientiously perused the page which was to be so fateful.

George ran his blunt finger-tip down the column. He was a steady, promising, well-grown boy of nineteen. His Sunday suit was of navy-blue serge, he wore a very stiff high collar, very large shirt cuffs, and a tie the colour of Ella's eyes; but, scrub as he might for the weekly clean up, the black would not come out of his broad, broken finger-nails. The which was a matter of greater concern to Ella than to him.

'There ain't no name of Dingle there,' he said.

'No one wants me!' said Ella with a mock despair. 'If my father had wanted me 'tisn't likely he'd have taken hisself off and left me alone.'

'Your father was drownded,' the blacksmith declared. 'For what else did he take off his new boots?'

George was still poring over the paper. Presently he lifted his head from it. He wore his hair in the fashion set by the Apollo Belvedere, dressed high in front, with a mop of light-coloured curls. 'If so being as her father don't inquire for her, why shouldn't Ella inquire for him?' he asked.

It was a new idea. They listened, spellbound in a minute's silence, turned astonished eyes on each other.

'To think o' that now! Blame me! Why shouldn't she?' the blacksmith asked.

240

Mrs Gall, who had been hitherto the only person of initiative in the family, gasped with astonishment at the unsuspected cleverness of George.

'Well done you, George!' said Ella, and bestowed a congratulatory pat upon the broad shoulder of the young man. 'If father's alive that will fetch him. Let's do it! Let's do it now!'

They composed the advertisement that very evening, taking those of cases which seemed similar to Ella's for their guide. When George had written it out in his best round hand, and Ella read it aloud to her foster parents, it met with general approval.

'Ella Dingle, aged fifteen, would be glad to hear of or from her father, Joseph Dingle, chemist, late of Dulditch, who is believed to have left England thirteen years ago to join his brother abroad. Apply, care of Mr John Gall, blacksmith, Dulditch, Norfolk.'

'Right affectin', ain't it!' Mrs Gall cried, and a tear actually trickled down the side of her nose.

The blacksmith, gaping at an exhibition of scholarship on the part of the boy and girl entirely beyond his own powers, slapped his knee and pronounced an emphatic 'Ah!'

Letters came with great rarity to the family of Gall, but after the Sunday afternoon that had witnessed the literary triumph of the younger generation the visits of the postman were looked for with extraordinary interest. After a few weeks, however, knowing nothing of the time occupied in the transmission of foreign mails, they lost confidence in their chances of a reply to the advertisement.

One morning, Ella Dingle, coming out of school, walking sedately as became the dignity of a pupil teacher, and surrounded by a bodyguard of little boys and girls whose homes lay in the same direction, saw, lounging down the road ahead of her, beneath the avenue of chestnuts which happened at that time to be in flower, a strange gentleman.

Unknown people flew through Dulditch in motor-cars, or struggled through on bicycles, but a stranger pedestrian on the familiar roads was a sight of great rarity.

A gentleman, too! Ella, from the accident of her birth, was held to be peculiarly endowed with the faculty of recognising the genus. But the less initiated, observing the cut of the clothes, the fashion of the moustache, and the indolence of the lounging walk, could have made no mistake here. The school-children instinctively touched their caps, and curtsied their 'manners' as he passed. The pupil teacher, of too high importance to make reverential greeting to unknown passers-by, only looked at him as they crossed upon the sun-and-shadow-chequered road with eyes round with curiosity and interest.

The gentleman condescended conspicuously to return her gaze. Moreover, as the children, who looked back to see, reported, having passed, he turned and retraced his steps, following the girl and her escort at a few dozen yards' distance.

Ella was in the habit of looking in on her Daddy and his assistant at their work before she crossed the green yard to the back door of home. She loved the ring and the roar of the forge, and liked to stand on the threshold of the smithy to watch the roaring blaze, to hear the clink and the hammer of the mighty blows on the red-hot bars, and to see the red sparks fly, lighting up the dear black face of Daddy with his big beard, and the not disagreeable face of the assistant with the smoke-dyed auburn curls. The two men never paused in their work to greet the girl, but they loved to see her standing there, and she knew they loved it.

As she turned to go indoors she saw that the strange gentleman who had followed her was watching the forge also, leaning upon the low wall which divided the yard from the road, his gloved hands idly dangling his walking stick among the nettles which grew beneath.

'Mother, there's a strange gentleman looking over the wall!' Ella said with some excitement. 'He walked home from school behind us all, and now he's looking over the wall.'

'He'll keep!' said Mrs Gall. She was busy dishing up the pickled pork and the light dumplings for the noonday meal. 'You come and eat your dinner.'

'He looked hard at me, mother. "You'll know me next time!" I felt inclined to say to him.'

'Don't you go to say no such thing, then!' Mrs Gall was irritable that morning. 'What should he look at you for, pray? You ain't nothin' so much, to look at!'

In her heart she thought that a sight more beautiful than Ella Dingle was not to be met with on a summer's day.

Since she had been raised to the dignity of pupil teacher, Ella's hair must not hang about, 'just anyhow,' as had been its habit, but must be put away neatly. Braided in two thick tails tied with ribbon its own colour, it now hung down her back; beneath her straw hat her 'bright face, crescent-browed,' her round fair cheeks, and eyes like 'little glistening seas,' and soft, innocent lips, were a sight for jaded and weary eyes; she wore a skirt of lilac linen and a white cotton shirt; and

242

altogether was, to say truth, a charming picture of rural health, and youth, and innocence, and simple beauty.

The children from the cottage near, walking back with 'Teacher' to afternoon school, were eager to impart the information that the strange gentleman of the morning had given them pennies, and had asked them for the name of the young lady who had walked with them.

And when Ella came out of school he was there again.

He was lounging in his walk beneath the flowering chestnuts, idly swinging his stick, as in the morning; but when Ella emerged from the school-yard his gait became more purposeful. With a quick step he approached, and to the girl's unbounded astonishment spoke to her, raising his hat.

'You are Miss Ella Dingle, I think?'

Ella's cheeks, so childish and fair and round, turned of the pink of apple-blossom. She gave a little gasping assent.

'May I be permitted to have a talk with you, Miss Dingle?'

Ella tried to swallow down her choking surprise.

'Perhaps these little people who are gaping around might be dispensed with?'

The pupil teacher raised the voice of authority waveringly, and the school-children reluctantly drew off.

'Here! Have you got a shop anywhere, with sweets to sell? Go in, and buy them,' the stranger said, and scattered a handful of coppers.

For a moment he watched the retreat of the scampering throng, then, feeling in the inner pocket of his coat, produced a letter-case. From this he took a scrap of paper, and held it before Ella's eyes: 'This comes from you?' he said.

It was the advertisement from the *People's Friendly*.

'Oh!' Ella cried, and falling a step back from him looked with an alarmed questioning at the stoutish, middle-aged stranger. 'You are my father!' she said.

He smiled upon her, took the advertisement from her fingers, replaced it carefully in the pocket-book which he thrust again into his breast pocket. 'I am not your father, but I come from him,' he said. 'I am your uncle, Ella.'

'If so be as I'd had time to think on't, I never could ha' brought myself to part from her,' Mrs Gall said many times afterwards, talking Ella's departure over with husband and neighbours. 'Never could I ha' brought myself to part wi' my Ella! But 'twas the comin' like a clap o' thunder upon us, and bein' all to be done in a jiffey, that kep' me up.

'On the Monday he come: Ella brought 'm in, along of her, when she come from school – "Here be my uncle," she say. You might ha' knocked me down! Then he laid it all afore me: how her father were alive, after all, and had seen the advertisement, and sent for 'er. He weren't drownded – Joseph Dingle weren't. He'd took off his boots to make as though he was a-goin' to do away with hisself. I put the question to him: "I ha' long wished to know, sir," I sayed, "why the man changed his boots." "'Twas his cunnin'," he say, "and to put people off."

'That was o' th' Monday. Tuesday, he come again, and brought his wife, what Ella was to make th' acquaintance of, to travel with. Wednesday they both come, and took her off in a carriage. There wasn't time so much as to think about it afore 'twas over, and she was gone.'

There was not even time for Ella to make the discovery that she did not wish to go, – until the last moment when it was too late; until the hired carriage with the uncle and aunt in it was waiting for her beyond the gate of the green yard that lay between the cottage and the forge; until her berth was booked in the ship to take her to America; until there was no possibility of altering plans. Then how she cried! Turning coward at last, how she clung to them all in turn, begging not to be sent away!

'Daddy, you are my real father. I don't want any other father but you! George, we shan't go any more walks o' Sunday afternoons! Mother, oh, mother! I shall want you so. Don't – don't send me away!'

Mrs Gall, for the child's good, had to be severe with her in the finish. ''Tisn't grateful to your uncle and aunt,' she reminded her. The uncle and aunt were seated in the carriage at the gate, the little tin trunk containing all Ella's worldly goods perched upon the box by the driver. 'Less than twelve months, and you'll be back with us again, for a stay. Your uncle have give me his promise. Ameriky ain't so far off, after all. And you'll write, ye know, Ella!'

The neighbours standing in the road to see Ella Dingle go said the scene was 'heart-rendin'.' 'But Mrs Gall, she had allust held her hid up so high about Ella bein' th' daughter of a chemister. Now she've got what she wanted.' They hoped she was satisfied.

Poor Mrs Gall, putting on a brave face, after her habit, was, in fact, desolate, inconsolable. She got no pity on any side.

Mrs Hustler, hearing of departure of Ella too late for interference, came down, and, as Mrs Gall afterwards reported to her husband, behaved 'right nasty' about it.

244

'I wish, in such an important matter, you had consulted Mr Hustler, Mrs Gall.'

Mrs Gall stared, wrung her nose on one side in a scornful snuffle. She had never been in the habit of courting the interference of the vicar in her affairs!

'You are quite satisfied, I hope, of the respectability of these people?'

Mrs Gall was contemptuous of the question. 'Ella's father was a gentleman, we all know. A chemister. Her uncle and aunt you only want to look at! Soon's Mr Dingle what was at Dulditch, and is now a-rollin' in his thousands in Ameriky, see the notice in the paper what we put in. "Go," he say to his brother, "and fetch the girl." Straightaway he come, the very fust ship, and bringed his wife with 'm – thinkin' as how 'twould be more agr'able for Ella, he being a stranger. Very thoughtful, I took it of 'm.'

'We know of the dangers to which young girls are exposed, Mrs Gall. The fiends in human form who lay traps to destroy them. We read our newspapers.' (Mrs Hustler dropped her voice, her shoulders moved with a shudder.) 'Poor young girls, and innocent children, decoyed from their homes and safety to an existence of shame and degradation and misery! One does not like to *think*, even, of such a case in connection with your dear, good girl. I mention it just to show why Mr Hustler and I felt you could not be too careful.'

No! she got no consolation.

And she needed it as time went on, very badly. For no eagerly expected letter, telling of her safe arrival, of her happiness with her father, rolling in money, and speaking of her speedy return to visit her foster mother's home, ever came from Ella to Mrs Gall.

Time went on – quickly for those who have their loved ones about them, weary, and weary-footed for the bereaved with eyes that ache and hearts that hunger, – but brought no news of Ella Dingle.

From the moment that the hired coachman touched his horse with his whip, and Ella, seated between her 'aunt' and 'uncle,' was driven away, her round childish face looking backward, the blue eyes anxiously straining for her last look at the forge, and her Daddy, and smoke-grimed assistant George, none that ever knew her set eyes on the petted, pretty child again.

It was as if the earth had opened and swallowed her. Better – far better – for her if it had.

'HA' you broke th' sticks for th' mornin's fire, and drawed th' water from th' well, and picked th' peas for th' dinner, and dug up th' new p'taties, Bob?'

'I reckon I have, missus. I reckon I done all them jobs, and more, while you was a-snoozin' a-bed this mornin'. Slape! I never see a woman slape like ye!'

'And wha's bed for, but for slapin' in? Turnin', and groanin', and growlin', half th' time, ain't what th' Almighty give us beds for.'

'Ah! I slep' well enough arter a day's wark, times gone by!'

'Now you ha' got to do yer wark i' th' night sayson, I s'pose? Theer was you, when I'd dozed off, a-hollerin' out "Hold ye! Hold ye!" Thought you'd got yer tame o' horses i' th' bed-chamber, steads o' yer wife, did ye?'

'A lot more soothin' to me they'd be, if so be as I had 'em there,' Bob said, heavily joking, after his kind.

He fetched his stick from the corner – he had no need to fetch his hat, because, except in that hour when, laid on the pillow beside his wife, he dreamed of his horses, it was never off his head.

'And wheer may you be off to now, I'd like ter know? Swaller yer brekfus', and off you go, stick in hand, like a gentleman! Fine to be you, nowadays, I say!'

'Ah!' said Bob, who had his own ideas on the subject. 'They're a-cuttin' of th' hay, acrost to th' home midder, and I'm a-goin' to see 'em a-doin' of it,' he explained.

'A-goin' to get a mardle, you mane, while I stop at home and do th' day's wark.'

'I scrubbed th' kitchen for ye, Sat'day.'

'And who should scrub it but you that do th' messin' of it? Bringin' in th' muck off yer old boots, to trail about.'

'Do you bless yer stars I don't wear 'em to bed, like poor old Tim Tucker done, when his dropsy wouldn't let 'm stoop to take 'em off!'

The couple were by no means out of temper with each other; the exchange of such pleasantries was all in their ordinary mode of conversation. His wife followed her Bob to the door:

'If so be as ye're bent on gallivantin', ye might call at 'Lizer's for her little M'y, at home wi' th' whoopin'-cough; 'twill give th' woman a free hand at th' wash-tub.'

'Lizer's M'y, attired in a clean 'pinny,' it being Monday morning, her tow-coloured hair parted on one side, and tied with a scrap of blue ribbon over the right eye, went off placidly, under escort, hand in hand wi' Gran'fa'. Their way led them past the village shop, at whose window, temptingly filled with biscuit-tins, innocent of biscuits since before M'y was born, the pair stopped: 'You got a ha'p'nny, Gran'fa'?'

From the inner depths of the buttoned pocket of Bob's often-washed trousers a ha'penny was disentombed, and laid forth in the purchase of 'nuggets'; a favourite confectionery, renowned for its character of 'Stay by-er,' being extremely difficult to get rid of when once lodged upon the tooth.

As the pair, hand in hand, emerged from the shop, 'Mother, she's a-goin' to fry some meece for my supper to-night,' M'y said.

Bob received the information with no surprise. 'Meece is good for th' whoopin'-cough,' he admitted. 'So's a bit o' tarred twine twisted round th' t'roat. I mind when one o' my little uns – Jarge he were – him as was arterwards kilt i' th' war in Afriky, – went about, for a matter o' months, wi' tarred line tied round his t'roat. Smelt, he did!'

They had climbed a low bank, and looking over the hedge, surveyed a field of young turnips in whose blue-green rows, hoe in hand, a man was at work. 'Hello!' called the man.

'Hello!' responded Bob.

'What, you tarned nuss?' demanded he of the hoe.

'I'm a-doin' a good tarn to 'Lizer, seein' arter her little un wi' th' whoopin'-cough. They look well, th' turmits du.'

'They grow agin, this m'ist weather, and set theirselves i' th' drills, fast as they're wed out. This here's the second time I ha' been over this job. A swelterin' one 'tis, too.'

'There's harder wark 'n that, bor, take my ward for it; and tha's to du nothin'.'

'S'elp me, I'd like to try, for a change,' the worker said, and spat on his hands and addressed himself to the turnips again.

'Did yer Jarge what was kilt in Afriky be shot with a gun or stabbed with a sword?' M'y inquired as the pair pursued their way.

Bob could not tell her. 'We knowed no fudder than that he was kilt,' he said.

'Did his mother cry when he was kilt?'

'Ah: th' woman cried.'

'Did you cry?'

'No.'

'What did you do, Gran'fa'?'

'I went and seed arter my hosses.'

'Did you have another little boy, 'sides Jarge?'

'One more.'

'What did he call hisself, Gran'fa'?'

'He called hisself Billy.'

'Was Billy kilt in Afriky?'

'No, Billy he got squashed to death with an ingine, out in Canada.'

'Did his mother cry?'

'I don't remember as how she did. He'd been away a sight o' time. You can't be allust a-cryin'.'

'Did you cry, Gran'fa'?'

'No.'

'What did you do?'

'I went and seed arter my hosses.'

'What are we a-goin' in here for, Gran'fa'?'

'We're a-goin' ter set down i' th' home midder, and see th' hay cut. Don't you go a-gallivantin' arter th' cutter, now! I once see a little un's two feet cut off, that played i' th' grass too close to the cutter.'

'Could she play when her feet was cut off?'

'No. They took her to th' 'orspittle, and she died. You ketch hold o' my coat, and suck yer nuggets. Here! we'll set down i' th' shade by Harbart, what's a-sharpin' th' knives for th' cutter.'

'Hello, Bob!'

'Hello, Harbie! Ye're a-cuttin' o' th' midder-hay at last!'

'Look like it. There's a sight o' stuff, but 'tis all laid by the rain, like.'

'That was a swelterin' day we done th' job last!'

'Ah, you're right, bor! Th' sw'at runned off my forehead and sizzled on the knives I was a sharpin'.'

'To-day there's a m'isture in th' air, and no sun to spake of. Labour's a pleasure, sich a day.'

'I'll chenge places wi' yew that han't got none.'

'You'd be wholly a fule to do it, Harbie.'

'You, a-walkin' out wi' yer stick, and all; and a-sittin' down where ter plase ye.'

'You try gittin' up at five i' th' mornin', bor, and nothin' afore ye all day but the chimbly corner, and yer missus's tongue!'

'I'd be a-thinkin' "Here be I – nothin' to do, and my pansion a-comin' in."'

'Wha's th' good o' my pansion to me? My old woman she take my five shillin's a week. Do I ever see a farden of it?'

'Gran'fa', here's th' cutter a-comin' round. I'd like to be Joe Balls, a-sittin' to drive th' hosses, Gran'fa'.'

'That 'ud be fine!' Gran'fa' said. He looked wistfully at Joe Balls on his coveted perch. He would rather have sat there than on the throne of kings. It had been his place last year.

'Was them two hosses yours, Gran'fa'?'

'They was mine. Th' black mare, o' th' offside's, Gipsy, and t'other's Albert. A tricksy one he were, to break in. Hulled th' muck-cart over by th' gate-post once. He's a old hoss now.'

'Like you, Gran'fa'.'

'Ah, you're right there! Only Albert he han't had to give up wark for th' sake o' takin' th' pansion.'

When the cutter came round again it stopped for Joe to descend from his throne, to unharness his horses, and re-harness the pair led up to the machine by him who had sharpened the knives.

Albert and Gipsy, being left in the shade of the tree to take their lunch, it was Gran'fa' who took on him the happy task of putting on their nosebags, of fastening bracken about their heads to keep away the flies. The old man stood, his arm thrown over Albert's neck, while the old horse munched his corn. No backward thought gave Albert to those fiery days of youth when he had wrecked the tumbril by the Long Meadow gate; but to Bob, gazing out beneath his battered hat, memories of old days came. Memories of days of poverty, struggle, hardship; grey days; days black with sorrow of loss; when salt taste of tears had been in the mouth if none had fallen from the eyes; days of rough weather, of aching bones, of soaked skin; all dear now, and precious to look back on, being of a time when labour had sweetened all.

Round and round went the cutter; M'y, seated, safe as in an arm-chair, on the broad back of Gipsy, surveying the lessening square of the grey and silver grass. The last nugget was displaced from its clinging hold of her tooth. It was her slipping from her seat on the black mare's back which aroused the old man.

'Don't yer want no dinner to-day, Gran'fa'?'

Then he lifted the arm that had grown cramped about Albert's neck, and prepared to depart.

'You've forgot yer stick, Gran'fa'.'

'You can kerry it home,' he told her. It was his badge of freedom from labour, in a way – no working man carries a stick on working days, – but to-day he was not in love with ease. 'You can kerry it yerself, M'y.'

So May passed a leg over the stick and rode it down the field, like a horse, while Gran'fa' lingered still a minute to pat the horses' necks.

He snuffled as he joined the child; and the eyes which had not shed tears when his two sons were killed were wet at the parting with Albert and Gipsy.

BLUE BEADS

SHE lay all day long on her bed, and often she lay and moaned. She was crippled by rheumatism, and sometimes she moaned because the pain was acute and she could not forbear, but oftener for a distraction from the monotony of silence, listening to herself as she did so. The only other diversion she had was when Alice, the fifteen-year-old maid-of-all-work brought her food at stated periods. The food she was glad to see because it marked the passing of the long hours, more than because she needed to eat. Also because sometimes she could prevail on Alice to talk.

She had enjoyed a life with the average amount of happiness; she had been young; she always thought she had been pretty – which is as useful as the real thing, when once the prettiness is gone; she had had plenty of friends. But now she was old and ugly, and distorted with pain; and she lived by herself in Acacia Cottage, in the depth of the country; and Alice, her maid-of-all-work, made her only society.

Alice was lumpy, and fat, and red-haired. Sometimes she was attentive to her mistress, and sometimes she neglected her. But it was necessary to put up with Alice, because it was difficult to find a girl who would endure the loneliness of the situation. She was recently from school too, and sometimes would read to her mistress portions from her prize books, and sometimes she would talk.

The moaning which was the expression of the sufferer's pain or her boredom had been unusually noisy, one autumn afternoon, and Alice, coming leisurely the steep stairs to the bedroom, tea-tray in hands, was irritated by it:

'That ain't no arthly good your a-carryin' on like that, miss,' she said, as, kicking open the door with her foot, she entered. She carried the tray to the big four-post bedstead, beneath the shade of whose drab moreen curtains lay the shrivelled, twisted little old lady who was her mistress. 'Your a-groanin' don't make the water bile quicker, nor yet the toast get brown.'

She set the tray on the unoccupied side of the bed, and went round to the other side, to lift the old woman higher on her pillows.

'I groaned aloud with pain, Alice. Night and day I am in pain.'

'"Tis very mel'ncholy for me that ain't,' Alice said. She threw a white woollen shawl over the arched back and shoulders. 'I suppose you don't think o' that?' she asked, and the invalid's only response was a shriek of pain, as she tried to raise herself in bed.

'I should wish to be dead if I was you, miss.'

The poor mistress wept a little at that: 'I do sometimes long for release,' she admitted.

The tea-cup shook in her cramped fingers: 'Climb on the bed beside me, and give me my tea, Alice.'

So Alice clambered up, and held the cup to the shaking lips; her manipulations were not skilful, and as much of the drab-looking, half-cold fluid fell on the sheet as went down the poor throat.

The mistress took one slice of the divided round of buttered toast, Alice, by invitation, ate the other.

'You've got on your new afternoon frock, Alice. You look very nice.'

'The one made out o' that old 'un of yours.'

'And the nice warm petticoat, Alice?'

'Here it be,' said Alice, and pulled up her frock to show it. 'What I want next is shoes.' She held up one coarse foot in a boot through which the toes were bulging. 'These here has seen their best days, miss.'

'If your feet were not so big you could have mine,' the mistress said. 'I shall not want them any more.'

'You won't,' Alice said, and turned her prominent, large blue eyes to stare at the old woman when she whimpered over the thought.

'If you're a good girl, and kind, and will stay with me, I'll give you some new boots at Christmas, Alice.'

'I'd a sight rather have the blue beads.'

'The blue beads?'

'Yes. Out of that little leather box on your dressing-table.'

'You're not to interfere with the things in that box, Alice!'

'I can't help a-seein' 'em when I'm a-dustin'. I think they're pretty. They'd go nice with my eyes and my coloured hair. I should like to have 'em.'

'You could not possibly wear them, Alice.'

'Couldn't I? Why not?'

'They wouldn't be suitable.'

'Didn't you never wear them?'

'I wore them. I was a little girl when I wore them. A pretty little, little girl.' She laid down the piece of toast she was nibbling and whimpered at the recollection.

'I ain't such a very big one, miss. Leastways, I ain't old.'

'The cases are quite different. What was seemly for me would not be so for you. Although I lie here lonely and helpless all day long, I am a lady, Alice. I think you sometimes forget that I am a lady. My father was a gentleman; and my grandfather before him.'

'My gran'father was hanged,' Alice said, pleasurably recalling the fact.

The old mistress turned her head on the pillow and looked at the girl beside her, sitting upright on the bed, and giving forth that disturbing piece of intelligence as if it were a matter for pride: 'You never told me that before, Alice. Is it really true?'

'He were hanged, safe enough,' said Alice equably. 'And so were my cousin Joe.'

'You should certainly have told me!'

'Why? I never give it a thought.'

'Do you mean they – *murdered* people, Alice?'

'That they did, miss. The old chap, he did for two of 'em at once. An old man and woman they was, as lived back of a little shop. He were a woodman, gran'father were, and one day when he was a-passin' he'd got his chopper handy, and he went in and downed 'em both at once.'

'Killed them? Really *killed* them? How horrible!'

'Bashed both their hids in. They ketched him, through his chopper – and what was on it. The perlice did.'

'What a terrible man!'

'I never heard mother say as he were. Mother, she finely took on at his hangin'; and so did my gran'mother.'

'And your cousin Joe, Alice?'

'That weren't in these parts. We read it in the paper, else we shouldn't have knowed. He took a little boy into a field and done him; cousin Joe did.'

'Murdered him? What for?'

'His clo'es, I suppose, and his boots. He'd sold 'em for sixpence when they catched him.'

'And he was hanged? Hanged for sixpence?'

'He wanted the sixpence,' Alice explained, serenely.

The old woman, peering up at the girl beside her with her dim, blear eyes, forgot to moan, in the grip of the interest she felt. Her life had been long, and she had known many people, but never one nearly related to murderers before!

'It is a terrible family history!' at length she said. 'You must be thankful, Alice, for a better bringing up than they could have had. You must give thanks for your church, and your school, and your teaching, and all the good influences which have been brought to bear upon your life.'

'Yes,' said Alice.

'And if I were you I would not mention to anyone else in the village that story. It might tell against you in people's minds.'

'I don't see that. It ain't as if I wanted to down any one with a chopper, like gran'father, nor yet to strangle a little boy with a boot-lace like my cousin Joe.'

'But these things tell against a person. Take my advice and do not speak of them.'

'May I have the blue beads to wear when I go to church, come Sunday? I'd put 'em back in th' box again.'

'My blue beads? No. Certainly not. And get off the bed, Alice. I wish to be kind to you, and to allow you to talk to me; but you are not to take liberties.'

Her mistress spared Alice to go to church on Sunday afternoons, and from one week to the next the old lady dreaded that couple of hours when she found herself shut in the house alone. Alice would come in the bedroom to display herself, in her short black frock and her long black jacket, her great hands and wrists emerging bare from her sleeves. She wore her large green straw hat pushed to the back of her head, exposing all her copper-coloured hair combed in straight thick bands down her soap-polished face; she always blacked that portion of her foot which showed through her broken shoes.

'I'm now a-goin', miss,' she would announce in tones of joyful anticipation; and having walked across the room to make a survey of herself in the long plate-glass of the wardrobe, would depart, lumbering down the stairs, to let herself out and turn the key noisily in the lock; a sound full of terror to the lonely old woman, moaning upon her bed.

Alice had not been many Sundays in the place, and, so far, had not been successful in attracting to herself one of the hobbledehoys who hung about the four cross-ways by the village school, appraising the fashion and beauty of the female population walking past, or waited for the emerging congregation at the church-gate. But on this auspicious afternoon, when the yellow leaves from the lime-trees by the church-wall fluttered slowly through the heavy air to find a resting-place upon the nameless graves, when the sun beyond the fresh ploughed fields was sinking, a dull red globe in a sullen sky, and a white mist hovered over the wet meadows, and hid on all sides the distant prospect, a youth did accost Alice as she issued from the churchyard-gate.

'What fine blue beads we've got!' he said, and put out a clumsy finger and thumb, pretending to grab the necklace at Alice's throat.

He expected to be told 'to git along,' to 'shut his ugly mug, for fear the top of his hid would fall off,' or such-like familiar exhortations for his pains; but Alice had not longed each Sunday afternoon for a young man 'to walk with' to rebuff him so.

'They're pretty, aren't they? Do you like 'em, really?' she asked, and grinned up delightedly into his sheep-face.

'They're same colour as my eyes, and go wi' my hair. Tha's why I wear 'em,' she explained.

'You wasn't a-wearin' of 'em las' Sunday. I seen ye las' Sunday, and the Sunday afore.'

'Why didn't you speak to me, then? I hadn't got no one to walk with.'

'I was a-walkin' along of Tatty Chivers, what was housemaid down at Potter's. She've left her place, Tatty have.'

'You may walk along of me, if you like.'

'I don't know as I keer to.'

'You jolly well will, when you've tried it. I had a young chap to walk with, afore I come here. You're the first I have happed with, since.'

With a little more pressure Sheep-face put himself alongside, and where Alice liked to take him for her constitutional allowed himself to be dragged.

They walked beneath the dripping trees along the road, meeting other couples as happily mated as they. Alice cheeked them as they passed. She was surprisingly blest. Her reproach was taken away. She was as good as any of them – she had a young man to walk with! They crawled between wet hedges down muddy lanes; they stood still to look at nothing over gates; and by this time the arm of Sheep-face was around that substantial waist of Alice.

⊰✳⊱

When Alice reached home she was an hour later than her allotted time. 'I don't keer if I am!' Alice said, and put out her tongue at the white face of the kitchen clock which she felt to be accusing her. 'There'll be

254

a hullabaloo!' she promised herself, knowing that her mistress should have had her tea long ago. She got it ready in a hurry, stuffing slabs of bread-and-butter and chunks of cake into her mouth as she did so; for she was hungry; making love to Sheep-face had been an exhausting exercise.

'Now for a wiggin'! And if she ask where I've been and what I've been a-doin', she'll hear the truth, 'on't she!' she said, with her tongue in her cheek, as, tray in hand, she kicked open the bedroom door.

But not a question on the subject was put to her, the mistress being full of another matter.

'Alice, where are the blue beads that were in the leather box on the dressing-table?'

'The blue beads? What, them you wore when you was a little girl, miss?'

'Where are they?'

'Why, where should they be but in the leather box on your dressing-table, still?'

'They are not there. I crawled out of bed to look for them. They aren't there.'

Alice put down the tray upon the side of the bed, and crossed to the dressing-table. The beads were clutched in her hand. It was easy, her back to the bed, to slip them back into the box. 'Finely you must have looked, miss!' and turning round, box in hand, she held up the beads for inspection.

'Bring them to me.' The old woman took them eagerly in her stiffened fingers; they were warm from the hot hand that had held them.

The eyes turned on the girl were eloquent of accusation and reproach. Yet not a word of either dared she speak. She was so helpless and alone. It was so difficult to find a girl to 'do' for her!

'I wore the beads when I was a little girl,' she said; 'I'll wear them now while I live. They shall be put with me into the coffin.'

She began to cry miserably as she always did at the thought of her own demise. She cried into her tea-cup. The three front teeth which were all that remained to her rattled against the brim; her slice of bread-and-butter was flavoured with her salt tears; but she contrived to keep the string of beads safely clutched in her hand; and when Alice saw them again they showed their alluring bird's-egg blue through the lace of the night-gown around the shrivelled, brown throat.

Alice sulked for two days. It was very uncomfortable for the mistress when the maid sulked. The meals were hardly any break in the blankness of the day if Alice, carrying them in, would only answer her anxious attempts at conversation with monosyllables. On the third day the baker was to call. Little tit-bits of interest which Alice gleaned from him – the amount of loaves they took in at the rectory; the enthralling fact that down at Potter's he now left none but Standard loaves; his remarks on the weather, and the state of his invalid wife's health – she carefully retailed, when in a good temper, to her mistress upstairs. So that 'Baker's Day' was a red-letter day at Acacia Cottage.

Was Alice going to sulk through it? The old lady heard the wheels of the baker's cart stop at the gate, heard the loud opening of the door, heard his voice rumbling on, beneath her window. She waited for Alice to come, and waited in vain. Then she rang her bell.

'I should like a glass of milk, Alice.'

''Tisn't your time for it, miss.'

'All the same, I should like it.'

From the look that Alice turned on her, from the sound of her footsteps as she departed, thumping down the stairs, to do her errand, the poor mistress knew the maid still sulked.

She felt for the beads beneath her night-gown, caressing them with a distorted, shaking hand. She had worn them when she was a little girl, dressed by her mother. At her parties, at the pantomime, at all the little gala functions of her childhood, she had worn her pretty pale-blue beads.

And Alice! Ugly, slipshod Alice, with her great coarse throat!

'Has the baker been?' she asked when the milk was brought. 'Aren't you going to tell me what he said?' the question came with a sob of reproach.

'No,' said Alice.

'You are not being kind to me as you promised, Alice. You are being cruel to me.'

Alice turned to go away.

'Alice!' Alice stopped short. 'Alice, I've just been thinking – since you like them so much – I'll – I'll leave you my blue beads when I die.' The words were accompanied by a burst of weeping.

'Will you, miss?' Alice came eagerly back to the bed. 'I'd like to have them, finely. Perhaps you'd better put it down in writin', miss, if you wouldn't mind.'

All Alice's good humour was back. The baker had been extra communicative. All kinds of interesting remarks he had made. The maid-of-all-work neglected her work downstairs to repeat them, sitting on the side of her mistress's bed. And even when at length she went she quickly returned, bringing pen, ink, and paper. Holding the poor mistress in a sitting posture with her arm around her, she helped her to scrawl the few words 'My blue beads are for Alice,' and to sign her name.

⇒⋆⇐

But on the next Sunday Alice must go to church without the beads.

At the church gate was Sheep-face, sure enough, but with no eyes for her. A new housemaid from Potter's had appeared, wearing a long white scarf whose two ends fell over her shoulders at the back; and these ends Sheep-face held, and with loud guffaws drove the young lady in front of him.

Alice called after the pair certain expressions not worth recording. But the new housemaid, entering into the spirit of the joke, began to frisk and curvet like a horse; and Sheep-face yelling encouragement, gambolled after her. The other girls, in service, and younger girls 'not out yet' of her own class, all had attendant swains. No one looked at Alice, in her long black jacket with only the frill of white lace round her great red throat.

Standing unnoticed beneath the lime trees, she watched the last couple away. Then she turned, and running, swiftly as bad boots and clumsy movements would allow, made her way to a village four miles off, where her mother who was a widow lived, keeping house for her brother who was an under-keeper.

Through lane and sheep-walk and meadow-path she went, by a short-cut that she knew; across fields, knee-deep in wet turnip-tops, over fresh-ploughed lands in which she sank to her ankles; plunging heavily along, not feeling the weariness of the way because of her ardour to achieve the goal she had in view.

But that goal was not her mother's cottage. She passed the back of it, not giving it a look or a thought, and made her way to a meadow near by. A meadow bordered on two sides by a thick plantation, where in the spring-time she had watched her brother at work; where the young pheasants had been reared.

The keeper's wooden hut stood there still, its wheels sunk in the long lush grass. Its interior was filled with half-emptied sacks, with rusty traps, with bags of poisoned meal for the benefit of the rats. With none of these familiar objects had Alice business now.

Along one side of the hut, high up against the roof, ran a little shelf where stood several empty bottles, and one or two dirty jars covered with dust and cobwebs. One summer evening Alice had watched her brother putting poison into the wasps' nests in banks and hollow trees.

The wasps had been a pest that year. Alice knew exactly which jar he had used – a piece of rag tied over its mouth; she had been forbidden to handle it, for fear of accident. But she took it in her hand now, and holding it beneath her jacket carried it back to Acacia Cottage.

Before she went to bed that night, she wrote a letter. She was fluent with her pen, having been reckoned a good scholar at the village school.

'My dear Swetehart,' she wrote. 'You was crule to me today. Was you ashamed I had no long taled scarf for you to drive me by. I thort you and her did look a fool. It was diffrunt when I wor my blue Bedes. Will you wate for me nex Sunday at the chech gate and I will ware them again so as you are not ashame to walk along of me. You shall have a swete kiss afore we part like we done afore – your loving swetehart Alice'

Then followed numerous noughts and crosses to represent love and kisses, and a P.S.: 'Look out for the Blue bedes.'

On the Saturday morning it happened that the doctor paid a visit to his incurable old patient. He took the maid-of-all-work aside when he came downstairs and warned her that her mistress was losing ground.

'I find her heart much feebler,' he said. 'You must be very attentive, and never leave her for long. She might die at any moment.'

Alice opened wide her prominent blue eyes with their sand-coloured fringes. 'Do you think she'll die afore tomorrow?' she asked.

It was impossible to say. He left some medicine to be given on emergency. Her heart was in such a condition that at any minute it might stop. She must not be left at night. Alice must make up a bed in the same room.

Alice did so, and slept like a top, although the poor old woman moaned through the whole night. Just before dawn, however, the mistress slept; she awoke to find the maid standing in her coarse night-gown by her bedside, her red, short hair standing off thickly from her face and shoulders.

'Why do you look at me like that?' the startled woman asked; for Alice's face was within an inch of her own.

'I thought you wasn't going to wake no more,' Alice said. 'You looked for all the world as if you was dead.'

The sick woman cried at that, and sent Alice to dress, and told her never again to hold her face so close to her own, to frighten her so.

At dinner-time she had revived in courage and ate a tiny bit of the chicken Alice had cooked for her, it being Sunday, and a spoonful of the sago pudding.

'You're going to church, Alice?'

Alice was already dressed; all but the green hat and the jacket.

'You won't be late Alice! You won't leave me alone long, today?'

Alice wasn't a-goin' just yet, she reassured her. Not till her missus had drunk the physic the doctor had give her. Nice physic it were, he had said, and would keep her quiet till Alice come home.

It did keep her quiet, after quite a short time. Very quiet. So quiet, that Alice, without much trouble, and meeting with no resistance, could take the blue beads from beneath the lace of the night-gown and fasten them about her own throat.

Sheep-face, in anticipation no doubt of the promised kiss, was at the church-gate after service. Alice saw him as she issued with the rest from the porch, waiting beneath the now leafless limes. She fought her way through the little crowd in the churchyard to get ahead of the new housemaid from Potter's with the long white scarf.

'I ha' got on my blue beads,' Alice told him, drawing his attention to the ornament.

'They're mine. My missus left them to me in a will. And she's dead.'

THE SMALL-HOLDER

HE had taken Boxer, his old cart-horse, to be shod, and his way home from the blacksmith's led him past the public-house. For twenty-four hours, without cessation, the rain had steadily descended. Over his old coat Job Mason wore a sack slung about his neck; more sacks were disposed upon the back of Boxer, but spite of such attempt at protection, man and horse were wet to the bone. The brim of the old 'bowler' which for years had protected the old man's weather-beaten face hung limp upon his brow; rivulets of rain-water trickled from it down matted streaks of sodden hair, to drip from nose and cheeks and chin. Two more hopelessly drenched, depressing-looking objects it would have been impossible to find in twenty miles of road on that depressing day.

From the White Hart's open door issued sounds of mirth, a shouted fragment of a song, loud talk in many voices. Old Mason, sitting sideways on his horse, had his face turned to the inn as he passed. His name was called by half a dozen voices; and presently one of the carousers came, stumbling to the door, and invited the horseman to come in.

'Come on, Job, bor! Come on!'

Job shook a rejecting head; there was a momentary disturbance of the rain-water supply on the old hat, and streams, increased in volume, ran down the back of his neck.

'Come and have a pint, man, and warm th' cockles of yer heart.'

Apparently unmoved by the invitation, Job held on his way. More than a pint of White Hart beer it would have taken to kindle his heart to any warmth of hope or happiness again, he knew.

'I'm beat,' he said to himself as he jogged along. 'Tha's what I am. Beat.'

He thought with longing of the warm stuffiness of the ale-house kitchen. It was not because the place held no attractions for him he had turned a deaf ear. How pleasant to him would have been the sound of the iron-clamped boots, shuffling on the gritty floor. What comfort there was in companionship, what cheer in the loud laugh, the jest and song, heard a thousand times before, and therefore the more readily understood. To be warm and dry, seated with a pint of beer placed before him by the landlord's friendly hand, how agreeable that would have been!

The shouting of the score of farm-labourers followed him as he rode on through the joyless rain, falling pitilessly on the soaked cornfields on either side, where under happier conditions the men would have been at work. The clover-plant was growing tall and green above the ears of the uncut barley, the wheat, standing in melancholy shocks, was turning black, and here and there was a suspicious blur on the spikes which showed that the corn was growing again. In a field near which the roused-up river poured along, the oats stood a foot deep in water.

''Tain't their prop'ty,' Job said, thinking of the convivial party left behind. 'Whativer come they git their wage. As for me, I ha' struggled. I'm dead beat. These here floods ha' finished me. My heart's broke.'

'He've got his gruel, ter yare, poor old Job have,' one of revellers said, looking after the dreary figure of the old man. 'A sight better off Job'd ha' been if so bein' he'd kep' like one of us, 'stids of takin' on's fifty acres o' land. And han't knowed a night's slape since.'

'Ter yare 'll finish 'm,' another added. 'Th' poor ol' beggar have had to pull his barley stack to bits, and hang the rotten stuff out to dry.

Some of it I seen spreeded on's barn door and his hedges. Two of 's shape what he bought at Hildermaze Fair was drownded, las' wake, in a ditch tha's mostly dry, other summers. How th' old feller is a goin' ter mak up's rent, ter yare, pass me!'

It 'passed' Job also. How he was going to do it was a question he was for ever asking himself. He was asking it as, having turned his old horse into the shed, he set to work to wipe him down with a handful of straw, and to make him as comfortable for the night as might be. As he crossed the black slush of the little horse-yard, and reached the door of his home, he asked it. He asked it as he entered of the anxious-faced wife, of whom he had already asked it a thousand times.

'How are we a-goin' ter make up our rent, ter yare?'

His wife had always the same answer ready: 'Somehow we'll manage,' she said.

There was nothing of definite comfort in the reply, yet, because the words were so familiar, perhaps, they comforted him. The ear of such as Job is not attuned to catch unknown harmonies, is almost as good as deaf to a phrase heard for the first time. In many a crisis of their lives – and they had known trouble, loss, illness, difficulty of all kinds – that sentence had been on the lips of Job's wife: 'Somehow we'll manage to pull through,' she had said; and 'somehow' – God and they alone knew how – they had done so hitherto.

'You're wholly wet,' she said, looking at him as he stood dripping on the fresh-washed bricks of the kitchen floor. 'Git out o' yer clo'es, bor, and let me dry 'em.'

He would only divest himself of his sack, however, sitting to steam as he was over the fire while he drank the tea which she had ready for him.

'You reek like a washin' day!' she told him, and herself pulled the draggled hat from his head and swished the water from it. 'This ain't th' best cure for your rheumatics, I fear me, Job.'

There was a cold dumpling of apples and blackberries for his supper, with bread and cheese, and a bowl of cold potatoes. The dumpling made in a basin was set before him, and he dug it out and conveyed it to his mouth without the medium of a plate.

'The White Hart's full,' he told her. The fact rankled.

'They're a-havin' a better time than their wives and child'en at home,' she commented. 'Drinkin' away th' money that should be for th' helpin' of 'em through th' yare!'

'I don't get no chance to drink away my money,' Job reminded her, not without bitterness.

'Tea's best for you,' she told him complacently, and poured him another steaming cup.

As he drank it he asked again the familiar question: 'Barley growed inter the 'arth agin, and whate only fit for th' muck'up – how are we a-goin' ter pay our rent, this yare?'

'We shall worrit through, somehow,' she said; and again the comfort of the words stole warm about his heart. Yet he persisted in his plaint.

'I'm dead beat. My heart's broke.'

'Not you! For shame ter say it! I'm wholly shamed on yer, Job.'

But presently when he was warmed inside his reeking clothes, and the dumpling of apple and blackberry had disappeared, she sprang a new misfortune upon him.

'I wanted you to get a warm, and your tea, fust,' she said, '– but Job, bor, the cow's ill. There, set ye still! All's done as can be done. I ha' fetched th' veterinny. A drink he gave her, and left another to be give, come six o'clock.'

'Is she bad?'

'She's bad, Job. The veterinny allowed as much, though by no means did he give out no hopes. "Worse cows ha' got better," was what he said.'

'Tha's done me!' Job said. 'I thought I'd got enough, but tha's done me!'

'Hape o' rubbidge!' his wife encouraged him. 'Yew ain't done while you've got ter see ter th' cow, Job.'

Through the melancholy soak of the evening rain he went out to minister to her; and again through the vapoury turbidness of the night. Looking up at the sickly moon with her wan circle, 'Kape on a-rainin' – Job, ironical in his bitterness of spirit, addressed the elements; 'I wouldn't lave off if I was you. You ha' done yer warst. Kape on. Kape on.'

In the morning when his wife awoke she found his pillow empty, and flew from her own with a scare at her heart. The grim fear that had haunted her of late, as she looked upon the ruin of their prospects and listened to her husband's hopeless talk, had taken tangible form. Something dreadful she had feared would happen to Job. It had happened. He had got up in the early morning and had killed himself. She should find him hanging from a rafter in the outhouse where a convenient hook had been placed on which to suspend a dead pig.

Flinging an old cloak over her nightgown, bare-footed, she scurried to the outhouse – empty even of the corpse of a pig. In all the tumbledown home premises she sought for what she greatly feared to find. Then through the straw-yard she plunged, ankle-deep in black water, knowing nothing of it, to the shed where the cow lay ill. There, in the poor light of a grey dawn showing through the broken roof, she saw her husband lying beside his cow, fast asleep in the straw; his tired head pillowed on the great heaving side of the sick beast.

'Job!' she called. 'Why, whativer ha' come to ye, bor, ter go to bed along o' th' cow?'

He lifted his head, stared stupidly about him, got stiffly to his feet. And presently the sick cow had also struggled upon all fours.

'Why, th' old girl's better,' Job said. He looked at her anxiously for a minute. 'She'll do,' he said to his wife. He patted the poor beast with a horny, caressing hand, then walked to the open half-door of the shed at which his wife stood looking in: 'Why, blame me, if it ha'n't left off rainin'!' he cried.

He felt an extraordinary ease of mind. The cow was going to live; the rain had ceased.

'I told you as how we should worrit through somehow,' the wife said.

MEDLARS

'A MEDLAR-TREE, is it? I'm not sure that I've ever seen one before.'

'You see it now, Londoner. For theer 'tis, safe enough; and the only tree in the orchard that give any promise of fruit, t' year. You know why, don't ye?'

He turned a staring and angry gaze upon me, and asked the question in the tone which, to me, accustomed to the milder manners of the city man, and his more resigned acceptance of the inevitable, sounded ferocious. He was a portly, healthy-looking farmer-man, with a stiff, hard-featured face, and a head as devoid of ideas as one of his own turnips; but with an unbounded belief in himself, and distrust of, and contempt for, the world which lay beyond the two hundred acres he tilled. Of the world of London, from which almost unknown region I had descended upon him in the form of paying guest, his fear, his scorn, and his ignorance are about equal.

'You know why?'

He had asked that savage question of me as we had walked over the shrunken swaths of hay, and picked our way among the mouldering hay-cocks, emitting anything but the fragrant aroma I had expected to enjoy in such a scene. 'You know why the hay, which was a good crop, has been ruined by incessant rain, and is only fit for manure, don't ye?'

He had asked it again as he pointed out the few blighted ears in the field of waving barley; as he called on me to notice the ravages of the fly among the turnips. 'You know why they're sent, I s'pose?'

I knew, at any rate by this time, the answer he expected to that question: 'To ruin the poor farmer.'

To conciliate my embittered host I generally repeated that formula; yet sometimes rebelled; as when he cursed the poppies in the wheat, and the golden field of charlock that blazed in molten glory where some more profitable crop should have grown.

'They're sent by Providence to ruin me,' he had declared, answering his own question when I remained silent.

'Why should the Almighty have been more interested in your affairs than in mine?' I asked him. 'He may have sent the charlocks and the poppies for me. I believe he did, come to think of it. My eyes are pretty well weary of staring at ledgers and brick walls, I can tell you. The Almighty may have thought the feast of colour would be good for them, and so planted the glory of the scarlet and the gold here, where I have come to revel in them for my refreshment and holiday.'

My host glared at me with staring eyes; a twist of a stiff lip conveyed a scorn and disapproval of me beyond words.

'You've got a rummy way of argeying,' he said. 'It show you don't know much of what you're a-talkin' of, young Londoner.'

He turned a belittling gaze upon me from his greatly superior inches. That it was unlikely such a meagre creature could be of account in the arrangements of Providence was obviously the thought in his mind.

'Yes, that is it,' I said, undaunted. 'It is for me; and the benefit of my tired eyes. It is why the honeysuckle is trailing over the hedge, there; why the forget-me-not and the river-mint fill the ditch on the other side of it –'

He struck at the hedge with his stick as I spoke, and a company of small birds shot up from it with a rushing sound. I followed their flight with my eyes.

'What birds are those,' I asked, 'that show such a melting of soft yellows and greens against the pearl grey of the sky?'

'Canaries, Londoner,' my host told me, and executed a slow wink for his private edification. In his not too pleasant way, he was exceedingly proud of his own ready wit.

But being in an acquiescent, undisputatious mood when he, standing in his orchard, asked me why it was that the medlar bore fruit while the apple-trees were barren, I replied with a prompt docility it was because apples were of value, and medlars of none. I added, at the moment basely desirous of conciliating him, that it was undoubtedly a well-worn device of Providence to ruin Mr Short, who was a farmer.

My host with a grunt assented: yet presently wished to qualify a portion of my statement.

'Medlars aren't much of a fruit in the market, yet if they haven't a money valley, they *have* a valley,' he announced, dispassionately.

'It's like this here,' he explained to me as we turned away from the orchard, and bent our steps across the rough lawn to our seats in the farm-house porch – there is no 'vally' in roses, and jessamines, and clematises, and they are allowed to climb and fall, and climb again, in beautiful untrammelled freedom, in my host's great untended garden. 'The gentleman that live at the Hall, and shoot over my farm, send us a brace of birds, now and again through the winter. They come in handy to my missus. I don't say 'tisn't our right to expect 'em, but they come in handy. You onderstand, Londoner?'

'Quite. Quite. Present of game. Very pleasant.'

'Bein' so, my missus took it in her head last year 'twould be encouragin' to make a return. You follow me?'

'Certainly. Question of barter. All presents are.'

' "Here's a small crop of medlars," said my wife to me. "What good are they to us? Let's put 'em in hamper," she said, 'and send 'em off to the Squire" (we call him that, for short. He isn't the real sort. Only one of those London chaps with money in his pockets, come down to fling guineas at the pheasants).'

'You must remember the poor London man has not your advantages, Mr Short.'

'That is so, Londoner. I make allowances. So my wife, she packed the medlars into a small hamper, and done 'em up top and bottom, with leaves, and sent 'em off to the Squire. Mighty gracious he was about it; stopped the missus coming out of church on the Sunday, and said as 'twas his fav'rite fruit, and he were much obliged. We reckon that present o' medlars brought us in a hare and a brace o' pheasants, extry.

'Next day I happ'd to be walking round the vicarage garden with our parson. "I didn't know as there was a medlar-tree at the Hall," says he to me. "Howsever, a medlar-tree there is," he say, "for the Squire have sent me a small hamper of the fruit. Very kind, I take it of him," the parson said; "for 'tis a fruit I don't often get, and very delicious."

'I didn't let on to my missus – for where's the use of talking to women? – but, two days after, she come to me: "There must be a good crop, gen'ally, of medlars, t' year," she say; "for Doctor (he'd been to see her for rheumatics in her knuckles, that day) was telling me as he had had a handsome present of the fruit from our parson. Won'erfully pleased with 'em he was. They're a very agreeable fruit," he say, "and wholesome for children."

'A day or two later I was in our village shop, buying my quarter-pound of baccy – Yes, thankye, Londoner, I'll have a pipe of yours. I can smoke my own, any day. – Says the man that keep the shop to me: "I've a little token," he say, "as I was going to ask your acceptance of, Mr Short. 'Tis a small hamper o' medlars as Doctor was so kind as to bring us yes'day when he come to our youngest. I'm not much of a fruit eater, myself," the man went on, "but medlars are reckoned something of a treat. Said I to wife, we'll send 'em where they'll be appreciated."'

'And did he send them?'

My host looked up from the pipe he was filling from my pouch.

'He sent 'em safe enough. In the very hamper I sent 'em away to the Squire in.

'My missus, she took and made 'em into a jelly. "It'll come in handy next summer when we have our paying guests," said she. I'll ask her to put a jar out for you at tea. They're a save to the butter.'

'And what will you do with the medlars, this year, Mr Short?'

My host had filled his pipe. He stuck it between his thick lips, struck a match on the underneath part of his corduroy breeches, fixed me with his stony stare as he applied it to his pipe.

'I shall send 'em to the Squire again. What do *you* think, Londoner?' he grinned.

A COUNTRY CHURCHYARD

There is a wedding at our village church, this breezy, leafy, laughing day of June, and I, who have known the bride and her groom since I taught them their collects in the Sunday school, have promised to be present.

Either I have mistaken the time, or the ceremony is postponed; for I find myself arrived at a church empty but for the presence of the parish clerk, who is pushing hassocks into positions before the altar rails. There is a chill and musty smell about the place. It is more cheerful in the sunshine among the graves.

The churchyard is trim, its paths well kept, and in the carefully mown grass borders roses now in full bloom have been planted. The sky is blue above, the birds sing, the soft breeze stirs the branches of the lime and chestnut trees in the road; their moving, light shadows dance upon the graves.

We do not live remote from our dead in Dulditch. They are not dragged from us with pomp of black horses and silver hearses to lie in huge strange cemeteries in unvisited graves. Every day, on work or pleasure bent, we pass the low stone wall dividing the living from the dead; the wind, which wafts the pink petals of the chestnut flowers to lie upon the graves, carries the voices of the children as they hurry by to school. Beyond the neighbouring meadows, golden now with buttercups, show red roofs of farmhouse and barn; the 'milky low' of the cows and farmyard cries are all about the deaf ears of those who lived and worked and played amid such sounds.

Most of the graves of those who have passed to their rest through an unbroken uniformity of days are nameless, but in many instances I remember the names and histories of those who lie beneath.

There sleeps soundly poor Anna Dunn, whose asthma would not let her sleep on earth. There, safe in the shelter of the porch, lies old John Laws, with whose rheumatic bones the rain and wind were wont to play such havoc. By the two jam jars sunk within the mould, in readiness for the flowers which she no longer remembers to bring, I recognise the last resting-place of Jemima Barnard's husband; I cannot believ that the old man would change the quiet of his peaceful grave for the racket of Jemima's tongue, and her dirty kitchen corner.

The parish clerk comes shuffling out of the porch, and with a hand shading his eyes looks down the road for the wedding party who still delay their coming. He makes his way among the graves to me.

'They're a-keepin' of you waiting, ma'am. They aren't so hasty to the marryin' as some.'

I would not hurry them, I tell him. I have been looking at the graves.

'There's hist'ries theer!' he says, being a parish clerk not devoid of imagination. 'Have you ever marked this one?' he asks, and points to an old stone, sunken and lichen-covered, but on which the carving of a couple of cherubs' heads is still in fair preservation. By its side is a similar stone, I notice, of like ornamentation.

'He was a Frenchy, this chap were,' the old man tells me. 'I don't know as iver he let on to mortle ear what they was, but there was troubles in his own country, and he come here. All them as was alive that day see him a-walkin' t'ro' th' village. A livin' skelinton he were, and his butes was nearly off his feet. There was sech a cu'rous look about 'm, or so my gran'father telled my father, that the children follered 'm as he went.

'To th' White Hart he come; and well as he could, in his Frenchy way, he arst for bread. But afore they brought it he showed th'insides of his breeches pockets. Empty. A joky man he were at th' White Hart, them days, as my gran'father telled my father. 'We pay for all we git, I' this country,' says he. 'You'll git nothin' for nothin', this part o' the' warld, Frenchy,' he says.

'At one o' th' cottages he arst agin. But sech a cur'ous way with his tongue he had that the woman she was frighted, and slammed th' door in's face. Then he come on theer.' The parish clerk turned and pointed across the buttercup meadow to the gables of the farmhouse.

'There weren't no fine drorin'-rooms built on, them days; the missus as lived there warked her own dairy, raired her own turkeys, managed the farm, bein' a wider and a business woman. There ain's none like her, not in our days, accordin' to what my gran'father telled my father. Like a man she were, with no woman'y softness. So when th' folk what was alive then see 'm a-goin' there, "You've come to th' wrong shop, Frenchy,' they called out.

'Hows'ever, wholly wrong they was. Fot arter she'd spoke to 'm for a time, she oped th' door wide, and arst him in. And till his dyin' day, twenty yare later, that door weren't never closed agin 'm agin.

'He warked for's livin', Frenchy did. Done odd jobs in house and garden – sech a garden as 'twas for flo'ers in his time han't been seen since, my gran'father telled my father – and sech-like occupations that don't need th' headpiece of ploughin' and sowin'. A tidy sum, beside, he arned by trimmin' the hairs of the folks as was willin' to trust theirselves in his hands.

'I don't know if you're aweer, ma'am, as how in them old ancient times the farm labourers took their wittles along o' their missuses? Strange it seem they di'nt know no better, but so 'twas; and the folk o' th' farm didn't hold wi' settin' down wi' Frenchy. So the missus she up and called 'm to her side; and theer he sot beside her till the day of 's death. And when he died, this is what she done –'

He stooped down and pointed with a horny finger to the time-worn tombstone, where, beneath the carven cherubs and the name Henri de Rougon, the word 'Gentleman', enclosed in brackets, could just be deciphered.

'A sight of talk it made in th' parush, my gran'father telled my father; for what was the man – a-trailin' over harrowed fields and a-sleepin' in barns – but a beggar till th' missus fed and clothed 'm? "A cur'ous kind of a gentleman," my gran'father say to my –

The old man broke off his recital there, and with a hurried 'The Reverend' made his way over the graves to the church, into which the clergyman had turned.

At the same time the wedding party appeared, walking two and two beneath the chestnut avenue to the gate. On they came up the path, between the ranks of those with whom there is no more marrying; the little band of relatives, each broadly smiling; the small bridesmaids from the village school, in cotton frocks and hardly suppressed giggles; bride and bridegroom, awkward, shy, beaming, happy.

When I had seen the boy and girl made man and wife; had walked with them to the churchyard gate – the pink petals from the horse-chestnuts fell on them, standing there, and on the graves, impartially; had wished them God-speed, and watched them starting hand in hand, upon their way; I turned back to the pair of tombstones with the carven cherubs, and a little while I stood there full of thought. And first I looked about me, over the forgotten graves, the sunken time-defaced tombstones, and wondered what histories – perhaps fragrant as this; unrecorded by the feeble pen of man, but written, surely, for remembrance by the angels – were hidden there; and then I made a mental picture of the refugee and his protectress. The farm-mistress, capable, industrious, upright in figure as in principle; beautiful in her homely way, and wholesome in appearance as in character; doing her duty to God and man, with no thought perhaps of doing it beyond that it lay to her hand and must be done. And the chivalrous little

Frenchman living beside her, bowing his head to all requisitions and vexations, but with what a charming grace; never, in the alien land and among people of a coarser fibre, losing the polish of his courtly manner; his life and service dedicated to the hand that rescued him, until, 'the good God having consulted His list,' it was the turn of Henri de Rougon (Gentleman) to go home.

The flowers I brought to do honour to the simple wedding are still in my hand. Here is a rose for your grave, brave gentleman of unhappy country, time, and fortunes: 'May such good things betide you as befall dead men.' And for yours a rose, dear farmer's wife of a sincerer age, noble lady, brave 'comfortress of unsuccess'.

In the church tower near by there is a stir and a hum. The jackdaws who make their home there fling themselves screaming into the blue. A moment, and how joyously the wedding peal strikes upon the ear!

AFTERWORD

'Happiness comes all in a row,' said little Margaret prettily to us one day, speaking of the manner in which each new childish delight pressed close upon its neighbour's heel.

In chronicling such trifles as these from the simple annals of the poor there is danger of much monotony of shade. It is trouble, pain, privation – suffering of all kinds which seems to come 'all in a row.'

There are lives which viewed from the outside are altogether hopeless, sad, and dreary, from whose contemplation the onlooker shudders away, terrified at the possible desolation of human history. But after all, and spite of our boasting, it is only from the outside that we are permitted to behold. The heart of the peasant, like the heart of the king, is unsearchable. The insignificance, to us so pathetic, of his poor life is probably unperceived by him; the perpetual, patient struggle perhaps only seems without reward; the mind which looks to us such a barren plot must be fruitful of some profitable, appropriate thing.

May it not be possible, if hardly by us conceivable, that to Wolf-Charlie, even, has come his god-like hour? If 'to endure and pardon,' as the great prophet has it, be the wisdom of life, surely such as the Gal La'rences and the grandmother of Jarge in India may be accounted wise. If it be true that 'the lives good for most people and intended for them are the lives of sheep and robins,' then must the poor of Dulditch give thanks that they have 'fields to lie down in and banks to build in', and are not called by heaven to the 'sorrow of its thrones.'